SNOW WHITE

Timeless Fairy Tales Book 11

K. M. SHEA

SNOW WHITE

Copyright © 2018 by K. M. Shea

Cover design by Myrrhlynn

Edited by Jeri Larsen

All rights reserved. No part of this book may be used or reproduced in any number whatsoever without written permission of the author, except in the case of quotations embodied in articles and reviews.

This is a work of fiction. Names, characters, places, and incidents are either the product of the author's imagination, or are used fictitiously. Any resemblance to actual persons, living or dead, or historic events is entirely coincidental.

www.kmshea.com

ISBN: 978-1-950635-02-3

❦ Created with Vellum

CHAPTER 1
OF LOVE AND FAREWELLS

Snow White was born into a world of love and farewells. It was with much love that her mother—taking in her wisps of dark black hair, piercing blue eyes, and creamy white skin—named her Snow White. (Though sometimes Snow White still questioned her naming skills, as she had yet to meet another being named after a weather pattern who was not a mage.) Sadly, it was also with much love that Snow White's mother left her, dying a few short months after giving birth to her.

It was with great love that Snow White's father—King Matvey of Mullberg—raised her. Laughter and warmth lived in the palace, and Snow White never doubted her place in his heart.

Which is why it was with great love that Snow White welcomed Lady Faina to the palace as her father's new wife when she was nine years old.

Lady—now Queen—Faina returned all that love, and together they giggled and laughed...which was the only thing that made life bearable when Snow White's father left them both, dying in a hunting accident when Snow White was a mere thirteen years old.

Snow White survived, *Mullberg* survived, only because of

Queen Faina, who held Snow White when she cried and would serve as regent until Snow White turned twenty and took the throne herself.

Snow White hoped that day would never come.

If I become queen, I will die the day of my crowning as my heart ceases to function, Snow White thought as she sat in on a meeting with her stepmother and the lords who served on their Cabinet. *Unless, maybe, they let me wear a blindfold so I do not see the immense crowd staring at me.*

Snow White tucked her chin and did her best to blend in with the bookshelves behind her. Mullberg's Cabinet was a unique feature on the continent, as no other country had such a council. It was comprised of advisors who each served as the minister of a department, and the lords who served on it were all of a decent sort. But they also had the unfortunate propensity to try to include Snow White in the discussion—something she'd rather avoid at all costs.

"Do we need to be more concerned with Verglas, to our west?" Queen Faina asked the lords. "They've deposed their king, after all—though they did crown Prince Toril as their new monarch."

"It's about time they got rid of that tyrant," Lord Dalberg grunted. "Torgen was a madman."

Snow White's lips twitched into a brief smile. *I have never heard a truer statement. I cannot imagine why his country bore his cruel reign as long as they did.*

"After reviewing the reports, Your Majesty, I don't imagine the new Verglas monarch will have any negative affect on Mullberg," Lord Kleist said.

The rest of the advisors nodded and voiced their agreement.

Snow White's chin itched, but as the lords were looking at Queen Faina, the *last* thing she wanted to do was draw their attention to her position in a padded chair just a bit behind her stepmother.

"Very well," Queen Faina said. "Then what of our internal defenses?"

The lords briefly talked amongst themselves as they shuffled on to the next topic.

Though Snow White listened to them, she allowed herself the luxury of studying the stuffed bookshelves of her stepmother's study.

Leather-bound books with gold embossed titles were stacked on every surface. The shelves were so crammed, Snow White doubted even one more tome would fit. The few open spots held things like rolled up maps and stacks of old letters and correspondence.

But it was the books that held the most interest for Snow.

Basic Astronomy, Rotation Based Agriculture, Theory of Magic, An Endeavor in Economics...

Snow White longed to pluck one of the books—*any* of the books—from the shelves and read, but she shook her head. *I can borrow them later. I really should be focused on this meeting.*

With a slight sigh, she ripped her eyes from the shelves and returned her attention to the discussion. She self-consciously tidied the stack of papers sitting on her lap—reports she had read in preparation for the meeting.

"Despite the rumors of a pack of trolls in the north, the Veneno Conclave representative who checked into it could find no evidence of the creatures." Queen Faina set a sheaf of papers down on her desk and raised her gaze to the dozen lords who cluttered up her private study.

Lord Kleist shook his head, making his grizzled white hair flail. "Again we chase our shadow for no reason," he grumbled. "It's the work of those seven brats, I tell you!"

Snow White glanced at her stepmother, trying to judge her reaction.

"Perhaps." The beautiful queen squeezed her eyes shut and rubbed at her temple.

Snow White shifted slightly in her chair, concerned at the sight of her stepmother's tells for one of her terrible headaches. *We should try to send for a mage with healing magic. They should be able to do something.*

Lord Sparneck grunted. "Baroke ought to keep his spawn in line. His son, Marzell, is the ring leader of those...*hermits*. Though they try to paint themselves as heroes and go around calling themselves the Seven Warriors, they *dare* cry out against our Queen?"

"Really, Your Highness," Lord Dalberg puffed up his chest. "You ought to have them arrested for their traitorous talk!"

Queen Faina opened her eyes—though her nails turned white as she pressed her fingertips into her temple. "All they do is talk, Lord Dalberg. I'm inclined to ignore them as long as it remains that way. They have taken no action, and though they criticize my regency, at the very least, they are smart enough to leave Snow White out of the matter."

When Queen Faina glanced at Snow White, she offered her a sincere smile. Though the gesture of affection warmed Snow White, the dark circles under the queen's eyes concerned her.

Yes. A mage must be sent for.

"Indeed," Lord Kleist studied Snow White. "If Princess Snow White were to make more public appearances and take up greater responsibilities, perhaps they would be silent."

At her name, Snow started to hunch her shoulders as dread hit her stomach like an anchor. *Oh no. No, no, no. Please don't be THAT good of a Cabinet Minister, and instead resume not seeing me!*

Blithely, Lord Kleist continued, "Marzell was your playmate as a child, was he not, Your Highness?"

A dozen set of eyes swiveled to gaze speculatively at Snow White.

Snow White felt her cheeks heat with a blush as her heart throbbed with such force in her chest, she was certain everyone in the room could hear it. Her cursed shyness closed around her neck like a noose, making it hard to even think straight with the Cabinet's attention on her.

She tried to open her mouth to answer, but as the lords stared at her, her heart beat faster and faster, and her palms sweat. *Say something—anything!*

"Princess?" Lord Kleist repeated.

Am I so inept and stupid that I can't manage a single word? Snow White wanted to shrink in her chair, and her eyes flicked around the room as she looked for a way to escape.

Faina placed a cool hand on Snow White's arm. "Breathe, darling," she murmured. "Look at me."

Snow White nodded at her stepmother and gulped. "I," she started but paused to swallow with great difficulty. "I am not yet ready for more," she said. She hated how her voice shook as she forced the words past her lips. "I h-have...much left to learn."

"You turn eighteen in roughly a year," Lord Dalberg said. "Soon, you will rule."

That was enough to make Snow White blurt out, "Not until I am twenty!"

Now that was elegantly put, Snow White internally grumbled. *What an excellent job of assuring them so they remain unaware of how I dread my future.*

Faina smiled at her, then returned her gaze to the Mullberg lords. "Snow White is a princess," she said. "She will not be forced to move because of the childish pranks of *boys*."

Lord Sparneck tried to scratch his chin, squashing the bulky ruffle that encased the neck of his doublet. "As you say, Your Majesty," he said doubtfully.

"What other matters do we have left to discuss?" Queen Faina asked.

Snow White released a shuddering breath and sagged in relief as the lords shifted the topic of concern, leaving her unnoticed once more.

It remained that way until after the meeting was adjourned and the lords left.

Faina flopped back in her chair and held her right hand over her eyes. "Though we haven't a single problem in Mullberg, for some reason, each meeting seems more tiring."

"You have a headache again." Snow White stood and brushed off the red skirt of her velvet dress.

Faina sighed. "Just a small one."

"I read of a tea recipe that is supposed to promote blood flow and proper humors." Snow White straightened the papers her stepmother had scattered across her desk during the meeting. "I'll send word to the cook, and she will brew it for you."

Faina cracked a smile and lifted her hand from her eyes long enough to give Snow White an affectionate wink. "Not another one of your nasty brews you pour down my throat in an effort to fix me?"

"With centuries of knowledge at our fingertips, I'm certain I will eventually uncover something that will help you," Snow White reasoned. "Even if I have to send for books from all corners of the continent."

Faina laughed. "Anything but that." She opened a drawer of her desk and removed a dark-colored piece of molasses candy. She offered it to Snow White—who refused—then popped it in her mouth. "We already spend twice our clothing allotment on your books!"

Snow White finished stacking the papers and moved the queen's sapphire gem inkwell to its proper place. "If I can find something—anything—to help you, it will be worth the expense."

"Such a skilled little scholar you are." Faina finally dropped her hand and motioned for Snow White to crouch in front of her. "And I am quite blessed to have such a dedicated step-daughter."

Snow White lowered her head, and Faina straightened the red ribbon that held Snow White's black locks back from her face and retied the bow. "Linus delivered the volume of myths and legends you asked for the other day." The Queen's close proximity brought a faint whiff of the sticky sweet candy she was so fond of. Snow White blinked. "I only asked if we had a copy. I didn't mean to imply you needed to purchase one."

Faina winked and patted her cheek. "If I am blessed to have such a dedicated step-daughter, I am *doubly* blessed to have a dedicated step-daughter who also happens to have a great thirst for knowledge. It will serve you well when you become queen."

Snow White straightened but stared at her feet. "I don't see how. All the knowledge in the world can't make me speak clearly before a crowd. I have no excuse for my terrible shyness—for neither lack of education nor childhood trauma is responsible for it. Something must be defective in me."

"You are *not* defective," Queen Faina said sternly. "You are smart, kind, and loyal. No—it is only that every ruler has her strengths and weakness. A *good* ruler will work to improve them."

Snow White mashed her lips together. She'd been shy all of her life and had undergone lessons, practice sessions, and more in the name of fixing herself. But no matter how hard she worked, the moment she held a stranger's attention, her throat closed up, her mouth went dry, and it was difficult to even *breathe*.

Faina must have caught Snow White's disbelief, for she stood and gently took Snow White's hands in her own. "I know you try, Snow White. That is why I believe one day you will become a brilliant and beautiful queen."

Snow White offered her stepmother a wry smile. "I'm glad you, at least, think so."

"Everyone does—even those stuffy ministers of ours. It's why they persist in asking you questions at meetings." Faina rolled her eyes as she brushed her beautiful auburn bangs from her eyes.

Snow White nodded, hoping her misery did not shine through.

She hated her shyness, not just because it made her feel like a dolt for being unable to say the simplest of things, but also because she was horribly aware that in doing so she was letting down her country and her people.

If only I were braver—or better.

"That was the last meeting for the day—thank goodness." Faina briefly squeeze her eyes shut. "You're free to do whatever you wish until dinner. The book of myths should be in your room."

Snow White glanced at one of the many shelves crammed in the study. "I saw a book about economics."

"Go drag it off to your book den," Faina chuckled. "Heavens know I'm not going to read it."

Snow White plucked the volume from the shelf and joined the queen at the entrance to the study. "You're going to go rest in your room?"

Faina grinned—though it was less playful and more tired. "I'm returning to my quarters, but not to rest as you would have me. I intend to imbibe in *my* weakness and vice as a ruler: my vanity. The seamstress is to fit me for a new dress."

Snow White wrinkled her nose. "You are not vain."

"Quite the opposite, my love: I am as shallow as they come—but at least I am aware of it. And that is half the battle."

Shaking her head, Snow White followed her stepmother into the hallway, cradling her borrowed book as if it were a precious treasure.

❧

SNOW WHITE PLUCKED at the full sleeves of her green gown.

Though the majority of the continent took its fashion cues from Loire, Snow White's stepmother insisted they embrace Mullberg customs and designers—so as to keep the country's clothing industry and styles within its borders. As such, instead of the smooth sleeves favored by the Loire Princess Elle, both Snow

White and Queen Faina had sleeves stuffed at the shoulders and elbows. (The style, in Snow White's opinion, looked better on Faina. Snow White, being rather petite, thought she looked childish.)

Snow White's puffs were a delicate gold brocade—though the gathering at her right elbow had become rather lopsided due to her propensity to rest books there when she read outside in the gardens and enjoyed the late summer breezes.

"We're late."

Hearing the tightness in her stepmother's voice, Snow White glanced at the Queen's back. "They can't start the meeting without you, Stepmother."

Faina glided in front of Snow White, her back stiff as she gave no indication of hearing her.

Snow White frowned slightly in concern. Faina was usually unshakeable and playful where Snow White was unbearably shy and sarcastic. But for the last year, she seemed to have lost some of her sparkle. *Her headaches have been increasing in frequency and pain; that must be the cause. And yet the Veneno Conclave has not been able to help her.* Snow White stifled the rather un-righteous desire to smack the latest mage healer that had visited the palace not a week ago and informed Snow White she was acting hysterical over "*mere headaches.*"

They cannot be "mere headaches" if they are affecting her so!

Snow White pushed one of her black curls out of her face and continued to follow Queen Faina to the meeting with the royal treasurer and four of his understaff.

They rounded the corner, and Faina collided with a servant carrying a load of clean linens.

Faina bounced backwards but was unharmed and stayed on her feet.

The maid, however, who had tried to leap out of the way at the last moment, slammed into a wood-paneled wall, banging her head on the gem-encrusted frame of a painting.

Snow White hurried forward, reaching for her stepmother's hand.

"Clumsy fool!" Faina shouted.

Snow White froze with her hand half extended, surprised by the unfamiliar and harsh tone.

The maid blinked rapidly as she scrambled to her feet. "My apologies, Your Majesty. Apologies!" She tried to curtsey without spilling the linens. "It was my fault. I'm sorry!" she babbled.

Faina's eyes narrowed. "I will have you thrown from the palace," she said in a low tone that was barely above a growl. "For your insolence in *touching me!*"

"Stepmother," Snow said. "It was an accident. I do not think she could see where she was going with—"

"*Silence!*" Faina snarled.

Snow White snapped her mouth shut and stared at her stepmother in shock and hurt.

"You are merely a stupid girl who cannot even manage the simple task of speaking her mind—" the queen broke off and moaned, swaying slightly as she pressed her hands to her temple. "It hurts," she whispered.

Snow White and the maid exchanged nervous looks. Snow White tipped her head, trying to hint to the maid that she should escape while she could.

The maid took a few steps but gazed back at Faina with concern.

The Queen hunched her shoulders and shook her head. When she raised her gaze again, her soft brown eyes were glazed with tears. "I'm so sorry Snow White. I-I don't know what came over me!"

Snow White took a step closer to her. "Is it your headache?"

"Yes, no, I don't know." Faina started crying in earnest, tears spilling down her cheeks. "Something is *wrong* with me. I don't know myself anymore."

Snow White embraced her stepmother, though concern

nipped at her heels. She didn't know what to say. Her dull tongue failed her again as she tried to summon encouragement or words of wisdom.

But all she could do was hug her stepmother while she cried.

꙳

SNOW WHITE WISHED the flooring would open up beneath her and swallow her whole.

"Your Highness, do you have anything to add?" Lord Kleist asked.

Snow White kept her eyes on Faina's desk, but she had to lick her lips before she could force anything from her mouth. "No."

"I see," Lord Kleist deflated in disappointment.

Why, why must I be so stupid? Snow White pressed her lips together in her anger with herself. *I know every lord in here! I have spoken to them before. But with such a large group...* Snow White looked up and immediately regretted it, for most of the lords were studying her.

She took in a shuddering breath and tried to keep her posture straight—she was representing Faina, after all.

The Queen had been struck with such a horrible headache she was unable to leave her room. Snow White had volunteered to go in her stead to the meeting with the Cabinet. Hah! What a mistake that was—she was barely better than putting a wooden puppet in Faina's chair. Her nineteenth birthday had already come and gone, and no magical change had occurred. She was still just as shy and tongue-tied as ever.

"I heard two more healers from the Veneno Conclave will soon arrive to see to Queen Faina?" Lord Dalberg inquired kindly, bringing her attention back to the meeting.

Snow White nodded mutely and stared at the desk again.

"That's very good of them," Lord Dalberg said.

Lord Sparneck snorted. "They can come all they like. It won't do Her Majesty any good unless they finally *heal* her!"

Snow White nodded slightly—though she doubted anyone noticed. *I agree whole-heartedly with that observation. For the sake of the people—they're mages. They use MAGIC to heal terrible wounds and cure illnesses, yet they cannot banish a headache?*

"You are too harsh, Sparneck," Lord Kleist said.

Lord Sparneck grunted. "If you say so. Next, I propose we talk of the seven idiots."

Multiple lords groaned. "Give it a rest, Sparneck!"

"Other countries are tangling with cursed royalty and goblin attacks. If all we can complain of are seven youths—"

"They are not *youths*," Sparneck insisted. "They are as mule-headed as dwarves. Instead of the Seven Warriors—as they fancy themselves—we ought to call them the seven heretic hermits, or the seven dwarves!"

"All they do is stir up rumors and complain of non-existent attacks on cities and people. Queen Faina has stated repeatedly that we are to ignore them until they pose an actual threat," Lord Kleist said. "Unless Her Highness Princess Snow White wishes to pursue them, they hardly matter."

Snow White's stomach rolled as the lords shifted their attention back to her. She kept her gaze on the desk and stared at a polished ruby gem that served as a paperweight.

Her ears rang, and she pinched the skin of her right wrist to make herself say, "N-no. That is...continue to ignore them."

Her heart pounded awkwardly, but when Lord Sparneck grunted and let the matter drop, she could breathe once again.

"What else are we to discuss?" Lord Dalberg asked.

Snow White straightened a few papers while she listened to the lords chatter about the other topics that needed to be presented.

She paused when she came across a scroll, tied shut with three rose-red ribbons. All three ribbons had the remains of a wax seal on them. After comparing the bits of remaining seal, Snow White was able to make out the royal Loire seal.

Why would Loire send a message so sealed? Stepmother didn't mention an impending war. And though there have been some mishaps over the last five years, politically speaking, the other countries seem solid. Is Erlauf planning for another take over?

Curious, Snow White opened the scroll, unwinding it a little. She glanced at the lords and advisors, but somehow their conversation had changed to complaints about the weather.

"Though spring is nearly upon us, we're shin-deep in snow!" one lord complained.

"It was a difficult winter," another lord admitted.

Snow White half listened to the conversation as she skimmed over the first few lines until she realized what she was reading.

What?

She glanced at the date marked at the top of the scroll, then frowned as she read the letter. As soon as she finished, she skimmed it a second time to ensure she hadn't misunderstood it. Unfortunately, she hadn't.

The scroll contained an invitation to a summit held by Loire. The invitation had been sent to every country on the continent—excluding Zancara, of course—and was meant to discuss the *"widespread attacks against our countries."* Based on the verbiage of the letter, the other countries in the continent weren't encountering the occasional band of goblins or black mage, but had endured multiple assassination attempts and outright attacks against them.

Snow White knew the continent was encountering *some* problems—who could miss it when Ringsted was walled off by a chain of massive storms?—but the letter also referenced other attacks and battles she hadn't even heard whispered rumors of!

The date on the scroll confirmed the summit had been held nearly a *year* ago.

Why did Stepmother not mention this? Even if we haven't had any problems in Mullberg, for Loire—of all countries—to hold such a summit is not a good thing. Did she send a representative and not tell me?

Snow White paused, then shook her head. *Impossible. She would have discussed such a matter with our advisors. Did she refuse the invitation then? And if so, why?*

Snow White grimly rolled the scroll back up, though she rested her hand on it.

As soon as this torturous meeting is over, I will go ask her, she promised herself. *I'm sure she will have a reasonable explanation.*

Reluctantly, Snow White forced her attention from the scroll and listened mutely as the lords argued about the effect the late snow might have on the crops.

༄

THE MEETING DRAGGED on longer than Snow White had imagined, so it was the nearly afternoon when she scurried to Faina's quarters, scroll in hand.

She knocked on the door and opened it, entering without hesitation. "Stepmother?" she called as she slipped inside.

The queen's private parlor—of which the far wall was made entirely of windows and overlooked the palace gardens—was empty. Not even a maid was present.

Snow White started up the winding wooden staircase that led to Faina's loft bedroom. When she had climbed high enough that her head poked above the pink rock tile that made up the flooring, she paused.

Faina stood in front of her giant mirror, studying her reflection. Her purple, velvet gown sported a train that fanned elegantly around her, but her normally warm and smiling face was as smooth as marble. She murmured quietly—though Snow White couldn't quite make out the words.

Slowly, Snow White climbed the remaining few stairs. She glanced at the ornate mirror—which was taller than she was. It had been a gift for Faina's birthday some six years ago, if Snow recalled correctly.

"Stepmother?" Snow called as she slowly drew closer. "Are you feeling better? Where did the maids go?"

Faina ignored Snow White and kept speaking—though now Snow White was close enough to hear her. "There can be none," she muttered. "I will not allow it."

"You won't allow what?" Snow White adjusted her grasp on the scroll so she could press it against her lips as she studied her stepmother with concern. *She must be having another one of those days.* Over the past few months, sometimes the queen's headaches became so debilitating it made her act short of temper and perhaps a little strange.

Faina gave no indication she had heard Snow White. "Mirror, Mirror, on the wall," she said, her voice several notes lower than its usual cadence. "Who in this land is fairest of all?"

Snow White shivered when a cloud passed over the sun, dimming the warm light that streaked in through the windows. "Faina?"

"*Snow White?*" Faina hissed.

Snow White blinked. "Yes?" she asked cautiously. *I'll have to send to the kitchens for some tea and the medication the last mage healer prescribed. But first I need to get her back to bed.*

Faina twisted with such abrupt swiftness, it was almost unnatural. She stared at Snow White, her lips a thin line and her eyes ringed by dark circles. "*You.*"

Snow White kept her facial expression pleasant despite her stepmother's hostility. "Yes, I came to check on you. You look a little fatigued—would you like to rest some more?" *So much for asking her about the summit...*

Queen Faina narrowed her eyes, but she held Snow White's gaze as she crossed the room and lingered at a small end table placed by her bed. She opened a wooden box that sat on top of the table and pulled out a small dagger with an ivory hilt.

Snow White straightened. "Faina—I know you're in pain, but you can't hurt yourself. Try to sleep—I'll send for your medicine."

"This dagger isn't for me, stupid girl," Faina snarled as she stalked across the room. "It's for you."

Snow White backed up until she fell against the loft banister. "W-what? Faina, you're scaring me."

Faina's face twisted in rage. "You might be the fairest, but not for long. I'll cut your heart from your pretty chest and *eat* it!"

CHAPTER 2
FLEE

"Guards!" Snow White shouted. "Help!" She tried to scoot toward the stairs, but her stepmother blocked the way.

Faina's red lips curled mockingly as she raised the dagger. "And then *I* will be the most beautiful of all!"

"*Guards!*" Snow White screamed, but no one came. She tried to back away from her stepmother and sidle around her, but the queen stalked her with the efficiency of a predator, guiding her farther and farther away from the only exit.

Snow White chucked the scroll at her stepmother and attempted to dart to the side. Faina—moving as fast as a snake—dodged the scroll and scuttled to intercept her. She jabbed at her with the dagger.

Snow White yelped and retreated. She backed up into a trunk, knocking her feet out from under her.

Queen Faina loomed above, her eyes gleaming with a maniac light. "Farewell, little Snow," she breathed, then lunged at her.

Snow White grabbed a pillow and thrust it up to block the dagger.

But as the queen started to stab the dagger at Snow White, the rage on her face broke, and her eyes bulged with horror.

"No!" Faina screamed, abruptly pulling back. She flung the dagger across the room with such fierceness she fell to her knees, crashing into the trunk Snow White had tripped on.

Snow White scrambled to a crouch, and though she angled herself so she had a clear shot at the stairs, her forehead wrinkled with worry. "Faina?"

A sob wracked Faina, making her shoulders shake. She stared at the ground and shook her head.

"Are you..." Snow White hesitated, not knowing what to say.

Faina raised her face and wiped tears from her cheeks. "Snow, I—that was..."

"Not you," Snow White said firmly. "I know you, Faina. You would never hurt me. It was just your headaches—"

"Headaches don't drive people to try to kill their step-daughters!" Faina swallowed, disgust twisting her mouth. "There is something *wrong* with me. It seems I cannot control myself, and I have become a danger to you. A danger to our *kingdom*!"

Snow White boosted herself to her feet—nearly tripping on her skirts in the process—and offered her hand to the Queen. "We'll call for another mage. If we can explain it to the Veneno Conclave—"

"It won't make a difference," Faina interrupted, though she took Snow White's hand and allowed Snow to tug her to her feet. "You have paraded a dozen mages through my rooms since these mood swings started. This is not an illness of the body, but of the mind. You must have me imprisoned."

All words left Snow White. She could only stare dumbly at the queen as horror built in her heart. "No," she finally spit out.

Queen Faina rested her hands on Snow White's forearms and squeezed gently. "You *must*, for your own safety."

Snow White shook her head. "No. We can post guards in your room. If the healers cannot help you, surely a Lord Enchanter or Lady Enchantress could."

"We cannot wait any longer—we must act," Faina said. "I just tried to *kill* you."

"You stopped yourself in time," Snow White argued.

"And next time I might not," Faina said. "You are the future queen and my precious step-daughter. I will not place you in danger for my sake."

Snow White's fingertips felt numb, and everything in her screamed in horror. *No, I cannot lose Faina. This cannot be happening!*

"I cannot recall everything I have done during the day, Snow White," Queen Faina continued. "There are times where I come to myself and have no recollection of what or how I spent the previous hour. Whatever twisted darkness has burrowed into my soul is too dangerous to allow free reign anymore. You *must* call for my imprisonment."

Snow White pressed her lips together. "I can't—I *won't!*"

Faina groaned. "You stubborn girl—now is not the time for you to jut your chin like your mulish father used to! I cannot make the orders myself, nor am I able to end this."

Snow White paused, mentally picking over the Queen's words. "What do you mean?"

"I have tried to tell the Cabinet I am a risk. I attempted to speak to the commander of the guard, and I have even..." she shook her head. "Regardless, whenever I do so, I am stopped. Either by a headache so fierce I cannot breathe, or I find myself unable to speak—or move. I *need* you to do this, Snow White."

"No," Snow White said. "You are my stepmother!"

"Snow White!" Faina sighed, exasperation veiling her voice. "*Please.*"

"NO!"

Faina blinked, then chuckled. "You could face our ministers with that ferocity."

Snow White glared at her Stepmother. "I fail to see how you can find humor during a moment in which you are asking me to have you *arrested!*"

"Because if I don't laugh, I might lose myself entirely," Faina said gently. She squeezed Snow White's arms, then stepped back. She turned her attention to the trunk they had both tripped over and opened it.

"If you are really so opposed to the idea, then you must flee to safety." Faina rummaged around the trunk, removing a thick letter that was sealed with the Mullberg coat of arms—a rearing ram.

Snow White took the letter when the Queen offered it to her. "What is this?"

"A letter for your maternal grandfather. Go to his lands of Trubsinn and give him this letter. You will be safe from me, and he will know what to do," Queen Faina said.

Snow White paused as she considered the request. "I don't want to leave you."

"You *must*, Snow White. If you will not have me imprisoned, I must know that you are out of my reach." Queen Faina briefly shut her eyes. "I am so tired. Even in my sleep, black nightmares haunt me. I don't know how much longer I can fight this. Go—so I know you are safe."

She has been fighting her headaches for years. How long has she waged this war alone? I need to do whatever I can to help her. Snow White ran her fingers across the parchment, then nodded. "I will do as you ask. And then I will return with Grandfather—and help from the Veneno Conclave. You'll get better, Stepmother."

Faina smiled fondly, though she studied Snow White with an unusual intensity. "You are sweeter than I deserve," she said.

Snow White snorted.

"You are," Faina said firmly. "No matter what happens, remember that I love you. You may not be a child of my blood, but you are the daughter of my heart."

Snow White flung her arms around her stepmother.

Faina embraced her tightly, then pulled back. She kissed her on the forehead. "You must go now."

"I'll go pack," Snow White said.

Faina shook her head. "No, you must leave this minute. Boris will take you to Hurra. A squadron of guards will be waiting there to escort you to Trubsinn."

"Why the hurry?"

"Please, my love. For my sake, leave," Faina said.

Snow White studied the sallowness of the queen's skin and did not miss the way her fingers shook.

She must be in a far worse state than I ever understood—obviously! Faina would never seek to hurt me. Irritated with herself for failing to notice the depth of her stepmother's troubles, Snow White nodded. "Very well."

Faina swept down the staircase, her purple dress swirling behind her. "Give the letter to your grandfather the *moment* you arrive. Do you understand, Snow White?"

"Yes." Snow White obediently said.

Faina stalked through her private parlor and flung the door open. "*Boris!*" she shouted, then turned back to Snow White with a trembling smile. "Be safe," she said. "No matter what happens, I am so very proud of you. And I know you have greatness tucked in your heart."

Snow White frowned slightly as she studied her stepmother. "That is an awfully strong goodbye for a temporary parting," she said.

Faina ignored Snow White's words and enveloped her in another hug. "You were the light of your father's life, and mine as well. Be brave, my love."

Though Snow White clutched the letter in her hands, she couldn't help but feel there was something *strange* about the send-off. Before she could question Faina more, Boris appeared at the door, dressed in drab, brown clothes.

"You called, Your Majesty?"

Queen Faina nodded and rubbed her eyes. "Yes. It is time—deliver Snow White to the city of Hurra as we discussed."

Boris bowed. "As you command, Your Majesty. This way, please, Princess Snow White."

Snow White quirked an eyebrow at her title, but slipped out of Faina's room and began to follow Boris down the hallway. Just before they turned off into a separate passageway, she looked back.

Queen Faina still was at the entrance to her room. However, she sagged against the doorway and appeared to be brushing tears from her eyes.

There is definitely something she is not telling me.

"Your Highness?" Boris called from the hallway intersection.

"Coming!" Snow White hurried after the man, holding the missive for her grandfather against her torso.

˜

"I APOLOGIZE for the hurried pace, Your Highness," Boris said, his deep voice drawing Snow White from the worries that ran an endless path through her brain.

She looked up from contemplating her horse's black mane. "There is nothing to apologize for," she said, offering him a wane smile. "Things are...this is..."

Boris—atop a dusty chestnut gelding—nodded. "Yes," he said.

Snow White relaxed marginally, thankful it was Boris and not a different groom who was escorting her down the road to Hurra.

Though Hurra was only a three-hour ride by horseback, making the journey with an absolute stranger would have been nearly unbearable when compounded with all of Snow White's concerns about her stepmother.

Thankfully, she knew Boris quite well, for it was he who had taught her how to ride and groom her first pony when she was a tongue-tied little girl. Since then, he had served as her groom and guide whenever she went riding through the lands.

Snow White adjusted her grip on the reins and rubbed her

thumb on the amethyst studded buckle that held the two reins together. "Boris...did the Queen prearrange this?" she asked. "You didn't seem surprised when Faina gave the orders...and she said a squadron of soldiers were waiting in Hurra to escort me to Trubsinn."

Boris scratched his beard, and they rode in silence for several long minutes as he contemplated her question. "She warned me three weeks ago I might be called upon to get you out of the palace fast-like," he said finally.

Three weeks? She's been planning this for that long? Or rather, she's been preparing for this for so long? Snow White uneasily tugged the collar of her bright red cloak shut and shivered in the icy cold air.

"She said you wouldn't need any possessions—your grandfather would have everything you need. And you'd be back," Boris added.

"Yes—Grandfather has a room and wardrobe for me since I visit him every summer," Snow White agreed. "I am rather glad she thought to send me there. Trubsinn is south and much closer to the Veneno Conclave."

Boris grunted and stared at the snow-covered farmland that encroached on either side of the road. Though spring was due to come any day, Mullberg was still blanketed in a thick cloak of snow.

Snow White patted her horse's glossy neck. "We've been traveling for some time. How far are we from Hurra?"

He squinted up at the sun. "Half an hour, likely." He paused, then added, "I'm to take your horse when we part ways—the soldiers will have a fresh mount waiting for you."

Snow White nodded, then mashed her lips together to keep her lower lip from trembling. "Watch Faina, please? Or tell the other servants to. I'm afraid she might do something drastic."

Boris bowed his head, but he did not reply.

The remainder of the journey was spent in silence.

It wasn't until the tall, pointed peaks of the familiar timber-framed buildings of Hurra appeared on the snowy horizon that Snow White straightened.

The city was surrounded by a low wall which was designed more to keep out wild animals than for actual fortification. The tall shops and homes of Hurra, rising at least three to four stories high each, were constructed out of naturally curved timbers carefully fitted together, strengthened by crisscrossing beams fitted to the walls, giving the city a rather boxy feel.

Snow White nudged her horse along so she obediently followed Boris to the center square, where the public fountain gurgled happily. Together they dismounted and peered around the city.

"It seems the guards are not yet here," Snow White said.

Boris grunted and took her mount's reins while she cupped her hands under one of the fountain spouts and drank deeply.

The water was icy cold and made her hands sting, but it was refreshing enough it blew away the haze that had clouded Snow White's mind since Faina had all but booted her out of the palace.

"Princess..." Boris scuffed his booted foot on the grungy cobblestone ground, kicking up a small patch of dead moss.

"Yes?" Snow White prompted when he didn't continue.

He glanced at the letter she held—the corner of which peeked out from underneath her thick red cloak. "The Queen has been concerned...That is to say she has..." He furrowed his forehead, lowering his thick eyebrows. "I don't know that you or I know everything she's thought through."

Snow White tilted her head as she tried to decipher his words. "It would seem so," she said carefully.

"Perhaps," Boris returned to staring pointedly at the corner of the letter. "You ought to see if *somehow* you can learn more afore you go south."

He's telling me I should open the letter for Grandfather and read it myself. But why?

Snow White moved to tug the correspondence out of her

cloak, and Boris took several large steps backwards. "Of course, if I'm not here to *see* you do something, like—mayhap—read a royal letter, there is nothing to stop you from doing as you please. You *are* the Princess."

Snow White paused. "Of course. If Stepmother asks, you can tell her you delivered me to Hurra safely, and as far as you are aware, I am waiting patiently."

Relief twitched across Boris' craggy face. He secured Snow White's horse to his and mounted up. He started to twitch the reins, then paused again. "You can't come back alone, Your Highness. No matter what the letter says, it's too dangerous. No one will let you enter Glitzern Palace."

Snow White blinked. *There must be a great deal more going on than I understood.* "I see. Thank you, Boris."

He nodded but didn't cue his horse forward. Instead he carefully studied Snow White. "You're stronger than you think," he said. "You'll find a way."

Snow White clenched the letter, making it crease. *I stand corrected. Things must be a great deal* worse, *and I was too oblivious to notice it. And I had better read this letter before the soldiers arrive.* "Thank you, Boris," she repeated. "Safe travels."

The groom clicked to his horse, and the beast carried him from Hurra's city square.

Snow White waited a moment to make certain he didn't look back before she unceremoniously broke the seal, her stomach churning as she dreaded what she might read.

Lord Trubsinn,
If you have received this letter—and received Snow White with it—the worst has happened. I have tried to harm her.
The murderous haze clouding my mind and the periods in which I do not know myself have only gotten worse. Whether this is the corruption of my soul or the work of someone dastardly, I do not know, but frankly it does not matter. I must ask you to end this for me.

I have tried myself—for I could not ever live with harming Snow White—but whatever dark madness has taken me will not let me imprison myself or even take my own life.

Snow White nearly threw the letter down, unfinished, at this revelation. "What?" she whispered.

Send troops to end my misery. While I once had hope of escaping this darkness, I cannot take the chance of false hope if it puts Snow White in danger. And though she does not think she is ready to be a ruler, she will make a wonderful queen.
Keep Snow White safe in Trubsinn until I am taken care of. If she learns of this, I fear her gentle heart would crumple.
Thank you for having the strength where I do not. Thank you for guarding the precious treasure my late husband left in my care. I leave her to you.
Faina

Tears blurred Snow White's eyesight, and her fingers trembled so badly she could barely make out the smudges of words on the paper.

No.

The word echoed through Snow White's mind in an absolute refusal.

No, I cannot lose Faina. I have been saying goodbye all my life, and I will not let her go as well! Not when this can be stopped!

Simultaneously, her heart twisted. *It's my fault she is resorting to this. If I had the strength of character, the bravery to open my mouth and talk! I should have imprisoned her as she asked. Because of my refusal, she intends to die.*

Snow White shook her head. "No," she whispered. "No!" *I have to fix this.*

Snow White impatiently wiped tears from her face, then roughly refolded the letter.

This is why Boris warned me I couldn't return. I can't go back and give the order to imprison her. He's right; it is too dangerous. If Faina has really been this sick...why didn't she TELL me?

Snow White wanted to kick something—or perhaps throw a snowball—particularly because she knew Faina hadn't discussed the matter with her in an effort to shield her.

Snow White hadn't just failed in her role as princess of Mullburg, she had failed as a daughter.

I was always so grateful she understood me, that she didn't demand more than I could give. But I would have tried even harder—I would have done anything—*if I had known the result would be this!*

Snow White stood and clasped her hands behind her back. She circled around the city fountain, giving her something to do and a way to warm up. *I will right this matter. But I cannot talk to the Cabinet. They will roll right over me and agree that Faina should be...*

She gulped. She couldn't even *think* it.

And Grandfather would lead the charge if he believes I really am in danger.

She frowned with that realization and edged away from the fountain. Slowly, she joined the crowds of people that passed through Hurra. (It wouldn't do any good to puzzle through all of this only to be swept off to Trubsinn when her escort arrived, and unlike the rest of the villagers in Hurra, the soldiers would definitely recognize her from her lengthy visits to her Grandfather's lands.)

When she felt she was safe, she refocused on the problem.

Snow White was effectively banned from Glitzern Palace and the capital city of Juwel, which left her with...the rest of the country. But that was hardly any help. She had a land full of citizens, but she was too cowardly, too cursed *shy,* to know what to do with it!

She paused long enough to inhale deeply. *Enough. I have to be logical about this. Getting myself upset isn't going to help Faina! If this were a problem a tutor posed to me, how would I solve it?*

Snow White mulled it over for a few minutes before a few ideas started to form.

She needed someone to stand with her; that much was obvious. She needed to be in control, or the lords of the Cabinet would ignore her and have Faina slain as the queen requested. So, she needed someone to support her position.

But who was crazy enough to stand against the Cabinet?

Snow White frowned bitterly. *Not me.* She crushed the letter in her hands. *I can't seek help from the Veneno Conclave. While they are willing to aid ailing monarchs, they have a strict policy of staying uninvolved in country politics. With Faina's life hanging in the balance, this would most definitely be something they wouldn't even consider.*

Could I go to one of our neighboring countries? Verglas to the west, or Arcainia to the south? If I can convince them that Faina's sickness might have something to do with whatever is plaguing the continent—as that summit discussed—they might help. The idea made her skin crawl. She would have to travel alone, and she'd have to request an audience and *talk.* She'd do it if it meant saving her stepmother, but there were too many risks. How likely was it that she would be able to convince other monarchs of her identity when she wouldn't have a royal escort?

Moreover, time was not on her side. If she disappeared, her grandfather—never mind the Cabinet—was sure to do *something.* It would take too long to journey to an ally and explain all that had happened.

She needed support immediately. Which unfortunately meant she would likely have to settle for backup that was perhaps less than ideal.

I could try to go to the army. As the princess, I think they would listen to me. But there would be no stopping word from getting back to the other nobles.

Snow White clenched her jaw in frustration as she passed a fabric merchant's store and dodged a farmer with a cart of hay, angry with herself, and even with Faina for her silence.

Though Faina's headaches had been around for years, the quick escalation of whatever madness was taking her had caught the country unguarded. How could they have missed this?

Snow White pushed the matter from her mind—it was unimportant at the moment, as it had no effect on the plan she chose, and she needed to remain focused. Slightly lifting the hemline of her dress, she hopped over a melting pile of slush.

I need my supporters to be independent of the government. There is the Verglas Assassins' Guild, but they would likely eat me alive, and their skills are exactly what I don't *want, not to mention they are also too far away. I need someone closer...*

Snow White blinked when she heard the pounding clop of many horse hooves on the city streets. Curious, she peered behind her and almost fell over.

Her grandfather's soldiers had arrived. Guessing by the way they scanned the crowd, they were looking for her. They must have somehow learned she was in Hurra, even if she wasn't waiting for them in the city square.

Curse it! Why does Grandfather have such competent men? Snow White darted up a dirty alleyway, holding her breath as she picked her way through muddy snow and piles of what she *hoped* was disintegrating food.

The alleyway intersected with a smaller street that mostly held forges, blacksmiths, gem cutters, and the like.

They are unlikely to think I would come to this area, but unfortunately I might not hear their horses over the pounding of all these hammers.

Snow White moved to stand under a small awning that

stretched out of a blacksmithy, buying herself a few moments to think.

It seems stupid to stay here in Hurra where I could be found, but moving on without a plan is foolhardy, and I have yet to settle the matter of whom I choose to ask for support.

She bit her lip and edged closer to a brazier for warmth. Two men who appeared to be waiting on a horse receiving a new shoe were there as well, though they only smiled and nodded to Snow White—oblivious to her real identity—and continued talking.

Impulsively, Snow White glanced from the cheerfully crackling fire to her letter. She tossed the crumpled letter into the fire, settling a little as she watched it burn.

That's one matter, but what next?

Her nose twitched from the smoke of the brazier and the hot metal being pounded out in a swordsmithy across the street.

"Did you hear about the mountain hag?" One of the men asked his companion, interrupting Snow White's thoughts.

Mountain hags were twisted magical entities with the nasty habit of eating human hearts. Though they were usually found in Kozlovka, occasionally a few skirted Verglas—for the Snow Queen's magic kept them from entering those lands—and ended up in Mullberg.

"Where is it?" the second man asked as he tugged on his mittens.

"In the north. Around Perlen, supposedly. It was seen by two villagers, but it hasn't attacked the village. Yet."

"Wasn't Perlen almost flattened by an ice giant not long ago?"

"Nah. There was an ice giant in those parts, but the Seven Warriors took care of it afore it damaged any villages or cities."

Snow White blinked at the exchange. If she had any social charm, she'd ask the men what in Mullberg they were talking about. *They make it sound as if magical creatures of ill will are running wild!*

The second man grunted as he adjusted his cloak. "The Seven Warriors will take care of the mountain hag as well, I expect."

"They move faster than the army," the first man agreed. "It's a real blessing as it means they end it before any damage is done."

Who are the Seven Warriors—oh...

The Seven Warriors, also known as the "Seven Heretic Hermits," were the men Lord Sparneck was forever complaining about. But Lord Sparneck made it sound like they were rabble rousers who did nothing but complain about the state of the country.

If these two men could be trusted, they were doing a great deal more than that.

I was unaware the Seven Warriors were fighting creatures.

The epiphany was a grim one, for it meant it was possible that the countless reports of monsters and creatures that the army looked into were not false rumors. Instead, it seemed the creatures had been taken care of long before any soldiers arrived.

And I never did talk to Faina about the summit. Are things grimmer than I believed? Is Mullberg not as untroubled as the many reports claimed?

Snow White wanted to grumble, but she settled for biting her lip.

I need to focus on Faina. If I worry over too many things, I'll never complete any of them. Faina first, and then I can further investigate these reports. Besides—it's not as if I can look into them when I am banned from Glitzern Palace.

Snow White stared at the fire with such focus, she almost didn't notice the mounted Trubsinn soldier until it was too late.

She quickly pulled up her hood and remained still as he rode past.

I really will have to leave Hurra before I have a proper plan —blast it!

Snow White sighed, then slipped away from the warmth of

the brazier and started up the street, heading for the nearest exit —which happened to be the northern gates.

So. Faina. Allies. What am I going to do? It is a fairly hopeless situation. Perhaps I ought to send word to the Seven-Heretic-Hermit-Warriors and ask for their help. Snow White snorted in amusement at her own joke as she turned left at an intersection—this road was thankfully not a smelly alleyway, but housed a tinsmith, gemsmith, and arrow fletcher.

Just as she passed the gemsmith, she stopped in the middle of the road.

Wait...the Seven Warriors. That's it!

The Seven Warriors—or, as her Cabinet had referred to them, the seven warriors/hermits/mule-headed dolts—were led by Marzell. She at least knew him, and she remembered him as a kindhearted boy even though he was several years older than her when they played together. If he couldn't help her, at least he might be able to give her the names of those who could!

Her mind made up, she mentally paged through all the reports she had read about them and reviewed the mutters she had heard at the various meetings with advisors.

The Seven Warriors lived in the Luster Forest due east of Hurra. It would be a bit of a walk, but she should be able to arrive just after nightfall. (Lord Sparneck had found their location and helpfully marked it on several maps during one of his rants.)

Something like hope started to beat in Snow White's heart as she turned onto the main road that cut through Hurra, making her way to the north gates.

It will be difficult—facing seven men with me being...me, I suppose. But I cannot fail again.

Spying two Trubsinn soldiers talking not far from the gates, Snow White edged closer to two chattering girls who—laden down with baskets and sacks—were also leaving. By keeping her head turned in their direction, she hoped to pass it off as if she were involved in their conversation—though she didn't know how convincing it would be, as she had a bright red cloak, whereas the young ladies had gray and brown capes.

Her heart buzzed in her throat like an angry bee as she passed the soldiers.

They didn't call out after her, even as she crossed the threshold of the gates and left Hurra.

I made it!

Smiling slightly, Snow White parted with the girls and pointed herself east, in the direction of Luster Forest. "Be brave," she muttered to herself as she charged through slush and snow. "For Faina's sake."

☙

"BE BRAVE," Snow White grumbled as she pulled her cloak closer and followed the small trail that cut through Luster Forest. "I should have told myself to *be smart*! I was an idiot for setting out in the late afternoon in the belief I would be able to find a place I had never visited before."

She scowled at the snow-covered forest, where every stretch and corner of the woods looked like the previous bit.

She had reached the forest faster than she had calculated but had wasted an inordinate amount of time wandering around the trails, trying to narrow in on the location Lord Sparneck had marked out.

I swear I've circled the correct area nearly five times now!

Snow White squinted in the dim light of the trees, trying to make out the fabled home of Marzell and his friends.

The forest was dark. Though the sun hadn't set quite yet, the pine and fir trees blocked out what bits of light remained, and the leaf-bearing trees that had dropped their leaves in the prior fall resembled skeletons glopped with wet snow.

I'll have to leave and come back tomorrow. I don't relish the idea of finding a place to stay in Hurra and continuing to dodge Trubsinn soldiers, but I'll die of the cold like a proper idiot if I try to stay out all night. I'll be walking back in the dark as it is, which is dangerous enough.

She sighed as she turned on her heels and started back the way she had come, pressing her lips together to form a grim line.

A frigid wind tugged on Snow White's cloak, nearly managing to whip her hood off. She clenched her jaw to keep her teeth from chattering as she listened to the sounds of the forest—still hoping she might stumble across Marzell's place on her way back to Hurra.

There were no voices, no sounds of humanity. An owl hooted—but that was hardly reassuring.

Snow White jumped when a winter hare ran across her path. A stick cracked, and something rustled under a pine tree.

She sped up from a brisk walk to a trot, her lungs burning from the exertion and the cold. *I'm going to get eaten by something—if not a wolf, then by a twisted magical creature!*

For a moment, Snow White almost wished she hadn't heard the two men talking at the brazier so she could have continued on oblivious to the very real dangers in Mullberg she had been told were all false sightings.

Something thrashed in the forest, and Snow White's heart squeezed. She threw herself into a sprint—her cloak flapping behind her—as fright spurred her on.

The crackling of branches and crunch of underbrush followed her.

Her breath coming in frightened gasps, Snow White ran. She was too terrified to make a noise as the thumping closed in on her.

Her heart nearly burst when she heard growling, and something came flying out of the woods and collided with her.

CHAPTER 3
ANGEL, THE APPRENTICE

Snow White hit the ground with a yelp. Icey slush seeped through the layers of her dress, chilling her further, but she scrambled to her feet and grabbed a thick branch before she turned to see what creature had attacked her.

...*A woman?*

A young lady who didn't look much older than Snow White groaned as she sat upright. "That hurt. I hate trees. And forests." She scowled at the surrounding foliage as if they had personally offended her.

Snow White gawked at her "attacker" and clutched her branch to her chest.

The young lady rose to her feet so she could dust dead leaves and snow off her cloak. She glanced at Snow White. "Sorry about that. I didn't mean to scare you—though you must already be off your rocker if you're wandering around a forest this close to nightfall."

Snow White swallowed, her muscles going lax as her fear finally seeped away.

"Are you hurt or something?" the young lady asked. "Or do you just not talk?" She fished around in a satchel that hung from her shoulder and held out some sort of crystal. "Shine," she ordered. The crystal hummed as it shed a pure white light that illuminated the young lady's features.

She was medium height and had bark brown hair that fell to her shoulders in a jagged cut that looked like it might have been hacked off with a knife. Her clothes were unusual. She wore tan trousers and laced leather boots that drooped from her calves as if they were a size too large for her. Her blue tunic was a lovely color, but it also looked as though it were a size too large as it spilled halfway down her thighs and was strapped to her waist with three leather belts. Her cloak was plain but serviceable, but her satchel was covered with pouches and pockets and had sprigs of dried herbs hanging from it.

Realizing she was still waiting for a response, Snow White opened her mouth. It took several tries before anything emerged from her throat. "I-I'm f-fine."

The eccentrically dressed young lady squinted at her and held the glowing crystal higher, further illuminating her face. She had a slightly stubbed nose and an overly round face, but her eyes were a breathtaking shade of silver that Snow White had never seen before.

The silver-eyed stranger went from a relaxed stance to tensed. "You're the Mullberg Princess, Snow White."

Shocked she had been so easily recognized, Snow White took a staggering step backwards. "No, I'm..." she cringed under the strange lady's sharp eyes and finished lamely, "not."

"You are Princess Snow White," she said firmly. "No sense hiding it. Unless..." Her silver eyes narrowed in suspicion. "You aren't cursed, are you?"

Snow White blinked. She was so surprised she was able to speak without fumbling. "Cursed?"

"Do you have to kiss your true love to avoid some sort of dire —and stupid—consequence?"

Snow White shook her head.

The young lady leaned back so she was almost peering down her nose at Snow White. "You weren't cursed by an evil mage, or sorcerer, or witch...were you?"

"No."

She slapped her hands together in a praying gesture and closed her eyes. "I ought to sing a hymn or something. This is a first for me in a *long time*. A princess who is not cursed, how wonderful —*wait*." Back came the narrowed look. "If you're not cursed, why are you—a princess—running around a forest at night."

Snow White bit her lip and took another step backwards. *I'm not certain I can trust this girl.* "Who are you?" she asked nervously.

The young lady scratched her chin. "Fair enough of a question, I guess. I'm Angel. I'm an apprentice to an herb wizard. See?" She gestured to the dried herbs on her satchel for emphasis, then thrust her hand out.

Snow White slowly took it and was surprised when Angel firmly pumped her hand. The apprentice's unusual manners dispelled some of Snow White's tension, allowing her to murmur, "How do you do, Angel?"

"I was doing a lot better before I found you." Angel planted her hands on her hips and frowned at Snow White as if she were a problem to be solved. "But now you know I'm a minor magic user, so spill it."

Snow White studied the self-professed apprentice herb wizard with a wary eye.

Angel stood with confidence—or perhaps expectance was more accurate. The herbs on her satchel looked like lavender and rosemary—neither of which, according to multiple books Snow White had read, could be used for mischief or dark purposes. She held the bright crystal with no signs of illness, which meant she wasn't a being of darkness taking on a guise and was likely what she claimed to be.

Snow White sifted through her options and the possible

outcomes for a few moments before deciding the risks of explaining the situation to Angel were minimal.

She might not be able to help me directly, but she may be able to aid me so I can return to Hurra without freezing to death. Besides, news of Faina will break as soon as any lords start to move against her.

Snow White nodded and took a deep breath. "My stepmother, that is Queen Faina..." she trailed off as the hard reality of everything she had lived through came crashing down on her. Her fingers tingled with numbness, and she barely felt the first of her hot tears when they spilled from her eyes.

Angel's stance softened, and though she sighed, it had more of a sad, sympathetic sound to it. "What is it?" she asked gently.

Snow White rubbed her cold nose and stared remorsefully at her hands. "Something is terribly wrong, and I've made it even worse."

THE REST of the story spilled from Snow White's lips with a surprising amount of ease. She didn't care that they stood in the middle of a rapidly darkening forest, nor did she even mind her wet dress.

She numbly explained the situation to Angel—who asked a few very pointed questions but otherwise didn't interrupt.

Snow White filled Angel in all the way to her escape from Hurra and her plan to ask the Seven Warriors for help.

"Seven of them, you say?" Angel asked when the story was over.

"Yes."

"All males?"

"To my knowledge, yes."

Back came the suspicious slant to Angel's narrowed eyes. "They aren't cursed, are they?"

SNOW WHITE

Snow White tilted her head. *She seems to be very concerned about people being cursed.* "No."

Angel exhaled a deep puff of air. "Good—we avoided that one. Though it does sound like something suspicious is troubling Queen Faina. Not a curse—I don't *think*—but something. I don't know enough about dark magic to make a half-decent guess." She nodded, then adjusted her hold on her glowing crystal. "Well then, shall we be off?" Angel strode off without waiting for an answer, plowing into the dark forest.

"Are we going back to Hurra?" Snow White asked as she rushed to follow the other girl.

"And lose time? No!" Angel snorted like an irritated horse. "We'll find these seven fellows of yours and go from there."

"*We'll?*" Snow White felt like she was mentally as well as physically scrambling to follow the eccentric apprentice.

"Yes, we'll," Angel brandished her crystal higher. "My goal is to search Mullberg. Helping you for a bit won't be too big of a detour. Especially as Queen Faina's odd behavior might serve as a new lead."

"What are you searching Mullberg for—and why are you in Luster Forest at nighttime?" Snow White asked. She nearly rammed into Angel's back when the apprentice herb wizard abruptly turned down a different trail.

"I'm on a quest, you could say," Angel said. "I'm searching for my master. He's been taken by some rogue mages."

"And you've tracked him to *Mullberg?*" Snow White asked.

"Yep. It's fair embarrassing with the Veneno Conclave being here and all, but it is what it is," Angel said.

"How long has your master been missing?" Snow White asked, ducking under a branch.

"A little over six years," Angel said.

"Six years?" Snow White stopped walking for a moment. "Are you sure he isn't dead?"

"*Yes.*" Angel's voice was as gentle as granite.

That's a touchy subject. Snow White grimaced in sympathy, then resumed trotting after Angel. "Although I greatly appreciate your help, are you certain you can help me?"

"You're questioning my skills when you're the one without magic wandering around a darken woods?" Angel asked as she departed from the trail and plunged into the snowy underbrush.

"Er, that's not what I meant," Snow White said. "Isn't your master part of the Veneno Conclave—as all magic users are? Given the political ramifications, I'm not c-certain they would approve of your actions." She hesitated, then added, "And I understand that you would want to prioritize finding your master. I feel the same way about my stepmother, even though it has become clear to me the state of our country isn't quite what I thought it was."

"I have a hunch that if I help you with Queen Faina, I might uncover a clue about my master's whereabouts." Angel held back a branch of fragrant pine needles so Snow White could pass through without getting slapped in the face. "And as for the Veneno Conclave, they can go throw themselves into a manure pile for all the good *that* lot has done," she said hotly.

Another touchy subject. I seem to be an expert at poking people where it most hurts, a skill that will surely make it easier to overcome my shyness. Hah. Aloud, Snow White said, "I see." She shivered in cold and disgust when her slushy dress wrapped around her ankles. "Um. If I m-might ask..."

"Spit it out," Angel advised when Snow White's pause to summon more courage grew rather lengthy.

"How are we going to find the house?" Snow White asked.

"What do you mean?" Angel asked as she paused by a large fir tree.

"I looked quite thoroughly for their home, and I couldn't find a sign of it," Snow White said.

"No trouble there." Angel marched through the prickly branches. "We've already found it."

When Snow White finished pushing her way through the scratchy tree and popped out on the other side, she could make out the dim shape of a cottage crouched among the trees.

It resembled a misshapen farmer's hat. It was round, the roof curved up and down like the squashed brim, and the steeply pitched center part of the cottage served as the crown of the hat. The walls were made of moss-covered stones, and plaster covered with dead tendrils of ivy.

Snow White stared as Angel marched for the front door. "How did you...?"

"I saw it earlier," Angel called over her shoulder. "Given its secret location in the forest, I worried it might belong to a mage—or worse, someone cursed—so I gave it a wide berth. But after hearing the description of your Seven Warriors, I suspect it is likely their home."

Snow White hurriedly joined Angel at the door, almost tripping on a pile of logs in the dim light. As Angel pounded on the door, Snow White tried to twitch her red cloak into place so she at least looked somewhat presentable.

They waited for several long moments.

"I don't hear anything," Angel announced with a frown.

"Perhaps they are gone? Based on what I heard in Hurra, one could conclude they travel frequently throughout Mullberg to put down magical monsters..." Snow White trailed off as Angel abandoned the door and stalked around the perimeter of the building.

Snow White glanced at the door and timidly knocked again.

Angel flattened her face against one of the glass windows. "Yep, they're gone. It looks like they'll be back, though. The coals in the fireplace are still hot and glowing."

"Should we wait for them? Or perhaps we should go to Hurra since we have no way of knowing how long it will be before they return." Snow White backed away from the door and considered the oddly shaped house.

"Nah." Angel marched up to the front door. "We'll just break in."

"We'll *what?*" Snow White squeaked.

"I'm not willing to sit out here in the cold because your seven heroes are off being do-gooders," Angel said.

"But it might not even be their home!"

"We'll figure that out when we get inside, and if we're wrong, we can leave." Angel tugged on the door and frowned. "Locked," she said as she poked a finger at the iron keyhole.

"How unfortunate. We should go," Snow White said.

Angel released a cross between a roar and a shout as she kicked out, driving her right heel into the door. Her kick landed just next to the lock, and the door cracked and swung open.

Angel nodded in satisfaction, then stomped inside.

Snow White was not so quick to follow. She spent a moment gaping at the fractured door frame. Angel had apparently kicked the door with enough force that the lock ripped straight through the wooden frame. Fragments of wood hung from the cracked frame, and the ground was littered with splinters.

"I am reasonably sure this is the right cottage," Angel announced as she rummaged through a rack of weapons tipped against the wall. "If not, we've stumbled on the home of a murderer."

Snow White tried to shut the door, but the damaged frame made it so the door no longer fit properly. "Um," she said.

"You should add a log and some kindling to the coals and dry yourself out," Angel said as she unabashedly climbed a set of rickety stairs that led to a small loft area.

This feels rather ignoble. But I might get sick if I don't warm up soon. Reluctantly, Snow White crossed the cottage. She took a dried log and thrust it into the fire grate, remembering to add some smaller branches when the coals did nothing.

It took a minute, but eventually the branches flamed up, and soon a strong fire crackled in the brick fireplace.

SNOW WHITE

Snow White's teeth chattered as she held out her hands, warming herself.

"Yep, this is it," Angel called from the loft. "Between the various bedrolls and straw mattresses, we've got seven sleeping spots. But I thought you said some of these men are lords?"

"Some of them are," Snow White said.

"What?" Angel bellowed.

"Some of them are," Snow White called in a louder tone.

Angel grunted. "If that's so, then they are downright rooting in dirt compared to their usual standards." She pounded back down the staircase, jumping the last few steps. "That's good news for you. Only men with iron-shod standards for heroes would do something like this. If you cry a bit, they should be willing to help you."

"Um," Snow White said again, at a loss as to how she should respond to the apprentice's blunt words.

Angel frowned at Snow White's sodden dress. "You're more wet than I realized. You really ought to change."

"I haven't any extra clothes with me," Snow White said.

Angel glanced speculatively at the loft. "You could borrow something from your future heroes."

"*No*, thank you," Snow White said firmly. *I'd rather die of cold than greet Marzell and his friends in their clothes, having broken into their house!*

Angel shrugged and went back to poking around the cottage. "I don't blame you. Their clothes and linens reek—I don't think anything in here has been cleaned in a decade."

The area around the fireplace was marked off with a wooden bench and several straight-backed wooden chairs, each carved with an intricate ram pattern.

The wall behind the chairs was covered with copper pots and pans that hung from nails. Even higher up the walls hung dried herbs—dill and thyme based on the tangy scents—and there was a shelf of worn but well-made wooden dishes and clay mugs.

There was a long wooden table with matching benches, a small shelf of books, and what appeared to be a crude writing desk of sorts covered with papers, inks, and dull quills. But the majority of the lower floor of the cottage was dedicated to a wide variety of weapons and what looked like rolled-up canvas paintings.

Most of the wooden flooring was spattered with flecks of paint and bits of dried herbs, and though the dried herbs were a strong scent, they were nearly eclipsed by the pungent smell of unwashed dishes and sweat-crusted clothes.

"Are they art enthusiasts?" Angel mused as she prodded a barrel filled with rolled up canvases.

As warmth finally returned to Snow White's fingers and toes, she shrugged tiredly and leaned back against the wooden bench. "Who knows," she murmured.

Angel made a duck-like noise in the back of her throat and continued to poke around.

Snow White's heavy eyelids threatened to shut as she basked in the warmth. *I'll close my eyes for just a few moments,* she thought. *I can't do anything until Marzell and his friends return anyway.*

She felt her tension melt away as she gave in and shut her eyes, listening to the fire crackle and the occasional clang as Angel accidentally dropped one of the many weapons cluttering up the cottage.

I hope they can help me. I hope I can right this wrong...

෴

SNOW WHITE DIDN'T KNOW how much time passed, but it seemed like only a moment before Angel said offhandedly, "Your Seven Warriors have arrived. Looks like they're stabling their horses in a lean-to behind the cottage, and then they'll be in."

"What?" Snow White stirred, blinking blearily as she tried—and failed—to sit up from her curled-up spot by the fire.

"No, no—you should stay there," Angel instructed through a crunching noise. "If they find you sleeping by the fire, it will underline your innocence."

Snow White tried to peel her protesting eyes open but failed. "What?" she repeated, struggling to keep up with Angel.

Angel didn't respond, but there were more crunching sounds.

"Are you *eating their food?*" Snow White asked, her voice rusty with sleep.

"Just go back to sleep—or pretend to," Angel coached.

Voices rumbled outside the door, returning Snow White to reality like a bucket of cold water. She snapped her eyes open and finally succeeded in sitting up, just as the door swung open.

CHAPTER 4
THE SEVEN WARRIORS

Cloaked men filled the doorway, and Snow White felt her stomach curdle in dread and a bit of fear.

Angel seemed to have no such anxiety, and instead, she waggled a shriveled carrot she had been munching on at the men. "Hello. Welcome home!"

The closest man—who was also by far the tallest—seemed to tilt his head as he studied them, but it was hard to tell, as his face was shadowed by his hood.

A shorter man pushed to the front, an unsheathed sword clenched in his hands. "Who are you?" he growled.

"Never mind that," Angel said. "You lot are a bunch of pigs. You're lucky it's not summer, or your pigpen would have been irredeemably claimed by flies and bugs."

"*Angel!*" Snow White hissed. She unintentionally drew the attention of the shorter, sword-wielding man and shrank under his sharp gaze.

Angel took another bite out of her carrot. "Oh, yeah. That's your princess. You probably ought to bow or something."

Outside a muffled voice asked, "Who is inside?"

The sword-wielding man took a step closer to Angel—who

looked unperturbed by the possible threat of violence. "A mad woman," he said.

The taller figure turned around and murmured a few indistinguishable words.

"What?" the muffled voice called.

There was a scuffle as someone pushed his way to the front. He flipped his hood off, revealing coppery brown hair and a kind face. "Snow White?" he asked, frowning slightly at her.

Snow White almost sighed in relief. "Hello, Marzell." She boosted herself to her feet, staggering a little when her weary muscles protested, and smiled at her childhood friend.

Though it had been years since they played together, Marzell still had a boyish face and lips that persisted in curving in an ever-present but gentle smile. She was grateful—it made it easier to talk to him if she could recall the days she had spent playing with him.

"What are you doing here, and who is your friend?" Marzell asked as he entered the cottage, glancing curiously at Angel—who had moved on to poking a basket with her toe.

Angel waggled her fingers at him but made no effort to pay him any mind as she continued to riffle through the food supplies.

Marzell pulled back slightly at her lack of care, but when he settled his gaze on Snow White, he paused, then bent over in a bow. "That is to say, Your Highness...why are you here?"

"It is a long tale," Snow White's voice faltered slightly when she glanced past him at the other men who crowded up the door.

A man with sunflower blond hair emerged between the tall man and the sword-wielder. "Did you say princess?" He blinked in curiosity as he eyed Snow White. "Oh. It is her." A moment passed before he grinned widely. "Have you also fallen prey to my handsome good looks and legendary reputation?"

"Shut your yap, Aldelbert," the sword-wielder said.

"I take offense to that tone!" someone behind Marzell objected. "Apologize to My Lord!"

"Why don't you make me?" the sword-wielder scoffed.

"Princess," Marzell glanced back at those crowded behind him. "Please allow me to introduce you to my friends. The one with the sword is Oswald—he's the third son of Lord Lowenstein."

Oswald huffed through his nose and finally put his sword back into its scabbard. He had shaggy strawberry-blond hair and was roughly Marzell's height—though he was scrappier in build and seemed to charge forward instead of walking like a normal person.

Snow White nodded to him. "How do you—" She couldn't finish the nicety because Oswald studied her with a narrowed gaze, then snorted and thumped into the cottage, making for the weapon racks.

"Uncouth mutt," one of the other men muttered.

Oswald whirled around. "What did you say, wimpy?"

The first man placed his hand on the hilt of a sword. "Say that again," he said in a low, emotionless voice.

Oswald placed his hands on his hips. "*Wimpy*—ouch!" He crashed to the ground when the other man threw his sword scabbard, smacking Oswald in the head.

"That would be Rupert—he's Lord Hugel's nephew and heir," Marzell said.

Rupert glided in Oswald's direction, moving slowly but purposefully. He had dark hair that Snow White thought might have been black—it was tough to see with only the light of the fire. The darkness of his hair made the pallor of his skin extra white. He had a slighter build, but if the welt on Oswald's head was anything to go by, that did not mean he lacked strength.

"Surely you must know *me*!" Crowed the man with hair the shade of sunflowers. He was built rather like sketches and paintings of heroes found in some of the books Snow White had read. He was wider through the shoulders, tall, and was strikingly handsome.

Another young man popped out by the handsome man's feet,

a harp in hand. "Everyone knows My Lord!" he said before strumming a chord on the harp.

They looked expectantly at Snow White, who felt her cheeks turn red in embarrassment.

She fought off the desire to hide her face and instead mumbled, "I apologize."

"What was that?" the handsome man said.

"I a-apologize," Snow White hesitated. "I don't..."

The man strumming on the harp was so shocked, he plucked too hard and broke a string. "You don't know *My Lord*?"

"Impossible!" the handsome man declared.

"This is Lord Aldelbert and his attendant, Wendal," Marzell explained as the attendant—Wendal—zipped past him. "Aldelbert is Lord Chita's only son."

Wendal plucked a rolled-up canvas from one of the stuffed barrels and marched up to Snow White. He thrust it in her direction. "Here," he said. "I'm certain you only need to view My Lord in his finery, and you will recall seeing him in the halls of Glitzern Palace, Princess."

Not likely. If he came for public events, I probably spent the whole time wishing to be struck dead before my speech came up. Still, Snow White took the canvas and smiled nervously at Wendal, who waited patiently for her to open it.

Snow White rolled it open, revealing a portrait of Aldelbert, dressed in a silken tunic, holding a golden cup and a bunch of grapes while smiling roguishly.

What am I supposed to say to this?

She wavered for a moment and was relieved when Angel joined her, leaning in so she could also see the portrait.

"Is he trying to marry a rich old lady?" Angel asked.

"I beg your pardon?" Wendal sputtered.

Angel tapped the painting. "Because this seems like the kind of thing you would give a rich old lady."

Aldelbert laughed loudly. "Hah-ha! I like your fire, poorly

dressed woman! Wendal, select a portrait for her as well, to reward her!"

Wendal scowled but started for the barrel. "She doesn't deserve it, My Lord," he said.

"Yeah, that's fine," Angel said. "I don't really want a 'reward' like that either."

Wendal ignored her and selected a painting—making Snow White wonder if *all* the rolled-up canvases were paintings of Aldelbert. On his way back, he was nearly run down by one of Marzell's remaining compatriots—a broad-shouldered young man who had shockingly bright red hair.

The red-haired young man yawned as he trudged inside—not even noticing Wendal's squawk of outrage. He plopped down on one of the benches set by the table and teetered for a moment before abruptly falling forward, hitting the table with a loud thud.

Angel raised an eyebrow. "Is he all right?"

"Yes, he's fine," Marzell said. "That's Gregori. His family owns Waldberg Imports."

Angel shrugged, unimpressed by the information, but Snow White eyed him with new respect.

Waldberg Imports was one of the biggest merchant suppliers in Mullberg, and the family was richer than half of the nobles in Snow White's court.

Marzell moved farther into the cottage, leaving his last companion—the silent young man who was the tallest of them all—to shove the door back into the cracked and damaged frame.

The silent man seemed to glance in Snow White's direction before he mumbled to Marzell. "Needs repairs."

Marzell frowned slightly at the door. "So it would seem. Ah—princess, allow me to introduce my final companion, Fritz."

Fritz whipped off his hood and smiled slightly. He had ashy brown hair and hazel eyes. Though he was rather tall—standing next to him, Snow White would have to fold her head back on her neck to look up at him—he was lean and moved quietly and with purpose.

"Fritz is actually a forester," Marzell explained. "We wouldn't be able to survive like this without him."

"That means he's the only useful one out of the bunch," Angel said in not-a-whisper. "So you'll want to make sure you convince him." She swatted in Fritz's direction with the rolled-up canvas painting of Aldelbert.

"I have many uses!" Aldelbert protested.

"I am unconvinced," Angel said.

Snow White was only vaguely aware of Angel's verbal jabs and Wendal's scoffs. She met Fritz's gaze and for once was glad she was scared stiff. It meant she couldn't utter even a squeak when the tall forester stared at her.

He's huge. And intimidating! And I didn't miss how he shoved the door back in the frame—he must be their best warrior, too.

Her spit got lodged in her throat when Fritz bent over in a bow.

"Snow White," Marzell said, drawing her attention away from the forester. "Can you tell us, now, why you are here?"

Snow White licked her lips. "Ah. Yes. There is something wrong with my stepmother."

"Queen Faina?" Marzell asked.

Snow White nodded.

Oswald snorted. "Any one of us could have told you that! She's ignoring the steady creep of monsters and fiends slowly invading Mullberg." He squeezed one eye shut as he peered down the length of a dagger.

"It's not just that..." Snow White trailed off when Oswald, Rupert, Marzell, and the quiet Fritz all stared at her.

"Yes?" Marzell kindly asked.

Rupert leaned against the questionably steady stair railing. "You've broken into our house, Your Highness. Now is hardly the time to be coy."

Marzell frowned at Rupert and shook his head, but the young heir merely shrugged.

"She tried to hurt me today," Snow White finally blurted out. "She's been prone to fits of anger and rage for...quite a while. But prior to today, she only shouted." She hesitated and glanced at her audience.

Angel had moved on and was once again digging through baskets of food. But besides her and Gregori—who snored from his splayed-out position on the table—everyone else watched.

Snow White gulped and stared at her feet. *I have to speak. I have to do this—or else...* She couldn't finish the thought and instead forced her mouth open. "She tried to...stab me. With a dagger. And she said she'd eat my h-heart. But she stopped herself in time."

Marzell folded his arms across his chest and his frown deepened. "That does sound serious."

"That sounds *crazy*," Oswald muttered.

"I am not often inclined to agree with the angry troll, but in this case, I concur," Rupert said.

Oswald growled. "Why you—"

Fritz set a hand on Oswald's shoulder. When the scruffy young man looked up at him, he shook his head.

Oswald grumbled and casually kicked the paint-spattered floor, but fell silent.

"She's not mad," Snow White argued. "It's not her fault. There's something wrong with her, but I don't think it's her doing."

"People don't choose to go mad, Your Highness," Wendal said with a note of sympathy to his voice.

"No!" Snow White shook her head and clenched her hands in fists. *How do I explain this to them?* "It's like she's not herself when it happens. She—I!" Snow White broke off, unable to articulate everything.

Angel set a gentle hand on Snow White's forearm and

squeezed. "Snow White is here because Queen Faina sent her away," she said. "Snow White was *supposed* to go to her maternal grandfather's and carry a letter to him from Faina. The letter essentially asked Lord Trubsinn to send troops to Juwel to kill Faina. Apparently, the Queen has tried to end her own life, but whatever it is that has her in its grips won't let her."

"Queen Faina has always been such a sound judge of character," Aldelbert said, making hope rise in Snow White. "Obviously so, for on the occasions I saw her at court, she always called me a handsome boy."

"As My Lord says," Wendal said.

"It's definitely madness," Oswald muttered.

Snow White clamped her jaw shut, her anger making it a little easier to meet his gaze. "Faina is *not* m-mad!"

With a grunt, Marzell set a pot of water to boil over the fire. "Then what is it, Your Highness?"

Desperation clawed at Snow White's thoughts. *I hadn't thought I would need to convince them! Angel believed me readily enough, and she doesn't even know Faina.* Snow White glanced at Angel. "You're an herb wizard's apprentice, Angel. Could it be something founded in magic?"

"*She?*" Aldelbert pointed a finger at Angel in horror. "This scruffy, dirty specimen is a *magic user?*"

Angel chomped her teeth together like a snapping wolf. "Put that finger any closer, and I'll bite it off."

Aldelbert stared quizzically at his finger, but Wendal scowled in outrage. "Come, My Lord. You should remove yourself from such a close proximity to this creature. Who is to say she doesn't have fleas?"

Angel snorted. "You pigs are the ones who sleep in filth!"

"Angel." Snow White's desperation gave her the courage to grab one of the apprentice's hands. "*Please.*"

Angel sighed and scratched her head. "It's hard to say. She's not cursed—those don't come and go on a person like that—and curses are what I have the most experience in. But I've encountered enough dark magic over the years to say it's possible it might be affecting Queen Faina. There's certainly a lot of it swirling around the continent these days, making it far more likely. It's impossible to know for sure, though, unless you are in her presence."

Snow White drooped. "There have been mages with healing magic in the palace over the past few years. Would they have noticed?"

"I imagine so," Marzell said, though he glanced at Angel for confirmation.

Angel shrugged her shoulders. "Not necessarily."

Marzell raised an eyebrow. "You think a Veneno Conclave *mage* would miss such a thing?"

"Call me a cynic, but with the way the continent has been plagued the last few years, they seem rather incompetent, or at the very least cowardly," Angel grumbled.

"What is it about Queen Faina's actions that make it hard to say if someone—or something—is using magic on her?" Rupert asked.

"From the way Snow White tells it, these moods or fits, you could say, have come and gone for a year," Angel said. "It would take an *extraordinary* amount of self-control and courage to fight off such magic for so long."

Snow White licked her dry lips. "P-perhaps whoever is doing this to her has done that on purpose to make it more gradual, so we wouldn't notice until it was too late?"

Angel nodded. "That's a distinct possibility. Given what dark magic users are running around, I can say they're certainly capable of doing such a thing—though it's awfully gutsy to do so when the Veneno Conclave is camped out in the front courtyard, so to speak—even if the Conclave has lost its teeth in recent years. Still, I'm not saying it couldn't be done. Particularly given that such a crafty spell would be much harder to find—which would explain why the healers never noticed it. There are a couple other possibilities, of course. Ancient cursed—or magical—artifacts can be responsible for such things. They can hold people under sway, provide extra power, or possess rare magic. Although, they are rarer than unicorns these days."

"So it's even less likely that an *object* could be responsible for this than a dark mage," Marzell said.

"Mmmm, yeah."

"I still say it's madness," Oswald announced.

"Oswald," Marzell said in a warning tone.

"What? After all we've seen, you can't really expect me to believe Queen Faina's been holding off some black demon!"

Rupert adjusted his sword belt. "He was chiding you for your insensitivity and lack of sympathy, not for your thoughts, you raging monkey." Rupert paused, then sneezed loudly and with enough force to make him bend over.

Oswald curled his upper lip. "At least I'm not a delicate spring flower who can't breathe without a coughing fit."

"I'm not delicate—this is just hay fever," Rupert grumbled before another sneeze took him.

"Has the little lord been outside doing too many manly things for his gentle constitution?" Oswald laughed, then choked when Rupert yanked him by the collar of his leather doublet.

"Hardly. It's the terrible fungus odor *you* emit that makes me so!" Rupert tried to punch Oswald but was tipped off balance by another sneeze.

Oswald slipped a dagger from his belt and jabbed it at Rupert. The lordling blocked it with his sword, then kicked out at Oswald like an angry horse. Oswald leaped backwards and threw his dagger at a rope securing a hanging basket of onions. The rope snapped.

Rupert leaped out of the way, but a dozen onions tumbled from the basket, hitting the wooden table with a rattle.

Gregori—the one built like an ox and sleeping soundly—

briefly stirred. His snores halted, and he muttered something into his arm as he slightly adjusted his position.

Rupert and Oswald froze—Oswald balanced on one leg, and Rupert clamped his hands over his mouth to strangle a sneeze.

Both remained that way for several long seconds until Gregori's snores picked back up.

Rupert sneezed loudly, then wiped his watering eyes. "Idiot," he snarled.

"Sickly heiress," Oswald snorted.

The two exchanged glares and tip-toed away from the table, renewing their fight by the weapons racks.

Snow White watched them with no small amount of calculation. *Good, with those two distracted, I might find it easier to bring Marzell around.* She cleared her throat, then forced herself to look her childhood friend in the eyes.

"Will you help me look into this, Marzell?" she asked. "I want to save Faina."

Marzell sighed and rubbed the back of his neck. "I want to believe you, Princess, but I'm afraid Oswald's idea of madness makes more sense."

"But you haven't even *seen* her," Snow White said, her heart stuttering in fear.

"I don't have to," Marzell said gently, "because my friends and I have been living through her actions for the past few years. Princess, Snow White, Faina has been slipping for years."

All the air left Snow White's lungs. "What?"

Marzell motioned for her to take a seat on the wooden bench by the fire. As she did so, he plopped down in one of the carved chairs. Fritz stood at his back, looking a bit like a vengeful ghost in the flickering firelight as he hadn't yet taken off his cloak.

Snow White thought Aldelbert and Wendal would join them, but the attendant nudged his master toward the still quarreling Oswald and Rupert instead.

Once settled, Marzell steepled his fingers together. "For at least five years now, Faina has been making increasingly poor decisions as a ruler."

Snow White started to shake her head.

Marzell raised his hands in supplication. "Hear me out, please. My friends and I came here and have lived in the woods because we so strongly disagree with her."

Angel, who thoughtfully watched Gregori slumber, raised an eyebrow. "Is it really possible for that bright-haired idiot to feel strongly about anything besides himself?" She asked, nodding at Aldelbert.

Snow White would have cracked a smile if the moment had been less tense, but she kept her gaze on Marzell.

"There have been attacks on our borders—not attacks from other countries, but from terrible creatures: chimera, hell hounds, goblins... Queen Faina has chosen to ignore them," Marzell said.

"That's not true," Snow White objected. "I've sat in on dozens of meetings with the Cabinet. She has sent troops to investigate the reports!"

"Weeks—sometimes months—after the monsters have already been taken care of," Marzell said.

"If it was a serious problem, I would think there would be no suppressing the news," Angel said as she moved to stand behind Snow White's bench. "I've been traveling the continent, and no one has heard of any trouble stirring in Mullberg."

"It's been subtle," Marzell agreed. "At first the creatures were only on the very fringe of the country—and even now, they do not venture very far in. They only harry those on the outskirts of civilization. But given the sad state of the rest of the continent, it's rather obvious that there is a trap waiting to snap on Mullberg. The Queen has done nothing to stop, much less prepare for it."

"If she hasn't moved, it's because she didn't know," Snow White said. "Her ministers—*our* ministers—told her countless times she should round you and your companions up, but she said no."

"I'm not saying Queen Faina's heart isn't good, but merely that if she really is mad, it's been brewing for a while," Marzell said gently.

Snow White's lower lip trembled briefly, not with sorrow but rage. *How dare he declare Faina mad! When she has suffered and fought against whatever this is. Just—I—how dare he!*

"Can you think of no situation where the Queen neglected to act, and there was a dangerous outcome?" Marzell asked in a coaxing voice.

Snow White froze as she thought of the invitation from Loire to join the Summit.

Marzell leaned back in his chair. "You see?"

Snow White blindly shook her head. "I cannot believe it. I *will* not! Faina needs to be saved."

Marzell sighed. "Regardless, I'm afraid we can't help you, Your Highness."

"Your decision seems awfully final, even though you've been in the woods and have not seen Queen Faina yourself," Angel said.

Marzell gestured around the cottage. "I don't have to. We saw the queen start to slide years ago, and you stated yourself that Faina would have to have extraordinary self-control to resist for even a year, did you not?"

Angel shrugged. "Even so. It seems dangerous to decide without investigating the matter first. Not to mention it is your *princess* asking for aid."

Snow White stared at her hands and gripped the material of her skirts. *So, I've failed on my first attempt. I thought Marzell and his friends would be the most likely to help, but it seems I was wrong. I'll have to come up with something else, for I cannot go to Grandfather or the advisors. They likely won't stop to question what is wrong with Faina, but will end her life as she requested.*

She pressed her lips in a thin line, angry with Marzell and his assumptions, angry with the protectiveness of her noble subjects, and angry with herself for failing to have the strength to make them listen to her.

What do I do now? Where do I go?

"You can spend the night here," Marzell said, jarring her. "It's too late for you to leave now anyhow. In the morning, one of us will escort you to a city of your choice."

Snow White nodded, but she did not lift her gaze.

Marzell sighed and awkwardly stood. "If you'll excuse me, Your Highness," he murmured before leaving the area.

Fritz, strangely, remained behind, as did Angel.

The apprentice set a hand on Snow White's shoulder. "We'll figure out something, Your Highness."

Snow White again miserably nodded her head. When she finally lifted her eyes, it was only to look at the fire.

I have to succeed, she thought, swallowing heavily as Fritz shifted quietly. *I will not let my stepmother sacrifice herself!*

❧

LATE INTO THE NIGHT, when the winds howled like a hungry wolf and seemed to threaten to rip the roof straight off the cottage, Fritz stood in the shadows of the loft, watching a wide-awake Snow White stare into the slowly dying fire.

The apprentice—Angel—was passed out in a bedroll near to the princess, her head cushioned on her herb-covered satchel as she muttered angrily in her sleep.

Behind him slept Marzell and the other warriors, their deep breathing and occasional shifts in their cots puncturing the silence.

Though it was well past midnight, Fritz was not at all tempted to retire to his own cot. Instead, he watched the princess—Snow White—with a thoughtful frown tugging at his mouth.

The unusual combination of her deep blue eyes and glossy black curls marked her as a beauty, but her red lips—surprisingly expressive even when she said nothing—and slender figure only amplified the effect. Though she was perhaps not quite elegant—she was too timid and lacked the required self-assurance—she was graceful in her still thoughtfulness.

Fritz didn't believe in love at first sight, much less friendship at first sight.

He was a forester in both occupation and temperament, which meant he usually preferred to stand in the shadows for a time and observe a person's true nature when they believed they were alone.

And yet. *And yet.*

There was something about Snow White that drew him.

He shifted so slightly that not even a floorboard creaked as he watched her stare into the flickering flames of the fire.

It is impressive that her loyalty to Queen Faina brought her this far. She has only been frightened and uncomfortable since she arrived—as proved by her stammer and her inclination to stare at her feet. But she draws up her courage for the sake of her stepmother, a rare trait.

Most people wouldn't face their fears for their *own* wellbeing, never mind for someone else's sake. But it was clear Snow White was acting only because of the danger Faina was in.

Even now, based on the expression in her eyes and her body language, if Fritz had to hazard a guess, he would say that she was already planning her next move.

Which surprised him.

It was generally believed that the Princess Snow White was a pretty girl—soft-spoken and rather shy, but gentle and kindhearted. Marzell and those of the Seven Warriors who had seen Snow White in court functions had only affirmed the gossip.

As such, Fritz had hardly expected their princess to be strategic. She hadn't given up when Marzell mentioned his doubts, but instead questioned his thinking and pulled answers from the herb wizard's apprentice to explore possibilities most wouldn't consider or think of.

She was...unusual.

And there may be something to her words. When she explained the situation to Marzell, there was a specific phrase she used that caught Fritz's attention.

She may be more correct than Marzell believes.

CHAPTER 5
CONSTRUCTS

Snow White rested her chin on her knees as she studied the flickering flames, sorting through all the possible options she could take next.

She shifted slightly, drawing her legs closer to her chest, then glanced around to make certain she had not disturbed anyone.

Angel slept soundly in her bedroll, mumbling something and then snorting loudly—though she slept on.

Marzell and the others had retired to the loft area—except for Gregori. He still slept on the table. (Marzell had tried to prod him off the bench so he would come upstairs as well, but the large man had opened a single eye, and Marzell had left so quickly there was a breeze in his wake.)

Snow White returned her gaze to the fire and thoughtfully pressed her lips together. Though she was still disappointed at Marzell's refusal to help, and occasionally hot tears threatened to flood her eyes, she kept her mind focused on the problem before her.

If I wallow in self-pity, I won't do anyone any good, and I'll only fritter away valuable time. I need to make a plan as swiftly as possible.

Thus far, seeking out neighboring royalty seemed to be her

best option after all. She had narrowed it down from Mullberg's three closest neighbors—Verglas, Loire, and Arcainia—to merely Arcainia.

The Arcainian royal family had experience with twisted magic after King Henrik had been spelled several years prior. Additionally, the country's fifth prince, Prince Rune, was famous for his battle prowess against dark creatures, and the crown princess was known to be something of an adventurer. They would likely be the easiest to sway.

She sniffed and rubbed her weary eyes, but even the warmth of the fire couldn't tempt her to sleep.

Something that sounded like footfalls creaked across the roof, and even through the walls, Snow White heard something crackle outside.

A branch, probably.

She shivered and stood, tip-toeing over to one of the small glass windows. She tried to peer outside into the darkness, but she couldn't make anything out.

Nervously, she swallowed and turned back to the fire, startling with a jump and a hushed gasp when she saw something stood between her and the fire.

It took her a moment to realize it was Fritz, dressed in dark green clothes that looked black in the dim firelight.

When she stepped back, he hunkered down enough so he could also look outside. After a moment, he turned to her and slightly tilted his head.

"I-I thought I...h-heard something. Out there. But...it's dark," Snow White babbled, quaking under his scrutiny.

Fritz strode across the cottage—as silent as a shadow. He didn't disturb the snoozing Gregori, or Angel—who had somehow acquired a knife and slept with it *unsheathed*, casually resting on her stomach.

Snow White reluctantly followed the silent forester back to the fire and watched as he unrolled the bedroll she hadn't used.

He fluffed it up, then set another blanket on top of it before motioning to Snow White.

She slowly eased herself onto the bedroll, wringing her hands as she was *very* aware of Fritz's steady gaze.

To her surprise—and apprehension—he lowered himself into one of the carved chairs opposite.

Is he planning to sit here and make sure I don't do anything? But why? Snow White swallowed and tried to keep her breathing rate normal. She almost jumped out of her skin when Fritz broke the silence.

"Why don't you believe Queen Faina is mad?" His voice was deep, like a canyon cutting through the earth, but it was also strangely soothing and warm.

Snow White glanced up at Fritz. His gaze was steady, and it appeared to be sincere. He really wanted to know why, when Marzell and the others refused to even entertain the idea.

Snow White quickly shifted her gaze to the flickering fire. She clenched her hands into fists. *Be brave, for Faina.* "Because I know Faina. She's kind and thoughtful. She listens carefully to everyone, and she would never knowingly leave her people in danger. She would *never* hurt me. She was a wonderful parent, even though I'm not hers. Even after Father died, she'd hold me when I was sad and sit with me when I was sick. She sang to me when I was a child, and consoled me whenever I bungled a speech."

"She loves you," Fritz said.

Snow White laughed quietly. "Yes. With more patience and gentleness than I thought possible." She shook her head in despair. "Faina did everything she could to protect me, and I was too scared to offer help. I left her alone to face whatever has her in its grasp."

Silence fell, besides the occasional hiss of the fire and the ever-present howl of the wind.

Snow White took a rattling breath. *This tastes like defeat.*

Knowing how much Faina loved me, and how I have failed her already...I must get to Arcainia. She rapidly blinked her watering eyes.

"She's not," Fritz said.

Snow White wiped a tear. "I beg your pardon?"

"She's not mad," Fritz said.

Snow White snapped out of her mood and—if Fritz had been any less intimidating—she would have grabbed him by his doublet. "H-how do you know?"

"She stopped herself," he said.

Snow White stared blankly at him.

"Earlier. You told Marzell she threatened you, but stopped herself in time." Fritz waited until Snow White met his gaze. His hazel eyes were hypnotizing in their strength and assurance. "If she were mad, she wouldn't have broken out of it."

"But she stopped...because she loves me." Snow White moved so she kneeled and gripped the wooden bench as if it were a raft. "Whatever it is that has her, she threw it off because she wouldn't let it hurt me."

Fritz waited for a moment, then inclined his head.

Snow White briefly shut her eyes and sighed in relief.

She knew Faina wasn't mad. She never doubted her. But to have *proof*? "Thank you." Snow White smiled at Fritz, unable to verbalize the assurance he had just given her. "Really... t-thank you."

Fritz smiled slightly—a gesture that was more in the gentle crease at his eyes than the slight curve of his lips. It made him look a lot less foreboding, too. "My pleasure—and honor," he said.

Snow White sat down on her rear with a thump, still shaken by his support. "Even if this doesn't move Marzell, I can point this out to the Arcainian royal family when I talk to them." Words leaked out of Snow White, but she found she shockingly didn't care to try and control them. "It appears I need more proof than I thought. Either the situation is so unusual, or it is merely that people don't view me seriously..." she trailed off, the bitter taste returning to her mouth. "Not that I blame them," she muttered. "I can hardly t-talk when more than two or three people are present."

Fritz shook his head.

"No?" Snow White ventured after a few awkward moments of silence.

Fritz blinked slowly—thinking—and held Snow White's gaze, the thoughtful light in his eyes still glowing.

Something tapped against a glass window pane.

Snow White blinked, and when she opened her eyes, Fritz was standing, his hand on the hilt of a sword she hadn't realized he had strapped to his belt.

He held a palm out to her, indicating she should remain where she was, as he crept toward a window. He angled himself so he approached from the side and slid his sword out of its scabbard.

Snow White once again gripped the bench as she watched him. *That was just a tree branch, wasn't it?*

She was about to call out and ask as much when the small window by the door shattered, sending shards of glass flying.

A clawed, shadowy hand thrust through the broken pane.

Snow White opened her mouth in a silent scream, but Fritz shouted, "*A breach*," his voice strong and loud even as the four other glass windows in the cottage shattered as well.

He lifted his sword above his head and chopped it down in a smooth motion, slicing straight through the shadowy arm.

The severed hand fell with a thump to the floor, before it morphed into black smoke that disappeared.

"*Magic breach!*" Fritz corrected without so much as blinking.

Gregori shot upright, going from seated at the table to running for the weapon racks with one sliding movement. The large man didn't even blink when a trunk-like arm grabbed for him as he passed a window.

"*What now?*" Angel snarled as she sat up, her hair messy and piled on the top of her head. She scowled angrily in the dim light until she spotted Fritz slicing off another shadowy hand that clawed at the plaster walls for a handhold.

Immediately, she switched to cursing under her breath as she flung her satchel open and started digging through it.

Snow White squeaked when she looked past the apprentice. In the back corner, past the food storage area, a creature finally succeeded in dragging itself through a window and all the way into the cottage.

It was humanoid in shape, but it looked as if someone had slapped it together in a mockery of mankind. It was skinny in the torso and had long, rigid limbs that were jagged at the elbows—as if shards of bone poked out, and the creator hadn't bothered to shove them back in. Similar jagged ridges poked out of its shoulders, but what was most horrifying was its egg-shaped head.

Broad and bald at the top, its face pulled down into a narrow chin, broken only by its serrated smile—which almost reached its eerie eyes that were perfect circles of glowing white light. The *thing's* eyes were frightening, for it was not the white of warmth and purity, but a void of emptiness. A white of endless hunger and mindless destruction.

Snow White grabbed a fire poker and took a step backwards, putting herself so close to the fire she nearly singed her dress. "One got in!"

Angel turned around, but before she or Snow White moved, Fritz threw his sword—which stabbed the creature straight through its chest cavity.

It hissed as its body turned smoky, its white eyes the last thing to fade away.

Fritz snatched up another sword off a rack of weapons and spun around, stabbing his sword through a window—presumedly into another shadowy monster.

Gregori wrenched a crossbow off the wall and loaded a bolt in it before shooting the head of one of the monsters as it shoved its way through a broken window, turning it into a puff of smoke.

"I've never seen anything like these...*creatures* before," he said, his voice unexpectedly musical.

"They're not creatures," Angel said with narrowed eyes. "They're magic constructs. That's why they fade when the magic is interrupted."

Oswald *jumped* over the loft railing, eschewing the stairs as he landed on the ground in a crouch. Rupert was right behind him, though the slighter man rolled when he landed, putting him a little closer to Angel and Snow White.

"Gregori, saber!" Oswald called.

Gregori—who had just pulled a belt quiver of crossbow bolts from a rack, yanked a saber from the wall and tossed it at Oswald.

Oswald caught it midair and ran for a window—where another one of the black creatures was trying to crawl through.

Marzell trundled down the stairs, pushing his mussed, coppery hair from his face. "What's going on?" he asked, his voice calm despite the outright attack on the cottage.

"Unknown number of these constructs," Fritz gestured to a monster that poked its head through a window before Gregori shot it in the face, making it evaporate. "Attacking the cottage," Fritz finished.

"Plug up some of the windows," Marzell said as he retrieved a long, tasseled whip.

"Oh, sure. We'll get right on that," Oswald groused as he ran for the widow past the food storage—where *another* creature was halfway inside and pulling its leg through.

Aldelbert waltzed down the stairs, a bright smile on his face. "These monsters are that excited to see my handsome face, are they?" He laughed and skirted a clawed hand that swiped at him, then casually picked up a wooden shield and slapped it over one of the broken window panes. "Might anyone fetch me some nails? Oh—and a hammer!"

Snow White watched as one of the rigid constructs slipped

through an unguarded window. It swayed on its feet for a moment as it shuffled, until its glowing eyes locked on her.

It lunged in Snow White's direction, picking up speed so it ran, swinging its long, twisted limbs as its white eyes focused on her.

Snow White scrambled to raise her fire poker, but nearly choked on her heart that had jumped into her throat.

The monster closed in on her and swung its arms above its head. It leaped, straight into a shower of daggers. The magical construct popped like a puff of smoke.

Snow White squinted up at the rafters, surprised to see Wendal crouched there. He held three daggers between his fingers in each hand, and his usually jovial expression was serious as he tracked the monsters' path through the cottage.

"I'm still waiting for that hammer and nails," Aldelbert said, sounding slightly put-out.

"Wait until you die of old age. They aren't coming!" Oswald snarled.

Aldelbert sighed. "Fine." He held the shield in place with one foot pressed against it, then stretched to grab four hand axes. He eyed the shield for a moment, then threw the axes with a surprising amount of force, so they pierced through the wooden shield and dug into the plaster walls, essentially nailing the shield to the window pane.

"That is remarkably effective," Marzell noted.

"It won't matter if these monsters' numbers don't start thinning," Gregori rumbled, his red hair bright in the dim light.

Fritz exchanged nods with Rupert and slowly backed up while Rupert crept forward so they swapped spaces, leaving Fritz to guard Snow White and Angel.

"If these constructs really have that great of numbers, perhaps we ought to reinforce the door." Angel eyed the door as she tossed her knife back and forth between her hands. "It *is* broken, after all."

"And whose fault is that?" Oswald snapped.

"She's right," Marzell said. "Fritz—reinforce the door."

Fritz nodded and picked up one of the table benches with one hand. He took a step toward the door, when the frame buckled before the door was kicked in, tearing it off its hinges.

"Now *that* is going to be a pain to fix," Angel said.

Fritz shot-putted the bench through the open doorway, taking out the three constructs crowded there.

The constructs stormed the cottage, pouring through the open door like water.

Fritz and Rupert cut a path through them. Rupert moved in defined stances, his sword form exact as he pushed forward.

Fritz, however, fought more like a dancer. He never stopped moving, and instead of Rupert's meticulous methods, he surged high and low, whirling his sword around him as he sliced through construct after construct.

Though Marzell snapped his whip—taking down a construct with every hit—and Gregori loosened bolt after bolt, the creatures surged toward Rupert and Fritz.

Oswald barely had a moment to ram a giant copper pot into the small, broken window he guarded before he ran to join Fritz and Rupert.

One construct darted around Rupert. Its eyes fixated on Snow White as it lunged at her—its arm extended and its saw-toothed mouth opened with a whistling hiss.

Snow White jabbed her fire poker at it, but it slipped to the side like a shadow. Its mouth grew larger and larger until it made up half its head.

"No!" Snow White flinched backwards, stepping to the side of the fireplace.

The construct briefly recoiled, then fell apart when Angel stabbed it in the back with her knife. "They're here for Snow White!" Angel shouted as she swiped her dagger through another.

"We noticed," Rupert growled.

"But why?" Snow White asked as she wiped sweat from her forehead.

Rupert made a noise in the back of his throat. "A question perhaps best pursued when we don't fear you being kidnapped by magical constructs."

"They shouldn't have come," Aldelbert laughed as he armed himself with a spear. "But that's all right. They will learn to fear the house of Chita!" He corrected the way he held the spear, then ran at the incoming flow of constructs with a roar, disappearing through the open door.

"Aldelbert!" Marzell yelled.

"There is quite an impressive number out here!" Aldelbert's shout came back slightly muffled, but still just as casual and upbeat as ever. "Back, you fiends!"

"Gregori," Marzell called.

"Uh-huh." Gregori grabbed the other table bench and jogged for the door. He waited until Rupert cut a pathway open for him before he slipped outside, briefly holstering his crossbow on his back so he could hold the bench in front of him horizontally, ramming constructs through as he disappeared into the darkness.

"Aldelbert," Gregori called. "Get back here."

"The House of Chita never retreats!" Aldelbert said.

"I'll burn your best cloak," Gregori growled.

"Vile!" Aldelbert declared. "Unsportsmanlike!"

Fritz cut his sword in a high arc—ending one construct—then whipped around and stabbed another through. "Numbers?"

"Ahh, yes. Gregori—how does it look out there?" Marzell shouted as he snapped his whip at the face of another construct.

"Not good," Gregori said grimly. "I don't see an end to them."

"We are, in fact, 'pinned,' as Fritz would say, to the side of our cottage!" Aldelbert cheerfully added.

Oswald grinned as he skid to a stop at Rupert's right, adding to the wall that blocked Snow White from the constructs. He laughed—a slightly unhinged sound—as he lunged forward with his sword. "As if they're anything to fear. They're just constructs!"

Angel's forehead puckered. "Just because they're made of magic doesn't mean they can't hurt you."

"Huh?" Oswald glanced at the apprentice wizard, briefly turning his back to one of the monsters.

The construct slashed at him with its clawed, long-fingered hand.

Oswald hissed as the monster's nails tore through the sleeve of his shirt, opening up gashes on his bicep.

"Like so," Angel said sourly.

"We need to get Aldelbert and Gregori back inside," Wendal said as he jumped to a different rafter and threw another dagger from his seemingly endless supply. "They'll be squashed out there.

"We need to *stop* these constructs," Marzell said through gritted teeth. "Or we'll get overrun soon."

Fear bit at Snow White as she watched Marzell stand with Rupert, Oswald, and Fritz.

Though the four men held them back, the constructs mindlessly rushed forward, their white, empty eyes fixed on Snow White. They reached for her over the men's shoulders, their mouths opening unnaturally wide.

"Any ideas?" Angel asked.

"Don't fall down," Oswald advised as he beheaded two constructs.

"Perhaps Wendal should fix the windows, and we barricade ourselves inside?" Rupert frowned in concentration as he thrust his sword ahead of him. He destroyed one monster, but another latched onto his arm with a clawed hand, digging its nails into his wrist.

Rupert remained stone-faced in his pain and tried to stab the creature through.

It dodged and instead pulled Rupert forward, nearly managing to drag him into the oncoming rush of constructs before Marzell snapped at it with his whip, destroying it.

Constructs writhed through the hole in the defensive wall that Rupert's absence created, rushing for Snow White.

One construct lunged for her, its clawed arms extended as its mouth gaped open.

Snow White ducked, and it lurched over her, hissing when the dim light of the fire hit it.

Fritz stabbed it through before it could recover, and Wendal threw three daggers, eliminating the others as Rupert limped back into position.

Snow White watched Rupert with worry. Both he and Oswald were now injured, and it was only going to get worse. Though the constructs weren't horrible foes, their sheer numbers were already pushing the warriors to exhaustion. But how could they fight them off?

She bit her lip as she recalled the way the construct had recoiled right when it reached for her.

Something makes the monsters fall back. That's the second time a construct has gotten back here and stumbles at the last minute, but what causes it? Snow White carefully compared her actions in the separate occasions. *I ducked and no longer blocked the fire, so it shed direct light on them. Could that be it?*

Snow White scrambled for the pile of logs and branches placed next to the fireplace. She dug through the wood, ignoring the splinters that jabbed into her fingers as she searched for a branch that was the right size for what she had in mind.

Angel frowned as she stared at the weapons on the far side of the room. "If you stand back—" she started, then paused when she saw Snow White impatiently pushing aside a large log. "What are you doing?"

"I want to test something." Snow White ripped the seam of her kirtle—the linen skirts and shirt under her gown—and tore a long strip of it free. She tied it around one end of the stick, then thrust it into the flames. As soon as the fabric caught on fire, she scurried up behind the protective wall the warriors had formed.

"Snow White, get back!" Marzell shouted.

Snow White ignored him. "Fritz, I need an opening!"

The ashy-haired young man nodded. He drew back, adjusting his grip on his sword, then swung forward, dragging his sword diagonally so he offed two constructs and ended with his hands and sword at eye level.

Snow White poked her head into the hole between Fritz's open side and Rupert, then shoved her burning stick in front of her.

The monsters closest to her staggered backwards, mashing their serrated mouths as they covered their eyes.

"I've got it!" Snow White shouted. "They're weak to fire—or light. I can't tell which."

"And so the princess proves the ancient saying of brains over brawn. But I know one way we can find out if they're weak to light and not just fire!" Angel went back to digging through her satchel, ignoring the chaos that swirled around her.

"If you don't mind, Princess, I'll take that." Wendal hung upside down from the rafters, his hand extended.

Snow White passed him up the flaming stick, then ran back to the fireplace. She tossed logs on the flames, filling the room with more light as the fire grew.

"Snow White, take these!" Angel passed Snow White five or six crystals. "Follow my lead." Angel held an armload of them and turned to the dark constructs that still poured through the door. "Shine!"

The crystals started to glow, shedding pure light from their prism facets.

The constructs closest to Angel staggered backwards, clawing at their eyes.

"Shine brighter still!" Angel shouted. The light in the crystals grew in intensity, until Snow White had to turn her back to Angel.

She glanced down at the collection of crystals Angel had given her. "Shine?"

Snow White's crystals ignited as well, burning a stark white light.

She licked her lips and watched Angel brandish a crystal in a construct's face. The construct actually fell in its panicked efforts to evade her.

Wendal hung from the rafter just over the door. He held the makeshift torch out, causing the constructs outside the cottage to hiss and stop their forward progress.

Marzell, Rupert, Oswald, and Fritz made quick work of constructs left inside as they writhed—stumbling away from the crystals and the well-stoked fire.

"How much brighter do these get?" Snow White asked.

Angel struggled to hold more crystals than Snow White would have thought were able to fit in her satchel. "At least another level or two, why?"

If they get brighter than this, and outside is covered in snow... "Come on!" Snow White darted between the injured Oswald and Rupert, slipping outside.

As Aldelbert had proclaimed, he and Gregori were trapped against the outer wall of the cottage, angled apart from one another so they could guard each other's backs.

Unfortunately, the open space from the cottage to the tree line *teemed* with the magic-made constructs. Though the moon shone dimly in the sky and the glittering snow added extra brightness, the constructs were packed so tightly together, the area was a sea of black broken only by their eerie white eyes.

When they saw Snow White, they surged forward, a wave of teeth and claws as they struggled to get closer to her.

I really hope this works, or I'll have killed myself with my own idiocy!

Snow White held her crystal aloft, making the shadowy creatures halt. Those closest to her thrashed and struggled to get away from her, gnashing their jagged teeth.

"What now?" Angel asked, her arms glowing from the crystals she held.

Snow White sucked in a deep breath. "Shine!" she shouted at her crystals.

They flared even brighter. So brightly, in fact, that Snow White had to squint to see. The crystal's bright light hit the snow, which reflected some of the light and lit the area up. Snow White flung her crystals into the air, making the constructs smash together as they retreated from the light. Those closest to the crystals faded away—not turning into the foul bits of smoke, but evaporating as if the light ate away at them.

"I get it—Shine!" Angel started throwing fistfuls of her crystals as well, until the area outside the cottage was nearly as bright as day.

Marzell, Fritz, Oswald, and Rupert raced out of the cottage and fell upon the struggling constructs, cutting through them with ease.

"My Lord!" Wendal shouted as he joined them, his daggers still clenched between his fingers.

"Wendal—you're just in time!" Aldelbert laughed as he pushed off the wall. "Come, let us drive them away!"

The Seven Warriors waded through the writhing creatures, forming a half circle as they pierced the darkness.

Finally, the constructs left. They hissed as they fled, racing past the glowing crystals even as some of them faded away under the light's influence. They escaped the brightness, pressing into the shadows among the trees.

Snow White held her breath, worried they were only retreating to the shadows, and not really leaving.

But as she watched the constructs plunge into the darkness, they turned around to face her. They hissed in anger, and a couple snapped their teeth at her as they faded, their glowing, circular eyes the last things to disappear.

Marzell scooped up one of the crystals and threw it farther away. It landed harmlessly in a snow bank, lighting up the previously darkened area to show there was nothing there. Marzell shook his head as he collapsed to his knees. "They're gone."

"Finally," Gregori agreed as he and Aldelbert joined the others in checking the perimeter.

Snow White started to sag where she stood as her bones turned to jelly, and whatever miracle it was that had kept her upright and moving abandoned her. She just wanted to sink into the snow and *breathe* for a few minutes—or an *hour*.

But I can't, she thought grimly as she made herself face the warriors. *I have an advantage now. I have to use it.*

CHAPTER 6
UNUSUAL HERB MAGIC

It took her a few deep breaths and one false start before Snow White finally managed to speak. "You can no longer deny something dark is at work," she said. "A-Angel said those were *magic constructs*. That means *someone* with magic is involved in this—not just goblins and monsters."

It was easier to talk outside. She could stare past the Seven Warriors at the trees behind them and pretend they weren't looking at her.

Angel nonchalantly joined her, scratching her nose to hide her lips. "Speak louder," she muttered.

Snow White sucked a deep breath in before pitching her voice even louder. "Y-You said yourself that all the skirmishes and creatures are at the border. The '*outskirts of civilization*' you claimed." She gestured to Luster Forest. "We are nowhere near the border. This was a deliberate attack. Clearly, I was the t-target," Snow White stumbled over that admission, for it was actually rather terrifying. *Think of it later.*

When the warriors finally stopped poking at the shadows and strode back to their cottage, Snow White gritted her teeth and bit the tip of her tongue to give herself the strength to lift her chin up. "You also said the country is in a worse state than I knew. You were correct, obviously. But after this, I-I think it's safe to say it's also worse than *you* knew, for you have not seen the Queen and the pain she has borne while the rest of us were stupidly oblivious." Unable to stop herself, she added, "And Faina is *not* mad! If you still claim that is so, you are not the Seven Warriors you profess to be but are the seven idiots my ministers think you are!" Snow White could have happily bit her tongue off for so bluntly voicing what she was thinking. *That last bit is not likely to win them over.*

She winced and steeled herself for their anger.

"So, Princess Snow White *does* have claws," Oswald snorted.

Rupert sniffed, though he swayed a little as blood seeped from his wrist wound. "Just because she doesn't mouth off like you does not mean she lacks the gumption necessary to be a leader."

"No, but her inability to speak her mind was *not* encouraging," Wendal said as he retrieved his daggers from the snow.

Snow White nervously glanced from warrior to warrior, even as Angel chuckled softly.

"The Princess is right." Gregori thoughtfully brushed the fletching on one of his crossbow bolts as he glanced from the shadows to his friends. "This is the first clear sign we have that all of this is on purpose. Monsters and creatures could be written off as the state of the continent. A magical attack is a sign of more."

"Agreed." Fritz crossed the now empty yard and stood with Snow White.

Snow White almost fell over with the relief that at least two of the seven warriors believed her. *They still might help me—if Marzell bends, that is.* The thought made her grimace. But she felt a little better with Angel on one side and Fritz on the other—it made facing the other warriors not *quite* as intimidating. Though Snow White would have gladly tied her tongue.

In only a few hours Fritz went from intimidating to assuring. Normally I'd question such a speedy change in my confidence, but clearly I was in the wrong when I focused on his height and thought him intimidating. He is quiet like I am—not out of anger, but thoughtfulness.

"You agree with her, Fritz?" Rupert asked, thoughtfully eyeing the tall forester.

Fritz nodded.

If Snow White edged a step closer to him, she told herself it was due to the shadows that swayed in the trees. Not because being closer to him just felt *safer*.

With another glance at the woods, Gregori turned to stride back to Snow White and the cottage. "Of course, he does—he figured out she was right before any of you retired to the loft for the night."

"How do you *know* these things?" Oswald demanded.

"I'm a merchant."

"Yeah, a merchant. Not a shady information-broker!"

"They are rather similar." Gregori paused to nod to Snow White, then studied the damaged door.

Aldelbert placed his hands on his hips and he slightly tipped his head back to study Fritz's face. "How did you know, my friend?"

Fritz paused, and for several very long moments all the warriors were silent as they waited for his answer. "Gut feeling," he finally said.

"You!" Oswald stomped a foot in the slushy snow. "There was a whole story behind it, but you just shortened it because you're too lazy to tell it!"

"It's long," Fritz said plaintively.

"Doesn't matter—cough it up," Oswald demanded.

"Don't bother if you don't wish to, Fritz," Rupert said. "Whatever the reason was that convinced you, Oswald is obviously too much of a dunce to catch it, or he would have believed Her Highness as well."

Oswald twisted around to scowl at the dark-haired heir. "You didn't believe her either!"

Rupert was attempting to apply pressure to his wrist and didn't even look in his direction. "Perhaps."

"There was no 'perhaps' about it," Oswald complained as Gregori and Wendal brought the broken door outside and lamented the torn hinges.

"Your Highness," Marzell said.

Snow White gulped as she turned her attention to Marzell, who joined her, Fritz, and Angel.

Marzell's gentle smile was more pronounced than usual. "I believe I owe you an apology. You are correct. There is obviously something stirring—and clearly magic is at work. And instead of listening, I behaved like the stubborn advisors I act against. Please, forgive me." He bowed deeply.

Snow White licked her cold lips. "Will you help me, then?" she asked softly.

"We Seven Warriors will do everything in our power to aid you," Marzell promised.

Snow White's relief was so sharp, she briefly swayed on her feet.

Finally. I've taken the first step and secured some help. I can do this—I can help Faina!

"Thank you," she whispered.

Fritz cleared his throat. "Marzell," he said in his low, rumbling voice.

"Hmm?" Marzell glanced up at the tall forester, who nodded at Oswald and Rupert.

The two were still bickering, though they staggered and blood dripped from the wounds the constructs had inflicted.

"Oh, yes. Oswald, Rupert—inside! You, too, Aldelbert. It looks like you received a scratch or two in the kerfuffle." Marzell motioned for his friends to follow him inside as he ducked through the open door.

"I'm fine," Oswald complained, though he obediently followed.

"It doesn't hurt," Rupert stiffly insisted—though he sneezed twice, making Oswald snicker.

Snow White and Angel trailed behind them, stepping into the cottage—which was hardly any warmer than the outside thanks to the broken windows and open door.

Snow White was so giddy with relief, she didn't mind the numbing chill. She was so wrapped up in her first win—her first *helpful* action—she almost missed Angel's question.

"Are you well? You weren't hurt, were you?" she asked.

"No, I'm fine," Snow White assured her. "I was in less danger after you gave me some of your crystals—is it okay to leave them outside like that?"

"They're called starfires, and they'll be fine," Angel said. "I'll collect them tomorrow morning—once the sun rises. I'd rather leave them where they are so they can serve as a defense for the rest of the night."

Snow White nodded. "A wise plan. Where did you get them?"

"Oh, they're a small thing craftmages make by the bucketload when they're apprentices. I got these from a friend of mine—I promised his wife I would carry them around," Angel said.

"Considering the size of your satchel, you had quite a few," Snow White said.

"They're smaller than they look." Angel said it so confidently, Snow White found herself nodding in agreement before she caught herself.

Wait, I held them. They aren't that small at all! Before she could further pursue the thought, Marzell interrupted their conversation.

"Angel, you're an apprentice to an herb wizard, yes?" he asked, eyeing Oswald and Rupert as they plopped down together on the bench by the still roaring fire.

"Yep!" Angel smiled brightly.

"Could you take a look at Oswald and Rupert, then? I don't think Aldelbert's scratches need anything besides being cleaned, but Rupert's wrist and Oswald's arm are a different matter," Marzell explained.

"What?" Angel's good cheer fell from her face like a candle being snuffed out.

"Their injuries." Marzell gestured to the quarrelsome pair, both of whom were still teetering on the bench. "Surely you could use your herb magic to do something for them?"

Snow White saw Fritz carrying one of the wooden table benches through the door, and ran to help—holding one end steady so it didn't strike the door frame. (Though Fritz still carried all the weight.)

When he set it down, she twitched it back into its proper position while he left again—likely to get the second one.

"No, no, I'm afraid not." Angel slapped her too-big-for her tunic and shook her head. "I haven't learned much about herb healing."

Marzell frowned. "Isn't herb healing the *basis* for an herb wizard's career?"

Angel blinked rapidly. "To an extent," she said. "But we're also taught how to use herbs for some basic charms, cleaning, hygiene—all of that."

Marzell smiled tiredly. "Even that would be helpful. We don't want to risk either of them getting an infection."

Angel sucked her neck into her shoulders. "Yeah. That would be bad," she said—though she still didn't look overly eager to help.

Fritz returned with the second bench, which Snow White carefully placed as Gregori and Wendal still puzzled over the door.

"You can use any of the herbs and supplies we have," Marzell said. "I'll boil some water and retrieve bandages and wraps for you."

"I need to repeat: I don't know very much," Angel said.

"Nonsense," Aldelbert proclaimed as he watched Marzell set a kettle to boil over the fire. "Your satchel is *draped* with herbs. Surely you must know enough if you practice such a custom as that."

Angel winced. "Yes. Yes, I do carry herbs around because I know how to use them. What I meant is that I always frustrated my master because I was so *bad* at it. Really, as a forester, I imagine Fritz might be better at dressing wounds."

"Angel," Snow White called, momentarily garnering her attention. "You don't need to apologize. Oswald and Rupert will be thankful for whatever you can do."

Instead of looking reassured, Angel pressed her lips into a thin line. "Uh-huh."

Marzell patted her on the shoulder. "Thank you—from all of us."

"Yeah, sure," Angel said.

Snow White offered her a smile as she passed the apprentice on her way to take up a broom that leaned against the wall.

Snow White looked around for a moment—watching as Fritz re-entered the cottage, this time holding a hammer, some nails, and a piece of wood which he held against one of the broken window panes and hammered into place, blocking out the whistling wind.

Angel had reluctantly yanked some of the rosemary herbs off her satchel and grabbed some fronds of dill that hung from the rafters as well.

Marzell hustled up the stairs—retrieving the bandages, probably.

Snow White hesitantly started sweeping the slush and snow the seven warriors and some of the constructs had trekked into the cottage, pushing it through the door.

"Go over to the benches by the table and lie flat," Angel instructed the still bleeding Oswald and Rupert.

The pair did as they were told—with Oswald grumbling the whole way.

Snow White succeeded in pushing her first pile of snow out the still gaping door as Wendal and Gregori squinted at the busted hinges.

"I think we just ought to have Fritz shove it back in place for the night. We can fix it tomorrow morning," Gregori said.

"And leave the door as a weak point?" Wendal asked.

Gregori shrugged. "We can reinforce it. And if the constructs return, the shining crystals should make them stay back."

"True..."

"What are you doing?" Rupert asked.

Angel was plucking bits of rosemary off a stalk and sprinkled the fragrant herb over Rupert's wrist. "Magic," she said.

Rupert frowned. "Are you certain?"

Angel picked up a frond of dill. "*Who* is the herb wizard's apprentice? Me. Unless you gained instruction somewhere between the fireplace and this bench, shut your pie hole."

Rupert shifted but said no more, until Angel started smacking him in the face with the dill. "Is this necessary?" he grumbled.

"Absolutely," Angel said as she hit him in the face, making him squeeze his eyes shut.

Though most of Angel's movements were blocked by her body, Snow White could have *sworn* she saw silvery light briefly gather at Angel's fingertips as she smeared more rosemary across Rupert's wrist.

Her herb magic, perhaps?

"That is a very interesting treatment, Angel," Marzell said as he jumped off the stairs, bandages in hand.

Angel sniffed. "Do not question the power of healing herbs."

"Those are cooking herbs," Wendal called from the doorway.

Angel glanced down at the herbs she clutched. "*Obviously*," she said after a moment. "The best healing always starts in the stomach—remember that."

Rupert stared at the cottage's rafters. "That doesn't make any sense—" He broke off in a sneeze when Angel whacked him again with the dill.

"Hah," Oswald snorted, though he had his uninjured arm draped across his eyes.

Snow White went back to sweeping snow and slush out, moving close to Fritz—who was working on hammering a piece of wood across the next broken window.

She bit her lip. "Do I need to clean up all the broken glass, Fritz?"

Fritz shook his head. "We need to rest. As long as we all wear shoes, we can survive the night."

Snow White nodded. "That is logical."

"This is strange," Rupert said once he recovered from his sneeze.

"It's working, is it not?" Angel demanded.

"It is—my wrist feels better. That's why it's strange," Rupert said.

"Trust in the magic—and the herbs," Angel advised him. "Now you—the bossy one. Clean his wrist off with the boiled water once it has cooled enough, and wrap it."

Marzell laughed good-naturedly. "I'm Marzell," he reminded her.

"I know that. I'm just choosing to let you know you're bossy," Angel said before she stalked over to the bench Oswald occupied. "Now hop to it."

Snow White smiled as she studied her brisk, new friend. *She's quite unique. I've read books on herb magic, and none of them mentioned using so few ingredients to accomplish anything. Perhaps it is that her magic is strong enough to handle it—for none of them mentioned visible signs of magic, either.*

Snow White shrugged and returned to sweeping, thankful that the task gave her something to do so she didn't feel useless as everyone worked around her.

I guess I am in more danger than I thought. Regardless, I still count tonight as a win. Hopefully tomorrow will be just as productive—and far less dangerous.

⁂

FRITZ SIGHED with relief and stood easier when the first rays of the sun brightened the horizon. *Daylight. Given what we learned last night, the constructs are unlikely to appear now.*

He leaned against the outer wall of the cottage, his breath creating a mist in the cold air—though he could feel the sunlight in his bones.

Spring was finally coming. Another day or two of sun, and the snow would completely melt, leaving a muddy—but less frigid—mess.

Fritz glanced over his shoulder when the broken door shifted, letting Gregori, Wendal, and Marzell slip outside.

"No sign of any attackers?" Gregori asked.

Fritz shook his head.

Wendal began retrieving the glowing crystals—which were markedly dimmer than they had been when Snow White and Angel first brandished them—from the wet snow. "I'll feed the horses once I'm done here," he said.

"Thank you, Wendal." Marzell tugged on the fur collar of his cloak, shivered, then also began picking up crystals. "The princess and the apprentice are still sleeping," he added. "I would like to let them rest as long as possible."

Gregori folded his arms across his thick chest. "Is that wise? We *need* to discuss what happened last night—in more depth than you already have." He drummed his fingers on his thick forearms. "Her Highness is no fool. By the time she wakes up, she'll realize just what it means that she was targeted by the monsters."

Realize? She'll try to come up with a plan before she rolls out of bed. We survived last night because she realized the constructs' weakness and came up with an idea to defeat them. That kind of critical thinking does not come without a great deal of practice.

But rather than voice all his thoughts, Fritz nodded and added, "Yes."

Marzell sighed. "I know, but we won't be able to handle this alone. We'll have to talk to some officers from the army—or possibly some lords. Snow White *hates* speaking in public."

"She's going to become our queen as soon as she reaches age twenty," Wendal said. "That is roughly a year away. She will need to reckon with that fear soon."

Marzell shook his head. "It's not just a simple fear—the way some people fear spiders. It's..." He paused.

"She would fix it if she could," Fritz said simply.

"Yes!" Marzell jabbed a starfire in his direction. "That!"

Wendal shrugged and trotted off to retrieve the crystals tossed at the edge of their yard.

"You like the princess, Fritz?" Gregori asked.

The wind nearly whipped Fritz's hood off his head. "Yes."

"Why?" Marzell asked.

Fritz wasn't about to tell his companions about his strange draw—could he safely call it respect after last night?—to the princess. They wouldn't scoff at him for it, but they *would* ask more questions than Fritz frankly wanted to answer. Besides...did they really not see Snow White's strength?

Even though she's terrified of speaking to large groups and obviously hasn't ever experienced combat before, she's willing to do whatever is necessary for the sake of Queen Faina. And though she's got that hidden strategic streak, she discounts no one.

Fritz thought for a few moments before deciding on a sufficiently short answer. "She's nice."

Gregori nodded thoughtfully, then shifted his attention to their unofficial leader. "How are Rupert and Oswald?" he asked Marzell.

"Fine, by the looks of it," Marzell said. "Neither complained of any pain when I checked on them before coming out here."

"They weren't deep wounds," Wendal said as he dumped an armload of crystals by the door.

"No, but given what *gave* them the wounds, I didn't know what to expect," Marzell said.

"It's fortuitous the apprentice—Angel, was it?—was here," Gregori said.

"She's odd," Wendal said.

"Given whom you serve, you are not in a place to criticize," Gregori said.

Wendal yipped in outrage like a lapdog, and Marzell coughed to cover up his humor.

"Fritz, what do you think of Angel?" Gregori asked, ignoring Wendal's anger.

Fritz scratched his chin as he thought.

There's something a bit off about her, but I can't tell how, and I don't think I'd be able to pin it down. Regardless, she is sincere in her actions, and she'll help. Not hinder.

"She's nice," he settled on.

Wendal pointed a finger at him. "That's exactly what you said about the princess!"

"Snow White is nicer," Fritz corrected.

"That's not enough of a distinction!"

"It's fine." Gregori waved a hand through the air. "As long as Fritz likes them both." He turned to the broken door.

"Where are you going?" Marzell called after him.

"Back to bed," Gregori said.

"But we have work to do," Wendal said. "I'll see to the horses, but we really need to fix the door—and the windows—and we still need to speak to the princess."

"Do what you like," Gregori said. "I'm going back to sleep."

"But—" Wendal started.

Gregori eyed the slighter man and cracked his knuckles.

"Sleep well," Wendal said meekly.

Marzell chuckled as Gregori disappeared back into the cottage. "Right, then. Wendal, I'll go help you with our horses." He clapped the attendant on the back with a smile.

"Thank you," Wendal said before he led the way around the side of the cottage, to the small stable they kept.

Fritz ghosted along behind them, intent on retrieving the shutters they used on the cottage in summer, but his thoughts lingered on the princess slumbering in their home.

She has a difficult fight before her. I hope we can help. More importantly, I hope she wins. Or Queen Faina won't make it.

CHAPTER 7
THE CHOSEN

Snow White stiffened her spine so she wouldn't squirm and instead tried to smile pleasantly at Marzell as he plopped down on the bench across from her and Angel.

"I think it's time we discuss the events of last night," Marzell said as he poured Snow White and Angel a cup of tea from a lopsided, clay teapot.

"What is there to discuss?" Angel asked. "Magic constructs attacked; we repelled them. Unless you're looking for feedback about what areas of home defense you're lacking in?"

Marzell's chuckled. "No, I'm afraid not—though I *wish* that was all we had to discuss."

Snow White glanced from Marzell to Fritz, who stood behind Marzell with Aldelbert—though the young lord seemed more focused on finding a striking pose than adding to the conversation. Wendal—holding a mirror—scurried in whatever direction Aldelbert directed him to, bouncing candlelight off the mirror and aiming it at Aldelbert so he *glowed*.

Fritz offered Snow White a gentle smile—that was again mostly expressed through his crinkling eyes. Snow White shakily returned it, then quickly peered around the cottage for the remaining Seven Warriors when she felt Marzell's eyes on her.

Gregori snoozed by the coals—draped across the bench—and Rupert and Oswald were "testing" their wounded limbs outside. (By fighting, based on the clear tolls of blades clashing and the shouted insults.)

"You were obviously the constructs' target, Your Highness," Marzell said. "They were going for you. Whether it was to harm you or forcibly remove you from our protection was not evident, but regardless, they clearly had ill intent."

Snow White nodded, then cleared her throat and made herself speak. "It's a sign that Faina *must* be under the influence of magic, for they were made by magic—something she has no talent for."

"Yes," Marzell said. "It proves your suspicions are correct. But it also means that when Queen Faina sent you away, she undermined the intent of whoever is controlling her."

"We cannot guess their exact design," Gregori said from his spot by the fire, making Snow White jump in surprise. "It is possible they were satisfied when you were in Glitzern and under Faina's control, but now that you have left, you might be able to fight back. Or perhaps they meant to have you killed before you left, which would explain the Queen's fits of rage."

"Regardless, we can at least guess what their goal is," Marzell said. "It seems most likely that they want Queen Faina under their control so they can rule Mullberg. You, obviously, pose a threat to that."

Snow White nodded slowly and bought herself some time by sipping her tea—which was a pleasant lavender brew. "But why Mullberg?" she asked when she could no longer avoid responding.

Marzell folded his hands on the table. "What do you mean?"

"Mullberg seems to be a rather dangerous place to attempt a coup de'tat," Snow White said. "We have the Veneno Conclave in our borders, and we have enjoyed decades of peace. Any kind of action—like this—would be rather apparent and volatile."

"Not that volatile," Angel muttered, "considering all of this has already happened with no one the wiser."

"I'm afraid I don't know much of international politics," Marzell said apologetically. "But based on what Gregori has told us, I think the rest of the continent has fared even worse than Mullberg. Is that right, Gregori?" He called.

Gregori replied with soft snores.

"It's true enough," Angel said. "Lots of royal families have experienced curses and assassination attempts by rogue mages. And every country has tangled with dark creatures of some sort—most often abnormally large packs of goblins."

"Before I left Glitzern, I saw an invitation to a summit held last year in Loire. The invitation detailed some of the problems other countries have been having. With so many places floundering, it seems this is all part of a joint effort," Snow White said.

"It is," Angel confirmed. "We believe it is all the work of the Chosen."

"Who?" Marzell asked.

"The *Chosen?*" Snow White almost stood up in her horror and shock. "The villains who nearly took Verglas before the Snow Queen defeated their leader and splintered their forces?"

"Read it in a book, did you?" Angel asked.

"Yes, but my history teacher discussed it at length," Snow White said.

"Well, Prince Lucien of Loire is just as versed in history, it would seem. He was the one who put the pieces together and realized it was the Chosen," Angel said.

"Can we trust the opinion of one prince?" Wendal asked.

Angel yawned and glanced up at the ceiling. "I don't know *all* the particulars about it, but yes. It's been proven several times since the prince made his guess. The Chosen have been biding their time for centuries and putting together some sort of mad scheme which—surprise—they've been acting on for the past few years."

Snow White pressed her lips together as she took in the news and the implications it brought. *That means the struggle to free Faina is larger than Mullberg. Or rather, the mage that has Faina under his sway has bigger aspirations than just our fair country. Later today, I had better ask Angel what other attacks the Chosen have launched.*

"So perhaps it is merely that we are the last target on their list," Marzell said.

"They feared Mullberg," Aldelbert laughed. "The Chosen are frightened by our courage and inspiring good looks."

"Hah!" Oswald scoffed as he and Rupert trooped through the newly repaired door. "I dare you to say that with a straight face when you look at all the old buzzard-lords."

"I was actually referring to myself." Aldelbert smiled—then motioned for Wendal to move a little to the left so the mirror bounced beams of light directly onto his smile, making his teeth sparkle.

Angel tapped the worn wooden table with her fingers. "I'm not convinced Snow White was a target last night because they are afraid she'll take Mullberg back."

Snow White frowned, thoughtfully. "That would be preferable, I suppose. It means they won't expect it when we act. I *am* ornamental most of the time."

"Your Highness, you underestimate your worth," Marzell chided.

Snow White shook her head, but before she could reply, Angel interrupted. "I didn't mean to imply they thought you were useless, Snow White. I meant that they might fear something else about you."

Oswald furrowed his eyebrows. "Like what? She quivers like a mouse when more than two of us look at her."

Angel scratched her neck. "All I know is that when a royal is targeted, it usually is either a power play to injure their country, or it is done to wing them so they aren't on the top of their game.

The best example we have of the latter is the time Prince Severin of Loire spent cursed as a beast."

"It is most likely that they targeted me to tie up the monarchy," Snow White said, "as I have no reputation of work and lack any special skill besides reading books quickly."

Angel shrugged but said nothing more.

Rupert flexed his wrist, testing it, and pushed his way past Oswald. "If we cannot be certain why Snow White is being targeted, what do we do next?"

"We need eyes in the palace—on Queen Faina specifically," Marzell said. "We need to solidify her actions and feelings before we decide whom to reach out to."

Snow White nodded. "I thought the army would be the wisest choice, but I can see the wisdom in watching Faina first. Depending how she acts now, the Veneno Conclave may be our best choice after all."

Marzell drummed his fingers on the table. "Precisely. If there is a rogue mage involved, I don't know that they can stay out of it —even *if* this is considered a political affair."

"I assume we'll use Gregori's network to contact people within the castle?" Rupert asked.

Marzell nodded. "I'll have him make a list when he wakes for lunch. Additionally, I was hoping to send one or two of us to the castle so we could see Her Majesty in person."

"I have *many* friends at the palace!" Aldelbert said. "I volunteer to go!"

"Sorry, Aldelbert, you're out," Marzell said.

The young lord dropped the arm he had been pointing to the rafters and frowned. "Why?"

"You're a rather unique man. I'm afraid you're too easily recognizable," Marzell said.

"He means you're too loud and eye-catching, so everyone already knows who you are," Angel translated.

Aldelbert dramatically thumped a hand over his heart. "Curse this handsome face and my enviable body that draws all eyes to me!"

"That is *not* what I said at all," Angel said.

"Whom do you think I should send, Snow White?" Marzell fussed with the lopsided teapot, but though his mannerisms were casual, Snow White didn't miss the slight quirk of his smile.

Is he...giving me this chance to further prove myself to the rest of the Seven Warriors? Well—besides Fritz, anyway.

Snow White licked her lips and made herself say, "Wouldn't Wendal, Oswald, or Fritz be the best choices?"

Marzell blinked. "Why those three?"

Snow White glanced at Fritz—since their conversation by the fire, he was the easiest to look at while talking. (Besides, he seemed to merely listen, not weigh her words like a jury.) "Fritz is not a court figure and could easily be mistaken as a guard. Though Wendal is Lord Aldelbert's servant, without Aldelbert around, I doubt anyone would place him as such. And Oswald..." she hesitated.

"Out with it, Princess," Oswald growled.

"As the youngest of three sons, I doubt you visited Glitzern Palace or the city of Juwel much, and even if you did, I am certain most would pay more attention to your older siblings," Snow White said.

Oswald rubbed his chin. "She's not wrong," he said.

"I could not dare to leave My Lord's side," Wendal said.

"What, scared he'll off himself in his stupidity while you're gone?" Angel asked.

Wendal scowled at her.

Marzell stood and busied himself with removing the dried lavender flowers from the empty teapot. "I think Wendal and Oswald should go."

Oswald scratched his bushy hair. "Not Fritz?"

Marzell tapped the bottom of the teapot. "I want Rupert to come with me when I talk to Gregori's contacts. That leaves only three of us seven behind in the cottage with Snow White and Angel. Fritz is by far the best fighter among us. He needs to stay behind so we can be assured Her Highness is safe."

Snow White thought this would have stirred up an argument among the men with each professing to be the best warrior, so she was surprised when instead they all nodded and wore pensive expressions—include Aldelbert!

"A reasonable suggestion," Aldelbert said. "I like it! Fritz and I shall guard the womenfolk whilst Gregori naps."

"But My Lord," Wendal objected.

Aldelbert cut him off with a chop of his hand. "No objections, Wendal. This is for the good of the country!"

"How very charming," Angel drawled. "But what are we supposed to do while you are gone? Repair the cottage from last night's fun?"

"You could rest," Marzell suggested. "It was hardly a relaxing night."

Angel shrugged. "It wasn't the worst I've had," she said dryly.

Snow White mutely pressed her lips together. *I don't want to sit around without a purpose. While I would like to question Angel more about the Chosen, I imagine she'll be busy. With everything that is at stake, it seems foolish to sit around and do nothing. But what can **I** do that they cannot?* Nothing, unfortunately, came to mind, so Snow White held her peace.

"Right then!" Marzell grinned broadly. "We have our assignments! Oswald, Wendal, check our chest for discreet clothes before you head out."

"Aye-aye, sir." Oswald sarcastically saluted him. "What are *you* going to do?"

Marzell grimaced. "I'm going to risk waking Gregori—we need that list."

His words seemed to be a magic incantation to clear the cottage, for instantly Wendal and Oswald headed for the stairs.

"Let's look into those dreadful costumes, Oswald," Wendal called.

"Yeah, right behind you," Oswald confirmed.

"I need a stroll," Aldelbert announced, making a beeline for the door.

"Don't die," Rupert advised Marzell.

Fritz bowed gravely to Marzell before he turned to Snow White and gallantly held out his hand.

Snow White felt a little flustered, and to her horror she could feel her cheeks heat as she stared at his hand. "Um?"

"I get the feeling we're supposed to clear out to avoid becoming collateral damage," Angel said as she hopped off the bench and snatched up her cloak and Snow White's cape.

Snow White placed her hand in Fritz's and let him guide her away from the table and outside. "Why do we need to be outside?" she asked as Fritz released her hand and shut the door behind Angel.

Fritz held up a finger and cocked his head as he listened.

Several moments passed in which the only noise was the chirps of birds and the crunch of squirrels munching on acorns.

The forest's serenity was broken by a deafening roar that came from inside the cottage.

Snow White jumped when there was a loud crash that shook the doorframe.

"Sounds like he threw the bench again," Aldelbert said. He shrugged, then whistled as he started on his jaunty way. "Better Marzell than us!"

Snow White looked wide-eyed from the cottage door to Fritz.

"It's fine," he said.

Angel eyed the door as she offered Snow White her red cloak. "That doesn't *sound* fine," she said when there was another thump at the door.

"He won't throw anything breakable," Fritz said.

"Oh, that makes it *so much* better." Angel stalked across the yard—which was still covered with wet and heavy snow.

Snow White trailed after her, glancing back at the cottage. "I hope he gives Marzell those names."

Fritz nodded—to imply that he would—and took up the spot behind Snow White.

Snow White slightly shook her head and squinted up at the bright sky. *The Seven Warriors are moving. So, what, now, can I do to help?*

※

LONG AFTER OSWALD and Wendal had left—with a windblown Marzell and an amused Rupert departing not much later—Snow White sat on a dry tree trunk outside, drawing in the melting snow with a stick.

Angel was crouched nearby, grumbling to herself as she shoved her starfires back into her satchel. (Snow White could have sworn the satchel wasn't large enough to hold them all, but somehow the apprentice managed it.)

Gregori still slept inside, having returned to his nap immediately after Marzell got the names from him, but Fritz and Aldelbert circled each other in the yard, crossing their sword blades in a practice match. (They had been at it since the other warriors left.)

Snow White watched Fritz block a strike from Aldelbert before knocking the lord's sword from his hand.

"A good blow!" Aldelbert praised as he retrieved his weapon.

Fritz only nodded and experimentally swung his sword once before crouching in a defensive position.

Snow White smiled minutely at the sight, then returned her attention to her crude drawings. She rested her chin on her knees as she scrawled out a few notes, pausing when a shadow covered her musings.

Fritz—his sword sheathed—looked down at her.

"Are you done practicing?" Snow White asked. She had to lean precariously to the side to see around Fritz to espy Aldelbert.

The pretty lord stood at the opposite side of the yard working his way through several sword stances with a rare look of focus on his face.

Fritz nodded, then moved to stand by her tree trunk—carefully trudging around her snow drawings.

Snow White offered him a smile as she stabbed her stick in the snow, happy for the company.

Every moment she spent in the quiet forester's presence seemed to only put her more at ease. He had quickly become her favorite out of the Seven Warriors—though it was admittedly rather childish to have a favorite. But there was something about him that let Snow White relax—something beyond the peace and security he brought everywhere with him, that was.

Perhaps I need to loiter about with more foresters if they are all this calming. Though I do suspect it is a trait unique to Fritz.

Fritz finally looked up from Snow White's scrawl in the snow. "What is this?"

Snow White bit her lip and squelched the desire to stamp out her silly notes. "I'm trying to see if I can pinpoint when things went sour," she said. "Angel has mentioned a few possible ways magic could be affecting my stepmother. If I can narrow down my timeline, it might help confirm or disprove some of those ways, and then in theory we *should* be able to come up with a better plan to counter whatever it is that is happening."

Fritz crouched next to her and gestured at her marks. "Explain it, please?"

She hesitated for a moment. *It's just a visual for my thought process. I doubt it will birth anything useful. But I don't think Fritz will mind.* She snuck a glance at the forester, who was studying her snow records with interest. "If you like," Snow White said before she realized what she had agreed to.

She cleared her throat and adjusted her grip on her stick. "It's a timeline," she said. "Here is where Faina's health started to deteriorate soon after Father's death. Down here is where we are." She tapped her snow on the far end of her line. "It's where the magic holding Faina turned deadly, and she tried to hurt me before she stopped herself, and it marks last night's magical attack. Things haven't been this...*volatile* before. This day is the first day when whatever it is that has Faina became a real threat."

Snow White frowned in concentration as she stared at the point. "It seemed rather sudden, but when I approached her, it felt like one of the fits of anger she had been having for approximately a year. They first started about here." She pointed to the spot she had marked for the year prior. "She never harmed anyone during those times, but she *did* say she felt like she wasn't herself."

She trailed off and pursed her lips in thought.

"You think a rogue mage or black mage first attacked her then?" Fritz guessed.

"It's our best bet. But Angel said before it was pretty risky for a mage to manage a spell for that long. The longer he or she spent in Mullberg, the greater the chance that he—or she—would be noticed, given that we house the Veneno Conclave and magic academy."

Snow White's shoulders stooped, and she glumly added, "Her health was fragile then. It's possible they struck then because she was at her weakest, and they thought to take advantage of it."

"Maybe the Queen fought the magic," Fritz suggested.

Snow White finally looked up from her scratchings and watched Aldelbert laugh as he snapped his cape and posed with his sword outstretched. "I want to think Stepmother did. She's a strong person, but it seems a little strange that the attacker left it, then, as long as he or she did given the previously mentioned dangers in that."

Fritz and Snow White were silent as they considered the mystery.

Snow White eventually groaned and rubbed her eyes. "All the facts don't add up. We're missing something—something crucial. It's probably in all the things she *didn't* tell me." She frowned as she kicked her foot through the snow-etched timeline.

"That upsets you?" Fritz asked.

"It upsets me that she thought I was so helpless she *couldn't* tell me," Snow White said. "It upsets me that I *let* myself be so, so 'protected' she felt like she couldn't ask me for aid. I knew she was struggling with her headaches, but we all thought the anger was from the pain. If she had told me more of what she was going through..." She stabbed her stick into the snow.

"Perhaps she didn't notice until it was too late," Fritz suggested.

Snow White slumped. "Maybe," she agreed. She glumly peered up at Fritz. "Thank you."

He tilted his head and raised his eyebrows in a questioning manner.

"For listening to me." Snow White rubbed her hands together in an effort to warm them before huddling them close against the white fur that lined the neck of her cape. "For not dismissing me."

Fritz blinked slowly—like a thinking cat. "Of course."

Snow White turned her face up to the sun, enjoying its warmth. "When do you think Marzell and the others will return?"

"Dusk."

"I see." Snow White resisted the urge to sigh. *Why is it that the crucial things in life always seem to take more time than necessary? Nonetheless! I need to help wherever I can.* She glanced at the cottage. "Is there anything else that needs repair?"

Fritz speculatively studied the cottage as well. "The doorframe."

"That's right; it's still broken from Angel's entrance," Snow White said. "Can I help you fix it? Or were you going to train some more with Aldelbert?"

Fritz shook his head and stood, then offered his arm out to Snow White.

Snow White paused for a moment—besides the occasional function she had attended as a child with her father, she had never really been escorted by a man before. But Fritz was so natural, she hadn't even noticed it when he gently escorted her out of the cottage before Marzell woke Gregori.

Ahh, yes, Gregori.

"Will pounding on the frame wake Gregori?" Snow White asked as she set her hand on Fritz's arm.

Fritz shook her head. "No."

Thinking of the deafening roar, she asked, "Are you *certain*?"

Fritz smiled at her, flashing his teeth. "If we don't prod him, he won't stir."

"If you say so." Snow White felt her shoulders relax as Fritz led her back to the stables—to retrieve supplies, likely. Her steps felt lighter as she followed him, grateful he—and the rest of the Seven Warriors—believed her and were working to help her.

CHAPTER 8
DISCOVERIES AND IDEAS

"Most of those I met with do not work directly with Queen Faina," Marzell explained. "Glitzern takes its defenses too seriously to manage that. However, they did promise to talk with those who do and look into the matter. One of the officials even offered to request a meeting with Queen Faina."

Snow White, Angel, and five of the Seven Warriors were gathered inside the cottage—once again sitting around the table (with the exception of Gregori, who was sleeping on the lowest stair—an impressive and surely painful sleeping position) discussing the various servants and officials to whom Marzell had spoken.

Snow White jumped when the cottage door slammed open, cracking ominously on its repaired hinges. "Queen Faina has lost it," Oswald announced as he strode through the door.

Marzell frowned. "We know it is the magic that drives her to act so," he said.

"That's not what he meant," Wendal said as he also trudged inside—though he took the time to shut the door, *carefully*, behind him. "What our simple-minded friend attempted to explain is that whatever it was that held the dark magic at bay in Queen Faina, it's gone now."

"Simple?" Oswald narrowed his eyes and scowled darkly. "You're calling *me* simple-minded when you serve Lord Fruit Pie?"

Snow White blinked, and suddenly Wendal was holding a dagger. "Insult My Lord again," he said with a frightening smile.

"Oswald, Wendal," Marzell interrupted. "Please explain your discoveries in more detail."

"Gladly," Wendal said. "Oswald, you see, has very little going on between his ears in that frizz-covered head of his. This means he is rather unintelligent."

"*What?*" Oswald howled, then glanced at Gregori to ascertain that he was still sleeping.

"He asked for an explanation," Wendal said innocently.

"Why you—" Oswald took a step toward the attendant, but Fritz set his hand on the shorter man's shoulder.

"Oswald," he said.

Oswald sighed, and his puffed-up shoulders and chest settled. "Yeah, yeah," he said. He snatched up a crusty roll left on the table from dinner and started devouring it. "Since Her Highness left, things have gotten real bad," he said whilst chewing. "The Queen is enraged all the time—throws stuff at servants, yells, makes vague threats, that sort of thing."

"Shut your mouth or go out in the barn," Rupert said, looking disgusted. "Though even *that* might be too good for the likes of you, as we don't have a pig pen."

Oswald—his cheeks stuffed—scowled at Rupert.

Wendal cleared his throat and picked up the narrative. "She stays in her quarters most hours of the day. Since Snow White left, no noble—Cabinet member or otherwise—has been admitted to see her."

"Oh. Yeah. It's known Snow White is missing," Oswald added as he bit into another roll.

Marzell frowned. "I would hope so. It was Queen Faina who sent Snow White away."

"That is not what the animal means," Wendal said.

"Animal!" Oswald tried to say something more but swallowed his half-chewed roll wrong and nearly choked instead.

Wendal stood at the end of the table and placed his hands flat on top of it. "The Queen—and about half the servants in the palace, it seems—knows Snow White was supposed to meet up with her grandfather's men. And that she *didn't*."

Snow White frowned at the reveal, as did Angel and Marzell.

"Of course," Aldelbert chirped.

Everyone swung around to peer at him in surprise.

"Of course, what?" Angel asked.

"Of course, they knew she didn't travel to Trubsinn," Aldelbert continued. "How else would the rogue mage have known to send his constructs here?"

"Well, what do you know," Oswald marveled. "Aldelbert had something smart to say."

"Even a blind squirrel can occasionally find a nut," Rupert said.

Snow White cleared her throat, then regretted it when everyone shifted their gaze to her.

"Yes, Princess?" Marzell prompted with his kind smile.

She lowered her gaze to the half-eaten food spread across the table, staring at a shriveled apple with great concentration. "What if the rogue mage didn't send his constructs *here* per say, but instead, they happened to track me here?"

"The mage might have acted after realizing Snow White hadn't met up with the Trubsinn guards." Angel thoughtfully tapped the rim of her wooden bowl. "Knowing her location gives him a fighting advantage. When she disappeared, I bet it messed up some of his plans."

"Could the constructs report back to the mage to tell him—or her—where she is?" Marzell asked.

Angel scrunched her mouth shut as she thought. "Possibly? I don't know much about magical constructs—they're *old* magic. There hasn't been a mage skilled in them for a while. Black magic can reach past the normal boundaries of magic, and since that was obviously black magic we encountered last night, there's really no telling what the spellwork was that put them together."

"If the rogue mage figured it out, they didn't tell Faina," Snow White added. She blinked when she realized she had chimed in without thinking.

It's getting easier to talk to them, Snow White noted in surprise. *And yet, I can't talk like this with my ministers, whom I have known for years. Is it their proximity—that we spend all our hours together? Or perhaps the life-and-death event we shared last night?*

"Yes," Wendal agreed. "Oswald is right—the Queen very obviously does not know Snow White's location, which upsets her. If the rogue mage figured it out, he didn't share."

"I see," Marzell said. "If that's the case, we should probably try to keep the ruse up as long as possible. Depending how deeply the rogue mage has wormed into Queen Faina's mind, she might order her troops to find Snow White. I'd like to avoid that."

"She'll need a disguise," Fritz said.

All the warriors—or at least those who were awake—nodded at Fritz.

"Yes, that's true. When we travel to meet with potential allies, Snow White will need a disguise," Marzell said.

"You *all* do," Angel said. "It would be fair obvious where she is if word gets out that Snow White is working with the Seven Warriors, who just happen to be traveling with a nun or something."

"Another fair point," Marzell agreed. "We can try to find some disguises later—I'd like Gregori's and Fritz's input on it in particular—but before we get that far, we need to talk, Princess."

Snow White shifted slightly on the bench. "Y-yes?" she asked uncertainly.

"What outcome are you hoping for?" Marzell asked.

Snow White felt like a frightened deer surrounded by hunters as the warriors looked at her. "What do you m-mean?" she finally asked.

Wendal clasped his hands behind his back. "You said you wanted to save Faina. What does that mean?" He offered her a brief smile that softened the hardened edge to his eyes.

"I want her captured—unharmed," Snow White said. She rearranged her feet as she tried to put into words what she was thinking. "She's a danger to the people of Mullberg like this, but I don't want her killed for it."

There was a long stretch of silence, but everyone waited patiently for her to continue.

Snow White sucked in a deep breath and forced herself to look up—though she could only meet Marzell's gaze for a second before having to peer elsewhere. "I want Faina off the throne and contained so she won't hurt anyone—including herself—while we find a mage, or perhaps even a Lady Enchantress or Lord Enchanter, who can break whatever spell has been cast over her."

"So you are also concerned for the wellbeing of the country?" Rupert asked.

Snow White nodded. *Faina was a good queen—kind and thoughtful. It would break her heart if she comes back from all of this only to find out she endangered our people.*

After a moment, she added, "But it is more than that, too. The Chosen, Angel spoke of, are a concern. If Mullberg falters, it will surely cost the continent and be considered a win for the Chosen."

"Wise words—and a wise goal," Gregori said, surprising everyone as he sat up from his makeshift bed on the stairs. "Though the Queen's situation is precarious, if we plan it out well, I don't think it will be terribly hard to contain her or convince others to join us."

Snow White stared at her hands. "In her letter, Faina asked Grandfather to kill her. I am certain he would have done as she asked—as would any of our ministers."

"She tried to hurt you," Oswald said.

"The black magic *controlling* her tried to hurt me," Snow White said quickly, her voice sharp.

Oswald rolled his eyes. "You're really stuck on that, aren't you?"

"We can do it," Fritz said.

"Really, friend?" Aldelbert slapped Fritz on the back. "What makes you proclaim it to be so?"

"Things have changed," Fritz said. "Snow White didn't follow Queen Faina's plan, which seems to have interrupted the mage's schemes. The Queen hasn't struck out at anyone. It's possible the magic is making her fixate on Snow White. We can use that obsession and strike her while she's unprepared."

Angel stared at the forester. "I don't think I've ever heard you say so many words before."

"*I* haven't!" Oswald said. "And I *live* with him."

"But he's right." Gregori rocked to his feet, then leaned against the rickety stair railing, making it groan. "It's likely Queen Faina was afraid she'd start a civil war in her anger. But with the princess hidden, she has no reason to start one. We can capture her with one attack on the palace—if we're smart about it and prepare ahead of time with the proper allies."

"So it's not as hopeless as it seems?" Snow White asked. Her heart beat almost painfully so. Not out of fear, but the ache of *hope*.

Gregori offered Snow White a rare smile. "No. Not at all."

"Once the queen is securely—and safely—held, it really will be a matter of finding the right mage to help." Marzell smiled warmly.

"Except Snow White is taking on all the danger," Angel said.

"In what way?" Snow White asked.

Angel rubbed her nose with the back of her hand. "We can take Queen Faina without much bloodshed because she's fixed on you—the black mage is, too, most likely. They'll be out for *your* blood. And as we saw last night, whoever it is won't hesitate to harm you."

"Angel is right." Gregori ran a hand through his bright red hair as he thoughtfully studied Snow White. "Is that acceptable, Your Highness? For you to be the bait?"

Snow White pressed her lips into a line. When she realized everyone was staring at her, she glanced down at the table. "I'd rather have that than the alternative," she said. *I would take on all the risk and danger in the world if it means saving Faina and sparing our people—and the continent.* She nodded, solidifying her resolve. "I can't do much, but I can do this. I accept it."

"We'll protect you," Fritz said.

Marzell nodded. "With everything we have."

Aldelbert leaped to his feet so he could pose with his arm thrust out in front of him as if holding a sword. "It is an honorable and worthy task to guard a princess. None shall slip past us—we will laugh at death and trick its cold fingers! Oh—that was a good line. Wendal—write that down!"

"I already am, My Lord!" Wendal happily reported as he scratched away on a parchment paper with a feather quill and black ink.

"Now comes the matter of whom we ask to join us." Marzell slipped off the bench and strode to a chest—covered with quivers and bows—pushed against the wall. "I can manage all communications, but I'm afraid you'll have to meet with them eventually, Princess, or they won't believe us that we are working with you."

Snow White mutely nodded.

"Gregori—whom should we ask?" Marzell retrieved a slate and piece of chalk from the chest. He wiped the slate off with his sleeve before turning to the muscled merchant.

Gregori rubbed his stubbled jawline. "I would think the lords are likely to offer us troops. We could use royal soldiers if we flashed Snow White's name around, but then we'll rouse the Queen's suspicions."

"A bad thing to do when we're trying to keep this quiet," Marzell agreed with a sigh.

Snow White cleared her throat. "Wouldn't it be best to ask local lords? Their troops would be more readily available so we could strike faster."

Marzell nodded. "A good point."

"Yes, especially given we can't count on keeping whoever is controlling Faina in the dark for long," Rupert added.

"Precisely!" Marzell settled down on the bench again and held the slate in one hand and his chalk—ready—in the other. "Then whom do we begin with?"

Angel nudged Snow White in the side with her elbow. "If I might have a moment of your time, Princess?"

Snow White nodded, then followed Angel when she retreated to the other end of the cottage.

Snow White stood with Angel so their backs faced the warriors, but Angel angled herself so she could study Snow White's face.

The apprentice frowned slightly. "Are you truly fine with this?" she asked.

Snow White clasped her hands together. "With the danger of keeping my stepmother's attention on me?" she guessed.

"No." Angel gestured behind them, to the table. "With Marzell acting as the leader and communicator."

That is possibly the last thing I expected her to ask. Snow White smiled slightly at her friend. "Are you really asking *me* if I am upset with being kept out of the spotlight?"

"Yes, but only because I don't know that you are thinking it through, and Marzell believes he's sparing you the pain of talking to others," Angel said.

"What do you mean?"

Angel leaned her hip against the wooden counter, batting a sprig of dried thyme that hung lower than it should out of her face. "I mean, the lords are going to make a lot of inferences out of Marzell talking to them and making all the arrangements—even if you are there. They will consider him the leader."

"But he *is* a leader—a good one," Snow White said, feeling the need to defend her childhood friend.

"Yes, but he doesn't have the power behind his name that you do," Angel pointed out. "He cannot throw his position around like you could."

Snow White considered the matter for a few moments. *She's right. Politically speaking, it puts us at a disadvantage. But Mullberg is much more informal; the lords won't disregard Marzell for it. In fact, because of that they will likely take better to him than they would to me if I were forced to stammer my way through an explanation and request for help.* "I see your point." Snow White pushed one of her black curls out of her face. "But I don't know that it will ever matter. As long as I can be kept safe, and the lords believe the country isn't in much danger, they'll listen to Marzell. And really, I'm glad he's sparing me the pain." She hesitated, then added, "I'm not a very inspiring leader. Princess or not, I think they'll listen better to Marzell."

Angel tilted her head, the stubborn furrow of her forehead telling Snow White she was not wholly convinced. "You are certain you won't regret this?"

Snow White nodded. "Yes. I trust my nobles. Even if they choose not to follow Marzell, they'll have heard about Faina. They won't tell her what we're up to."

Angel snapped her neck in a rather painful looking nod, then smiled. "Very well," she paused. "If it helps, I—"

"Princess, Angel," Marzell called out to them. "We're going over possible disguises. Have you any preference?"

Angel set her hands on her hips and turned to face the warriors. "I'm an apprentice to an herb wizard. Why do *I* need a disguise?"

"We were rather hoping you and Snow White could be disguised in the same way," Marzell said.

"It would make it more believable," Gregori said as he eyed the wooden bench by the fire—likely planning his next nap location.

"You'd be a matched pair!" Aldelbert proclaimed.

Rupert rolled his eyes. "They're not horses."

"Obviously, or they'd make you sneeze—Lord Dewdrop," Oswald said.

Rupert narrowed his eyes at his friend and sneered back at him.

"I don't much care what disguise we have, but I will say I'd make a rather poor nun." Angel picked her way back over to the table, gesturing for Snow White to follow her.

"With your mouth? That was a given—*ouch*!" Oswald hissed when Angel picked up a tray to remove it from the table and "happened" to bash Oswald on the forehead as she turned.

"Oops, *so* sorry," Angel said in a voice as sweet as honey.

"Nag," Oswald huffed—under his breath so the fearsome apprentice couldn't hear.

"How will you seven be disguised?" Snow White asked.

Fritz scooted down the bench, making room so she could sit next to him.

"We haven't decided yet," Marzell said. "We were thinking we would build our disguise around yours."

"There are seven of you. I should think it would be the reverse," Angel said as she set the tray down on the wooden counter.

"We could don the costumes of daunting and debonair highway men!" Aldelbert cheered.

"We want to avoid detection, not get arrested," Rupert said.

"But it was a clever plan, My Lord," Wendal was quick to add (even though Aldelbert didn't so much as droop from the immediate refusal).

"We might have to split our costumes given that there are, as Angel said, seven of us. I would think it would be suspicious to see seven foresters or seven blacksmiths riding together—don't you think, Gregori?" Marzell asked.

"Mmmm," Gregori said as he got up and walked over to the fireplace bench.

"Don't you have an opinion, my friend?" Aldelbert asked.

Gregori frowned thoughtfully as he stretched out on the bench. "No," he said before turning his back to them.

"And Gregori is unavailable until breakfast," Oswald announced.

"Unfortunately." Marzell tapped his finger on his slate. "Do you have any thoughts on our disguise, Princess?"

Snow White shook her head and was grateful when Marzell moved on to musing over his goblet.

"We could be royal soldiers," Oswald said.

"We'll have to steal the uniforms," Wendal said.

"It's too risky given Queen Faina's new occupation as a shut-in," Rupert added.

"I don't see *you* making any suggestions," Oswald growled.

Rupert curled his upper lip in a sneer but then sneezed three times in a row.

"I was wrong," Oswald said. "It seems Lord-Heir is suggesting we pretend to be seven invalids."

Rupert started to snarl but was cut off by another sneeze.

Snow White sat, content to watch, but was surprised when Fritz leaned closer.

"You really don't have any ideas?" he asked in a voice that was barely above a whisper.

Snow White scratched her nose as she considered the idea. "For a disguise, it would be best to look like something that is common. The mountain ranges to the south and west hold the richest deposits of minerals, ores, and gems in the continent. Could you be jewelers—or luxury merchants?"

A slow smile crossed Fritz's lips—one that started with a glow in his eyes. "I have an idea..."

CHAPTER 9
IN DISGUISE

"Shouldn't we sing a song?" Aldelbert asked as he tugged on the bridle so his horse made a circle. "I feel like we ought to be singing a song."

"*No*, Aldelbert. No song," Marzell had to turn in the saddle to shout back at Aldelbert, who was positioned near the back of their group.

Aldelbert pushed the rust red hood of his cloak off his head. "But we're miners."

"I was unaware miners were known to be great singers," Angel said.

"They aren't," Snow White said. She peered up at the cloudy and drab sky.

"Aldelbert is merely highly misinformed as to what life is like for regular citizens," Rupert said as he adjusted the pickaxe fastened to the back of his saddle.

"This was an excellent suggestion, Fritz," Wendal said as he pushed up the brim of his floppy leather cap—which was frankly shaped like a sack—back up his forehead. "Taking on the guise of miners explains our numbers and gives us an excuse to carry excess baggage."

Fritz bowed his head in thanks.

"It was a wonderful idea," Aldelbert confirmed. "Remind me to give you a portrait of myself when we return to the cottage, Fritz, in reward!" He winked. "Wendal will make certain to pick out a good one for you."

"Just remember our cover story," Marzell said. "We're all cousins from Baroke lands, carrying gem and rock samples to Lord Chita."

"Yeah, yeah, except for Angel going as herself and Snow White acting as our remarkably pregnant cousin-in-law." Oswald scratched his cheek, further smearing the ash he had rubbed on his face before setting out. "How are you managing, Princess?" he asked with a drawl.

Snow White, resting her arms on the cushion of her pillow-belly, nodded. "This is quite comfortable." She kicked her horse to keep it moving when it eyed a green weed that poked up out of the mud on the side of the road, but she was unable to drag its head away from the weed as the horse was actually on a lead line tied to Fritz's horse.

It was a ploy to further confirm their cover story—which put Snow White in the role of Fritz's pregnant wife.

"You are all remarkably nonchalant considering your *princess* has gotten herself married and made a mother in one day," Angel said.

Aldelbert blinked. "Do you not understand it is a *disguise* and not real?"

"Obviously." Angel waved her hand through the air. "But I have seen more royals than I cared to over the past two years, and even the laxest among them would pause before getting pretend married to one of their subjects and falsify being with child." She squinted in thought before she added, "Though that might not be fair. Elle would do it, I suppose, but Severin would probably die of a heart attack. And Quinn could be as convincing as a pregnant mother as she would be posing as a thoughtless, dunderheaded flirt."

By Severin and Elle is she referring to the much-admired prince and princess of Loire? But how would an apprentice to an herb wizard come to know them? Unable to deny her curiosity, Snow White asked, "You know Prince Severin and Princess Elle?"

"No." Angel frowned when a breeze caught her cloak and made it puff up with air before she yanked it closer. "I said I've *seen* them—not fraternized over tea and dinner."

Snow White leaned back in the saddle as she carefully studied Angel, unable to shake the feeling that there was something *different* about her new friend.

"You'll find we don't have much use for formality here in Mullberg," Marzell explained. "We still have the caste system with various class levels, but it is a point of pride in Mullberg that the noble families interact with their tenants—not just as their lord but also their protector and provider. Similarly, the monarchs have always been more open and less separatist in their class."

"I was taught since I was a child there is nothing special about my blood, and that my role as future queen is a responsibility—not an excuse to be careless or disregard the welfare of my people," Snow White added.

"I'm starting to see why you planted your heels, then, about Queen Faina," Angel said. Though she was talking to Snow White, she curiously eyed Gregori, who was passed out—snoring—over his horse's neck and shoulders.

Snow White nodded but found she couldn't say much more, so she busied herself with adjusting the plushy pillow that served as her protruding stomach after glancing up and down the road to make certain no one was within eyesight.

She could see horses and riders off in the distance—the flat farmland that the road divided didn't make the best cover—but unless they were riding with a spyglass stuck to their eyes, the other travelers wouldn't notice Snow White adjusting her belly.

It took her a moment to make sure the knot of the cords that wrapped around her waist to secure the pillow sat in the small of her back and wasn't visible. Satisfied with the adjustment to her disguise, she leaned forward to pat her horse on the shoulder. "Where will we meet the lords Marzell has contacted?" she asked Fritz.

"A thicket of woods north of Fluss," Fritz said, naming a tiny farming village southwest of the city of Hurra.

Snow White nodded. *It shouldn't be too far, then. Perhaps an hour ride—and we'll mostly cross farmland and forests.* She shivered when the wind tugged on her mud-colored cape—which she had exchanged for her vibrant red cloak in order to fit her disguise.

A week had passed since Snow White first came to the Seven Warriors. Though the temperatures were still raw and cold, the snow had melted away, and the ground had thawed, leaving everything a muddy mess.

The road, thankfully, was only soft—not great for riding on, but better than squelching through the muddy farmland surrounding them.

Snow White chewed on her lip as she stared out at the puddle-filled fields. *Marzell said I wouldn't have to do much talking—merely be on hand to assure the lords this is true. But I wonder if they will have heard about Faina's actions by now. Gregori's contacts have reported that she only grows more volatile and enraged each day and that she commonly screams threats about me.*

Hopefully the lords hadn't heard that last part. Snow White was aware that the best possible scenario was to keep their capture of Faina subtle and quick and not allow it to balloon out of control and—at a worst-case scenario—turn into a civil war.

Oswald yawned and lazily slapped his horse's saddle pack. "Riders ahead."

"We're not blind," Rupert drolly said.

Aldelbert urged his horse into a trot and joined Oswald at the front of the party. He shielded his eyes—though it was more for effect than anything given that the sun was screened by clouds. "They're dressed in Trubsinn uniforms. How quaint!"

Marzell nearly lurched off his horse. "*What?*"

Rupert nudged his horse to the front, joining in on the fun. "He's right. I don't know how Oswald the Oblivious missed it, but those are Trubsinn soldiers and troops—looking for Snow White, no doubt."

"How many?" Gregori asked as he abruptly sat upright. (His sudden movement, surprisingly, did not alarm his mount.)

Rupert squinted. "A dozen?"

"Nay, two dozen, and all of them mounted!" Aldelbert beamed as he turned around in his saddle. "It seems that your grandfather loves you very much, Your Highness!"

Snow White smiled weakly. "Perhaps we should think about sending word to him, so he doesn't worry so much."

"Certainly, if you want him to realize who you're running around with and then drag you back home like a misbehaving child," Angel snorted.

Gregori raised an eyebrow at the apprentice. "Do you have a low opinion just of those in Mullberg or all mankind?"

Angel smiled widely. "I hate everyone equally."

"Charming," Gregori said.

Marzell watched the incoming soldiers with worry. "Aldelbert, fall back—ride with me. Rupert, if you stay with Oswald, you cannot bait him."

Rupert nodded, which turned into a sneeze.

"Don't worry yourself, 'Zell," Oswald drawled. "I'll make certain Lord Fragile doesn't fall off his horse." His snicker turned into a retching-choke noise when Rupert struck him in the throat with the heel of his palm.

Angel pointed to Rupert. "I feel like he hates a lot too."

"Most people, not everyone," Gregori said.

"Give it time," Angel said dryly.

"Stop talking—all of you!" Marzell hissed as the troops continued to march closer. "Act according to your roles."

"So, we really should sing then," Aldelbert said as he held his horse back long enough to walk shoulder-to-shoulder with Marzell's mount.

Marzell groaned. "Why would this strike you as a good time to sing? We should be as uninteresting as possible."

"You said to act in our roles. We're miners," Aldelbert objected.

"For the last time, Aldelbert: miners do not sing!" Marzell hissed.

(It was around this time that Snow White reflected that if the moment was not so tense, she would have been less likely to want to slap her hand over Aldelbert's mouth and would be more inclined to feel sorry for Marzell in his role of—apparently—matron of the Seven Warriors.)

"Here is your role, Aldelbert," Snow White called up to him. "You are a mute miner—you cannot utter a word."

"Oh!" Aldelbert beamed. "I see—I mean..." He nodded, then whipped around to face forward again.

Fritz twisted in the saddle so he could offer her a quick grin, but he straightened when the soldiers were within striking distance of a bow and arrow.

Snow White wove her fingers through her horse's mane and stared at the crest of its neck, unable to watch as they marched toward her grandfather's troops.

Her heart shuddered painfully in her chest, and her hands turned clammy as the hoofbeats of the soldiers' mounts grew louder.

"Hullo—let's move over," Marzell said.

Snow White slumped slightly in her saddle as Fritz—towing her horse behind—moved to walk on the very edge of the road, giving the troops more room.

She watched out of the corner of her eyes as the first of the soldiers drew even to their party.

The soldier in front nodded to Snow White and Angel—and several of his troops followed his example and did the same.

Angel smiled slightly and called out "Good day!" in a pleasant voice she had never used before. Snow White—internally cursing the blush in her cheeks—could only stare at her horse's ears.

She waited, holding her breath, as her grandfather's men moved past, murmuring between themselves. The soldiers paid their party no more attention than cursory nods. But with each passing horse, Snow White waited for one of them to spot her and call out to his fellows.

Marzell waited until the last of the soldiers passed before directing his horse back to the middle of the road, and Snow White's heart was finally able to settle back into her chest.

She made herself face forward—though she badly wanted to glance back and assure herself they really had just slipped away. She released the gulp of air she had been holding in, and Fritz glanced back at her with raised eyebrows.

"I'm fine," she whispered. She listened with a cocked ear, assuring herself the soldiers wouldn't be able to hear her hushed voice. "It is merely that that was...harrowing."

Fritz nodded. "You did well."

"Indeed!" Aldelbert proclaimed in his booming voice.

"Aldelbert—hush!" Marzell hissed too late.

"They didn't even glance at us!"

Angel and a grim Gregori twisted round to look back at the guards.

Oswald didn't wait. He kicked his horse—which took off like a shot, flicking up clods of dirt with its strides.

"There goes our chance at subtly," Angel grunted before she also kicked her borrowed mount.

"Go!" Gregori shouted.

Rupert urged his mount after Oswald, and the rest were not long after him.

When Fritz nudged his horse into a trot, then a canter, Snow White's horse obediently copied it—still tied to Fritz's saddle.

Snow White—usually a fair horsewoman—clung to her saddle as her horse kept pace. (It was incredibly disconcerting to be riding a horse at a canter without any way to control it.)

Fritz glanced over his shoulder, his eyes lingering on Snow White for a moment before he looked past her. "They're following!" He shouted above the thunder of their horses' hooves.

"We can't fight. We'll have to lose them," Marzell shouted.

"In the woods," Fritz yelled. "Or they'll be able to track us!"

What woods? We're surrounded by farmland!

As if answering her thoughts, the road curved slightly, letting her see past the galloping tangle of their party, to Oswald—who was far ahead of them.

Beyond Oswald was a smudge of green on the horizon.

"*That's* the forest?" Snow White shouted, her outrage getting the best of her worries and shyness.

Surprisingly, she must have been loud enough to hear over the snorts and stomps of their mounts, for Gregori offered her a grim nod. "Hold tight!"

Deciding the disguise was useless, Snow White crouched low —squishing her pillow, but giving herself an ounce more of control and balance.

She risked glancing over her hunched shoulder and immediately wished she hadn't.

The soldiers—their horses galloping in a military formation—were hot on their trail. Snow White couldn't have thrown a rock and hit them, but it was a close thing, and their mounts were gaining.

"Halt!" The lead soldier shouted at them.

The Seven Warriors paid the order no mind.

Instead, Wendal and Gregori maneuvered their horses so they

brought up the rear. They exchanged nods, then yanked on the knots that held their saddle packs and miners' gear tethered to their saddles.

The knots gave, spilling equipment across the road.

Snow White heard the soldiers shout in alarm. When she glanced back, she saw the roadblock had forced them to slow down some as they pressed to the sides of the road to avoid the pickaxes and stakes littering the rest of it.

In return, Snow White, Angel, and the warriors surged ahead, finally gaining on Oswald.

The forest Fritz had referred to grew on the horizon. Snow White could now make out the trees, though they were still uncomfortably far away from the woods and the safety it represented.

"Oswald—you idiot!" Rupert howled when Oswald was within hearing range.

The frizzy-haired warrior turned around so he could scowl and reined his horse in a little so he dropped back to the group. "What now?"

"We pray they don't catch us before the woods," Marzell yelled.

Snow White risked glancing back at the soldiers again.

They were still chasing after them, though they hadn't regained their ground yet.

"We split in the woods," Fritz shouted. "Gregori, Wendal, Rupert, and Oswald—keep riding on the main path, but split off in pairs before the trees thin."

"Aldelbert and I will follow you, Fritz, but you and the princess will turn off immediately from us?" Marzell guessed.

Fritz nodded.

"I'll go with the others," Angel drawled. "My herb magic might come in use." Though her horse was cantering just as fiercely as the others, she sat calmly and with assurance.

Snow White gulped as they thundered closer and closer to the forest. Another glance back at the soldiers revealed they hadn't shaken them, but they weren't following as close as they first had.

"Here we go!" Marzell shouted as they entered the first layer of trees.

Fritz waited until the road curved before he slowed his horse to a trot, then directed it down a small path covered in dead leaves that veered off from the road.

Snow White's horse followed, and Marzell and Aldelbert were quick to follow, as well.

On the road, Oswald whistled, and Gregori shouted, "Faster!" making enough noise to keep drawing the soldiers deeper into the forest.

Though her horse's trot was nearly bouncy enough to throw her from the saddle, Snow White crouched low against its neck and glanced back.

Sooner than she would have thought possible, the soldiers zipped past the entrance to their tiny path, pointing down the road—where Oswald continued to whistle and Gregori yelled.

Fritz kept them trotting through the forest, following the trail as it wound away from the road. He stopped only when they could hear no other horses than their own, and even Oswald's piercing whistle had faded.

"That was close," Marzell muttered. Though he spoke softly, his voice was loud in the ear-ringing silence of the forest. He wiped sweat off his forehead as he looked overhead, studying the few birds that nested in the evergreens and the bare branches of the leaf-bearing trees.

"Indeed. Good strategizing, Fritz," Aldelbert praised.

Fritz nodded, even as he turned around to check on Snow White.

She smiled at him and finally sat straight in her saddle, her fingers white with tension as she kept her hands tangled in her patient mount's mane.

"You deserve to have some sense jostled into you, Aldelbert,"

Marzell grumbled. "Though Oswald made the situation much worse by taking off. We *might* have been able to recover if not for that."

"It cannot be helped," Aldelbert shrugged, not at all bothered by the trouble he had caused. "This is our first stealth mission. We are used to coming to the daring rescue of quaint villages, not escorting a hiding princess around the countryside. Oh!" He grunted in pain when Marzell—who rode in front of him—released the prickly branch of a pine tree which smacked him in the face.

Fritz shrugged. "He's not wrong."

"This is an *unusual* mission," Snow White agreed—quietly. The forest air was colder than the farmland was, and although she had to clench her teeth to keep them from chattering, it was not due to the cold, but from relief.

"All of us are too understanding," Marzell sighed. "But it's about time for you two to separate. We'll keep along this path in case they double back and find it."

Fritz nodded as he pulled his horse to a halt and swung off. "We'll lead the horses and go by foot without a trail."

Snow White, following his example, slid from her saddle, landing shakily.

"Will you two be all right?" Marzell asked, his eyes flickering from Fritz to Snow White and narrowing in concern.

Fritz nodded again as he untied the rope tethering Snow White's mount to his and handed it off to her.

Snow White took it and peered up at her childhood friend. She tried to find the words that would assure him, but Aldelbert beat her to it.

"Of course they'll be fine!" He said. "Fritz is the father of her pillow—he'll keep her safe." He beamed down at them like a proud grandfather.

Snow White felt her jaw drop as she stared up at the bright-haired lord.

Fritz didn't even blink. He took his horse by the reins and started to lead it into the forest, leaving the pathway.

Marzell rubbed the bags under his eyes. "Aldelbert, you need to learn what is acceptable to say to friends, and what is acceptable to say to a princess."

"Whatever for?" Aldelbert asked as he nudged his horse into a walk and continued down the trail. "Snow White is not just a princess, but a friend as well!"

Marzell only sighed deeply.

Despite the seriousness of the situation, Snow White smiled, amused by Aldelbert's words—which lessened the tension in her shoulders. Feeling lighter, she followed after Fritz, affectionately patting her horse—which was spattered with mud and had a sheen of sweat on its neck and chest.

Fritz led her deeper into the forest's embrace, weaving around thorny bushes, fallen logs, and dry saplings. He frequently paused to glance back at her, nodding in silent encouragement when she met his eyes.

The woods were quiet—except for the occasional caw of a crow and the random nicker from their mounts. They walked in the near silence for a while—making Snow White internally marvel over the size of the woods.

Do I know this forest? I don't recall another woods between Luster Forest and Fluss.

She stopped when Fritz held up a hand and halted his horse. He held out his reins, and it took Snow White a moment to realize she was supposed to take them.

Fritz gave her an encouraging smile, then disappeared into the muted browns and grays of the forest as he jogged away from her.

"Good boy," Snow White murmured when his horse blew its hot, hay-scented breath in her face.

Fritz's gelding smacked its lips and tried to eat one of her black curls, which she yanked free before he could chew on it. She patted his neck when he sighed, then pulled on her horse's lead line when it eyed the only green weed in the area.

"We're safe," Fritz announced, nearly making her jump with his sudden appearance.

He flicked off the hood of his brown cloak and smiled with more warmth as he strode back to her. "The soldiers chased the others—who split up and gave them the slip." He gestured for her to follow and led her about five horse-lengths south.

Snow White blinked in surprise when she realized she could see the edge of the forest.

"We won't go any farther." Fritz reclaimed his horse's reins with a gentle tug so they fell from her grasp. "If we do, they might see us if they go to the entrance or exit of the forest."

It took her a minute, but Snow White realized she could visually follow the gentle curl of the treeline and see the far exit of the forest—which was almost within shouting distance.

"Will we regroup before we head to Fluss?" She asked.

Fritz shook his head. "Not entirely. The soldiers might decide to keep chasing. With scattered numbers, they won't be able to follow us all."

"It will be easier for us to slip off to the meeting place, then, as well," Snow White said.

He nodded.

Snow White looked down and grimaced at her cockeyed belly. "Do we keep our disguises?" She grunted as she yanked her belly straight.

"You and I will," Fritz said. "The others might not. Folks around these parts know them."

"So they would vouch for them if the soldiers stopped them?" Snow White guessed.

Fritz nodded. "Are you all right?" His normally bright hazel eyes slanted down with his slight frown. "I didn't mean for you to ride like that at a canter."

"It was a little unnerving, but I am unharmed," Snow White said. "Though I would like to avoid a repeat performance."

Fritz smiled with his eyes. "Understandable." He turned back to his horse and set about double checking the saddle and tack, testing its tightness, before doing the same to Snow White's borrowed mount.

Snow White stared at the forest floor—which was mostly covered by moss and dead leaves. *I need to prepare myself. Soon I'll be facing the lords. I should be able to recognize them, but I don't know that I will know them.*

During social events, Snow White found it easier to sit in the public eye if she was doing something to keep her mind busy. As a result, she had spent hours looking into the crowds and memorizing the names and faces of those present.

Faina had encouraged the game, saying it would help Snow White when she was queen, but she had to wonder if her stepmother was merely mollifying her.

Faina...

"Snow White?"

Snow White shook her head, breaking free from her thoughts. She forced herself to smile as she looked up at Fritz—who had moved to stand directly in front of her.

His forehead was wrinkled slightly with concern as he studied her. "Are you well?" he asked.

"I will be," Snow White said firmly. Her smile turned sincere as she studied his hazel eyes.

Fritz shifted his weight as he reached out and pressed the back of his hand against her forehead.

She laughed. "No, I am not running a fever that you need to check for. I really am well—all things considered."

Fritz slowly removed his hand. "I am sorry—for all you have been forced to live through."

Snow White shrugged. "If Faina's life wasn't threatened, I wouldn't mind this nearly as much. It's taught me..." she paused.

Fritz waited in expectant silence.

She hesitated as she stared up into his face, not out of fear, but surprise. *I've been meeting Fritz's gaze for a while, and I don't feel the burning compulsion to look away. But why? Have I really become that close with him and the other warriors in such a short time?*

When Fritz slightly tilted his head—still waiting for a response—Snow White hurried to finish, "It's taught me that I can—and need—to do more."

The expression in Fritz's hazel eyes turned thoughtful, and the wind ruffled his ashen hair.

Perhaps it is that he feels safe—but no, that makes him sound like a tame kitten. It is more that he makes me feel safe—like I can take a chance and push myself because he'll make sure to catch me if I fail. She was so intent on wondering why—even now—she didn't feel the familiar companions of shame and embarrassment; Snow White nearly missed his words when he spoke.

"Perhaps," he said. "But you have not given yourself enough credit. You've faced great difficulties, and you still pushed forward. Not many would do all you have done for the sake of another."

"Thank you." she hurriedly muttered, hating it when she felt a blush warm her cheeks.

Fritz nodded as he adjusted the hood of her cloak, pushing her black curls back to do so.

At that moment, Snow White was very awkwardly forced to consider how...*tall* and lean he was. She ripped her gaze away—mostly because she knew if she stared at him much longer, she was going to turn bright red.

Faina is going to laugh herself sick when I tell her how I ogled one of the Seven Warriors.

"Are you ready to remount your horse?" Fritz asked as he offered her his hand.

Snow White dropped her chin—making her hood fall even

more over her face so it hopefully shielded her red cheeks—then set her hand in his. "Yes."

Fritz started to approach the horses, then froze, every muscle in his body tensing. He abruptly spun around and tucked Snow White behind him with one neat move. Then, just as abruptly as his caution appeared, it drained away from him.

Snow White stuck her head out from behind Fritz as she heard something thrash through the forest.

Oswald—with a twig jutting out of the nest of his hair—scowled as he and his horse squeezed between the branches of two evergreens. "Don't push Gregori today. He's a real bear," he grouched as he fished pine needles out of the folds of his clothes.

Fritz and Snow White stared silently at him.

"And you!" Oswald jabbed a finger at Fritz. "You could have answered me when I used our bird-call signal!"

"Didn't hear it," Fritz said.

"Uh-huh, right." Oswald eyed them with suspicion. "Well, I'm here."

Snow White and Fritz exchanged glances. "Were we supposed to expect you?" Snow White finally asked.

"Yeah? Marzell insisted I ride with you. He said something about needing two of us with Her Highness to act as a chaperone, but I don't know why. It's not like we're taking you dancing or something." Oswald rolled his eyes.

Fritz nodded. "We'll mount up."

"Yeah, yeah, just hurry it up. Gregori and Marzell are all worried we'll arrive late—as if this were some kind of party. Ugh." Oswald snorted and let his horse follow Snow White and Fritz over to their mounts. "This is why I left home—politics. There's nothing worse—except maybe dancing at balls." The warrior shivered in horror.

Snow White stifled a smile as Fritz held her horse's halter while she boosted herself into the saddle. When she glanced down at Fritz and met his eyes again, another blush heated her cheeks.

Enough, she sternly told herself. *Oswald has a point. I am not some young maiden who flutters over handsome men. I have to save Faina.* Sufficiently chastised, she nodded and cleared her throat.

"Can we go?" Oswald asked as Fritz vaulted onto his mount's back.

Snow White and Fritz nodded.

"Of course, I would get stuck with the mutes in the group," Oswald grumbled as he kicked his horse, weaving his way through the thinning trees. "C'mon! We've got prissy lords that Marzell says *we can't keep waiting!*"

CHAPTER 10
THE FOUR LORDS

"I don't like it." Lord Gossler, one of the four local lords Marzell had contacted, scratched his beard.

Snow White swallowed hard, but she stood safely behind Marzell and Gregori. It was they who were receiving the most scrutiny.

"Is there something we have said that you do not believe?" Gregori asked. "The explanation of the Chosen, perhaps?"

"No, that is the most believable piece, actually," Lord Gossler said. "We've all heard of the troubles facing the royal families across the continent. Though I do expect you might be exaggerating things a bit, or believing it to be worse than it really is."

Angel made a noise in the back of her throat.

"Then is it the Queen?" Marzell asked.

Lord Gossler shrugged. "No. The Queen's behavior has been questionable for a while, but since Snow White disappeared, everyone within a day's journey of Juwel knows she has been acting mad. A spell from a rogue mage makes sense, for even King Torgen of Verglas did not act half as crazed before he died, and everyone knew he was rotten to the core."

"We had been wondering if there was something else at work,"

Lord Vitkovci—the eldest and most senior of the four lords—said. The wrinkles around his eyes seemed to deepen as he sighed. "But the idea seemed far-fetched given that the Veneno Conclave lives within our borders."

"If you believe that Queen Faina has some sort of dark magical influence moving her, then what is it you object to?" Gregori asked.

Lord Leyen adjusted his thick silver glasses that made his eyes appear to be larger than they were, and looked past Gregori and Marzell to Snow. "Personally, I am not sure it is at all wise for Her Highness to run around with the pack of you. Though it was wise of her to seek you out first, should she really *stay* with you—a group of all men?"

Snow White held in a wince, though against her will her gaze dropped to the ground. *So much for going unnoticed.*

"So I guess I'm just baggage now, is that it?" Angel drawled.

"You'll have to excuse our practicalities, but as an apprentice to an herb wizard, you haven't much clout," Lord Gossler said. "Certainly not enough that her grandfather—should he know it—would feel comfortable leaving her where she is."

Snow White glanced at Angel in concern. But instead of seeming offended, Angel's shoulders were shaking...in *laughter*. Snow White frowned a little as the apprentice continued to laugh silently with such force she had to grab her horse for support.

"Additionally, it doesn't feel right to keep Lord Trubsinn in the dark over this matter." Lord Holdenberg rested his hand on the gentle slope of his bulging belly. "He is the last of her kin. Ought he not be told what it is we have planned?"

"If you do that, he will undoubtedly march on Queen Faina—as we have warned—which will ruin any chance we have of a surprise attack," Marzell said.

"And in doing so, he will likely start a civil war," Gregori added. "And those who are *not* aware of Queen Faina's recent actions might feel the need to defend her. All of this would only add to the poor state in which our continent finds itself."

Lord Leyen squinted as he took his glasses off and cleaned them with a handkerchief. "I am certain our fellow lords would see the truth in what you've told us eventually."

Marzell and Gregori exchanged glances.

They don't know how to respond, but there is one way to convince the lords they don't want that. Snow White opened her mouth to speak, but nothing came out. *Blast it! I thought I was getting better!* She swallowed and tried again, but she couldn't produce even a squeak.

She gritted her teeth and curled her hands into fists. *How can I be so inept that I cannot manage this small thing?*

Gregori must have caught onto her frustration, for he stepped away from Marzell. "Do you have something to say, Snow White?" he asked in a lowered voice.

Snow White nodded, relaxing slightly as hulking Gregori stood between Snow White and the Lords, momentarily hiding her. "Tell them it will be their lands the troops will march on," she whispered.

Gregori cracked a smile and bowed slightly. "Spoken like a true merchant," he murmured before turning back to their audience. "Her Highness wishes for us to point out that should war come, it will be *your* lands and crops the troops will march over to reach Glitzern."

Lord Holdenberg frowned and played with the jewel studded rings on his fingers.

Lord Leyen almost dropped his glasses and frowned slightly as he put them back on.

Lord Vitkovci—the least upset at the thought—nodded. "Yes, there is that," he acknowledged.

Lord Gossler coughed and scuffed his foot on the flattened grass. "I suppose there is wisdom in attempting to subdue the queen without putting our country through the wringer. Very well, we can keep our efforts between us."

"*Unless* Snow White is placed in more danger." Lord Vitkovci held a finger up in objection. "The moment she is harmed, we inform Lord Trubsinn." He frowned. "But that does not settle the impropriety of Her Highness staying with seven men."

"I *am* a woman—or at least I was the last time I looked," Angel said—her voice shaking still with her silent laughter.

"Yes, apprentice, you have already pointed that out," Lord Gossler said with obvious patience. "However—"

"And regardless of my position, I am a magic user," Angel continued, thoughtlessly talking over the noble. "I have been selected and trained by the Veneno Conclave. I'm registered with them, in fact. Do you mean to say that a registered magic user—from the very organization that lives within your borders—is not legitimate company?" Angel smiled and rapidly blinked, making her dark eyelashes flutter.

Lord Gossler shut his mouth with a clack.

"Ahem—er...that is to say..." Lord Holdenberg coughed and looked uncomfortable. When he could think of nothing else to say, he glanced at the other lords. "Leyen?"

"I suppose she is correct," Lord Leyen said slowly.

Lord Vitkovci nodded. "Moreover, she is not with strangers, but her peers. Marzell, Rupert, and Oswald are of noble birth, and Lord Aldelbert already has a title due to the status of his family."

Aldelbert, who had been humming in the background—appearing to be oblivious to the conversation—smiled dazzlingly. "Indeed I do, good sir! And as a fellow lord, I have to say if you really think we'd be so dastardly, I don't want *you* around Snow White. No telling what *you'll* do if we leave her with you if *that* is where your mind goes."

Rupert erupted into a timely sneezing fit, or Marzell might have reached back and strangled the blond-haired lord based on the strain in his smile.

"Pay him no mind, Lord Leyen," Marzell said. "He's merely protective of Her Highness."

Lord Leyen squinted at Aldelbert. "I see."

"Before we settle this, though, Your Highness—Snow White." Lord Vitkovci shuffled so he viewed her straight on. "We need to ask: are you truly comfortable with all of this?"

Snow White's innards started to churn as the other lords joined him in directing their attention to her. *Stand tall. Don't look down—all right, never mind. That seems impossible. Just don't blush.*

"Do you *wish* to stay with the Seven Warriors—and the apprentice," the elderly lord was quick to add when Angel started to open her mouth. "Do you agree with all the plans we have made?"

Snow White nodded, but the lords kept staring at her, waiting for more.

I have to do this. Spit it out—no matter how terrible it feels!

She cleared her throat, then managed to say—in a much higher-pitched tone than usual, "Y-yes. I don't wish to risk Faina's life," she said, almost choking on the last word.

Lord Vitkovci nodded. "Very well. Then it seems we are finished here."

"We'll begin to muster our troops as you requested," Lord Gossler said. "But it will take at least two weeks."

"Particularly because we wish to avoid rousing anyone's suspicion," Lord Leyen added.

Marzell bowed slightly. "We are glad you have chosen to join us. Since our timeline is tentative, perhaps we ought to meet ten days from today?"

Lord Holdenberg nodded, making his jowls bounce. "That's reasonable. By then we can start planning the attack."

Gregori nodded. "My contacts in Glitzern Palace will have more information about Faina by then, as well."

"Excellent," Lord Leyen said. "We will see you in ten days,

then—and hear from you sooner to schedule the time and place, I assume?"

Marzell nodded. "Yes. Of course. Thank you."

The lords exchanged glances, bowed to Snow White, then strode for their horses—which were standing with the handful of guards that accompanied the men.

Snow White exhaled with relief when they returned to their men—though she watched a moment longer as Lord Holdenberg mounted a hot-blooded but beautiful horse. She shook her head, then offered Fritz a brief smile when he stirred at her side. She would have liked to bask in his calmness, but Marzell started talking.

"I thought that went well—better than I expected," Marzell said as their party formed a circle.

Gregori shrugged. "They agreed to the plan, anyway, and it seems they will not betray us."

Snow White slightly shook her head.

"You disagree, Snow White?" Aldelbert asked as he planted his hands on his hips. "But how could they resist us when I'm here?"

"You're a stale fruitcake," Oswald said.

"Take that back, you uncultured swine," Wendal growled.

"Enough," Marzell warned.

Rupert thoughtfully rubbed his chin. "Was Aldelbert right, Your Highness? Do you not agree?"

Snow White glanced over her shoulder at the mounted lords. "I merely think it is a very tenuous agreement," she said finally. "If they knew just how bad Stepmother has acted they likely wouldn't have agreed to refrain from telling Grandfather."

"Right enough," Marzell agreed. "Thankfully we're dealing with a shortened timeline, so hopefully they won't learn of it until we already have Faina secured."

Snow White slowly nodded, but she wasn't convinced it was that easy.

Despite my inability to talk, the Mullberg nobles have been patient and kind with me. They show me honor, but I'm not entirely certain they respect me. If they believe they know better than us, they may tell Grandfather even if they swear to my face that they will not.

The familiar pang of failure squeezed her heart. She had never before been bothered by the lords' and ladies' treatment of her—rather she was grateful for their kindness. But this was just another example of how she had failed Faina—and failed her country.

A monarch should not be doted on or treated with kid gloves. But Faina really did try to help me.

"How will we travel back home?" Oswald asked.

"We'll split the group in thirds," Marzell said. "Angel, Aldelbert, Fritz, and Snow White will ride together. I'll ride with Wendal and Gregori while you and Rupert will be together," Marzell said.

"What? I don't want to ride with *him*," Oswald complained.

"I also request a change in companions," Rupert said. "Can I not switch with Fritz?"

"Fritz is the least recognizable out of all of us," Marzell said, "since he is a forester and doesn't have a title. No one will press him if he claims Snow White is his pregnant wife, and Snow White's disguise will also explain Angel's presence."

"It's still not fair," Oswald grumbled.

"Enough," Marzell said, sounding much like Snow White's childhood nurse. "Get onto your horses. I want to hear no more arguments from either of you."

Oswald and Rupert grumbled but did as they were told.

Snow White smiled and followed the duo to the horses, where she mounted up onto her gelding, only half listening to the others as they approached their horses as well.

I'm disappointed with the meeting, even though I shouldn't be. The lords agreed to aid us. They're going to give us troops and help, and we will move faster but...

She bit her lip as she thought. *It is a much more fragile agreement than I thought we would get. Consequently, it's not quite the reassurance I was hoping for. I'm concerned, still, that Faina's safety is not yet guaranteed.*

❧

FRITZ ADJUSTED his grip on his horse's reins and glanced at his traveling companions.

Although Aldelbert had been instructed by Marzell that he was to act as himself, and he had abandoned his drab cloak for a bright blue one Wendal had packed ("just in case!") he switched back and forth from humming to whistling.

He really wanted us to sing in our disguises.

Fritz cracked a smile, then studied Snow White and Angel.

Angel was grinning like a mouse that had feasted on cheese and laughed randomly even though no one was speaking.

Snow White, however, was far more pensive. Her red lips were pressed together, and the crinkle by her blue eyes said she was worried.

Though her pillow belly was back in place, Fritz had buckled the set of extra reins he had packed to her horse's bridle, so she was in control of her own mount. She held her reins in one hand and patted her horse with her free hand.

If she is concerned, it must be from something the lords said.

Fritz tugged back on his horse's reins, slowing it until his and Snow White's horses were shoulder-to-shoulder.

It took her a moment to realize he had joined her. Then she offered him a smile—one markedly better than the weak one she had used the past few days—though Fritz could still see some tension in her shoulders and the set of her chin.

"Hello, Fritz," she said. "Are we very far from Luster Forest? I know we've traveled a different route this time."

When she didn't say anything more, Fritz nodded to the forest that was not even a league away. "There it is."

She blinked. "Oh, I hadn't realized that much time had passed."

"Are you pleased with the way things are progressing?" Fritz asked.

"Yes, of course!" Snow White nodded so violently she almost dislodged her hood from its perch on her head.

Fritz waited patiently for her to continue.

She's cautious about sharing, but if you give her time to think through her words, she will share. It was a shame the lords hadn't realized that. Nor—Fritz thought with a rare feeling of dislike—did they seem to realize just how brilliant she was.

"It just...the outcome was perhaps not as definitive as I had wished for." She shifted slightly in the saddle and unconsciously tugged on the puff of her belly. "I didn't really care for the caveat Lord Vitkovci added that they would remain silent as long as I was not placed in serious danger."

"You see that as a possible threat on Faina's life?" Fritz guessed.

"Yes, though I hope it does not come to that," Snow White sighed.

"They are concerned for you. Though Queen Faina has ruled well, they are *your* subjects, for she is only the regent. They will always be more concerned about your wellbeing," Fritz said.

Snow White patted her horse again. "I did not ease their worries, either, by behaving like a mouse. It's so *frustrating*! I am doing better talking to all of you. I thought I might be able to face the lords—particularly as there were only four of them."

"You are trying to run when you have just learned to walk," Fritz said.

Snow White cocked her head. "What do you mean?"

Fritz took a minute to mentally arrange his words so they would make sense. "You faced your fears in coming to us, but you grew to know us and trust us quickly because of our circumstances. You have no such bond of trust with the lords. Additionally, the lords have more power with them—it's like comparing a farm horse to a prized stallion."

Snow White scowled. "You are *not* a farm horse!"

Fritz smiled, warmed by her stout defense.

"Oswald might be a fuzzy pony, and Marzell would be a lady's palfrey, but you are at least a war steed," she grumbled.

He could tell the moment she realized what she was saying as her eyes bulged and she gaped up at him, unable to verbalize an apology.

Fritz couldn't help but laugh at her horror—and also a little bit due to the pleased feeling that she was so comfortable with him she had blurted out such an example. He asked, purposely continuing the banter to put her at ease, "Would Aldelbert be a circus horse, then?"

Snow White stared up at him for a moment—likely to try and gauge if he was making fun of her—then shook her head. "No, Wendal would be the circus horse—it would mean he's used to thriving in an uproar and doesn't shy from Aldelbert's...eccentricities. Lord Aldelbert would be a carriage horse—showy and beautiful."

"He will preen if he hears you called him beautiful," Fritz said.

Snow White laughed, her body language relaxing some. "You might be right, though. You, Angel, and the rest of the Seven Warriors are my friends. Talking to you was a breakthrough, but it was the lowest step on a staircase of improvement—is that what you mean?"

Fritz nodded but added, "You cannot be angry with yourself for failing to conquer your fears in one shot."

Snow White shrugged with her whole body. "Perhaps. But I'm still mad that I sat in Glitzern for so long, making excuses for myself. My subjects—both noble and peasants—are kind people. Would they really have thought poorly of me if I stammered and embarrassed myself? I told myself they would, but I think I might have been wrong."

Fritz studied the princess for a moment. *I don't think she really wants a response to that...but I do not like to leave her looking so sad.*

Fritz hesitated and wondered if he should dare.

Mullberg royalty had always been approachable, but Snow White had smudged the line even further in the way she treated him no differently than the other warriors. And if Fritz was being truly honest with himself, he hoped she might be partial to him—at the very least she seemed to reach for him most often. (Though that might be a bias colored by the pull he felt for her.)

Regardless, I don't think she'll mind.

Fritz moved before he gave himself more time to ponder it—or talk himself out of it. He shifted so he held the reins in one hand like Snow White did, then leaned across the narrow distance between their horses and briefly held her hand, squeezing it gently.

Snow White blinked in surprise, then offered him a shy smile. "Thank you, Fritz," she said, squeezing his hand in return. "For everything."

"It is my honor," Fritz said truthfully.

They rode hand-in-hand for a few quiet minutes.

It wasn't until they reached the border of the forest and Angel —still laughing—turned around to talk to them that they shifted.

"Snow White—oohhh. What are you doing?" she asked, speculatively eyeing their hands.

"Um," Snow White said.

Angel—half hanging out of the saddle—looked back and forth between Snow White and Fritz. "Oh...*oh*!" She chortled to herself and wriggled her eyebrows at them before her expression froze. "Wait...*again?*"

"Pardon?" Snow White asked, glancing at Fritz when he released her hand.

"Every time!" Angel said. "Every time it's in a *crazy* and

dangerous moment. There has got to be something wrong with all the royal families of the continent."

"I don't think I know what you're talking about," Snow White said.

Fritz did not entirely share her confusion. *She is likely referring to my...respect for Snow White. But what else is she talking about?*

Angel batted her hand at them. "You don't know it. Yet. But you will. *Wow*, that's all I can say." She released a bark of cackling laughter, keeping Fritz and Snow White from enquiring further.

Fritz wasn't certain this was a bad thing.

CHAPTER 11
TEA AND MARRIAGE

Though her conversation with Fritz had helped Snow White see the folly in both her impatience and her belief that being able to talk to the Seven Warriors meant she would have an easier time facing the lords, she was not fully satisfied.

"I need to fix my shyness," she told Angel the next day as she mended a hole in one of Wendal's shirts.

Angel, who had been sunning herself in the spring sunshine, squinted at her. "What?"

"I need to fix my shyness," Snow White repeated. "Or end it."

Angel snorted. "I have got some disheartening news for you: we all have personal struggles. They cannot be fixed, nor do they have an end. They are something we are forced to fight our whole life."

"My shyness is not a struggle, but a flaw," Snow White objected.

"It's a battle," Angel said. "You aren't shy because it suited you to be so or because you were raised to be shy. It is a facet of you, and you must learn to excel in spite of it."

Snow White glanced from her sewing to the apprentice.

Angel yawned as she watched Fritz school Marzell and Rupert

on archery—correcting their posture and form as they loosened arrows at the haybales the forester had set up at the start of the morning.

"What?" Angel asked when she felt Snow White's gaze.

"Then what is *your* personal struggle?" Snow White asked.

"Magic." Angel responded without hesitation, but in a flat tone that did *not* invite further conversation about the topic. She scratched her side and glanced at Snow White. "Is this because you don't want to do the lads' mending?"

"No—not at all," Snow White said. "I offered to do it. It is a small way I can express my thanks."

"Then where is this coming from?"

Snow White paused in the middle of pushing the needle through the sturdy but faded shirt fabric. "I was disappointed with myself for not being able to clearly speak to Lord Vitkovci and the others yesterday at our meeting."

She paused and nodded her head in greeting when Aldelbert strutted past, toting an axe. As she watched, he stopped at a pile of logs nearby and started splitting them and neatly stacking them for firewood.

"Fritz said I was trying to run before I learned how to walk," Snow White finally continued. "And I agree with him. But I am at a loss of how I am to get better and keep improving."

"Practice?" Angel offered. "The more you interact with nobles, the better you will grow to be."

"I have been around nobles my entire life, and that did not seem to help me," Snow White said.

"Yes, but now you are desperate to improve," Angel pointed out. She leaned back on the wooden stool she had claimed and watched Aldelbert attack the logs. "I can tell you from personal experience: when it seems like your world is ending, and all is crashing down upon you, you'll find new courage to try where before you were too afraid."

Snow White inspected her stitches, pleased with their precise placement. "You are correct. Though it is still disheartening, for I fear it means I won't get much practice when I very badly need it. I have grown comfortable with the Seven Warriors. Speaking to them is nothing like addressing the lords and ladies of nobility."

Angel and Snow White jumped in surprise when Aldelbert thunked his axe into an old tree trunk and shouted. "Ah-hah!"

They watched—Snow White with a curious frown and Angel with an arched eyebrow—as the sunflower haired lord strode over to Fritz, Marzell, and Rupert, and began talking to them in a hushed tone as he gestured back to the cottage.

"They certainly are an odd bunch," Angel said as the four men trooped past them and entered the cottage—Rupert arguing with Aldelbert along the way.

"They are heroes," Snow White said firmly. "They are kind, brave, and generous."

"Though their words certainly don't reflect that," Angel grunted.

Snow White smiled faintly and returned her attention to Wendal's shirt. *Fritz's cloak is the next piece I get to work on, and I want to finish mending it before nightfall.*

They sat in silence as Snow White put the last few stitches in Wendal's shirt, then pulled out Fritz's cloak, carefully inspecting the tear.

She changed the thread of her needle to match the shade of Fritz's brown cloak and just as she was about to start the first stitch the cottage door swung open.

"Ladies!" Aldelbert called in a terrible falsetto voice. "I do say, ladies!"

Snow White and Angel turned to look at the flashy man.

He had a blanket tied around his hips, creating a black skirt of a sort, and he had a pink ribbon tied around his forehead.

"Yes, Aldelbert?" Snow White cautiously asked.

Aldelbert laughed, then slapped his hand over his mouth.

"How silly of you to mix up the two of us, Snow White. I am the cousin of the handsome and magnificent Aldelbert, Aldelfreda."

"Has he finally lost what little sense he had?" Angel asked.

"The noble ladies and I were wondering if you would join us for some tea and streusel!" Aldelbert called.

Angel hefted herself to her feet. "This sounds strange and possibly disturbing—for I can guess who the other 'ladies' are. But I'm always game for refreshments. Coming, Snow White?"

Snow White set Fritz's cloak aside with a furrowed brow. "I... yes," she said, more than a little curious.

"Come in, come in," Aldelbert called—still using a falsetto voice.

Snow White and Angel lingered at the darkened doorway, but Angel bowed. "After you, Your Highness."

Snow White grabbed a fistful of her skirts and cautiously poked her head inside.

Nothing could have prepared her for the sight that greeted her.

Marzell stood just inside the cottage, an awkward and slightly embarrassed smile twitching across his lips as he adjusted the blanket he had clamped under his arm pits, so it resembled something of a dress.

An extremely hostile Oswald was perched on the bench by the fire. He wore a white headdress—whose origins Snow White could only wonder about—and locks of his wild hair poked out under the headdress' brim and the blue feathers that ornamented it. His arms were folded across his chest, and a white table cloth was wrapped around him, almost so he resembled a long—and angry—candlestick.

Rupert sat next to him, his eyebrows lowered as he looked at his companions with apparent distaste. (Though his only female ornaments were a lacy apron and a ribbon threaded through his hair.)

Fritz stood behind them, a bow clipped to a short lock of his hair and his gray cloak put on backwards.

Gregori was passed out, snoring, in a chair, as expected, but someone had arranged a white fur on his head so it resembled a wig, and a square of linen was tied across his shoulders to serve as a shawl while an empty tea cup had been shoved into his right hand.

Wendal—who sported a similar blanket-skirt like Aldelbert, though his was a drab brown—smiled and clapped his hands when Snow White and Angel entered the room. "Welcome, Your Highness and Angel. We are so glad you could join us today," he said.

One thing was clear to Snow White: Somehow, Aldelbert must have convinced the Seven Warriors to act—and dress up to a certain extent—as the rich, noble ladies Snow White had confessed to fearing.

Angel crowded into the cottage after Snow White, then whistled. "I really don't know what to say to this," she said. "Am I supposed to compliment your fashion choices, or would that make you feel worse?"

"It would make us feel worse!" Oswald snapped.

"Oslivia, mind your manners," Aldelbert chided.

"Yes, Oslivia, conduct yourself in a noble manner," Rupert said.

"Shut up...Ruth," Oswald muttered.

As the warriors shuffled awkwardly—obviously uncomfortable but choosing to soldier through anyway—Snow White found she had to stare at the ceiling, not due to her shyness or to stop herself from snickering like Angel, but to keep from crying.

They have no reason to do this, she thought. *None. They fight to keep people safe and act with honor, but I never thought they would embarrass themselves all for the sake of another—much less me.*

She sniffed a little but didn't dare lower her gaze, yet.

They are far kinder and nobler than I ever thought. And I have done nothing to deserve their loyalty. But I will strive to become someone they are proud to have helped.

Her resolution steeled, Snow White finally let her eyes fall.

"Please sit, Your Highness," Aldelbert instructed. "Don't mind Grandmother Grotchen—she sleeps through all social calls. Cousin Fredia, come sit! You will like Fredia, Snow White. She is nearly as quiet as you!"

Snow White smiled a little when Fritz glided across the cottage and perched on the edge of a bench pulled up to the table.

When he met Snow White's gaze, he pinched the front of his cloak and bobbed what was likely supposed to be a curtsey. "How do you do, Your Highness?"

"Fredia is a stupendous alto singer," Aldelbert said.

Marzell grinned. "Indeed, he—er, she—might even be considered a tenor or baritone!"

Gregori's white fur wig sagged as he snored away, but Wendal eyed the sleeping merchant as he carefully seated himself on the bench. "Today's tea is chamomile with a hint of honey," he announced. "If you cannot pick out the subtle honey undertone, you are an uncultured swine." He looked expectantly at Snow White, who guessed she was supposed to reply to the obvious jab.

"Pardon me..."

"Wendelia," he supplied.

"Wendelia," Snow White carefully repeated. "But perhaps you are too hasty in your judgement."

"I disagree," Marzell said. "Ladies ought to be able to do such things like..." he stared at his tea cup with a furrowed brow.

"Taste the subtle undertones of tea," Wendal supplied.

"Yes," Marzell agreed. "That."

"Snow White, when are you getting married?" Rupert asked as he stirred his tea.

When the five (awake) Warriors all turned to peer at him, he frowned.

"What?" He sneezed into a handkerchief embroidered with yellow flowers. "My mother asks me that every time I see her!"

"Marriage is a common conversation topic," Snow White said encouragingly.

"And...parties?" Fritz asked more than stated.

"Oh yes, of course, we should discuss who dances with whom," Aldelbert said.

"Dance partners often reflect real life politics and power struggles," Marzell agreed.

"I can't believe you're making us do this," Oswald grumbled as he straightened a feather in his headdress.

Aldelbert dropped his falsetto voice long enough to give his disgruntled friend a smile, and to say "Why? As heroes, we should be secure in our glory and masculinity while recognizing the strength and nobility of women, as well!"

Angel studied Aldelbert over her teacup. "I would like to meet your parents one day," she said. "They seem like they would be interesting folk."

"Lady Chita taught My Lord most everything he knows about fighting," Wendal said proudly.

Angel pursed her lips. "That explains a lot, actually."

Snow White's heart warmed as she watched her friends.

Oswald winced when he set his tea cup down with too much force, and Marzell absently plucked at the top of his blanket-dress.

Wendal asked Angel for herb suggestions for tea, and the apprentice reluctantly recommended chives—drawing a disgusted look from even Oswald—and Rupert sipped primly at his tea.

Fritz glanced at Snow White, and when their eyes met, he offered her an easy smile.

They aren't just heroes. They are my friends, Snow White realized as she returned Fritz's smile. *My amazing, unfathomable friends.*

SNOW WHITE

THE EVENING OF THE LADIES' tea debacle, the Seven Warriors gathered in the stables to wash up.

Fritz, having gone first, checked on the horses—a towel tossed over his shoulder—as the others shivered in the nippy, spring air.

"Why are we out here while the girls stayed inside?" Oswald demanded through chattering teeth.

"Because we should not appear in a half-dressed state in front of ladies," Marzell said. He shivered as he stripped his shirt off, then scooped up warm water from a bucket and washed his face.

"But *they* could have come out here after they finished washing! Then we'd at least be warmer," Oswald complained.

"Why don't you admit your true complaint: You *like* being dirty," Rupert asked. He dunked his head in his bucket of water, then unfolded upright. His wet, black hair was plastered against his face, and he promptly sneezed.

"At least the water is warm." Gregori tossed Rupert a towel. "We usually don't bother with such things, but Her Highness insisted."

The others nodded in thankfulness, but Oswald screwed his mouth up as he glared at the steaming water.

"Oswald!" Aldelbert looked unusually morose as he posed proudly with his shirt off. "I'm afraid you must do this task."

Oswald glanced at him with a furrowed forehead. "Huh?"

"For even my handsome good looks will not be able to distract or cover up the terrible odor you will give off if you do not bathe," Aldelbert declared.

Wendal, who had finished almost as quickly as Fritz, strummed his hand harp. "Tis true," he said. "Also, even someone as glorious as My Lord cannot be friends with a dirty pig."

Oswald growled and looked like he might jump the attendant, until Gregori handed him a bucket.

"Bathe," was all the merchant said.

Oswald sneered a little and grumbled under his breath as he also stripped off his doublet and undershirt. His mutterings stopped, however, when he thrust his hands into the bucket. "Her Highness is quite clever," he finally said as he peered down at the steaming water.

"Indeed," Wendal nodded. "She has far more intellect than I would have credited her with before meeting her."

Every time we encounter a new challenge, it has been interesting to witness her tackle it, Fritz thought, but "Yes," was all he said aloud.

"I have grown fond of her—even if she does not properly appreciate my portraits," Aldelbert announced. "Even the dirty apprentice to the herb wizard is quite likeable!"

"She was always smart, even when we were children—Snow White, that is." Marzell sucked in his breath before he also dunked his head into his bucket of water.

"Is that why you always had such hope for her rule?" Rupert asked as he hurriedly buttoned his shirt.

"I always assumed you were just sweet on her," Oswald grunted as he finished washing his arms.

Marzell laughed. "No, no she was and will always be just a friend. Besides, even as a lad, I was vaguely aware whoever married her would have a dragon of a mother-in-law to deal with."

Fritz blinked. "What do you mean?"

"Faina is *fiercely* protective of Snow White," Marzell said as he toweled off his hair. "Any man who approaches the princess with marriage in mind will likely find himself being cross-examined and questioned…for months."

"You don't think Faina will try to choose her husband for her?" Gregori leaned against a horse stall, patting the cheek of a bay mare when she poked her head over the door.

"No," Marzell shook his head. "She's protective of Snow White, but she also dotes on her. I imagine she will tell the princess to marry for love."

"A shame she likely won't do so," Rupert grunted.

Oswald squinted at him. "Whaddya mean?"

"As Wendal alluded, Snow White is clever," Rupert said as he drew his towel over his shoulders like a cloak. "She's aware she's too shy to bend her subjects to her will. She'll marry someone to consolidate her power and politically support her."

Oswald rolled his eyes. "More politics," he muttered before he dunked his head into his bucket with a splash that nearly got Rupert.

Fritz frowned at Rupert's observation, privately disagreeing. *Perhaps some time ago she would have believed she needed to marry for power. But once Faina is rescued, I don't think it will be necessary.*

"You disagree, Fritz?" Wendal asked.

Fritz shrugged.

Aldelbert laughed and slapped him on the shoulder. "Come now, you should share! You are our forester. You often see what we don't and protect us from our own stupidity."

"Some of us more than others." Oswald's words were nearly lost as he pressed his face into his towel and rubbed his hair.

Wendal, who happened to be casually strolling by, rammed the base of his hand harp into Oswald's gut, making him gurgle. "A sound observation, My Lord!" He brightly said as he ignored Oswald's strangled curses. "One I agree with, so I would also like to hear your reasoning, Fritz." He adjusted his spectacles and peered at Fritz with an encouraging smile.

Fritz paused in the act of peeling a hay bale into flakes for the horses. *Snow White is soft-spoken, but she is improving. Everything she has done for Faina's sake is proof enough.*

Fritz finally said, "She's getting better."

"Ah, true," Wendal agreed.

Rupert shrugged but nodded. "I suppose. She doesn't turn red whenever she addresses the group of us anymore. And even at her worst, she was better spoken than the angry monkey."

"*What* did you call me?" Oswald howled.

"Funny how you answered to that even though I never specifically said it was *you* I was referring to," Rupert said.

Aldelbert laughed. "Friends, why do we fight? Oswald is an honorable and skilled warrior," he declared.

"Yeah! So take that," Oswald sneered at Rupert.

"I might if I thought Aldelbert was an excellent judge of character," Rupert said dryly.

Wendal's harp was replaced with his daggers. "Was that an insult to My Lord?" he said with false brightness.

Fritz smiled slightly as he watched his companions carry on. Though many of the Seven Warriors always seemed to be on the verge of fighting, Fritz had come to learn it was their strange way of affirming their friendship.

When Marzell joined him in observing the spectacle, he glanced at the young lord and smiled.

Surprisingly, Marzell didn't seem to join in Fritz's amusement at the almost-a-fistfight. Instead, he carefully studied Fritz. "You really like Snow White, don't you?"

Fritz shifted carefully. "Of course," he said.

Marzell waved his hand out. "No, I phrased that wrong. You *care* for her, don't you?"

Fritz hesitated.

He'd finally come to the conclusion that the draw he felt for her was, in fact, attraction. And yes, he had come to care for and admire Snow White. If he was any less cautious, he would perhaps say he was interested in her.

But it doesn't matter. She will only remain with us until Faina is safe, and I am not so far gone to believe I love her after knowing her for such a short amount of time. There is no use brooding over what could be or might happen. I need to focus on helping her however I can now.

In the end, Fritz settled on a shrug.

Marzell raised both of his eyebrows. "Really?"

Fritz slowly nodded three times, then smiled.

Marzell rubbed his hands together. "I see. Maybe I can help you!"

Fritz—who had gone back to watching Wendal yank on

Rupert's hair while Rupert rubbed a fistful of straw against his glasses—narrowed his eyes and returned his gaze to Marzell fast enough to make his neck crack.

Marzell grinned cheekily at him.

"That's not what I meant," Fritz said.

"Oh, I know what you meant," Marzell said cheerfully. "But I also know what you're really feeling. Worry not, my friend. Snow White is a *special* girl." He patted Fritz on the back, then cleared his throat when Fritz did not let up on his half-glare.

"Right," Marzell said. "I better go stop them, or we'll all be just as dirty when we go back inside as we were when we came out here. I say—Wendal, Rupert, stop that!"

Fritz shifted his feet so he stood wider as he watched his friends bicker and laugh.

With luck, Marzell won't do anything. No matter how I feel or don't feel, Snow White's mission to rescue Faina needs to take priority. If her predictions come true, Mullberg's problems will affect the rest of the continent. And that is a much more important endeavor to focus on than whether or not I really love Snow White.

&.

SNOW WHITE PEERED through the open shutters of the little cottage and watched the Seven Warriors in the yard.

Gregori was snoozing—splayed across a bench—but Snow White did not miss the crossbow and quiver tucked under his makeshift bed.

Oswald and Rupert were wrestling in a fairly even match. Though Rupert had superior skill, whenever he stopped to sneeze, Oswald would wriggle out of whatever hold he was stuck in. (At least until Rupert shoved a fistful of moss into Oswald's mouth after the warrior mocked his sneezing for the fifth time.)

Whenever Gregori shifted in his sleep, both Oswald and

Rupert would freeze in mid-motion—making them look like eccentric lawn ornaments.

Aldelbert stood in a spot of sunlight and sorted through two barrels of portraits with Wendal's help.

The attendant would select a rolled-up canvas, unwind it, and hold it in front of him for Aldelbert's inspection. The paintings ranged in size from as small as Snow White's hands to larger than Wendal, but Aldelbert studied them all with a critical eye.

"This is such hard work," he declared. "To judge a painting of such a handsome specimen as myself, that is. For anything that bears my image is worth treasuring!"

"I'm happy for you that your self-confidence is so undefeatable," Marzell said dryly. He sat near Fritz—who was fletching arrows—re-reading some of the letters the lords and Gregori's contacts had sent.

Five days had passed since the meeting with the lords, and though Snow White could hardly believe it, things were going smoothly.

The lords, thus far, were rallying their troops without catching Faina's attention—or the attention of the Cabinet Ministers or other lords visiting the area.

Though Queen Faina was still said to be seething during all of her waking hours, she hadn't hurt anyone. (Though the servants reported it had been a close call once or twice.)

If things continued like this, their plan just might work!

...Which didn't sit quite right with Snow White.

First plans almost never survive contact with the enemy. I thought we would need to plan alternative methods. I'm glad it's going well, but considering that the rogue mage who has Faina in his thrall sent those constructs after me the night *I disappeared...this seems oddly quiet. Or maybe I'm just being silly, and I'm one of those people who is never happy or satisfied.*

"Oh, I think I see it!" Angel crowed in triumph, dragging Snow White from her thoughts.

She reluctantly closed the shutters, cutting the cottage off from the sunlight and fresh air the rare—*pleasant*—spring day proved, and curiously watched Angel dig through her satchel.

The apprentice had almost her entire right arm shoved in the bag as she sifted through it, peering at its contents.

In addition to the armload of starfires Snow White had witnessed the apprentice shove in, Angel had previously unearthed a cloak and mittens for Snow White to wear days prior, and was now supposedly uncovering a dress for her.

How does that leather satchel have room for all of that? Is it actually larger than it seems?

Angel yanked a velvet blue gown with a pale-yellow kirtle from her satchel. She shook it out, but miraculously the garment was not at all wrinkled.

"This should do nicely." Angel held the gown out for admiration. "It's heavier cloth, so you'll still be warm enough."

Snow White nodded, but her eyes kept straying to Angel's satchel.

"Do you not like it?" Angel asked.

"No, it's not that. It's quite beautiful. It is merely that..." Snow White paused, trying to find the politest language to frame her question. Eventually she ran out of patience and blurted out, "How can your satchel hold everything?"

Angel laughed. "It's magic. I have a craftmage friend who is lending it to me—it's spelled to hold more and weigh less than it ought to be able to handle." Angel passed the bag over, which shed a few sprigs of herbs.

Snow White reluctantly peeled the flap back and peered inside, and her mind reeled.

The satchel was almost like a doorway of sorts. With the flap held back so light could fall inside it, Snow White could see a mound of objects. The item closest in reach was a starfire perched on a black cloak, but Snow White could see she'd have to stretch her arm—which was longer than the satchel was deep—to grab it.

"...Thank you." Snow White passed the satchel back as she dumbly stared at the cottage wall. *It's magic. There's no use in even trying to explain it.*

"Did you still want the dress?" Angel asked.

Snow White nodded and took the gown. She climbed the rickety stairs to change in the small area the Seven Warriors had cornered off with blankets for that very purpose.

The gown was soft and comfortable—the velvet sleeves with the yellow ribbing peeping out in the Mullberg style at the shoulders and elbows were a warm caress on her skin—but best yet, it smelled *clean*.

"Thank you, Angel," Snow White called as she descended the stairs. "I can't tell you how grateful I am."

"Of course! I'm happy to help since we're friends now!" Angel winked.

Snow White smiled slightly. "Is *that* why you didn't offer this the night we broke in here and instead suggested I wear the warrior's clothes?"

"Oh, that!" Angel laughed again. "That was for the fun of it. You had these great big moon eyes that seemed to get bigger with everything I suggested. I was wondering how much I could make them bulge. Besides, I trust you more, now."

"I see." Snow White kept her smile in place and did not let her surprise flicker across her face at Angel's expression of trust.

There's something about her that I haven't been able to figure out, but it seems like she has no interest in acknowledging it or confessing. That she essentially just professed she didn't *trust me when we first met is rather telling, even if she did not mean for it to be.*

Snow White threw open one of the shutters again. "Shall we go outside to join them?"

"Certainly!" Angel said as she settled one of the sturdy but plain cloaks across her shoulders and brushed off her blue tunic.

Snow White led the way, cautiously opening the cottage door —which still creaked ominously on its hinges.

Aldelbert turned around—curious at the noise. When he saw Snow White, he grinned hugely and bent over in a flourish-filled bow. "Your Highness!" He trumpeted. "Your new dress does you credit!"

Behind him, Wendal nodded in agreement and clapped to show his approval.

Oswald—who had Rupert in a headlock at the moment—squinted at her. "You look like you're going to a ball instead of living in the forest—oof," he grunted when Rupert ground his elbow into Oswald's gut.

Rupert threw Oswald over his shoulder and to the ground. He panted for a moment, sneezed, then bowed his head to Snow White. "Ignore the yowling tomcat," he advised. "If something is not covered with layers of dirt, he cannot wear it."

"Why you—!" When Oswald recovered, he launched himself at Rupert, and the wrestling match began anew.

Snow White ruefully shook her head as she pulled her fraying red ribbon from her hair, undoing the bow. (The days of living in the cottage had not done the ribbon any favors. It was shedding bits of cloth at an alarming rate, but she'd have to make do.) She approached Marzell and Fritz, self-consciously clearing her throat as she plopped down on a three-legged stool. "Do they always fight this much?" she asked.

"Hmm?" Marzell looked up from the letters. "Oh. No, not always. They were *nearly* civil over the winter, but I suppose that might be why they are worse now. They can finally be aired outside."

Fritz glanced from Marzell to Snow White, then quietly said, "You look very nice."

"Ahh, yes—my mother would be horrified with my manners," Marzell winced. "Fritz is right—you look lovely, Your Highness."

Snow White blushed and busied herself with retying the red bow in her hair, giving her the excuse to only mutter, "Thank you."

Marzell nodded and returned his attention to his papers. Fritz however, watched Snow White as she pushed her black curls back.

The heat of Snow White's blush intensified under Fritz's scrutiny. She tried to say something, but—irritatingly—was unable to make her mouth move.

What happened to "it's easy to talk to the warriors?" she thought with no small amount of self-disgust.

Fritz nodded to himself, then set aside the arrow he was working on. He picked up his cloak, digging through the folds, and unearthed a royal blue ribbon. He smiled slightly—perhaps shyly, even—and held it out to Snow White.

Snow White paused. "For me?"

Fritz nodded, and his smile grew a little. "Yes."

Snow White hesitated, then took the ribbon. "Thank you, Fritz. It's a very pretty shade," she said.

'It's a very pretty shade?' I sound like an idiot!

She yanked her red ribbon from her hair and carefully drew the blue ribbon through her curls instead.

"Where did you get a ribbon?" Marzell asked as he curiously studied Fritz.

"Juwel," Fritz said. "When you sent me to pick up the letters from Glitzern Palace," he said, nodding to the ones Marzell held in his hand.

Seemingly bemused, Marzell glanced from Fritz to Snow White. "That's very thoughtful of you, Fritz." He ran his thumb along the edge of one the letters. When Snow White finished tying her curls back, he glanced at Fritz.

Fritz blinked at his friend.

Marzell looked at Snow White, then back at Fritz.

Fritz raised an eyebrow.

"You are *incredibly* stubborn," Marzell grumbled as he gathered up the letters. "And for no reason at all!" He shook his head as he strode off, making for Aldelbert and Wendal.

Snow White blinked in surprise at his sudden exit and shifted her gaze to Fritz.

Fritz's smile was a little bigger and much warmer now.

"Um," Snow White said with all due intelligence.

She was grateful for the distraction when Angel sashayed outside, scratching her side as she gnawed on what looked like a radish.

Wendal gave the apprentice a slightly withering glare. "Do you have even an ounce of elegance in you?" he asked.

"Does it look like I do?" Angel grinned and waggled the radish at him.

"I feel sorry for your master," Wendal grumbled as he unrolled another painting for Aldelbert's inspection.

"Me, too," Angel said as she admired her radish.

"What's wrong, Aldelbert?" Marzell asked.

The blond-haired lord was staring at his rolled-up portraits with narrowed eyes. "My portraits are moving," he announced. "I do not know if it's because they are so filled with my glory they cannot stand to be hidden, or for some other reason."

"What?" Rupert, who pressed one foot against Oswald's back and held the other warrior's right arm twisted up, released him. He backed away and peered into the woods.

Instead of taking advantage of the moment to leap on Rupert, Oswald rolled and snatched up both his sword and Rupert's from where they had tossed the weapons at the start of the wrestling match.

Snow White exchanged a concerned glance with Fritz.

Fritz stood and silently maneuvered himself in front of Snow White, holding his sheathed sword in his hands.

"Do you hear something?" Marzell asked after a few heartbeats.

Oswald tilted his head back and sniffed the wind as Rupert glared into the forest.

The pair glanced at each other, then nodded.

Marzell cursed under his breath and hurriedly shoved the letters into the barrel with Aldelbert's paintings.

Wendal snatched up a spear that leaned casually against the cottage and tossed it to his master.

Aldelbert caught it with ease and grinned as he whirled it above his head. "We're ready!" he declared.

Gregori awoke sometime during the quiet preparations. He rolled off his bench and hit the ground. When he jumped upright, he held both his crossbow—now loaded—and his quiver.

The perfect synchronization they worked in made Snow White realize she hadn't been alone in thinking things were too quiet. The Seven Warriors were clearly prepared for whatever creature was about to arrive.

"Snow White, here." Angel dropped two fistfuls of starfires onto her lap. "Since this attack is during the day, I'm a bit doubtful these will help, but one never knows." She wasn't looking at Snow White but rather south of the cottage, where the Seven Warriors were slowly gravitating.

"Thank you," Snow White said as she also stood.

She could feel the faint vibrations through her boots.

Whatever it is that's coming, it's big.

CHAPTER 12
A NEW KIND OF CONSTRUCT

Soon, the woody groan of splintering trees reached Snow White's ears.

She breathed twice as fast when two trees at the edge of the yard swayed, then abruptly tipped forward, snapping like matchsticks.

Standing in the hole the trees had left was a foul creature.

It was made of jagged branch-like bolts of—assumedly—magic molded together to form something half-human/half troll-like in shape. It had short legs, a stooped back, and long arms that it leaned on, but it was a watery black color. It had a curved—almost shield-shaped head—and its eyes were actually the darkest part of its body; they were a bottomless black, and like the constructs', they were also perfect circles.

Snow White gulped as she stared up at it. Even from this distance, she could see it towered over the warriors and was easily twice their size.

It was forged by magic, for certain. But it felt more solid—more threatening—than the other constructs had.

Before the creature moved, Gregori shot it in the chest.

The bolt stuck out of the monster's chest like a porcupine

quill, but it didn't even look down at it. It roared—a deep groaning sound like a thousand falling trees—then snapped its mouth shut—which clamped imperfectly due to the splintering edges of its mouth.

Yes. This one is going to be much *harder to defeat.*

It lurched forward, putting its weight on its arms and hefting its body forward. Though the movement should have been awkward, it was startingly fast.

"Angel, what can you tell us about this thing?" Marzell asked as he yanked two hand axes from the barrel of portraits.

"It's not alive—it's magic made," Angel called.

The monster pounded toward the cottage but skidded to a stop—leaving trenches in the dirt—when Aldelbert stabbed his spear into its side. It whipped around to face him and pounded its shadowy fists on the grass, making the ground shake.

Aldelbert staggered but held his ground.

"Any idea how to stop it?" Wendal asked. He shook his hands, and his daggers slipped into place between his fingers.

"I'm trying to figure that out," Angel said grimly. "It's much stronger than the previous constructs. It can take both damage and light—the rogue mage put a lot more effort into this thing."

"You don't say?" Rupert grumbled as he shifted into a waiting stance.

Oswald had no such desire and instead flung himself onto the creature's back, scurrying up it until he stood perched on its shoulder blades. "Just *die!*" he grunted as he stabbed his sword into its back again and again.

The monster didn't seem terribly bothered by the attack. It tottered on its feet for a moment, then heaved itself backwards so it landed on its back.

Oswald jumped ship with a few curses.

Fritz and Rupert rushed the creature. Before they even reached it, the monster flung its arms above its head, shoved its claw-like fingers into the ground and performed a flip so it was once again standing.

"Holy haybales, that thing is fast," Oswald complained as he staggered away from it.

Gregori scowled as he shot another bolt at the monster, this time hitting it in the face. "It also appears to have no weaknesses."

"That's impossible," Angel shouted. "Every type of magic has weaknesses and tradeoffs."

The monster roared, making the deadly crossbow bolt snap off like a toothpick. It ran for Gregori, but its entire body jerked sideways when Marzell threw one of his axes, striking it in the side of its head.

"If that's so, it's not an obvious one," Marzell said grimly.

"Snow White, do you see any possible way to kill it?" Fritz shouted back to her.

Snow White stepped closer to Angel and shook her head. "No..." She didn't dare pull her eyes from the monster as she mentally catalogued its every move.

"Its exterior seems impermeable, but it moves fast when usually that would logically make it slower," she muttered.

Angel glanced curiously at her but didn't say anything. Instead, she yanked a sprig of herbs off her satchel and grimly set her shoulders.

The monster spun on its short hind legs, whipping its arms around.

Its hand connected with Rupert, sending the warrior toppling head over heels.

Aldelbert took advantage of its preoccupation and again jabbed his spear at its gut.

The monster whirled around to face him. It reached for him, its claw-like fingers making a snipping motion.

Wendal stepped in, throwing a dagger. It hit the creature squarely in the eye—or rather it *caught* the monster square in the eye—the weapon's blade was too thick for its eye hole and caught on the rim, so it stuck out of the monster's eye socket like a pin in a pin cushion.

The monster reared back and started to roar, but it cut itself off when it seemed to realize the dagger had not punctured, but was stuck.

"Nice shot, Wendal!" Aldelbert praised.

The attendant made a tisking noise. "It did nothing, though."

The monster hit itself in the back of the head, making Wendal's dagger pop out of its eye, then planted its fists back on the ground, tearing up the brown grass.

"I don't know about that," Snow White murmured, her mind whirling as she tried to make sense of the creature's actions.

"There is one bright side to all this," Marzell said as he chucked his remaining axe at the monster. This time it struck it at the knee joint, but it only clipped the creature and bounced off instead of digging in.

"What's that?" Oswald grumbled. "It hasn't damaged our home?"

"No." Marzell sprinted for the side of the cottage, snatching up a wicked-looking mace that had been propping open a shutter. "It does not seem to be targeting Snow White."

"Quite right!" Aldelbert laughed. He rolled his shoulders back, then rushed the creature, diving past its arms so he stood underneath its chest and belly. He stabbed his spear upwards, heaving with his entire body.

The monster didn't even look down at him. It kicked forward with its left leg, striking Aldelbert with precision.

The young lord collided with a stack of firewood, scattering logs everywhere.

Wendal half walked/half crawled in his direction, keeping his eyes on the monster as he tried to stand between it and Aldelbert. "Are you badly injured, My Lord?"

Aldelbert choked and struggled to sit up. It took several

moments before he managed a wheezing breath and waved his hand.

Oswald and Fritz tried to attack the monster simultaneously from either side. Both stabbed their swords into the monster's abdomen.

The creature rocked back so it stood entirely on its legs, then tried to hit Oswald and Fritz with its claws curled into fists.

Fritz avoided it, darting around to the monster's back and stabbing it there. Oswald ducked, then had to retreat to avoid getting stomped on when the monster turned to face Fritz.

Is it playing with them or just occupying them? Snow White watched with narrowed eyes as the creature tried to smash Fritz with its fists, but the forester danced out of reach. *It moves fast and seems to have an impenetrable exterior. So why hasn't it laid waste to them? As Marzell pointed out, it doesn't even seem to be going for me, so why is it even here? Unless...*

Snow White did a complete circle, studying the edges of the forest before she looked up at the roof of the cottage.

"It's a trick!" she shouted.

Another one of the creatures was perched on the roof. It climbed around on the "brim" of the hat-shaped building, moving almost noiselessly.

When Snow White pointed at it, the monster snarled. It threw itself off the cottage, almost landing on top of Snow White and Angel.

Angel brandished her herb sprig at it, which burst into flames. She mashed it into the monster's arm while Snow White scrambled away.

The monster slammed its fist down on Angel, but she dodged at the last moment. It then kicked out at her, this time catching her square in the torso.

Angel flipped head over feet and slammed into the cottage wall.

"Angel!" Snow White screamed.

The apprentice winced as she peeled off the wall, revealing her squashed satchel that seemed to have taken the brunt of the attack. "Well," she said, dusting herself off as if she hadn't just taken a hit that, if not for her satchel, would easily have cracked her ribs. "Its weakness is *not* fire."

The first monster moved even faster now. It sprang at Aldelbert and Wendal, swinging one arm at them.

They threw themselves to the ground, the monster's arm whistling as it passed just above them.

The monster snatched up two of the firewood logs with its free fist and threw them at Rupert, making him retreat from his press toward Snow White and Angel.

"We can't let them separate us from Snow White," Marzell shouted. He swung his mace, throwing it so it smacked the first monster on its chin, making its lower jaw crunch shut over its upper lip.

The monster tottered for a few steps as it tried to pry its mouth open again.

Considering it takes being stabbed in stride, it seems oddly upset about the mace. And it grew angry, initially, about Wendal almost hitting it in the eye, too.

"Gregori," Snow White shouted. "Aim for inside their eyes!"

She yelped when the monster targeting her tried to scoop her up. Angel barely yanked her away in time. "Or their mouths if they're open!"

"I'll give it a try," Gregori said doubtfully.

"Cover me, Fritz!" Oswald called as he ran up the back of the second monster.

Fritz stabbed the creature in the arm, momentarily drawing its attention away from Snow White.

The monster lunged for him, leaning on one front arm as it snatched at him. It got close enough that it sliced a slit in Fritz's leather doublet before he ducked, sliding between the monster's legs and popping out on the other side.

Its path cleared, the monster took a lumbering step in Snow White's direction, then stopped and snarled—the hissing noise of wind shrieking through empty tree branches—when Oswald stabbed his sword between its shoulder blades.

It pivoted slightly, and Oswald slid down its back, falling into a crouch directly beneath the monster's posterior.

Above him, the creature rammed its back into the side of the cottage—making the whole building shake.

"Why are these monsters so intent on smashing things with their backs?" Oswald grumbled as he scrambled out of the way of its feet.

Gregori had crept closer and closer to the original monster, stopping when he crouched behind the half-toppled pile of firewood. He narrowed his eyes as he loaded another bolt. "Aldelbert, get its attention and hold it somewhere behind me."

"Of course!" Aldelbert brightly said.

"Wait—no, My Lord, I'll do it!" Wendal protested.

"Nonsense, Wendal. While I like you, I'm not willing to share the glory of being bait with you!" Aldelbert paused—like an idiot—to pose with one fist under his chin and the other propped up on his hip.

"I don't know why you haven't died yet—if not by a monster, then by a man," Rupert grumbled as he jabbed the leg of the monster that was intent on Snow White.

"Skill!" Aldelbert proclaimed as he sashayed up to the first monster. He slightly stuck out his tongue as he narrowed his eyes in concentration, then jabbed upwards. He hit the monster in the chin, which made it gurgle oddly, though it didn't seem particularly bothered. Leaning on its fists, it tried to kick him.

"No—no unsportsmanlike behavior!" Aldelbert chided as he dodged it. "For I am far too cunning for you—whoops!" He barely avoided the monster when it leaned back on its legs—freeing its front right arm so it could try to grab him.

"Gregori, I have its attention!" Aldelbert announced as he ran across the yard, the monster right on his heels.

"Run to me," Gregori instructed.

Aldelbert course-corrected, making straight for Gregori's lumber pile. The monster thumped along behind him, the ground shaking slightly from the force of its steps.

Gregori carefully lined up his target, then shot his crossbow. The bolt hit the monster in the left eye, disappearing so deeply that barely the red fletching on the bolt's end was visible poking through the empty eye socket.

The monster reared back and roared with the strength and volume of a landslide. It clutched its clawed hands over its eyes and stomped its feet as it wildly thrashed around.

"Yeah, I'd call that a weakness," Angel said wisely.

"Aim for its eyes or mouth!" Marzell shouted.

"You don't say," Wendal growled. He hopped on top of Gregori's log pile. He threw four of his daggers in quick succession, striking the monster in its open mouth.

It released a terrible shriek as it fell to its knees. Its arms went lax as it tipped and hit the ground like a fallen tree.

Aldelbert was on it in a flash, spearing it in the mouth.

The monster shuddered, then its body seemed to liquify as it lost all shape and its mass evaporated, leaving behind Gregori's crossbow bolt and Wendal's daggers.

"Judging by its end, I would say these things are another magic-made work of the rogue mage," Marzell said. "Which is at least a little encouraging. It means we're not fighting against multiple black mages."

"That's wonderful," Oswald grouched. "Great effort. Now if we could have a little *help* over here?!"

"The second monster is still alive, in case you've forgotten," Rupert added.

He, Oswald, and Fritz stood in a semi-circle around the

second monster, jabbing at it with their swords whenever it tried to make for Snow White.

Snow White and Angel kept retreating, following the cottage exterior wall, and the monster stalked after them.

Snow White's spit tasted metallic, and despite the still cool temperatures, her hands were clammy. She wanted to do nothing more than run, but logically she knew such a thing would be a disaster and make the monster harder to contain.

Be brave, she reminded herself. *Imagine what horrors Faina has faced if it is her rogue mage that conjured these up!*

"Step lightly, Oswald, Fritz, Rupert," Marzell coached as Gregori loaded his crossbow and swung around to face the monster.

Unfortunately, the second creature was a little smarter.

It shuffled sideways—its front side facing the cottage—as it scurried after Snow White and Angel.

"Turn it around," Gregori said.

"How?" Oswald demanded.

Wendal threw three daggers, nailing the creature in the back of the head, but it did not shift to face him.

Oswald stabbed the monster in the lower back. The creature —leaning on its arms—kicked behind it like a mule.

Oswald avoided the kick by lurching backwards, but he fell over his own feet and hit the ground.

"As able as always," Rupert grumbled. He darted forward and stabbed his sword into the creature's gut, zipping backwards just as quickly to avoid getting stomped on.

"Like you have room to talk, Mr-I'll-get-myself-killed-by-stopping-to-sneeze!" Oswald sneered.

"Everyone, attack it on one side," Marzell called. "We have to get it to turn around so Gregori or Wendal can take a shot."

"What a bright idea." Oswald rolled to his feet and tried to stab the monster in its legs, but his blade merely chipped it, making a spark or two.

"I can't believe we didn't think of that first," Rupert added with a grumble.

"If you have air for sarcasm, you aren't fighting hard enough," Gregori rumbled as he shot the monster's back.

Wendal and Aldelbert joined Oswald and Rupert in attacking the monster's flank.

Unfortunately, instead of turning around, the monster lunged—one arm snaking out as it reached for Snow White.

"Nope!" Angel said as she yanked Snow White out of the way. She was barely quick enough—the creature managed to snag the hem of Snow White's dress with an outstretched claw and tear it through.

Snow White clamped her mouth shut to keep from screaming and took pains to keep her breathing deep and steady. *Don't panic. The warriors finished one construct. They can get another.*

"Should we move off the wall?" Snow White asked when she could do so without her voice trembling.

"I don't much like that idea," Angel grunted. "It keeps too many of your sides open, and it's harder to contain it."

"We might not have a choice," Marzell said grimly.

Snow White and Angel took slow steps backwards as the Seven Warriors tried to turn the monster with little success.

Snow White glanced past the monster, and her gaze met Fritz.

He nodded to her as he grabbed a long bow and pulled three arrows from a quiver. He backed up, then turned on his heels and ran, disappearing behind the curve of the circular-ish shaped cottage.

What is he doing?

"Aldelbert, get between this *thing* and Snow White. With your reach, you might be able to keep it back," Marzell called.

"Of course!" Aldelbert vaulted over his barrel of portraits, landing in front of the creature with a little hop. He wasted no time jabbing his spear at the monster, stabbing it in the face.

The monster made a hissing noise, then abruptly dove forward, nearly pinning Aldelbert beneath it.

Its head pressed into the ground, it thrashed its limbs, connecting with Marzell, Rupert, and Oswald. The force of its swing sent the warriors flying. Rupert flopped when he hit the ground, Oswald rolled a few feet, and Marzell groaned.

Snow White froze momentarily, her concern gluing her feet to the ground. *Did it kill Rupert? And what about Oswald?*

Gregori shot the monster twice on the side of its head and cursed as it scrambled to its feet.

Snow White blinked, and the creature was nearly on top of her and Angel.

Angel took a breath and grabbed a sword stabbed into the ground, but the monster backhanded her into the wall with such force she *bounced* when she hit it. It then scooped up Snow White, its clawed fingers biting into her sides as it squeezed her like a child holding a ragdoll.

"Snow White!" someone shouted.

Snow White screamed in pain as it tightened its hold on her and held her up for inspection. She tried kicking it and then stabbing it with one of the starfire crystals Angel had given her, but to no avail.

The creature brought its other hand up to cup her head and chest, and Snow White realized with stark clarity, *It's not trying to carry me off. It's going to crush me here and now.*

The monster started to curl a claw around her neck—to snap her spine most likely—when someone whistled.

Slowly, the monster looked up at the roof of the cottage.

Fritz stood on the edge, an arrow nocked in his long bow. His hazel eyes were cold with rage, and he unblinkingly loosened his arrow—striking the creature in its gaping mouth.

Before it could rear back, he loosened two more arrows—hitting it in the mouth each time.

The monster's fists loosened, and Snow White slipped from

its grasp before it topped backwards—almost falling on Wendal and Gregori.

It screamed—a grating noise of crackling wood—and shuddered violently. Then, like the first, its black, branchy body seemed to liquify before it disappeared, and only the arrows remained.

Snow White stayed where she had fallen on the ground, her heart beating frantically.

Fritz hopped off the roof and landed in a crouch next to her. "Are you hurt?"

Snow White shook her head. "I-I don't think so." Her waist still ached from the hold the monster had on her, but it didn't feel like its claws had cut into her.

Fritz offered her his hand. When she took it, he gently tugged her to her feet, his eyes scanning her. "Does it hurt to breathe?"

"No. I think I'll be bruised but nothing too bad." She bit her lip as she viewed Oswald with concern as he tried to boost himself up with a groan and failed. "I'm not sure about everyone else, though."

"No bleeding wounds around here, right?" Angel asked as she started plucking more sprigs of herbs off her bag.

"I'm fine—" Oswald started to say, then broke off into a muffled oath when Gregori prodded his back.

"Rupert and Oswald are the most injured, I think—Aldelbert, too," Gregori said.

"Rupert, how many herbs am I holding up?" Angel asked when she crouched next to the young heir.

Rupert groaned and didn't answer.

Marzell winced as he rubbed the back of his head. "Great job, Fritz," he said. "Are you hurt, Your Highness?"

Snow White shook her head.

"That's good news," her childhood friend grunted. "We'll have to talk about this, but for now, let's see what we can do for Rupert and Oswald."

"And for you and Aldelbert," Snow White added.

Marzell offered her a slight smile. "As you say," then approached Oswald, a limp in his step.

Snow White briefly shut her eyes. *That was even more terrifying than the first set of constructs. But it only proves we must stop that rogue mage, or he or she will do massive damage to my people. And if he and the Chosen had control of Mullberg, who knows what they would do to the rest of the continent.* "Thank you, Fritz, for saving me," Snow White said with her eyes still shut.

Fritz only squeezed her hand in response.

Snow White smiled and forced herself to suck in a deep gulp of air. She squeezed his hand as well, then opened her eyes. "I ought to see what I can do to help Angel."

Fritz took a step back from her, slowly pulling his hand from hers. "Don't injure yourself further."

"It's fine," Snow White said as she watched Rupert—even more white-faced than usual—sit up with a grimace. "I'm not hurt very bad in comparison." She offered Fritz another smile, then picked her way across the broken yard.

They fought to protect me, she thought as she approached Angel. *I need to make their sacrifice worth it. I need to make certain that when we save Faina, I listen to what they have to say and address their concerns.*

I don't care how many meetings I have to talk in to accomplish it—I will *stop* this march of darkness.

CHAPTER 13
AN ALTERED PLAN

In the end, it was Snow White who brought up the implications of the fight.

She waited for someone to mention it that night as Angel dressed the Seven Warriors' wounds by smearing minced garlic on their bruises and holding an onion up to their face. No one did.

She woke up early the following morning and waited for the discussion as she helped Marzell prepare the morning breakfast of oatmeal. It was never mentioned.

Finally, by noon, she had decided they could not continue in silence. "We need more help than soldiers and troops." She sat in a chair and glanced around the cottage before finally meeting Marzell's gaze. "We have to send for the Veneno Conclave. Now."

Marzell rubbed his eyes as Aldelbert led Oswald and Rupert in what he called his "Glory-Intensifying-Stretches."

"You're right," Marzell admitted. "This mage seems like they might be more than we can protect you from. It is our failing."

"No," Snow White said. "This is no fault of your own. Faina has a castle full of ministers, servants, and soldiers—none of them were able to protect her, either."

Marzell said nothing in return, and together they watched Aldelbert's eccentric stretch routine.

"Now lean forward to bow in all humility and graciousness, then reach for the sky and grab the greatness waiting for you!" Aldelbert told Oswald and Rupert.

"This is the dumbest thing I've ever heard," Oswald grumbled.

Wendal kicked him in the back of the knee. "Cease your complaining and thank My Lord for his graciousness, or I will take you out behind the cottage to end your pain."

"It *is* helping," Rupert said, sounding surprised as he stretched in the manner Aldelbert instructed.

"Of course. It's all due to my fabulous healing," Angel said.

"A bold claim," Rupert said. "I still smell like garlic."

"Your bruises are better, aren't they?" Angel demanded.

Fritz stepped out of the shadows of the cottage, lingering by Snow White's chair. "Snow White is correct. We need to send word to the Conclave now. I'll go."

Snow White tensed slightly. "What?"

"I know the fastest routes. And as a forester, I won't draw the attention Aldelbert, Rupert, or even Gregori would." Fritz nodded at the slumbering merchant draped across a basket of dried nuts.

"Wouldn't Angel be our best bet?" Wendal folded his arms across his chest as he considered Fritz. "She has magic and has told us before she is certified by the Conclave. They would instantly believe her. If Fritz goes, he'll have to have proof of some sort."

Angel pulled on her jagged locks and sighed. "Sorry to ruin your plans, but I am the *last* person you should send to the Conclave. I'm not really...liked by the powers that be."

"Won't they listen to you on something this important?" Snow White asked.

Something hard momentarily settled on Angel's face, and she seemed to look past Snow White, to something far and out of reach. "Hardly. I've gone to them before with news just as dire, and every time..." She shook her head and returned her gaze to Snow White with a false smile. "Let's just say hatred knows no boundaries."

"I can go!" Aldelbert volunteered. "I am a lord—and *very* admirable. It is certain they would listen to me!"

"If you didn't get robbed on your way to the Conclave or lost due to traveling without Wendal," Oswald snorted.

"I would have to accompany My Lord," Wendal said. "His father only allows him to be here because I made an oath to follow him everywhere."

"It's true," Aldelbert said with a sincere nod. "Father was very concerned I might break my neck whilst traveling with you all."

"Fritz really is the best choice," Rupert said.

Marzell nodded. "I guess so. We'll have to draw up some kind of formal document for Snow White to sign—to prove his claims so they'll send someone as requested."

"I will not wait for them," Fritz said.

"Explain yourself, man," Oswald snorted.

Rupert sneezed, then added, "You've chopped too much off your sentence again for us to understand what you meant."

"I will not wait for them to send a magic user before I return," Fritz said. "It will take too long. You will attack Glitzern Palace and take back Faina before they are ready."

"Very likely true," Angel piped in. "No one can accuse the Conclave of leaping before they look."

"We ought to tell the Conclave, then, to send the magic user to one of the lords that supports our plan," Snow White said. "For there is no guarantee we will have *succeeded* in capturing Faina by the time they arrive. Our plans may have changed, and we will not want a mage entering Juwel thinking it is safe territory."

"We should tell them, then, to go to Lord Vitkovci's lands," Marzell said. "We'll let him know to expect help."

Wendal leaned against the creaky stair railing. "It's settled, then?"

"Yes, I think so," Marzell said. "Wendal, help me with the wording, will you?" Marzell snagged a quill and inkwell and carried them back to the table.

"Certainly. Though shouldn't we wake Gregori for such an occasion?" Wendal asked.

"If you wish to, please do so," Marzell said as he sat down at the table, propping his arms up on its edge.

Wendal—some clean papers in hand—stopped next to Gregori's slumbering form. He reached out to prod the merchant heir in the shoulder but stopped just before touching him. "No, we ought to let him sleep." Wendal abruptly turned away from Gregori and joined Marzell at the table, dumping the papers on its paint-spattered surface.

Angel outright cackled as Snow White grinned slightly. She glanced up at Fritz to see if he shared their amusement.

He wore a hint of a smile—as usual, revealed only by the light of his eyes and soft set of his lips. When he met Snow White's gaze, he bowed slightly. "I should ready my horse."

Snow White stood and twitched her skirts off her chair. "May I come along to help you—or perhaps *try* to help you?"

The hint bloomed into a small smile, and Fritz bowed his head slightly. "Of course."

He moved to the cottage's front door and stepped through, holding it open for Snow White as she followed after him.

"Anyone notice that Fritz is more likely to speak complete sentences to Her Highness?" Oswald asked.

"It is possible he enjoys cultured conversation instead of exchanging grunts with a thuggish pig like you," Rupert said.

"Why you—"

Fritz shut the door before any more of their argument could leak through.

Snow White smiled and walked shoulder-to-shoulder with

Fritz as they strolled round the exterior of the cottage. "Your friendship—the Seven Warriors' friendship as a whole, I mean—is rather remarkable."

Fritz studied her with enough gravity to make her blush. "You mean because of the differences in class level and social standing?"

"No! Oh, no, not that at all!" Snow White stammered and could have happily yanked out her own tongue. *All the times I have wished I could talk more easily, I should have thought to specify that I would speak with elegance, not blurt things out with poor manners.*

She shook her head and continued, "I meant despite the differences in temperament. No matter how Oswald and Rupert argue, they usually stand and fight together. And though Wendal fawns over Aldelbert, he is willing to lend anyone in the group his strength. Aldelbert, even, has his place." Snow White linked her hands together and stared at the ground as she thought. "Some might find his personality condescending or obnoxious. But he really does treasure you all, and he does try to help."

"He has moments of great insight." Fritz ducked to enter the ramshackle stable, which—despite is dilapidated state—smelled of fresh straw and leather tack. "But what I value most about him is the strength of his heart."

"His heart?" Snow White asked. "Isn't it filled with love for himself?"

The smile was back, and this time Fritz grinned so wide, his teeth flashed. "It might seem so, but his actions reveal the real sentiment behind his words."

"I guess I will trust you that your words are true."

Fritz selected a bridle, saddle, and blanket to slip under the saddle as Snow White scooped up a few brushes and carried them outside.

Fritz hopped over the wooden paddock fence and approached a chocolate-colored gelding with a creamy flaxen mane.

Snow White opened the gate for Fritz and his mount and shut it behind them as Fritz secured the horse to the wooden fence.

Snow White patted the horse on the neck before she started brushing him. "Thank you for going to alert the Conclave."

Fritz stood on the horse's other side and was crouched down, brushing its legs, so Snow White was unable to see when he answered, "I am glad I can serve you."

Snow White winced slightly and leaned into the horse, taking comfort in the warmth it radiated. "I..." she paused and thought. "That is to say...are you doing this out of duty?"

She could have kicked herself. *Of course he is! That was my selling point to the Seven Warriors: save Faina and spare the country war and pain.*

Fritz stood up and gravely studied Snow White over the horse's sleek back. "Not at all. It is because *you* think it is wise, and it is necessary for your welfare."

Snow White was struck mute at his words and blushed like a lantern. *How can he say such things so smoothly?* she wondered as Fritz crouched down, disappearing from view once more. "Well," she said lamely.

"Be careful while I am gone," Fritz continued. "If you can manage it, try to stay near Angel."

Snow White cleared her throat and focused on brushing the horse. "You expect we'll have trouble?"

"I hope not, but given the attacks against you thus far, it is still a danger."

They switched sides, keeping the placid horse between them. (Snow White wasn't entirely sure if she was thankful for the shield of the horse, or sad.)

"I will be on my guard," Snow White said. "From the attack yesterday, I think we can say with certainty that the rogue magician has figured out where we are. Though I suspect he'll use Faina to strike next. Strategically, it would be the best option since he—or she—has failed twice already."

"Then I'll ride fast," Fritz said simply.

Snow White nodded slowly. She bit her lip, then stared at the horse's back with more concentration than necessary as she said, "I wouldn't want y-you to—that is—the road is dangerous, but I know you are a good f-fighter...the monsters might..."

Magic take it! Curse my stupid tongue! Though I might find simple conversations easier, it appears a meaningful conversation might still be out of my grasp. Perhaps I should consider a future as a court jester when this is all over.

Snow White's scowl broke when Fritz reached across the horse and placed his hand on top of Snow White's, stilling her brushing.

She slowly looked up, meeting his warm, patient gaze. She swallowed, then slowly said, "Be safe."

Fritz gave her his slight—but warm—smile, squeezed her hand once, then stepped away to retrieve the saddle blanket.

Snow White stepped back and watched as he tacked the horse up with sure and efficient movements.

"Shall I check with the others?" Snow White asked as Fritz slipped the metal bit into his mount's mouth. "You'll need provisions for the road."

"Wendal will have prepared them—with some help from Aldelbert." Fritz buckled two straps on the bridle, securing the horse.

"Those two do the packing?" Snow White asked. "Does that mean you can expect to find a canvas painting of His Lordship in your pack?"

Fritz laughed, making Snow White grin.

When his humor faded, they silently stood side-by-side. Snow White awkwardly dropped her gaze to her feet. *What do I do? Faina would always wish Father a safe trip and kiss him whenever he traveled, but I can't be that bold! Moreover, what if I'm just imposing on Fritz? Would he feel like he couldn't reject me because I'm a princess? Would a friendly pat on the arm be acceptable? But wouldn't that be awkward—*

Snow White stopped thinking when she heard Fritz's quiet chuff of amusement.

He snaked an arm around her shoulders, tugging her closer to his side. "Take care, Snow White."

Snow White relaxed and rested her head on his shoulder. "You too, Fritz." She clenched his cloak with her hand that pressed into his side. "Though it's unfair you always know the right thing to say," she muttered under her breath.

Fritz must have heard it, for he bent slightly over her and kissed the top of her head.

Snow White was caught between freezing like a statue and blushing with the strength of a lighthouse.

At that moment, Angel came strolling around the side of the cottage. "Wendal finished packing, but Aldelbert wants to know if you want a painting with Wednesday's outfit or Monday's, because obviously you could not possibly 'stand to go a single day without viewing greatness.'" She laughed at the quote, then studied Fritz and Snow White. "Am I interrupting something? Do I need to start whistling whenever I'm sent to find the two of you so I don't risk running into you canoodling?" She wriggled her eyebrows at Snow White.

Snow White glared at her friend.

Fritz merely smiled. He gently squeezed Snow White's shoulder, then slipped away from her to grab his horse's bridle and lead him to the front of the cottage.

Snow White cleared her throat and brushed her dress off. "Thank you for coming to tell us they are ready."

"I didn't hear a refusal. Does that mean I should just assume the answer is yes?" Angel cheekily asked.

Snow White rolled her eyes and followed after Fritz and his horse. "Go chew on some herbs."

"*Hurtful*! Your Highness, your love, it stings!"

"You are certain you can manage?" Marzell leaned on his longbow and tapped it in thought.

"Didn't you say you'll be within shouting distance?" Angel brandished a sprig of dried mint at him. "We'll be fine!"

"One of us could stay behind," Marzell offered.

Behind him, Gregori yawned widely, and Oswald and Rupert were involved in a shoving matching.

Aldelbert was charging out of the yard and into the trees, shouting "Onward! To seek the defenses of our castle!"

"My Lord, you've forgotten your spear," Wendal called as he trotted after him.

Marzell turned around to squint at his friends and fellow warriors. "Or maybe *I* should stay behind."

"It's fine," Snow White said. "You went through the trouble of setting the traps in case another magic attack was sent. You ought to check them and see if any were set off. As long as you remain within shouting distance—as you promised—we really will be fine."

Marzell pressed his lips together, looking very much like an unconvinced parent.

"Angel will be with me," Snow White added.

Oswald snorted. "That's hardly reassuring! What will she do if something attacks? Throw a clove of garlic at it?"

"No, my best garlic attack involves forcing a peeled clove up my target's nose," Angel said. "Want to give it a try?"

"It'll be fine, Marzell," Gregori rumbled.

"You are needlessly worrying," Rupert added. "We will have the cottage yard surrounded. Any attack would have to get through us before they could reach Snow White."

"Fine, fine." Marzell sighed, then fixed a pleasant smile on his face. "Do not hesitate to call for us."

"We won't," Snow White promised.

Marzell nodded twice, then followed his fellow warriors as they left the yard and stepped into the tree line, the browns of their cloaks allowing them to blend in almost immediately to their surroundings.

"Good luck," Angel called after them. She waved farewell, then marched back into the cottage. "Quick, Snow White, now is our chance!"

Snow White blinked twice as she tried to decipher the apprentice's words. "Our chance for what?" she asked as she followed her inside.

"I don't know," Angel confessed. "It's simply that we're not left alone often, so this seems like the ideal time to poke around the cottage or to burn some of those ruddy portraits Aldelbert keeps giving us."

Snow White smiled. "I'm cleaning the mushrooms Wendal found this morning."

"Such a diligent and good future ruler," Angel sighed.

Snow White shook her head slightly as she retrieved the basket of mushrooms.

"You'll make a good queen—though with *your* king, you two might go down in history as the quietest royals ever," Angel continued.

Snow White almost dumped the basket, but saved it at the last second and only scattered a few of the mushrooms across the floor. "*What?*" she squeaked.

Angel snorted and tossed her head like a horse. "You can't say you thought you and Fritz were keeping your mutual admiration a *secret?*"

"I don't know—mutual admiration? What makes you think— there's been no indication," Snow White babbled.

Angel patted Snow White's hand with enough enthusiasm to make her stop talking. "Don't you worry. Fritz is a patient lad. When you finally get the courage to say that you love him six years from now, he will undoubtedly accept."

Snow White stared open-mouthed at Angel as she flounced through the cottage.

"Though now that I reflect on the matter longer, I think you'll muster the starch to tell him much sooner. You have moved rather fast."

"Fast?" Snow White asked.

Angel didn't seem to hear her. "After all, you fell in love with him in about two weeks! For a shy girl, you do *not* poke around."

Snow White set the basket down and slapped her hands over her cheeks to hide her blush. "I don't know that I would call my deep admiration *love*, and at the very least I cannot presume to say that Fritz feels as I do."

Angel shook her head as she picked up the few mushrooms Snow White had lost. "It's odd. Folk stir up such a fuss about falling in love and are always so terrified of what the object of their affection thinks."

"It's scary," Snow White said, "to know someone has enough power over you to crush your heart or give you boundless joy."

Angel grunted. "Maybe so, but *falling* in love is easy. It's the years that come after love that are the real challenge."

Snow White brushed dirt off a large mushroom. "What do you mean?"

"Falling in love is frightening because it means your heart is no longer under your control, yes, but when the other person returns your affection—that is not the end of your trial but merely the beginning. It's the heartache and pain that come with life that test you. It's the times you feel like you have been beaten to within an inch of your life, like the whole world is against you. It's the years that pass and gradually change how you look—how you spend your time. *That* is the real challenge in love, and that is where it most often fails. People fall in love with an ideal—not a person."

Angel turned her silver eyes to Snow White, and Snow White felt as if Angel could see straight to Snow White's heart. "You are right about yourself and Fritz. Despite my teasing, I'm not certain you fully love him yet. But you don't need to fear it. The way you strive to save Faina, the tears you've shed and the fears you've conquered? *That* is love. Fritz knows that, and he values it. So, don't worry yourself over whether he returns your feelings or not."

Snow White rested her hands on the edge of the counter. "Instead, I should look ahead to the trials I might face and conquer them early."

"That wasn't quite what I had in mind, but given your strategic mind, I guess it's not a surprise that was your conclusion," Angel said wryly.

"If I had thought this way sooner—if I had attacked my shyness with everything I had—this fight we're in might not be quite so difficult." Snow White curled her hands into fists. "Maybe we wouldn't even be in it."

"Snow White." The slight sharpness in Angel's voice caught Snow White's attention. "You have to stop blaming yourself and agonizing over the past. If you made mistakes—which I'm not even saying you did—they are already *done*. What is important is your actions *now*." Angel thoughtfully looked at the ceiling, her silver eyes glittering. "Though I must confess, I'm not entirely certain how you are supposed to let go."

Snow White studied her friend, taking in the way she elegantly clasped her fingers and the fathomless depth to her eyes.

Angel sighed deeply.

"Is there something I can do to help?" Snow White asked.

The apprentice shook her head, and her eyes softened when she smiled fondly. "Not at this time. But I'm grateful you asked." Angel leaned over and ruffled Snow White's black curls as she might a pet or a younger sibling.

Snow White blinked at the somewhat odd expression of affection, then scooted a little closer to Angel so she could pat her back. "Thank you," she said, "for being here and helping me."

"Of course," Angel said. "It's my duty—and my pleasure."

Snow White slightly narrowed her eyes as she picked through Angel's words. *There is some kind of clue in there...*

"I'm going to clean the horse paddock next," Angel announced.

"What happened to poking around the cottage?" Snow White asked.

"Abandoned in favor of horses."

"I did not know you loved horses so much."

"I'm on fine terms with them, but I'm missing my pet," Angel admitted. Before Snow White had a chance to inquire, she continued, "You'll come so I can keep an eye on you?"

Snow White sighed. "I wish it did not sound like I am a child who needs minding."

"It's not that way at all. You are more like a precious jewel that needs a guard—so Fritz would say." Angel slyly smiled.

Snow White shook her head at her friend's forwardness. "Let me finish with the mushrooms, and I'll join you."

"Lovely! Don't take too long!" Angel skipped out the door, her oversized tunic flapping like an ill-fitting dress.

Once alone, Snow White mashed her lips together. *I do think she is overly optimistic about Fritz's feelings for me. I'm not an idiot—given the kindness he has shown me and the marked difference in his manners with me and Angel, I do think there is something there. Fondness perhaps...but love already?*

She shook her head, then started to blush again at the memory of Fritz kissing her temple. *By the crown—stop fussing! He kissed my head—that's hardly anything to be embarrassed about and certainly nothing worth fawning over.*

She scowled and used a towel to brush a clod of dirt off a mushroom with more force than necessary. *I'm not even entirely certain how to define my feelings. Angel is right: it has been only a fortnight or so. I am a princess. I cannot be impulsive in my feelings or let them get the best of me. For now, I must say—and believe—that I have a deep admiration for Fritz and hope that we continue our friendship after Faina is safe again.*

Finished with her internal strategy session, Snow White nodded, satisfied she had hopefully talked some sense into herself.

She set the mushrooms aside and peered down at her borrowed dress, brushing dirt off the velvet skirt. She made for the front door and opened it, then startled when she found an old woman just outside.

Her face was leathery and wrinkled, and her frizzy white hair half spilled out of its braid. She was stooped over—whether from age or long-borne strain, Snow White couldn't tell. "Hello, dearie," crooned the old woman.

CHAPTER 14
AN APPLE

Snow White held fast to the doorframe and glanced around the yard. "Hello," she said cautiously.

What is this lady doing here? Does she know one of the warriors? Did they let her through?

"You are so pretty." The old woman smiled, showing a few missing teeth.

"Um...thank you?" Snow White furrowed her brow as she studied the woman's drab, brown clothes. Something twisted deep in the pit of her stomach, and Snow White licked her lips and forced herself to ignore her desire to squirm under the old lady's gaze.

"I'm a peddler, and I have just the right thing for a girl as beautiful as you." The old woman started to dig through her basket.

Snow White bit her lip and considered calling for one of the warriors. *I am acting paranoid. She's just an old lady—and there's no possible way she could have silently gotten past them. They must have purposely given her passage, and this is just my cursed shyness.* "D-do you know the Seven Warriors?"

"Here, I have bodice laces in bright colors—perfect for such a pretty girl," the old woman held out the end of a royal blue bodice lace.

Oh, my. I hope this is not their idea of an intervention. But if the warriors felt I needed a new dress, I'm certain Aldelbert would have no such trouble telling me so to my face.

"No, thank you, kind lady," Snow White said, awkwardly clearing her throat.

The old woman bobbed her head. "Very well, very well. Then how about a comb? Yes, a beautiful comb of gold and rubies to match your blood-red lips."

Snow White shifted uncomfortably. *Perhaps they let her through because she's a bit mad, and they intend to help her find her way home?* "Um…"

"Here—take it!" The old woman held out a gold comb studded with red gems that sparkled in the sunlight.

"No, thank you. While it is lovely, I'm afraid I don't need a comb just now."

Though she wanted to do nothing more than shut the door in the old lady's face and hide, Snow White made herself step out into the yard. *Fritz said I have to take one step at a time in conquering my shyness. I can handle one old woman—even if it makes my stomach churn.*

"Whom did you speak to on your way here?" Snow White asked.

The old woman studied her and said not a word.

Snow White clasped her hands together to keep herself from fleeing to the stables like a scared lamb. "Which of the warriors did you see along your way here?"

"If you don't want any goods, let us share a snack." Again, the old woman dug in her basket and pulled out a shiny, red apple.

Snow White frowned slightly as she studied the fruit—which looked as though it had just been picked off a branch. *Apple season is in the fall. Most apples kept in cellars are shriveled by now and not even half as appealing.*

The old woman cut the apple in half with a blunt belt knife, then held out half of the apple to Snow White.

Snow White took it with great reluctance.

"Do you not like apples, dearie?" The old woman asked coaxingly. She bit into her half of the apple with great gusto.

Snow White inspected her half—it smelled sweet, and the fruit looked pristine and crisp. "I like apples quite a-a bit," she said as she again glanced around the yard.

I know—I'll take her to Angel. She'll know what to do.

Snow White nodded in satisfaction and raised the fruit to her lips. She was about to call for the old woman to follow her, when the lady herself interrupted her thoughts.

"Yes, yes, apples are your favorite fruit, are they not?" the old lady asked.

Snow White turned around as she bit into her half of the fruit. *How does she know that?*

The old lady watched—strangely enraptured—as Snow White chewed.

There's something off about this, something that can't be entirely blamed on my personal failings. Her tongue felt strangely numb as she chewed the apple, but she ignored it as she again turned in the direction of the stable. "Ang—" She was unable to finish calling for her friend—it felt like someone had her by the throat.

Her legs started to shake, and the numbness spread to her fingertips. *Something is terribly wrong.*

She tried to call for Marzell, but her throat still wouldn't move. She attempted to swallow the fruit, but it got stuck at the back of her throat.

Her legs gave out, and Snow White collapsed on the ground, her half of the apple still clenched in her fingers.

The old lady laughed, her voice changing from a scratchy croon to a full and familiar voice. "Yes, *yes,* fair Snow White."

Snow White shook with fear as the old woman straightened up to her full height. Her leather face faded—like a mask shattering—and Faina stared down at Snow White with a cruel smile on her lips.

"I *finally* have you!" Faina hissed. "She has resisted and resisted for years, and I had to scheme around her stubborn will. But no one can save you now, and she really will be within my power."

She?...What? Who?

Snow White's thoughts were slow to surface, and she felt a fog envelope her mind as it grew increasingly hard to think and impossible to keep her eyes open.

"*Snow White!*" Angel screamed.

Snow White pried her eyes open long enough to see the apprentice sprint across the yard—her expression glittering and dangerous.

Faina—it *was* Faina, wasn't it?—snarled. She said something, and a white doorway of magic blazed into existence. It glowed with a fierceness that seemed to upset Faina and shed bits of magic that hissed and fizzed.

Faina gingerly stepped through the doorway, disappearing from sight. Then, the magical passageway folded in on itself, growing smaller and smaller with each fold. Angel leaped for it, but the last bit disappeared just before her fingertips could reach it.

Snow White's eyes fluttered shut again as the numbness spread through her body. Soon she couldn't feel anything.

So, this is my end, Snow White thought. *I failed.* She would have cried if she could have, but she couldn't even feel her cheeks anymore.

She felt cold, and the world turned dark, though Angel's hysterical shouts were faint and muffled. Still, she struggled; she tried to move a finger or open her eyes again. In resistance of whatever held her in its grasp, an important thought surfaced.

That was Faina. I know it was. But then who was talking? And how could Faina resist for years? Unless...?

She tried to swallow but couldn't. Instead, the darkness embraced her, and she felt nothing more.

CHAPTER 15
POISONED

Marzell paused in the middle of shouldering his longbow. "*Snow White!*"

It took him a moment to recognize Angel's voice. The kind but shrewish apprentice had never sounded so frightened before.

Snow White!

Marzell turned on his heels and ran, dodging branches and underbrush as he sprinted down the path. He broke through the tree line, entering the cottage's rather torn up yard, and skidded to a stop.

Angel was crouching down next to Snow White, but the princess was still.

Her eyes were closed, her skin deathly pale, and a chunk of a red apple rolled out from the loose grasp of her fingers.

"Snow White!" Angel slapped the princess' cheeks, but Her Highness did not stir.

Aldelbert came bolting out of the trees. Unlike Marzell, he did not stop but kept running full tilt to Snow White and Angel. "What happened?" he shouted.

"Faina," Angel said grimly. "I don't know entirely what happened, but she put some sort of spell on her."

"Is she still breathing?" This came from Wendal as he shoved a branch out of the way and sprinted into the yard.

"Yes," Angel said.

Marzell forced himself into motion and reached Snow White by the time Oswald and Rupert bolted into the yard together.

"You said it was Faina?" Gregori asked. Sweat beaded at his brow as he jogged up to them, his eyebrows drawn together in concern.

Angel nodded. "She must have approached Snow White disguised as an old woman. I saw her drop her illusion as I came around the cottage."

"You say she put a spell on her?" Marzell asked.

Angel nodded. "I can't tell what—if we're lucky, it might be a curse. Those are easier to alter."

"But how could the Queen do such a thing?" Rupert asked. "She hasn't any magic."

"The rogue mage controlling her?" Wendal offered.

Gregori shook his head. "If that were the case, would the mage have not come here on their own rather than risk sending Faina?"

Marzell rubbed his eyes. "There must be a way to save her. There *has* to be."

Snow White is the princess—we can't fail her!

He glanced down at Angel, who was glaring fiercely. "Was there anything else you noticed?"

Angel curled her hands into fists as she sat back on her heels. "Nothing that will help us wake Snow White up," she said bitterly. "Only further proof that our old inaction with the Chosen may be the end of us yet."

Marzell cocked his head. "What?"

"We should get Snow White inside," Gregori said.

Marzell shook his head, forcing himself to concentrate. "Yes. If we can assess the situation, we might be able to figure out whom to send for."

"I should be able to pin down what sort of enchantment was placed upon her," Angel said. "But it will take me a little while."

"Please, do whatever you can. Aldelbert, Wendal, take Snow White inside," Marzell said.

Aldelbert nodded, his usually smiling face wrinkled with concern as he scooped Snow White up, almost stepping on the apple piece.

Marzell forced himself to watch as Snow White hung in Aldelbert's grasp like a ragdoll. "Rupert, Oswald, search the area," he said grimly.

Oswald and Rupert separated, moving in different directions as they disappeared back into the forest.

"Faina is gone," Angel said. "She used magic to leave."

"Perhaps, but we're taking no chances. Not after we've already —" Marzell cut himself off and took a deep breath. "Gregori, can you stand guard just outside the cottage—and prep a horse so we can send for help?"

Gregori nodded, then jogged off to the stables.

Angel had started for the cottage but lingered in the door. She paused and turned around. "Fritz?"

Marzell wanted to groan. "He's still at least a day or two away."

Angel nodded and disappeared inside the dim cottage, but her question did not fade so easily from Marzell's thoughts.

When Fritz finds out...this will—no. Snow White will survive this. I have to believe that.

🙠

FRITZ STIFFENED IN THE SADDLE. *Something is wrong.*

He tilted his head and listened. His horse's hoofbeats were steady and sure, and he could hear the honk of wild geese and the sweet trills of the songbirds returning to the area. Nothing *seemed* out of order.

He twisted in the saddle, scanning the surrounding farmland

with a critical eye. The land was hilly but easy to inspect, and though much of it was still dead and brown from winter, green was beginning to sprout.

No sign of trouble. But the feeling of dread in Fritz's gut intensified.

He frowned as he double checked that his saddle packs were secured.

He had already gone to see the Veneno Conclave and had spoken to several mages that worked for the council—the Conclave's ruling government comprised of the top enchanters and enchantresses. The mages had promised very prettily that they would send a carefully selected magic user as soon as possible, and they could watch for their arrival in a week or so.

Fritz was grateful they had agreed to help, but the trip was rather off-putting.

The Veneno Conclave and Luxi-Domus—the Conclave academia for magic—were gorgeous and ornate.

Frankly speaking, they were more ornamental and breathtaking than Glitzern Palace.

Fritz didn't begrudge them the beauty—it was likely due to skilled mages, anyway. But the place seemed overly showy, as if they could hide the Conclave's failures with gold and glitter.

But even in visiting the Conclave, Fritz had felt uneasy—as if someone had his heart and was digging their nails into it.

Better to hurry home, he decided. He nudged his horse, and the gelding willingly increased its pace to a quick trot. *I can stop and get fresh horses in rest cities if need be. But...I think I need to return home. Immediately.*

§⋅

AN HOUR LATER, Marzell had practically worn a path through the fireplace rug with his pacing.

"Magic take it!" Angel snapped.

Marzell swiveled to face the enraged apprentice. "What is it?"

"This is the one time—the *one time*—I want it to be a curse so I can patch in a stupid 'true love's first kiss' fix. But it's not a ruddy curse!" Angel slammed her fist on the edge of the table, though she was careful not to hit the still unconscious Snow White. (Lacking a bed downstairs, Aldelbert had temporarily placed her on the table to be evaluated.)

"I don't understand," Marzell said. "Can't you tell what it is that is doing this to her?"

Angel took a deep breath, then pushed her sloppily cut hair from her face. "I can, of a sort. But it's not good news. It's a spell that has placed her in a deep sleep."

"And that is worse than a curse?"

"With the right opposing force—like love and sacrifice—curses can be broken," Angel said. "It usually takes great force to undo it because they are stronger and deadlier."

"Isn't that *good* news, then?" Wendal asked. In his concern for Snow White, he held three of his daggers between his fingers and continuously shifted them. "Doesn't that imply whatever did this to her is less powerful?"

"If we're looking at sheer strength, yes," Angel said. "The problem is I don't know *how* this spell was placed on her. Did Faina throw it on her? Did she do something to Snow White? I can't tell."

"What does that matter?" Marzell asked. "Aren't spells easier to break?"

"They are, except this one is strange." Angel scrubbed her face with her hands. "It's like nothing I've seen—not because it's particularly terrible; it's just *weird*. The spell strands aren't like any kind of casting I've ever seen. It seems antiquated and outdated. But that's where the problem lies—I can't pick it apart since I don't understand the casting. If I knew how it started, I would be able to unravel it, but since we don't even know that, it looks like gibberish."

"Would a mage be able to work it out?" Wendal asked.

Angel shook her head. "No. It will take a Lord Enchanter or Lady Enchantress—and they'll have to be excessively well read or incredibly experienced. In fact, only the Enchanters and Enchantresses on the Council might be able to do something about it."

"If she is merely sleeping, we can take her to the Conclave," Marzell started.

Angel held up her hand to forestall him. "I'm afraid not. Though I can't read the spellwork, I *can* guess at the effects of it. She's going to get worse, and the more we move her, the faster she'll dwindle. If you carry her to the Conclave, she'll die en route."

Marzell cursed under his breath and resumed pacing.

"You said the spell seemed antiquated, Angel." Aldelbert peered at Snow White with a thoughtful expression. "What does that mean?"

"It's rather like weapons," Angel explained. "The techniques and methods used now are far more advanced compared to what was available centuries ago, wouldn't you agree?"

Aldelbert nodded. "Of course."

"The same goes for magic. It has changed over the centuries as magic users have grown better at using and controlling it. Our spells are now far more precise and work with a great deal more finesse. Enchanters and Enchantresses are able to bend their magic to their will to cast spells that would normally be outside the range of their powers. It's why all Lord Enchanters and Lady Enchantresses are skilled in things like illusions, rudimentary weather spells, curse breaking, and so on. Our spellwork is far more complex to account for those improvements."

Angel hesitated. She released a deep sigh as she stared at Snow White. "The spell that has cut down the princess is something rudimentary but extremely brutal. It bears none of the complexity of modern magic, but it has something darker at its roots."

"How could a rogue mage have that kind of knowledge?" Marzell asked. "Do the Chosen have those kinds of resources at their disposal?"

"Are we perhaps dealing with someone more powerful?" Wendal didn't look up from his daggers as he fanned them between his fingers. "A rogue enchanter or enchantress, perhaps?"

Angel shook her head. "There is no such thing. As for Marzell's question, I'm afraid you are right: they *do* have those kinds of resources. It seems they kept meticulous records—more so than the library of the Conclave. Compared to them, we are nearly ignorant in the old ways of magic."

Marzell ran his hands through his hair. "Is there nothing more you can do for her?"

"I'll keep looking, but the best course of action is to try and reach the Veneno Conclave and ask directly for the council's help," Angel said grimly. She glanced back at Snow White. "I could go—I have a method of reaching the Conclave far faster than a regular horse and rider."

Marzell shook his head. "No—we need you on hand to support Snow White with magic if necessary. We have no one else that can fill that position."

Angel nodded. "I understand."

She retreated back to the table, her eyes narrowed as she studied Snow White while something silver coated her fingertips.

Marzell sighed as he motioned for Aldelbert and Wendal to join him at the fireplace.

"What is the plan, leader?" Aldelbert asked, some of his spunk returning. "How shall we face this trial?"

"We have to send word to Lord Vitkovci and the others and tell them what has occurred," Marzell said.

"A reasonable action—they need to know things have grown more serious," Wendal said.

Marzell nodded, but indecision made him rock back on his heels. He knew if Snow White were conscious, this next part would upset her. "We will send a missive to Lord Trubsinn, as well."

"Objection." Aldelbert held his hand up like a boy in a schoolroom. "Snow White specifically wished not to tell her grandfather so as to safeguard Faina's life."

"I'm aware of this, but the situation has changed, Aldelbert," Marzell said. "Snow White lies on a table—possibly dying—because of Faina. We cannot let the princess die because of her affection for her stepmother."

Aldelbert lifted his chin in stubbornness, but he seemed to mull over Marzell's words and said nothing more.

"If we tell Trubsinn, we'll lose control of the situation," Wendal warned. "He'll sweep in, and we will no longer be part of the decision-making process."

"We lost that honor when Snow White was injured under our watch," Marzell said. "We were careless—I *let* us be careless. We knew Faina was after Snow White and that the rogue mage knew our location. We should have moved to a different cottage—or requested backup."

"We were following Snow White's orders," Wendal pointed out. "She knew what she was doing."

"Regardless, we let her place herself in harm's way. We never should have allowed that," Marzell said.

Wendal blinked several times. "I'm surprised I have to ask anyone besides Lord Aldelbert this, but you *do* understand what it means that she is the princess, yes? Her word *is* the law."

"Not when she's vulnerable as she was," Marzell said.

Wendal shrugged. "As you say, Lord Marzell. Do you want me to inform the others?"

Marzell folded his arms across his chest. "Yes, please. I want Oswald and Rupert to ride out with the messages. Oswald should take the message for Lord Trubsinn to Hurra. Some of Trubsinn's soldiers are still stationed there and will see to it that he receives the message."

"What of Fritz?" Aldelbert asked.

"What *of* Fritz?" Marzell asked, slightly confused by the question.

"We are the Seven Warriors," Aldelbert said. "We do not make decisions on the scale of this one without input from all of us."

"In matters involving us, yes," Marzell said. "But this matter is bigger than us now."

Aldelbert wrinkled his forehead quizzically.

"What is it, My Lord?" Wendal asked.

"I'm not certain anything involving Snow White is beyond Fritz," the blond-haired lord said with surprising astuteness.

"He'll find out when he returns here," Marzell said grimly.

"You think Snow White will hold on that long?" Wendal asked.

"Yes," Marzell said with an assurance he did not feel.

She has to hang on. We have to see her through this.

❧

FRITZ CROUCHED low over his horse's neck, ducking a branch. *Almost there.* He had to be within hearing range of the cottage now, and yet his unease drove him forward.

Finally, his horse trotted down the last bit of the hidden path and popped out of the trees and into the cottage yard.

Fritz nearly relaxed when he saw his six comrades sitting outside and Snow White splayed out on a cot. He paused and reassessed the situation, tensing when he realized Snow White was pale and still—so much, in fact, that she looked *dead*.

For a moment, the world stopped.

"Fritz!" Marzell wore the pinched expression he only used when he was deeply troubled, but it was the sight of Gregori awake and grim-faced that made Fritz clench his teeth.

"What happened?" Fritz dismounted, nodding his thanks when Oswald took his horse's reins and walked off to care for it.

Marzell shut his eyes as if it pained him. "Faina."

"She's still breathing," Wendal said. "But she's been unconscious ever since."

Fritz crouched next to Snow White's cot, grimly studying her.

It was just as bad as it had looked from horseback. Her skin was a deathly pallor, and when he placed a fingertip near her nose, he could barely feel her breath.

She's alive, at least. A flicker of hope flared to life in his chest. *She's still breathing. She can still make it.*

"You're back sooner than we expected—sooner than we *hoped* for," Marzell rambled. "We didn't know if—"

The forest exploded with the sound of alarmed birds chirping and tweeting as they suddenly took flight.

Fritz, still kneeling, twisted around and watched birds fill the sky above the forest.

"Angel," Gregori said.

Fritz raised his eyebrows.

"That likely was her," Gregori explained. "She's been staying near Snow White since...*it* happened two days ago, but she looked like she needed a break, so we told her to take a walk."

"She was the one who suggested bringing Snow White outside." Wendal slightly adjusted the pillow that cradled Snow White's head. "She said the sunlight might do her some good, seeing how darkness abhors sunlight. Usually."

"What happened?" Fritz asked, this time with more iron in his voice.

Marzell's shoulders drooped. "After you left, we were checking the traps we laid to see if anything had set them off. We were within shouting range of the cottage the whole time, but we left Angel and Snow White at the cottage."

"Angel wanted to clear the horse paddock, but Snow White was cleaning mushrooms and said she would follow her once finished," Gregori said, taking up the narrative when Marzell did not continue. "Angel went out to the stable, but a few minutes passed, and Snow White did not come. So Angel started back for the cottage."

The big merchant glanced at Marzell, who held up his hand.

"I can tell the rest," the young lord sighed. "Angel came around the bend and saw Faina. She had an illusion woven over her as a disguise—Angel thought it was that of an old woman, but she only caught the tail end of it as Faina was already removing the illusion."

Fritz slowly shut his eyes as if he could block out reality. "And Snow White?"

"Already collapsed on the ground, though Angel did see her briefly open her eyes," Marzell said. "Angel ran for Faina, but she used magic to escape before she reached her. We heard her shout around then and started back for the cottage, arriving just after Angel began checking on Snow White."

Dread filled Fritz, but he tried to ignore it. He rubbed his eyes, then gestured to the cot. "Angel has no idea what the Queen did to cause this?"

"No," Wendal said. "But after studying the magic around Snow White, she knows it's a spell—an old one that is unfortunately difficult to remove given its ancient spellwork. Angel had a go at it, but she said we'd need a Lord Enchanter or Lady Enchantress from the Veneno Conclave's Council to break it off safely."

Fritz nodded and tried to smother the painful twist in his chest and focus on the facts. *I need a calm head to work through this*, he reminded himself—though he really wanted to shout his anger and frustration.

"How did Faina accomplish this?" he asked. "She has no magic of her own."

"We haven't thought much about that," Marzell admitted. "It seemed less important than trying to find help. Angel can't do anything unless she figures out the origins of the spell."

A reasonable thought, but if we know how Faina was able to use magic, it might reveal much more about the spell.

"I sent word to Lord Vitkovci and the others," Marzell said. "They...didn't take well to the news."

"They got snooty and threatened to have us court-martialed for letting the princess come to harm," Rupert growled. "Never mind the threat Faina poses to everyone if she can wander about and use magic at her will."

Oswald returned from the stables, his hands shoved in the pockets of his trousers. "I carried a message to Trubsinn's soldiers in Hurra," Oswald said. "The soldiers reached him by messenger bird and have already heard back. He's marching here and intends to take out Faina."

"And Snow White?" Fritz asked.

Oswald shrugged. "He said he will send word to the Council and ask for their help. He should be here by tomorrow night—he'll take Snow White to a fortification in Hurra and leave her there until someone from the Conclave comes."

"He'd move her to his lands, but Angel thinks that might speed up the spell that has Snow White unconscious and could... kill her," Gregori said hesitatingly. "Taking her to Hurra is risky, but it's a necessary safety precaution in case the rogue mage decides to finish the job with a physical attack."

Fritz rubbed his thumb on his sword's crossguard. *It cannot end like this. She cannot die. Snow White would never give up on Faina, and I...* Fritz let his head hang, and he stared at the ground. *She lingers on death's doorstep. Is there nothing I can do to save her?*

Desperation stabbed him like a knife to the heart. *I can't let her go this way!*

"Is there anything else you remember?" Fritz raised his head and stared unseeingly at Snow White's pale face. "Was she lying a particular way? Was there something different about her hair or her dress?"

Gregori shook his head. "She looked like she had collapsed

where she stood. Angel said when she opened her eyes it seemed like she was fighting to stay conscious, but that is all."

Fritz nodded as he carefully inspected Snow White. He rolled up the sleeves of her dress, checking her arms and wrists for a mark, a piece of jewelry he had never seen before—*anything* that would give an indication of how Faina cast the spell.

"There was a piece of apple," Marzell said. "But given she and Angel were cleaning food, it was most likely from the cottage."

Fritz nodded as he inspected Snow White's feet, pulling off her slippers.

Nothing. Not a single clue as to what is killing her. No measure of how this happened. Snow White fought so hard for Faina, and it seemed like Faina had fought just as hard for Snow White. How could she cause her downfall this way?

Fritz set a hand on top of Snow White's and gently squeezed.

She didn't react—of course. She had a *spell* on her. She wasn't magically going to wake because he had returned home. But there was something about the moment, seeing that she didn't wake or blush at the contact as she usually did that felt like a slug to the gut.

Fritz shut his eyes and forced his shoulders back.

She will live. She has to. I can't... He ruthlessly cut off the thought and stood. He would not wallow, not while she still breathed.

Fritz would do everything in his power to help, even if it meant infiltrating Glitzern Palace alone.

ও

FRITZ TUGGED on his black leather gloves before he flipped up the hood of his coal-gray cloak.

"And where do you think you're going?" Angel asked, surprising Fritz.

When he had crept down the stairs—taking great pains not to

make the rickety stairs creak—she was mumbling in her bedroll by the fire, not far from Snow White—pale and deathly still—on her cot.

"To find out how the spell was cast, hopefully," Fritz said blandly.

Angel stood with her back to the fire and folded her arms across her chest. "I am guessing you intend to pounce on Faina in her room and hope to smack the secret out of her? As much as I applaud the show of devotion, I have to say you don't stand a chance. Faina is using magic—*strong* magic. Magic you have no way to defend yourself against. Not even I could hold out against it. Going there by yourself is folly."

Fritz checked his sword belt. "I can't watch her slip away and do nothing about it."

"Lord Trubsinn has sent word to the Veneno Conclave," Angel reminded him. "A Council Member will come to help."

Fritz stared at Snow White. "Do you really think they'll arrive in time?" he asked with no small amount of bitterness.

The fire crackled as a log shifted, shedding embers.

"I don't know," Angel admitted. "But I do know you won't return if you follow your plan and walk out that door."

"Then tell me what I can do to fix this!" Fritz grasped the hilt of his sword as he watched Snow White's chest move with her faint—*too* faint—inhales and exhales. "I will not stand by and let her slip away from me—from us!"

Angel sighed and crouched down next to the cot. "She's growing worse. Or rather, she's slowly fading away."

Fritz wanted to growl—or perhaps groan—at the admission. *There must be something we are missing! Some clue that can bring her back!*

"Did you hear Faina cast the spell?" Fritz asked.

Angel shook her head. "Whatever spell it was, it was already on Snow White by the time I left the stable. In truth, I came looking for her because she was taking so long, but also because I thought I could detect a faint stench of something rotten."

"Faina?"

Angel nodded. "The feeling left as soon as she magicked herself away."

Fritz tugged his hood off. "How could Faina use magic to escape so swiftly? I did not know it was possible."

"It requires powerful and rare magic," Angel's voice was wooden as she rested her chin on her knees.

Fritz nodded, and his mind relentlessly dug through the facts. He walked to a cottage window and nudged it open, sighing when he saw the sky.

It was still dark outside and would be for some time, but the eastern sky was starting to lighten from a true black to a rich purple.

He wasn't planning to attack Faina immediately but had planned to take the day to get into the palace. Seeing the light, he realized, *if I don't leave before Marzell rises, I won't be able to slip out.*

"This spell is cursed *simple*," Angel grumbled, her voice dark. "However Faina cast it, it was quick to cast on Snow White and quick to settle in. By all rights, that should mean it should be *easy* to remove."

The apprentice sighed and hung her head. "I should have listened to my master and learned how to use my core magic instead of running from it all the time." She muttered some more under her breath, but Fritz couldn't make out the words.

Fritz stared outside, his mood as black as the sky. He mentally reviewed everything his friends had told him about the circumstances they had found Snow White in. "And the apple?"

"Eh?" Angel asked.

"The apple from our food storage?"

"What apple?" Angel said, sounding confused.

Fritz spun around, his eyes narrowed slightly. His heart jolted in his chest, but he was afraid to hope. "Marzell said she had an apple piece in her fingers when he arrived. He assumed she had taken it from our food storage, as you said she had cleaned off mushrooms."

Angel shook her head. "There was no apple when I left her for the stables. It's possible she grabbed one on her way out, but Snow White isn't one for snacking. That is something I'm far more likely to do."

No apple? But why, then... "Could Faina have given it to her?" Fritz murmured. He knelt next to Snow White on her cot and held his fingers suspended above her lips. He hesitated for only a moment before he gently pulled her mouth open.

It was too hard to see into her mouth in the dimness of the cottage, but with her mouth open, Fritz was more easily able to hear her breathe.

There was something wet about her inhale and exhale, and it was slightly wheezy, as if something partially blocked her throat.

"I need light," Fritz snapped.

Angel dove for her satchel and pulled out one of her light-shedding crystals. "Shine," she breathed on it, making the crystal release a pure, white light. She scrambled back to Snow White's side, holding the glowing crystal above the princess's head.

It was still hard to see, but Fritz thought he could see something white and red lodged at the back of her mouth.

A bite from an apple.

Fritz ripped his gloves off and carefully pulled Snow White so she sat upright. "Support her back."

Angel scooted so she sat directly behind Snow White, still holding up the glowing crystal. "Do you see something?"

"A half-chewed apple piece. Could it—"

"Possibly." Angel's voice sounded as taut as Fritz felt.

He maneuvered Snow White so she tilted forward slightly. Fritz carefully stuck a finger in her mouth, trying to scoop the apple across her tongue without setting off her gag reflex.

It took three tries before he got most of it out. He wiped her lips with the inner lining of his cloak. "Should we try to rinse her mouth—"

Snow White coughed—a raspy sound that rocked her body.

Fritz wrapped an arm around Snow White's back, freeing up Angel who returned to her station at Snow White's side, peering intently at the princess' face.

Snow White coughed again, spitting up a little piece of apple Fritz hadn't managed to scoop out.

Fritz waited, every muscle in his body tight as Snow White sagged back against his arm.

Did it work? Was that what Faina used to cast the spell on her?

Each moment felt like an eternity, yet Snow White didn't move. The cottage was silent except for the crackling fire.

The flickering flame of hope in Fritz's chest snuffed out as Snow White remained pale and still in his arms.

It hadn't worked.

Angel must have come to the same conclusion, for she thumped her forehead on the cot's wooden frame.

His heart heavy, Fritz started to lower Snow White back into a reclining position. *It was a long shot, a baseless hope.* He knew that, but the bitter sting of failure and dashed hopes still ate away at him. Snow White was still unconscious, her life hanging on by a thread. He loved her, and yet he was failing her—and losing her.

Just as he started to ease his arm out from under her, Snow White's eyes snapped open.

She bolted into a sitting position, nearly smacking skulls with Fritz as he gaped at her, his heart finally beating again, but she didn't seem to see him.

Instead, her lovely blue eyes were narrowed with *rage*.

CHAPTER 16
THE CULPRIT

Snow White's mind fought its way through the haze, making her realize she felt something in her mouth.

What's going on? Why can't I open my eyes?

Something hit the back of her throat, and she coughed, spitting something rancid out.

Immediately she felt better. The white fog that had lulled her into nothingness started to clear. Her thoughts still felt rusty and her body wouldn't listen to her, but with each passing moment feeling returned to her extremities.

What happened? I remember the old woman who was really Faina. She did something to me...gave me an apple...but that's not what was important. What was it?

She could finally feel warmth again in her fingertips, but she felt like a horse was sitting on her. She tried to move but not even a single muscle listened to her.

Faina said something strange. It was as if it wasn't her speaking in her own body, but something else. They said she had resisted for years. But how could that be? Angel said a rogue mage wouldn't be able to hang around like that.

She was missing something vital. They all were.

Perhaps we made an incorrect assumption. We decided it was a rogue mage because it was the most logical option, but what if we're wrong? Angel said a magical artifact might be able to do something like this, but it seemed unlikely and didn't fit the timeline.

However, if we are to widen the scope...when did Faina really start going downhill? With the start of her headaches, I think. I thought they were an unrelated physical ailment, but what if they're an indicator instead? They started years ago, and it seemed that in these last few months, that she had a headache whenever she was angry or struck out.

But that doesn't exactly illuminate anything. Someone would have had to plant such an object, and they can't just have it sitting around the palace. Myself or a servant would have noticed it! It would have to be an extraordinarily small object to avoid detection, or something hidden in plain sight—given as a gift perhaps.

Snow White snapped her eyes open when the answer hit her like a lightning strike.

She sat upright, barely able to contain her blinding anger. *How could we have MISSED that?*

"It's that mirror," she hissed, her voice boiling with barely contained fury. "That *cursed* mirror! I'm going to shatter it myself when we march on Glitzern."

She could have screamed in her frustration and anger. A *gift* had nearly ruined Faina. A stinking mirror!

Snow White sucked in a breath of air to keep from snarling, then paused.

It was dark. She was inside the cottage. Angel was crouched at her side—her face ranging from shock to awe to anger. Fritz was on her other side, his eyes shining with *something*.

Snow White paused, her fury swapping out for confusion. Her revelation aside, the previous events replayed in her mind—the way she had fallen to the ground and couldn't speak or move.

"Did I die?" she asked, confused.

Angel made a strangled noise and threw her arms around Snow White, yanking her into a hug. "You little idiot," she said in a voice that was half a laugh and half a sob. "Didn't Faina ever teach you not to take food from strangers?"

"The apple was laced with something, wasn't it?" Snow White winced in chagrin. She remembered how the numbness had spread through her body as soon as she bit into the apple.

Angel's snort was enough of an affirmation to make her cringe. *That was an embarrassingly harmful mistake to make.*

Angel released her and scrambled to her feet. "Oi, warriors!" she shouted up the stairs. "Wake up—Snow White is alive!"

"What?"

"Her Highness?"

There were thuds overhead, and someone must have tripped on Gregori, for a familiar roar sounded from the loft.

Snow White pushed a curl out of her face but couldn't stop a smile from blooming on her lips when her eyes met Fritz's. "You're back," she said, feeling stupidly shy.

Fritz leaned forward, pressing his forehead against hers. "You were dying," he said, his voice quiet but strong. "We almost lost you." He rested his forearms on her shoulders so his hands were draped over her shoulder blades.

Snow White cleared her throat, overly aware of where their foreheads touched. She looked down, unable to keep his gaze thanks to the heat that blazed in his eyes.

"I'm sorry. I made a stupid mistake," she whispered.

Fritz pulled back long enough to kiss her forehead. "I'm just glad you're alive." His lips brushed her temple when he spoke, making Snow White blush hard enough to light up a corner of the room.

It was then that she knew. *I love him.*

It was different from how she imagined it would be. Instead of sweeping her off her feet in a glorious and romantic progression, her feelings for Fritz had slowly snuck up behind her and essentially walloped her upside the head.

It was not all-consuming like fire, but more similar to the

sudden thaw of winter into spring. She hadn't noticed it all that much, and now—suddenly—she was dimly aware that Fritz had become so important to her, she would do *anything* just to stay by his side. (She had come this far for Faina. In her heart, Snow White dimly realized she'd go just as far for Fritz.)

Her hands shook slightly as she dared to place her palm flat against his chest and briefly rested her head on his shoulder. He adjusted his hold on her into more of a traditional embrace, and set his chin on top of her head. She felt slightly lightheaded—not from fear, but from sheer giddiness.

She loved Fritz!

She opened her mouth to say something—she wasn't exactly sure what—but footsteps thudded down the stairway, and voices called out, "Snow White!"

Snow White reluctantly pulled back from Fritz's embrace and smiled as Marzell and Aldelbert ran down the stairs, Rupert following them at a much slower pace.

Wendal hopped on a crossbeam and lowered himself down like a stealthy thief while Oswald jumped over the loft railing.

Gregori was the last to join them, blinking blearily and looking like a recently awoken bear.

Wendal careened to a stop and looked Snow White over from head to foot as Fritz helped her stand. Aldelbert, apparently, had no such compulsions. He elbowed his way past Marzell, his expression unusually serious. He took Snow White's left hand and clasped it in his.

He studied her for several seconds—his face still crinkled with worry—then said in his usual obnoxious way, "You still look rather unhealthy, Snow White. Do you want to use some of my face lotions? They'll make your skin shine with health!"

"Aldelbert!" Marzell hissed.

Wendal pushed up the bridge of his glasses. "We are glad to see you up and awake, Your Highness."

Rupert nodded his agreement, and Oswald awkwardly scuffed his bare foot on the ground.

"How did you break the spell?" Marzell grinned broadly as he looked from Fritz to Angel.

"The apple you mentioned," Fritz said.

"Yes?"

Fritz blinked and moved slightly so his left arm was behind Snow White. When she veered slightly—not quite stable on her feet—he placed a warm and supportive hand on her lower back, steadying her.

"The apple," Angel started, "came from Faina, did it not, Snow White?"

Snow White nodded. "Faina disguised herself as an old peasant woman. I thought you all must have known her, for I didn't think it was possible for anyone to slip past you—obviously it didn't occur to me she was more than she appeared to be. I refused to buy anything, but she offered me an apple. When she cut it in half and took a bite out of her section, I assumed it was safe. She must have spelled it somehow."

"You're safe now," Fritz said. "That's all that matters." His hand crept round her lower back and stopped at her hip, leaving them in a half-embrace.

"Though we failed you in our promise to keep you safe," Marzell sighed.

Oswald scratched the back of his neck, and Rupert refrained from taunting him and looked at his feet.

They took my mistake badly—I'll have to address it later, though. We have far more important matters to attend to. Snow White wanted to jump with glee at the reminder and kick herself for failing to think of it before. "It doesn't matter—I believe I know how Faina is being controlled!"

Gregori muffled a yawn. "You know what spell the rogue mage is using on her?"

"No, because there *is* no rogue mage," Snow White said

triumphantly. "We assumed there was because it was the easiest plan to enact, but obviously we underestimated our enemy."

"What else could it be?" Rupert asked.

"Angel said it previously, when we first discussed Faina's affliction." Snow White whirled to face Angel and held out her hand to the apprentice.

Angel thoughtfully studied her. "I'm touched you bothered to remember every squawk that comes out of my mouth, because frankly I do not."

Snow White spun again to face Marzell and the other warriors. "She said there are some powerful magic artifacts that could hold people under their sway. They are incredibly rare, though, so we rejected the idea." Snow White shook her head and briefly covered her face with her hands. "I should have seen the inconsistency in our rogue mage theory when I first created my timeline, for that is where we can see the proof!"

"What you're saying sounds very important, Snow White," Marzell said. "But could you describe it in greater detail?"

"You're railing like you're off your nutter," Oswald said with a great deal more bluntness.

"I apologize. Right." Snow White cleared her throat and nodded to herself. *Be clear and concise.* She mashed her lips together, then launched into a better explanation.

"Approximately six years ago, Faina was given a mirror as a birthday gift," Snow White said.

"Six years...that would have been around the time Queen Ingrid of Arcainia died, Prince Severin of Loire was cursed, and the elves were cursed," Angel said.

"I am unaware of any of those events," Snow White said. "What's important is that the mirror was a gift. I don't recall who gave it—I'm not sure if we ever knew. That year was Faina's first birthday since Father had died, so many nobles and foreign dignitaries sent more gifts than usual. Regardless, it was soon after that Faina's health started to falter. She didn't have headaches yet, but she was much more fragile. Everyone assumed it had to do with Father's death—that her broken heart made her more delicate."

Snow White wished she could throttle her much-younger self.

Now that I think of it, that alone is a ridiculous idea. Having witnessed how Faina has fought for me, why did I ever think losing Father would break her? She's too strong and determined to let such a thing happen!

She shook her head and made herself focus. "I think the deterioration of her health—which, while slight, was *still* pronounced and noted by our staff—is an indication that the mirror—an artifact—started to inflict its magic on her."

"The timeline works better. Six years is an impossible timeline for a rogue mage to hold, but an artifact would keep at it," Angel said. "If it really is an artifact, that also explains the ancient spell placed on Snow White, as all artifacts were forged long ago—most well before the time of Verglas' Snow Queen. Usually an artifact would affect people much faster, but it seems plausible Faina held out longer than most."

"She did!" Angel said proudly. "After I bit the apple, Faina—or the mirror speaking through Faina—complained about the years she had resisted. I think it meant to ruin us sooner, but Faina fought it off."

"I agree this seems like a possibility," Wendal said as he adjusted his spectacles. "But only if you know for certain the mirror *is* an ancient artifact."

Snow White bit her lip. "I don't know how many artifacts exist, so I cannot say for sure. But the more I think it over, the more I am certain the mirror is somehow involved. Before I left Glitzern, when she nearly hurt me, I saw her *talk* to the mirror—not to her reflection in the mirror, but to the mirror itself." Snow White pinched her eyes shut as she struggled to recall the details of the moment. "I think she even asked it a question."

The Seven Warriors looked thoughtful, but Marzell nodded.

They seem like they might believe me—enough that we can send someone to look into it!

"It's the mirror," Angel said finally.

Snow White blinked. "How do you know?"

Angel tossed her glowing starfire on top of her satchel. "I can't say if your mirror is a rare artifact or not, but after seeing the magic Faina used yesterday, I can promise with nearly absolute certainty: it is the mirror."

"Can you further explain that?" Gregori asked. "You didn't know it was a mirror before Snow White brought this up."

Angel pinched the bridge of her nose. "Yes, it's my failing. I didn't notice the signs and connect them until Snow White brought it up. I can't really explain it more than that, but knowing what I know, having followed a trail for years…If we can get that mirror out of Glitzern and Juwel, I am certain we can free Faina."

Snow White skirted a chair to lean out an open window. She could still see the stars, but the sky was brightening with hints of dawn.

"We should send a message to Lord Vitkovci and the others. It's early enough we could still meet today, couldn't we?" Snow White turned around, her anticipation making it hard to stand still.

We can save Faina!

Everyone swiveled to look at Marzell. The young lord cringed and rubbed the back of his head. "About the other lords…we need to talk."

ঌ

THE SKY WAS a swirl of rose gold and royal purple as they rode through the forest. It was still dark, and the trees blocked the sliver of sun that had risen above the horizon.

Snow White's breath turned into a misty puff thanks to the

cold night, but she was warm—mostly because she was riding double with Fritz and was snugly tucked against his back.

She rested her cheek on his cloak-covered back, her arms loosely linked around his waist. Much of the hope she had felt earlier was gone, snuffed out by Marzell's guilty confession.

"Snow White, I'm sorry," Marzell said somewhere behind her.

A muscle twitched in her cheek. *Apologizing isn't going to save Faina if my grandfather arrives early!*

"We thought you were dying. We had to focus on saving you," Marzell said. He sounded unnaturally loud in the silence of the forest.

Snow White forced the thought from her mind and made her voice neutral, if not pleasant. "You did what you felt you had to," she said. "I understand."

And in a way she did. Marzell thought he would have the death of the kingdom's heir on his hands if he didn't act. But it still rankled her that he had chosen to alert Lord Vitkovci *and* her grandfather to her unconscious and gravely ill state.

And did he have to be so efficient about it? Couldn't he have waited a day to send word to grandfather? He's due to arrive in Hurra tonight! *We have a day to convince Lord Vitkovci, Lord Gossler, Lord Leyen, and Lord Holdenberg that not only should we follow the original plan, but we need to attack* today *to avoid a confrontation between Grandfather and Faina!*

"If I had known—if we had figured out earlier what spell Faina cast on you..." Marzell trailed off, sounding miserable. "I apologize for going against your wishes," he sighed.

Even farther back behind Marzell, Wendal snorted, "Who warned you? That is right: My Lord and I warned you. But what do *we* know?" he murmured as he nudged his horse so it passed Marzell and his mount. He road abreast of Fritz's horse, his golden glasses gleaming in the faint light as he studied the surrounding trees.

"I can't say I am not disappointed," Snow White said finally.

"But you were placed in an impossible situation. With luck, we can convince Lord Vitkovci and his cohorts, and none of this will matter."

Oswald, riding just in front of them with Rupert, laughed outright. "Good luck in that impossible endeavor," he said. "They're probably going to lock you in a tower room for your safety as soon as we arrive. So why do we have to be up and riding so early in the morning?" His voice took on a grumpy quality for the last bit—someone, clearly, was not an early riser.

"If you don't stop whining," Gregori called from the very back of the line, sounding like death itself, "you'll wish someone would offer you a tower for *your* protection."

"I'm just warnin' Her Highness that they're not going to listen," Oswald argued. "As far as the lords are concerned, we're children playin' grown up."

"I am the princess," Snow White pointed out, leaning slightly so she could peek around Fritz and peer at Oswald.

"Yeah, one that's been quiet and coddled her whole life," Oswald snorted.

Snow White winced and didn't reply. What *could* she say to such a truth?

Rupert, who was bundled up as warmly as when they were forging through snow, slipped his right foot out of the stirrup, pulled his leg up, and kicked Oswald in the side.

Oswald snarled and pulled a knife out of his belt, but Rupert ignored the blade as he sedately slipped his foot back in the stirrup. "That is how subtle you were," he said.

"I disagree with them, Your Highness," Angel—riding at the front of their dawn-riding caravan—drawled in a sing-song voice. "You are the princess—the future Queen of Mullberg. If you have the resolve, you can move the world."

"They shall listen to Snow White," Aldelbert said with absolute and completely unfounded confidence. "She is the princess, and we are a group of uncommonly handsome men. Mostly. How could they refuse us?"

"Wendal, are you such a faithful attendant because if *someone* does not stand by him, Aldelbert is going to accidentally raze his lands to the root?" Oswald asked.

He yelped when Wendal chucked a dagger at him, cutting it so close to Oswald that it sliced a corner of his cloak.

"Keep asking *why,* and you'll find out," Wendal said ominously as he again nudged his horse out of the line—this time to retrieve his dagger.

Snow White wanted to smile at their banter. She had more than a hunch that they were carrying on for her sake. But all she had the strength to do was lean against Fritz's broad back and steal his warmth.

She briefly shut her eyes, and for a moment everything felt hopeless.

Yes, she had her very timely realization about Fritz. But everything she had fought against was coming to fruition anyway. Every circumstance she had worked valiantly to avoid was taking place.

Because of a single moment of carelessness, when I already have a lifetime of such moments stacked against me.

But it doesn't matter. We must convince the lords. Faina cannot die!

"Are you well, Snow White?" Fritz murmured.

He was barely audible over Oswald's and Rupert's bickering, but Snow White felt the rumble of his voice through her cheek pressed into his back.

"I'm scared," she admitted. "I don't know if we can do this."

"*You* can," Fritz said.

Snow White switched positions, so it was her forehead she rested against Fritz instead of her cheek. "How can you say that with such confidence?"

"You unraveled the curse on the Queen. And when the worst happened and you were incapacitated, everyone moved as *you* predicted they would." He was quiet for a moment, then said, "You focus too much on what you are unpracticed in, instead of giving yourself credit where it is due. You are intelligent and well read, Snow White. You have the mind to lead. You just need more practice."

Unfortunately, I haven't got time for practice. I have one day.

Despite the negative thought, Snow White warmed a little at Fritz's praise.

"I like to read, yes," she said a little awkwardly, her forehead still against his back. "But I don't know that it is at all praiseworthy."

"You are more than ready to ascend the throne," Fritz said over his shoulder. "You are merely holding yourself back."

Snow White was quiet as she mulled over Fritz's words. They rode in silence, until Snow White cleared her throat. "Thank you," she said abruptly. "That is to say, um, I never thanked you for figuring out how to break the spell on me. Angel told me what you did…"

It had been strangely intimate to know Fritz had to fish around her mouth with his finger. Snow White wasn't quite sure how to react, except with gratitude—for both saving her and for being the one to do it. (If Aldelbert had attempted such a thing, Snow White would probably be dead right now.)

As time stretched on and Fritz said nothing, Snow White was profoundly grateful she rode behind him so he did not have to witness the awkward way she hunched up.

"I was desperate," Fritz said eventually.

"Hmm?" Snow White straightened like a turtle poking its head out of its shell.

"I could see we were losing you," Fritz continued, his words slow to come. "I couldn't sit and watch you fade. I would have tried anything…"

Snow White bit her lip in indecision, then tightened her grasp around Fritz's waist, squeezing him gently.

Fritz placed a gloved hand over hers and gently returned the squeeze.

Snow White smiled at the gesture and quietly contemplated his back.

Perhaps I finally do have a bit of courage. I almost died once, and I would have faded without allowing myself to admit my feelings for Fritz. But how am I supposed to proceed? No tutor or book prepared me to eloquently confess my feelings for a man!

Snow White made a face. *At least I know I am supposed to do such things in private. Not when we are in the middle of a riding party off to try and convince several lords to listen to us.*

She sighed gloomily. *I cannot let this turn into something I push off, though, or I'll die again before telling Fritz how I feel. But, curse it, it's embarrassing enough to try and talk freely. Telling someone that I care that deeply about them? I'd burn my library and run all the Cabinet meetings for the next decade!*

Snow White pressed her lips together in displeasure, then began mentally rehearsing all the instructions she would whisper/hiss to Marzell so he could convince Lord Vitkovci and his minions.

They had to succeed. No matter the price, Snow White would pay it—for Faina and for Mullberg.

CHAPTER 17
PRINCESS SNOW WHITE

The sky had warmed to a light blue, but the sun was still young and golden by the time they arrived at Lord Vitkovci's lands.

They rode to his manor home, but rather than entering it and stabling their horses, they stopped at a small thatch of trees that invaded a hay field.

Gregori went alone to the manor to request the presence of the older lord—and hopefully Lord Gossler, Lord Leyen, and Lord Holdenberg as well.

Snow White sucked in a deep breath and clasped her hands together, trying to hide her nervous shakes.

Angel smiled as she strolled past the princess. "You'll do fine."

Snow White blinked. "I don't intend to speak much. Marzell will be the one to explain the mirror to them."

"Mmhmm," Angel sidled away, sounding wholly unconvinced.

Snow White pressed her lips together, worry making her squint. *That's the plan—and it's the wisest course, as Marzell has been our speaker thus far. But why would Angel expect otherwise? She was present when we made the plans.*

"I see Gregori." Wendal rustled in the top branches of one of the trees. "And the four lords. They appear to be following him."

"Good!" Marzell hooked his thumbs on his belt. "He must have gotten through to them."

Oswald grunted. "Unless they're coming with him just so they can grab *Her Highness* and drag her to safety."

Rupert smirked and rested a hand on the hilt of his sword. "That is one of the most intelligent things you've ever said."

Oswald brandished a white snowdrop flower he had plucked, flicking it under Rupert's nose and making him sneeze three times. "I'm so *glad* winter is over," Oswald said with great relish.

Though Snow White was tempted to hide behind Fritz, she made herself stand shoulder-to-shoulder with Aldelbert. She stood a little straighter, though, when Fritz started to veer around her to take up his place behind her.

Though I don't like being out in the open, it feels a lot better to have Fritz at my back.

As if sensing her thoughts, Fritz paused when he stood next to her. He smiled with his eyes and slowly tucked one of her back curls behind her ear, his fingers brushing her cheek in the process.

Before she could blush, he eased into his assigned place.

Snow White cleared her throat, and lifted her chin up, when Rupert and Oswald reluctantly joined their lineup. Wendal climbed down from his perch, leaping off the tree *far* earlier than Snow White thought was wise—though he landed with a neat roll and trotted round so he stood a little behind Aldelbert.

"Here they come," Marzell said as he folded his hands behind his back.

Angel didn't move to join them and instead stood with their tethered horses, crooning to them with lilting words.

Snow White held her breath as she watched Gregori lead the lords away from the manor and across the gardens that spotted the front yard. They passed the gatehouse—Lord Vitkovci waving off two soldiers who moved to fall in behind them—and after another minute of walking, reached their thatch.

"Your Highness!" Lord Vitkovci's wrinkles around his mouth and the corners of his eyes amplified his smile. "I am both heartened and gladdened to see you are well again!"

He showed no signs of stopping as he—and the others—marched straight for her, so Snow White held out her hands to both assure them she was well and to forestall them from getting any closer.

Lord Vitkovci took her hands in his and squeezed. "I was very troubled—and disturbed—to hear how Queen Faina had attacked you, and that you had fallen prey to a spell."

Snow White smiled magnanimously, though she wanted to shoot Marzell a glare. *He did what he felt was right, but that doesn't mean I don't want to take a stick to his head for doing it!*

"It does my heart good to see you alive and breathing. When we heard…" He shook his head, unable to continue as his wrinkles briefly warred between joy and sadness. "But you have recovered, and that is what is important!"

"Indeed." The glass in Lord Leyen's spectacles glowed in the morning light. "News of your recovery is the most reassuring and heartening word we've received in months."

"Absolutely." Lord Holdenberg had his arms tucked around his slightly bulging belly. "With your wellbeing assured, we can march on Glitzern Palace with the guarantee of your future. Lord Trubsinn will be so glad to see you!"

"About that," Snow White said, her voice cracking slightly. "We have u-uncovered n-new information." She struggled to hold their gaze, but that made it much harder to talk without stammering. She took a deep breath. "Marzell…" she trailed off when she noticed the lords exchanging looks, then shook her head.

It doesn't matter. We have to convince them—even if they seem like they won't listen to us!

She cleared her throat. "Marzell shall tell y-you what we have learned."

"Right." Marzell nodded once and offered the lords a brief smile when they swiveled to face him. "Because of the type of magic used on Snow White, and because of some things Faina said when she attacked Snow White, Her Highness has uncovered the perpetrator of the dark magic plaguing Queen Faina."

Lord Gossler tugged on his beard as his eyebrows rose in surprise. "Truly?"

"Don't hold it in, man—tell us!" Lord Holdenberg barked.

"It is not a rogue mage as we assumed, but rather an artifact: a mirror that was given to Her Majesty for her birthday six years ago," Marzell said.

Lord Leyen frowned slightly. "I assume you have proof of this? For it is quite a jump to go from accusing a rogue magic user to an inanimate object."

Lord Vitkovci shook his head. "Artifacts are not mere things, Leyen. They are objects, yes, but forged out of great power. Most of them are legends, used by our ancestors centuries ago. The weapons of the Legendary Magic Knights of Sole are a more modern example, and even they are not as powerful as artifacts of yore." He looked from Marzell to Snow White as he stroked his grizzly white beard. "Sadly, though, most artifacts were lost in the grains of history. The few of any worth that I am aware of are kept at the Veneno Conclave."

"Yes," Marzell agreed. "But knowing that, isn't it plausible the Chosen saved several of their own?"

Lord Vitkovci grunted.

"I am willing to entertain the idea that it might be an artifact that has affected Her Majesty so," Lord Gossler said. "However, why do you believe it is this mirror?" He glanced briefly at Snow White but looked to Marzell for the answer.

"Snow White was able to pinpoint it with a timeline. As we said, Queen Faina received the mirror from an unknown giver at her birthday six years ago. It was then that her health started to fail, escalating into headaches, which then turned into the rage-fueled outbursts that plague her today," Marzell said. "Additionally, Angel saw Faina use magic in her escape. When Snow White suggested the mirror, she was able to confirm that the type of power she used could be given to her by such a thing."

Angel waved and waggled her fingers at the lords when they studied her, slumped against Gregori's large gelding. "Hey-o," she said.

"The princess' explanation sounds plausible," Lord Gossler said. "But I can't really say the opinion of an herb wizard's apprentice moves me."

"Regardless, it won't cost us anything to look for the mirror, particularly if Snow White can give us a description," Lord Vitkovci said.

Hope welled up in Snow White. *They're listening! They're going to do it!*

"We will discuss it with Lord Trubsinn when he arrives tonight," he continued.

Snow White bit her lip and grabbed fistfuls of her skirts when she realized she was wringing her hands. *This is the important bit. Come on, Marzell. You can do this!*

"About that," Marzell said. "You were planning to wait for Lord Trubsinn and attack Juwel tomorrow or the day after depending on the state of Lord Trubsinn's forces, yes?"

Lord Holdenberg nodded. "Yes, that is so."

"I propose that—knowing as we do, now, about the mirror—we move the attack up to today," Marzell said.

Snow White smiled slightly at the strong, even tone of his voice. *Yes, Marzell was the right choice to suggest this proposal.*

"Today?" Lord Gossler asked.

"Juwel will not be difficult to march on," Marzell said. "Queen Faina has neither consolidated her forces nor made a move to attack with the military. It seems the mirror spurs her to move personally—as seen in the way she personally set a spell on Snow White rather than have soldiers capture her, or something similar. The citizens of Juwel and the servants of the palace will pose no threat to your forces—*particularly* if they know you are merely there to capture Queen Faina for her own safety and have not come to execute her."

Lord Vitkovci held up a hand to silence Marzell. "I'm afraid I must stop you there. In our exchanges with Lord Trubsinn, we have concluded that Faina poses too great of a threat to Snow White. She must be killed."

No. Snow White's hearing turned fuzzy, and the pounding of her heart throbbed in her ears. *No, they cannot mean that.*

"But Snow White is alive!" Marzell argued.

"For now, but even if we kept Faina in a dungeon, it would do no good if she can use *magic*!" Lord Gossler said. "She'll escape the same way she gave you the slip."

Marzell shook his head. "You don't have to hold her captive. If you can free her from the mirror, she will no longer be under its control and will then pose no threat."

"We should look for the mirror and destroy it, yes," Lord Leyen said. "But we do not know for certain it is the mirror causing these fits. And we have no guarantees the change in Faina's temperament was solely because of the mirror. What if it was something more?"

"Or worse: there is a distinct possibility another dark force will be able to take the reins imbedded in her by the mirror and will kill the princess later," Lord Gossler added. "She might become similar to the mad King Torgen of Verglas and the way he acted before he died."

Lord Holdenberg shook his head and widened his stance so he more closely resembled a stubborn donkey. "No, we cannot risk Snow White again. We nearly lost her. For the good of our country, we must do whatever we can to protect her."

"No!" The words tore out of Snow White before she was

aware she was speaking, but she didn't regret it. "How can you just r-resign yourself to this? There must be another way!"

Lord Vitkovci sighed. "We wish there was, Your Highness. Make no mistake, we will hold off as long as we can and spare her. With luck, perhaps the Veneno Conclave Council Member who was to be sent here to save you will arrive in time and contain her. But when we face her, we must act with great purpose and swiftness. We *cannot* bandy about this time."

"But *why?*" Snow White took a step forward, leaving the warrior's lineup. "Why would you do such a thing? Faina is your *queen*. H-h-how can you plot her murder when she has served our country so well?"

"Queen Faina has ruled well and was a proper stepmother to you, Snow White. I admire her very much, but *you* are our real monarch," Lord Vitkovci said. There was a painful furrowing of his brow, but his mouth was set. "You are the future. She is only to be your regent for another year—an unnecessary thing given you are already of age," Lord Vitkovci said. "I am sorry that her end may be this way. It is a terrible thing given how she has served our nation. But we *cannot* gamble with your life, Your Highness. You are what is most important to Mullberg."

But I can't be. Faina and I have ruled together. She's done so much! What will this do to the people? Would they even understand, when I cannot? How could they ever trust the nobility when they prove they are willing to resort to murder for my sake?

How could anyone follow me, knowing I was too weak to protect my throne and my own stepmother?

Snow White couldn't stop her jaw from trembling as desperation set in.

The likelihood that the Veneno Conclave representative arrives in time is slim. And even if they do—will the lords allow Faina to be saved?

Numbness set into her chest. Her feet felt shackled to the ground, and she could barely stand. *I cannot lose Faina. I cannot!*

"This cannot be the end of this discussion," Marzell said, his voice pinched with concern. "There must be an alternate strategy."

"You can take it up with Lord Trubsinn if you like," Lord Gossler said doubtfully. "But he will likely be even more decisive given that this matter involves the life of his granddaughter."

"That is, we assume you mean to join us still in the attack, despite our differing opinions?" Lord Leyen asked.

That's it! If we can slip away, perhaps we can attack Faina ourselves? Surely some of the palace guards will help us. Snow White licked her lips and glanced at Marzell, wondering how she could hint to him her thoughts.

"Snow White will stay with my family until Lord Trubsinn arrives," Lord Vitkovci said. "I have a granddaughter her age. She will gladly welcome you inside."

Snow White clenched her jaw and forced herself to speak. "I have no n-need for hospitality. W-we won't take any more of your time."

"I'm afraid you misunderstand me, Your Highness," Lord Vitkovci said gently. "You *will* remain here. I meant my oath when I said we would let you go with the Seven Warriors unless you were injured."

"But..." Shocked, she couldn't get any words past her lips.

"We will do whatever is necessary to keep you from harm, Your Highness," Lord Leyen said.

"But I am a *princess*. You, you c-can't keep me against my will!" Snow White's voice cracked with frustration and a little fear.

"It is because you are the princess that we do this, Snow White." Lord Vitkovci extended his arm, a subtle order for her to take it and come with him.

Snow White stiffened and stepped backwards, slightly shaking her head. She almost yelped when Fritz—as silent as a ghost—stepped out in front of her, his hand on his sword.

"Do we need to call for our soldiers?" Lord Holdenberg asked, a hint of ice to his voice.

"No," Snow White said. "No, I will not allow this. I will issue a royal decree—"

"It will do you no good, Your Highness," Lord Gossler said. "Even your Cabinet would agree with us that this is the wisest path. I apologize that we are disregarding your wishes, but this is best for everyone."

It's not best for Faina. It can't be best for our people either.

Snow White swallowed hard, and her fists shook—not with fright or embarrassment, but with anger.

The Chosen are going to win. Even after we've uncovered their scheme, they're still going to win. Faina...

Hot tears clouded her vision.

It's not fair! I moved past my fear and sought out the Seven Warriors, I have faced magical monsters—I may have even figured out the source of Faina's pain! And after all of this, I still can't win.

Her heart throbbed painfully in her chest.

But Faina...she will die.

She shook her head.

No. No! I have failed at many things. I will not fail here!

Snow White took a deep gulp and internally muttered a prayer.

Fritz claims my intellect is more useful than I know. I just hope he is right.

"No," Snow White said.

Lord Vitkovci frowned. "No?"

"No, I am Princess Snow White of Mullberg. You will *not* hold me captive like a criminal, and you will listen to my orders." Though she had to spit the words out between clenched teeth, she found it easier to speak as long as she remembered that these lords would kill Faina if she gave them the chance.

Lord Leyen smiled slightly. "You are in no position to make demands, Your Highness."

Here it begins.

Snow White braced herself as she turned her blue eyes onto

Leyen. Though she wanted to scream, she forced herself to meet his gaze. "Lord Leyen. You own the smallest amount of land of those present, with the bulk of your acreage tied up in forests. As the Mullberg demand for local lumber has waned given that exotic cedar lumber is now in vogue, your lands have suffered. Your taxes were lowered for two years in a row, and you were advised—no, *I personally* advised you—to find a secondary trade for your people, something you have failed to do. Do *not* presume to speak to me of doing what is best for my people when you haven't even tried to aid those under your protection."

Stay brave. Use what I know. If I fail, the world may very well pay the price.

She swung around, her eyes landing on Lord Holdenberg. "And you, Lord Holdenberg. You claimed the floods two years ago wiped out your lands' harvest *and* stores and begged for help from the crown. And yet your clothing is made of the finest material—more expensive than Lord Vitkovci's, even—and at the last meeting, you rode an Andalusian horse—a breed not native to Mullberg that was obviously imported. It seems Faina and I have been unnecessarily lenient on you, and we should perhaps hold an audit to see just how you have used the crown's money."

Snow White narrowed her eyes at the pudgy lord, who wiped sweat from his forehead. "Y-your Majesty," he babbled.

Snow White ignored him, she was already moving on to Lord Gossler. "And surely, Lord Gossler, you do not think I have forgotten you? Or perhaps you think I am unaware of the bribes you've been taking from guilds. Or really, I say bribes, but we might as well call it what it is: extortion. You require extra taxes from some guilds that you have *not* reported. It is something I have let slide thus far given that you have kept the amount low—and frankly I have had greater concerns—but perhaps I ought to rethink the matter, for I cannot leave a crooked man in a position of power."

"And last but not least, Lord Vitkovci." Snow White smiled at the old lord.

He raised his eyebrows. "I have done nothing dubious, nor have I borrowed money and cheated the crown. I have no sins to pardon."

"You are correct," Snow White said evenly. "Your son, however, is an entirely different matter."

Lord Vitkovci turned ashen.

"The monarchy of Mullberg has always encouraged conversation with its people, which is how—six months ago—I received the first few reports of your *son* beating his vassals and punishing them for crimes they supposedly committed without any proof. Even now, there is a set of documents on my desk recording how I have meticulously built my case against him for the day I can press charges. Because unlike your son, *I am not unjust.*" Snow White hissed. "Your actions today may aid me in deciding whether he is beyond reformation or might learn if given the proper incentive—after an appropriate punishment, of course."

Snow White studied the lords' faces, watching the tell-tale trembling of their muscles and their darting eyes.

They were afraid.

It pains me that the truth makes them fear me, but I do not—and will not—regret this.

"I will crush each of you without moving a single soldier," Snow White promised as she stared each man in the face. "I *am* a princess. Though I might not speak well, I watch. I listen. I read. And I *remember well.*"

"Your Majesty, a good ruler would not threaten us," Lord Vitkovci said.

The sudden upgrade to her royal title did not escape her. *They finally are listening!*

Snow White smiled. "I'm afraid I *haven't* been a good ruler. Not yet, anyway. But I have always been just. Right now, much more hangs in balance in the world than your sense of duty. If

Faina falls and Mullberg trembles, there is no telling how we will tip the scale. And *that* is something I will use all of my power to prevent from happening."

She waited until they finally looked up and faced her. "I am *done* being passive," she said firmly. "And I will no longer allow others to dictate my decisions. Follow my orders, or you will discover how true of a monarch I can be."

Leyen stared at his feet. Holdenberg was still sweating profusely, and Gossler ran his hands through his hair.

It was Lord Vitkovci who went down on one knee. "What is it you command, Your Majesty?"

※

SNOW WHITE—WITH aid from Marzell—spent two hours explaining to the lords what the next move would be.

When the lords bowed and strode off to return to the manor to muster their troops—with Gregori, Oswald, and Rupert trotting at their heels—Snow White could not hold back any longer.

She darted behind the safety of a tree and plopped down, knock-kneed and breathing shakily.

I did it. I convinced them to follow me. I wanted to bite my tongue off on two separate occasions when I thought I might die of fright after stammering, but I made it.

"Well done, Snow White."

Snow White pushed her hair out of her eyes and weakly smiled at Fritz as he crouched down in front of her. She took the waterskin he offered and gratefully sipped at it. "Thank you. I feel like I was run down by a herd of Baris' wild horses."

Fritz smiled. "You reached beyond your fear and showed them who you really are."

Yes, and if Marzell hadn't shooed them off to collect their troops, I might have swooned like an idiot. She stared at the waterskin, mostly to distract herself from her self-satisfying desire to lean against Fritz and fall asleep.

Fortunately, Angel marched around the tree, yanking Snow White from her thoughts. "I knew you had it in you." The herb wizard's apprentice sounded just as smug as her smile looked as she planted her hands on her hips. "You've always been a bright one—or so magic-user gossip said."

"How did you *know* all of that?" Marzell asked.

Snow White shrugged. "It's all in the reports."

"The reports from *what*?" Wendal asked. "You cited proof from the treasury department, peasants, and what must have surely been reports from royal spies. Your advisors cannot know all of this."

"I meant *all* the reports," Snow White said, somewhat confused by their puzzlement. "I heard about Vitkovci's son when I was reading over reports recorded during the grievance days when peasants can bring their complaints before Common Courts in Glitzern. I had noticed Holdenberg's obvious discrepancies at the first meeting with him, and I've been keeping an eye on Leyen's accounts since Stepmother first granted him leniency. One of my spies heard grumblings from several different guilds, which is how Gossler's iniquities came to light."

"So, what you mean to say," Fritz said carefully, "is that you read *all* the reports... from every facet of Mullberg government?"

Snow White shifted slightly, aware that everyone was studying her with surprise. "I thought that if I cannot speak, I might as well make sure I am well informed. It's easier to talk when I have notes I can read off," she muttered shyly.

Angel whistled lowly. "Your tutors might have thought they were merely encouraging your mind when they made you a reader, but you have got to be the most knowledgeable—and *patient*—monarch I've met to make such an effort to read all of that. Most rulers just delegate."

"I wanted to be a good princess." Snow White cleared her throat and awkwardly rested her hands on her knees.

"I don't know that you'll be a 'good' queen," Marzell said slowly. "That seems too tame of a word to describe you."

"The Great," Aldelbert said. For once, he was not beaming. Instead, his expression was thoughtful as he studied Snow White with care. "You will be Queen Snow White, The Great," he said. "Because you will lead others to achieve what most deem impossible, even if they question their sanity along the way."

"So may it be," Fritz said.

"So may it be," the others echoed.

Snow White pressed her lips together, but for the first time in months, perhaps years, she began to wonder...

Maybe I can be a good queen. Perhaps it'll just look different from the way Papa ruled with great justice, and the kind firmness Faina achieved in her regency.

Perhaps the people won't mind a bookish queen.

But before I get carried away, we must prepare ourselves. This afternoon, we will save Faina, and I'm going to shatter that wretched mirror with my own hands!

༶

FRITZ WATCHED Snow White meticulously draw out the rough layout of the palace in a patch of dirt.

Gregori snoozed under the shade of a tree while Oswald and Rupert watered the horses, and Aldelbert and Wendal checked their gear.

"You already explained the plan to the lords so well, do you really think this is necessary?" Marzell asked as he opened a saddlebag and removed some provisions for an impatient—and hungry—Angel.

"The lords will return here so we can set out together." Snow White didn't look away from her illustration and instead paused, then backtracked and added details. "Regardless of whether or not they've set foot in these parts of the palace, it is best to give us *all* a clear depiction of the plan so we might notice any potential pitfalls, and so we are all working off the same mental image."

Marzell thought for a moment, then nodded. He looked like he was going to reply, but Angel prodded him.

"This isn't enough food," she said.

"Oh, sorry, were you going to share with Snow White?" Marzell asked as he dug in his saddle pack again.

Angel shook her head. "No, I'm just really hungry."

While Marzell gaped at the apprentice, Fritz stepped from one shadow to the next, drawing closer to Snow White.

Her forehead was puckered in her concentration, and she pursed her red lips as she studied her illustration with slightly narrowed eyes. She had been glorious when confronting the lords, and Fritz found himself watching her yet again. He'd been glancing at her more often than usual since she had woken up.

It's like I must constantly reassure myself that she really is awake and here with us. That the spell placed on her has been broken and she really does live again.

If Fritz had been any less loyal—or perhaps had any less concern for Mullberg's future and what could happen to the continent if they failed—he would give in to the temptation to wrap his arms around Snow White and ask her to stay behind.

But he knew she needed to be in the battle. She needed to lead them, because now only Snow White could save Faina.

Loving her is a careful balance of desiring to keep her from harm and recognizing the danger she must face.

Fritz shifted slightly. *At least I can be with her. I can protect her from the shadows, and I will slay anything—man, woman, or creature—that dares to even try to harm her.*

He didn't think she was aware of his feelings—or at least the depth of them. It seemed a little unlikely, after all, that he would fall for her so quickly.

But when he saw her—pale and deadly still...Fritz was not going to fret over a small thing like time.

He loved Snow White, and he had almost lost her. He would not let that happen again.

When this is over, and Mullberg has been saved, I will tell her. But until then, I'd rather be a source of strength, and be given the chance to remain close to her so I can guard her in this darkness. Her safety is more important than any petty comfort I might receive.

Snow White nodded in approval when she finished her sketch. She then looked up and caught sight of him, lingering in the shadows.

"I think it's finished." She tapped her stick on the ground, then strolled in his direction. "Or at least, it is close enough that everyone will reach a better understanding of the plan." Her blue eyes were still slightly narrowed in thought as she pushed a stray black curl out of her face.

I wonder how many realize that her beauty—her blue eyes and perfect curls—cloak a mind of equal parts love and cunning intelligence.

Snow White tossed her stick aside and brushed her hands off when she reached him. She offered him a smile that Fritz couldn't help but return, then paused. Her cheeks warmed to a fetching pink as she tucked her hands in Fritz's.

"Will you come look it over—and point out any inaccuracies?" she asked his feet.

"Of course." Fritz, still holding her hand, stepped out of the shadows and into the light. She walked at his side, her grasp on his hand tight, even if she didn't look at him.

For a moment, just before they reached her illustration, Fritz allowed himself a moment of hope.

Perhaps...it is possible she feels the same for me.

CHAPTER 18
MARCH ON GLITZERN

Snow White's mouth turned dry as she stared at the side entrance of Glitzern. *This is it. We're infiltrating the palace. We have three hours before, according to our scouts, Grandfather's forces arrive in Hurra. I hope we can secure everything by then.*

She breathed in deeply through her nose in an effort to calm her nerves as she stood in the shadows, watching servants flow in and out of the palace. Fritz stood at her side. Though his posture was casual, he never stopped searching the crowds, watching for potential threats.

Marzell stood with Aldelbert and Angel, chatting—though Aldelbert laughed a bit too loudly to avoid notice. Wendal and Rupert were busy supporting Gregori, who tilted from one side to the other as he slept on his feet.

"We should have hired a cart and pony to drag his giant carcass for us," Wendal grumbled.

"Let's just hope he actually *wakes up* when we enter—oof." Rupert sagged visibly when Gregori tilted in his direction, nearly flattening the leaner man.

A wagon full of straw rolled past. Oswald hopped out of it and trotted over to Snow White, Angel, and the rest of the warriors.

"The other lords are in place, as are their men," Oswald said. "We're free to proceed."

Snow White nodded once, then again as if she could nod conviction into existence.

"Ready, Princess?" Angel asked with a wink.

Beside her, Marzell wrinkled his forehead, but he refrained from asking Snow White to stay behind. (He had only made the request once and had taken her refusal surprisingly well.)

Perhaps he's concerned about what unflattering information I have on his family? He needn't worry; I don't have much, or I would never have sought him out all those weeks ago.

Snow White gazed up at the reddish-brown stone castle. *Wait for us, Faina. We're coming!*

"I am ready," she said. "Let's go."

She rolled her shoulders back, then strode across the courtyard—unable to keep all the stiffness out of her shoulders. Her red cloak flared around her, but no one gave her a second look until she climbed the five stairs that led to the secondary entrance.

The two guards posted there stood at attention, the ram of Mullberg emblazoned on the tunics that covered their chainmail. "Please state your business," the one on the left asked.

Snow White pushed her hood back so it only covered her hair, not her face.

The guard on the right swore when he saw her face, but the left guard kept a placid look on his face. "If you'd like to step just inside," he said calmly.

Snow White ducked into the castle, blinking in the much dimmer light. She stood aside, letting Angel and the other warriors troop inside like a line of ants.

"Your Highness," the left guard whispered. "What are you *doing* here? If the Queen finds you..." He stared at her, waiting for an answer.

Snow White wanted to suck her neck into her shoulders, but

she made herself look the soldier in the eyes. *If I told off four lords, I can talk to a palace guard.* "We're here to—" her voice stopped in a squeak. She cleared her throat, minutely shook her head, and tried again. "We're here for Faina. We mean to secure h-her for her own safety."

Relief rippled through both of the guards, but they moved to stand at attention. "Your orders?"

Snow White glanced at Marzell, hoping he would tell the men their plan.

Marzell merely raised an eyebrow at her and waited with the others.

Childhood friends are insufferable know-it-alls.

Snow White licked her lips. "Send word to the guards at the other palace entrance points. L-lord Vitkovci, Lord Gossler, Lord Leyen, and Lord Holdenberg are waiting with small squads of soldiers. You need to let them inside. Get word to the rest of the palace guard not to attack them but to pull back instead. We want to take Faina safely—when she's alone, without any palace guards or servants nearby. Most importantly, we want to take her by surprise. T-take precautions, and be subtle."

Lest she order someone to attack us and stir up even more trouble.

"Yes, Your Highness," the soldiers said in unison.

"Can you get word to Flora?" Snow White asked, naming the castle housekeeper. When the soldiers nodded, Snow White added. "Tell her to meet me in Faina's study. Thank you."

The soldiers bowed slightly, then strode off, moving at a quick clip.

Snow White tugged on her cloak, wishing she could cast it off. She was starting to sweat from adrenaline and anxiety. *What a wonderful combination.* But as she did not account for an uproar in this strategy caused by being recognized, she left the hood up.

"We made it inside!" Aldelbert puffed his chest in arrogance.

"That was disappointingly easy," Oswald complained.

Snow White led the way down the hallway. "Ideally, strategies are *supposed* to make things easy. It's when they go wrong that things get difficult."

"Do you think they'll manage to keep things quiet?" Angel asked.

"If things have been half as bad as my contacts claim, they'll make the effort," Gregori said. He was at the back of their group, his stance wary and his eyes wide open, as if he hadn't been napping mere minutes ago.

Rupert seemed to be thinking along the same lines, for he glared up at the merchant heir.

Oswald folded his arms behind his head and, instead of moving with the urgency that Snow White did, swaggered along. "The palace guards let the other lords in, and...?"

Snow White glanced at him and got the general feeling he was asking her just to give her mind something to fixate on and not because he had forgotten her painstakingly explained plan. "If we don't meet any resistance, we'll convene on Faina after I learn her location from Flora."

Wendal frowned thoughtfully. "You really think the guards will turn on you if Faina orders it?"

"Perhaps, but the likelihood is low." Snow White turned right at a hallway intersection and started up a stone staircase. "I'm more concerned there might be magical constructs."

"Oh," Oswald said. "*Oh*."

"If Faina is not aware of our arrival, could we not assume there won't be any constructs?" Marzell asked.

"Previously we thought a rogue mage had made them, but since Faina is likely under the influence of a magic artifact, wouldn't that mean she had to create them herself?" Rupert asked.

"Not necessarily," Angel said. Her voice lacked its usual carefree quality, and she narrowed her gaze as she cleared the last step and followed Snow White as she swept into the second floor of the palace. "If the mirror has a power source, it can feed off of it and cast the constructs itself."

"Could a mirror really be so *sentient*? And what kind of power source are we talking about?" Gregori asked.

"A human one," Angel said grimly. "As for sentience, it's best to follow Lord Vitkovci's example and compare it to the weapons of the Legendary Magic Knights of Sole. The weapons—while not technically alive—have preferences, goals, and rules they abide by."

Snow White paused outside an ornate door. She cracked the door open and pressed her head in the narrow gap, relaxing when she saw that although the curtains were drawn, there were no lit lamps or fire in the fire place. *It's empty. Thank goodness. I didn't think Faina would be here—she rarely came here since her headaches increased in pain and length, but I didn't know for certain.*

Snow White pushed the door completely open and motioned for everyone to enter. "Those weapons, though, they are not *that* old considering our continent's age," Snow White said. "I recall reading of some artifacts that are thousands of years old. Aren't they far stronger?"

"Yes," Angel said. "But we must hope one of those isn't what has Faina in its clutches."

"Why?" Aldelbert asked as he perused one of the sturdy bookshelves.

"Because if it is, there's a reasonably good chance we'll die," Angel said wryly.

Snow White grimaced at the dire prediction. "Wendal, when we leave the study, can you start to trail farther behind us?"

"Of course, Your Highness," Wendal said.

"Thank you. When we move, stay back as far as possible without risking yourself, and hide in the shadows if possible," Snow White said.

"You want to use him as back-up?" Aldelbert asked. "Wendal is excellent at that role."

"No," Snow White said. "I want him free to run and warn the other teams if we encounter constructs."

Oswald grimaced. "You are not the happiest ray of sunshine to be around, you know?"

Snow White eyed the documents piled high on the desk. *It looks like Faina hasn't done anything since I left.* She poked at a few of the papers before she replied, "I don't care about being optimistic. I care about finishing our mission with as few casualties as possible."

There was a knock, and the door cracked open. "Your Highness?"

Snow White smiled, at ease with the longtime servant. "Flora, come in."

A middle-aged woman in a simple dress—her hair pulled back in a tidy but simple braid—slipped inside. When she set eyes on Snow White, her crisp austerity drooped, and she smiled. "Princess, I am so glad to see you—unharmed."

Snow White nodded. "Yes, thanks to the efforts of my companions: the Seven Warriors and Angel."

"How do you do." The woman very properly curtsied to them, then shifted her attention back to Snow White. "Your Highness —you are in danger here."

"I'm aware of that, but Faina's condition poses a threat to more than just me," Snow White said.

"Then you are here...?"

"To subdue her—and hopefully free her from whatever is affecting her so," Snow White said.

Flora held her hand over her heart—which, given how carefully she held herself, was about the equivalent to a swoon for her. "So, you know there is something wrong with her? Something magical?"

"Absolutely," Snow White said. "Stepmother would never act this way. It is the work of dark magic, and we intend to shut it off and save her."

Flora's slight smile grew a little. "Thank you. She is our queen, but we fear..." she trailed off.

"No one is going to harm Faina under my orders," Snow White assured her. "But I'd like the matter to be as efficient as possible. To begin with, I need you to start drawing the servants back. You can remain near the kitchens and in the servants' wing, but I want everyone out of all other parts of Glitzern. We are receiving support and military help from four lords. I do not want their troops worrying about encountering servants."

Or having to rescue them.

Flora, a born taskmaster, straightened—her vigor renewed at the thought of labor to be done. "Yes, Your Highness. I will begin to do so immediately. May I help in any other way?"

"Yes. Do you know where Faina is right now?" Snow White asked.

"She was in her quarters not an hour ago," Flora said. "But I cannot be certain she has remained there."

If the mirror is controlling her, there is a good possibility she is still there. It was my first guess anyway.

"Excellent. Thank you, Flora. That will be all."

The housekeeper gave Snow White a quick curtsey. "Of course, Your Highness." She slipped out of the study and back into the hallway, a look of grim determination settling on her face.

Snow White leaned against a bookshelf, taking comfort in the leather-bound books. "And now we wait."

"How much time will you give her?" Marzell asked.

"A quarter of an hour," Snow White said.

"That's not very long," Oswald said.

"The longer it takes for us to move, the bigger the chance Faina will hear of it and will have time to prepare," Snow White said. "But at the same time, we cannot leap foolishly into battle. I'm trying to strike a balance between the two."

"Fifteen minutes should be adequate," Fritz said. "The servants will work together."

"We'll meet up with Lord Vitkovci and the other forces at Faina's rooms?" Rupert asked.

Snow White nodded. "They've been instructed to send a soldier to this study once they get their forces inside. I expect we'll see them soon, actually." Snow White trailed a finger down a book spine. "When they arrive, we will tell them our target is Faina's quarters, and they'll report back to their lord."

"Very well," Aldelbert said. "Since we have nothing better to do, you may all help me decide what pose I should strike for my next portrait!"

Angel snorted and studied a palm-sized statue of a charging ram fashioned from a single—*giant*—emerald.

Wendal, however, appeared to get a little teary eyed. "Always so generous, My Lord!"

Oswald shivered. "Ugh. Hey, fragile flower, want to have a go? I'd rather fight than listen to Lord Fruitcake."

Rupert snorted. "I always welcome a time to prove your own stupidity to you."

Snow White cleared her throat as the two boys circled each other. "If you upset a single paper or ruin a piece of furniture, I will require your presence at court for the next year."

Oswald scratched his scalp, and Rupert frowned thoughtfully.

"I bet I can find the most boring book in here," Oswald said finally.

"You're on."

Marzell rubbed his eyes like a tired mother. "You two could turn *breathing* into a competition."

Oswald—who had been perusing a shelf—paused. "How would we do that?"

"You could see who can hold their breath longer," Gregori said wryly. "If we're lucky, you *both* will pass out."

Snow White cracked a smile as she plopped down in an armchair. Fritz casually shifted so he stood directly next to her. "How are you feeling?" he asked as they watched Rupert hop on a stool to grab a book that Oswald was jumping for.

Snow White sucked a deep breath in. "Worried. I'm terrified that something will go wrong," she admitted. "I wonder if I have taken on more than I can manage."

Fritz shook his head. "You've proven yourself, and your stepmother loves you." He paused, then added, "No matter what happens, I'll see to your safety."

"No promises that everything will go perfectly? That's not a good sign," Snow White laughed nervously.

"The coming events don't matter as long as we get the outcome you desire," Fritz said. "And we *will* get it."

The assurance made Snow White sit a little straighter in her chair. "Thank you," she said. "I highly doubt we'll sneak through unscathed after witnessing the mirror's work with the constructs. But you're right. We can adjust our strategy for any circumstance."

Fritz smiled and took her hand in his just long enough to squeeze it before he turned to watch the door, brushing his fingers against the hunting knife strapped to his belt.

There was a hurried knock on the door in the pattern Snow White had meticulously insisted the lords learn for signaling purposes. "Your Highness?" A soldier holding his helm in his hands and bearing hair streaked with sweat poked his head inside the study.

He brought with him the faint metallic scent of blood.

Snow White stood up, her concern making her zero-in on the soldier and forget her usual shyness. "Enter—what's wrong?"

The soldier saluted and kicked the door shut behind him. "Your Highness. Lord Gossler's, Lord Leyen's, and Lord Holdenberg's troops have run into resistance."

"From Mullberg troops?" Snow White asked.

The soldier shook his head. "Monsters. Lord Vitkovci says

they are the magical constructs you discussed in your strategy meeting."

Rats! I knew it wasn't likely we would slip past without the mirror acting out somehow. But I had hoped it wouldn't happen until we were already confronting Faina! We haven't even had a chance to consolidate our forces. Time to change the plan.

"Lord Vitkovci has not encountered any?" Snow White asked.

"No. They are concentrated near the main entrance of the castle. Lord Gossler's troops stumbled on a herd of them, Lord Leyen another. Lord Holdenberg split his troops to support them," the soldier reported.

"What type of constructs are they?"

"There're two: one looks like a sort of shadowy human that disappears once stabbed. The other is much bigger, can't be stabbed, and moves on its front arms and back legs. There's a regular sea of the shadowy ones and three of the big uglies. Due to your instruction, they know how to defeat both types."

So it is *the constructs we've encountered before. I'm not sure if that's a good thing or a bad thing, but at least it means this mirror must not have many types of constructs at its disposal. Either that, or these are the two easiest to make—a very unhappy thought.*

"Have the servants evacuated those areas?" Snow White asked.

The soldier nodded. "Except the guards—they were joining forces with Lord Gossler when I passed through."

Snow White smiled slightly, gladdened to hear that in the heat of a fight, the palace guards stood faithful. "Excellent. Despite the lords' knowledge, I want Lord Marzell and Fritz to give you a detailed explanation on fighting the bigger constructs. They're far trickier, so you must be absolutely certain you know how to fight them. And I need a moment to plan our next move, anyway."

Fritz bowed slightly at the soldier, but Marzell smiled and hooked a leg of a wooden chair with his foot and pulled it closer to him. "Come sit down, man. You look like you've been running," he invited.

The soldier gratefully collapsed in the chair and wiped sweat from his face. "Thank you, Your Lordship."

"Of course. Now, Fritz, correct me if I am wrong, but the large constructs..."

Marzell's voice faded from Snow White's attention as she pressed her fingertips together and frowned in concentration.

We need to strike Faina now, but it would be foolhardy to go after her with just the Seven Warriors. If we had time, I'd have Wendal or Fritz scout her room, but it would take at least an hour for them to accomplish such a task without getting caught.

There is comfort, however, in that the constructs must take power to create—or run. The mirror only sent two of the large constructs after me, and it waited quite a while after its first attempt to send them. Even if it spent most of its power on sending the creatures and powering them at such a far distance, that there are only three of the big ones in the fight thus far is rather telling.

Unless the mirror has some other terrible construct that it hasn't shown off yet which requires even more power.

Snow White wanted to groan and flop back in her chair, but she kept her eyes narrowed and her back straight.

But if we free Faina, would that stop the mirror? I don't know that it matters—I'll take a hammer to the thing myself. So, what would be the best arrangement?

Snow White pursed her lips as she thought, a new plan slowly forming. When she was satisfied with it, she nodded, then turned her gaze to the soldier, who was still chatting with Marzell.

"Do you understand the constructs' weak points—and how to take advantage of them?" Snow White asked the soldier.

The soldier rocketed to his feet. "Yes, Your Highness."

"Will you be able to clearly and concisely relay these details to the lords?"

"Yes, Your Highness!"

Snow White smiled slightly. "Excellent. Your superiors did well in sending you. I do have a message for you to take back to Lord Vitkovci."

The soldier saluted her smartly. "It will be my honor to carry the message."

Snow White stood and tugged gently on her skirt. "Though I am thankful for your enthusiasm, there's no need to be so formal. Please, sit again. You'll be running back soon enough."

The soldier sank back into his chair, glancing around the study to gauge the reactions of the Seven Warriors.

Gregori winked at the man, but Oswald and Rupert were too involved in their book-themed competition to pay him any mind.

"What is your new strategy?" Fritz asked.

"Surely you will want me to go to the front lines, so I might inspire others with my dazzling swordplay!" Aldelbert declared.

"My Lord!" Wendal cheered.

"Angel, myself, and the Seven Warriors will continue to Faina's quarters," Snow White said. "I want Lord Vitkovci to join us with a small contingent of his men. The rest he can place under the order of whatever Lord is hurting the most—Leyen, I'd bet, if the soldiers are still mostly linking up with Gossler."

"Knowing the constructs are about, you still mean to go with us to capture Faina?" Marzell's forehead wrinkled like cracking ice. "It will be dangerous."

"It doesn't matter. I stand the best chance of getting through to Faina," Snow White said.

"Or seeing you might make her hysterical," Gregori pointed out.

"Either reaction should make her easier to capture," Snow White said. "If she's hysterical, it means she won't pay attention to any of you."

"A good plan," Fritz said.

Marzell eyed his friend. "I thought you would be on my side. Going to Faina's room will put her in danger."

Fritz shrugged. "I am on whatever side gives us a better chance of winning. I trust my skills enough to believe I can keep her safe."

Oswald just about dropped the book on forest fungus he was inspecting. "*Two* whole sentences from the mute lazybones? Slap my hands, and call me pretty!"

Rupert eyed Oswald. "*Why?* Fritz speaking so much is impressive—not disturbing."

"It's a good plan," Gregori said, disrupting the argument before it could begin. "If we encounter a great many constructs, we can always regroup. But I side with Snow White. If we give Faina too much time, I think it's likely there will only be more enemies, and we'll find it harder to fight our way to her."

"Sounds right as rain to me," Angel said in her sing-song voice. "Though if Faina offers you food, I'd suggest you refuse them this time, Snow White."

Snow White sighed. "I suppose I deserve that."

"You do," Angel said. "I lost several years of my life finding you collapsed like that. I hope you're sorry."

"Very much so." Snow White once again turned her attention to the soldier. "Do you understand what you are to tell the lords?"

"I am to instruct them again how to kill the large constructs, and tell Lord Vitkovci to divide his forces—leaving some behind to fortify the squads that need it most—and march with the remaining soldiers to Queen Faina's rooms where he will meet you," the soldier said.

"Excellent. Wendal?" Snow White turned to the attendant. "Would you escort this soldier back to the lords?"

Wendal frowned and glanced at Aldelbert.

"You can return here once he reaches safety. There is no need to wait for him to deliver the news," Snow White said.

He's my first choice since he's so sneaky, and I'd bet my favorite horse he knows the palace layout better than the other warriors, but I can send Fritz if I must.

Aldelbert made a shooing motion at Wendal, but the attendant ignored it and narrowed his eyes in thought. Snow White could see he made up his mind when he nodded and flicked his eyes to her.

Wendal bowed slightly. "I am your servant, Your Highness."

"Thank you, Wendal. Both of you stay safe," Snow White said.

Wendal motioned for the soldier to follow him out of the study. He already had three daggers in place by the time he slipped out the door.

"Your Highness." The soldier gave Snow White a choppy bow, then hurried after Wendal, strapping his helmet back in place before he pulled the door shut behind them.

Oswald stared at the shut door and scratched his cheek. "What's the point of sending a messenger if you have to send one of us to go with him?"

"Because I want to make certain our messenger lives to deliver the message," Snow White said grimly.

❧

WHILE THE WARRIORS waited for Wendal to return, they checked over their equipment and prepared again for the fight that loomed ominously ahead of them. (Aldelbert attempted to lead them in a round of glory stretches. Surprisingly, Oswald and Rupert followed them faithfully.)

Snow White circled the desk, paging through the stacks of reports that had built up in her absence. As she frowned over every new report, she only vaguely noticed Angel when she settled down in the chair Snow White had abandoned.

"You're doing quite well, you know," Angel said without any sort of preamble.

Snow White blinked. "I beg your pardon?"

"This whole leadership thing," Angel said. "You're leading no small number of troops into battle. Or at least into a strategic mission. And you're not just bossing around your little lordlings, but four adult lords as well."

Snow White grimaced.

"You disagree?" Angel asked.

Snow White shook her head. "Not exactly. It is merely that the thought of calling myself a leader makes me feel ill."

"You could think of them as your minions instead," Angel coached.

"*Minions?* That is not at all appropriate."

Angel rolled her eyes. "Of course it's not if you say it with such disapproval in your voice."

Snow White cracked a smile. "Though I appreciate your humor, I'm afraid as little as I like it, I must accept that I am indeed leading a large force of men. I *must* remember because I need to understand that every life under my command is precious and not to be taken lightly."

Angel scratched her nose as she studied Snow White. "I know you're upset because you feel like Faina coddled you perhaps too much, but she might have chosen not to push you because she knew you'd be a great queen and that eventually you would decide to move forward despite your fear and shortcomings. She likely knew she would do more damage by forcing it rather than letting you reason it out yourself."

"I don't blame her for it at all," Snow White said. "It is myself that I am most disappointed in."

"Snow White."

Angel didn't move from the relaxed, sprawled position in the chair. But her change of intonation—the serious edge that seemed to line her voice—made Snow White look up.

"Release the grudges you're holding against yourself," Angel said. "Or one day they will become your undoing."

Snow White set the papers she was holding back on her desk. "What do you mean?"

"If you continue to dwell on your short-comings, you will drive yourself mad. You are human. You *will* make mistakes. And while I admire your spirit—for it means you will work actively to make as few errors as possible and learn from them—I can say if you do not learn to forgive yourself for your past iniquities, years from now it will be *you* we are rescuing. Such thoughts open the doorway to darkness."

Snow White stilled as she puzzled through the thought. She could see the wisdom in Angel's words, but she didn't know quite how to respond. In the end, she said the only thing she could say, "Thank you, Angel."

The apprentice dropped the air of gravity and winked. "Always glad to help, Your Highness. Which is why, once this is over, I'm going to hold an informational meeting with you so we can discuss what you can accept from strangers and what you should *not* accept from strangers."

Snow White cracked another smile but stilled when there was a knock on the door.

Wendal opened the door and slipped inside. "It's done," he said. "I dropped the messenger off—practically on Lord Vitkovci's head."

"Did you meet any resistance?" Fritz asked.

Wendal sharply nodded. "We encountered three of the humanoid constructs on the way to the others. I dispatched them with no difficulties."

"Thank you, Wendal," Snow White said. "Are we ready to leave?"

The Seven Warriors exchanged nods and shrugs.

"I believe we are, Your Highness," Marzell said.

"Then let us depart for Faina's private quarters," Snow White said.

"Finally," Oswald grunted. He stomped across the study, his boots thumping heavily on the plush, blue rug. "Let's get to the *fighting!*"

"Brute," Rupert said as he adjusted his belt.

SNOW WHITE

Snow White and Angel left the study together. Angel suspiciously peered up and down the hallway, but Snow White started off, indicating the direction they needed to go. "It's this way," she called.

Fritz joined Snow White, stationing himself at her left side. His steps were quiet, and he moved as smoothly as water—especially compared to Oswald, who stomped with the force of a charging bull as he zipped ahead.

"Don't get too far ahead, Oswald," Marzell cautioned him. "You don't know where we are going."

Oswald grumbled, but he slowed down some.

Aldelbert trotted to catch up—with Wendal trailing the group as Snow White had requested.

"I must be on the front lines," Aldelbert declared.

"Why?" Oswald drawled. "So your shining greatness can blind the enemy?"

Aldelbert beamed. "I *was* going to say because someone needed to make certain you were not trampled, but your idea is—surprisingly—superior."

Oswald stared at Aldelbert. "I think I ought to hit you," he announced.

Rupert scoffed from his position in the back of the group where he lagged with Gregori. "So your intelligence level has fallen so greatly you cannot tell when even *Lord Aldelbert* is mocking you?"

"This way." Snow White ignored the argument and turned down a different hallway.

Oswald started to squawk a reply, but Fritz held up his hand.

"What is it?" Marzell asked.

Fritz stared down the hallway, his head tilted slightly as he listened. "Fighting."

Snow White squinted in concentration, but try as she might, she couldn't hear anything besides the quiet tap of the party members' boots on the stone floor.

"It must be the other lords," Marzell said.

"Do I need to take us a different route?" Snow White asked.

Fritz shook his head. "They're still far away. If we get too close, I will say something."

"We should be quiet, though," Marzell said. "There is no sense alerting the constructs to our movements."

"Message received, *leader*," Oswald said wryly. "We'll make like Fritz and keep our mouths shut."

Snow White furrowed her brow—still straining to hear any sound of conflict—as she led the Seven Warriors through Glitzern palace.

Unfortunately, Faina's quarters were with Snow White's in the royal wing—a small sliver of the castle that housed bedrooms for the royal family, a private parlor, and a nursery. This meant they had to cross a great deal of the castle to reach the wing—although perhaps the remoteness was actually fortunate, for it meant Faina was isolated, and the conflict was unlikely to involve anyone besides the lords and their forces.

They passed through the central part of the palace—where the throne room, ball rooms, dining hall, and other such rooms were located—without meeting anyone. But Snow White could have sworn she *felt* something.

It was a dirty, misty feeling—like the smoggy smoke that clogged up the air when someone tried to burn wet leaves. It made it harder to breathe. Even more unsettling, it simultaneously pressed down on Snow White as if it could flatten her against the ground *and* seemed to claw at her throat.

Snow White glanced at the rest of the party. She could sense their unease. Fritz grew that sharp edge he showed whenever he fought, and he moved more wolf-like as he carefully glanced ahead and behind them. Marzell shivered and rubbed the back of his neck, Rupert sneezed six times in a row, and Gregori fingered the trigger of his crossbow.

At the head of the party, Oswald slouched more than usual,

and Aldelbert peered at the back of the party to exchange a rare glance of concern with Wendal.

Most markedly, however, was Angel. She frowned as she stared in the general direction of the throne room, an unfathomable expression in her silver eyes.

Despite the odd sensation, no constructs sprang at them, and the feeling started to diminish as they exited the central part of the palace.

Conversely, it wasn't until roughly two turns before the royal wing that Snow White finally heard the faints sounds of the fight—the clash of weapons and raised voices shouting instructions. (She was fairly certain that was Lord Holdenberg who was bellowing so loud, he made the crystal chandelier overhead wobble.)

They proceeded down the few remaining twists in the hallway with markedly increased concern.

Wendal moved to the front of the party, though he pressed himself against the wall and slithered in the shadows.

When Snow White would point in the direction they needed to go, Wendal slipped ahead of them, made an inspection, then returned.

The royal wing was quiet as death when they stepped onto its threshold. Nothing in the hall stirred, even as Snow White motioned for everyone to press themselves into a small inlet in the wall that held a dried-out water fountain studded with diamonds.

"We must have beaten Lord Vitkovci here," Marzell whispered.

"It is understandable. He had to divide his troops before coming," Snow White murmured.

"Which door is it, Your Highness?" Gregori asked in his soothing tenor voice.

Snow White pointed to it. "The one with the Mullberg flag hanging above it."

"Do you hear anything, Fritz?" Rupert asked.

Fritz shook his head. "It is strangely still."

Wendal scratched his chin with one of his daggers. "She doesn't have any guards—or they were warned ahead of time by the servants and deserted their post."

"We would occasionally have guards at the entrance to the royal wing, but not often," Snow White said. "But we never had guards outside our bedrooms."

Oswald grunted. "Doesn't matter, does it? She still knows we're here. Or at least the mirror does, or the constructs wouldn't be attacking."

Rupert opened his mouth to speak, but Marzell slapped his hand over the dark-haired warrior's mouth. "So we need to prepare ourselves for a fight, then?" he asked, ignoring the dirty look Rupert gave him.

Snow White nodded. "I would agree with that assumption."

Gregori peered down the hallway, looking back the way they had come. "I believe Lord Vitkovci has arrived."

Snow White leaned out of the inlet, making eye contact with Lord Vitkovci and roughly twenty soldiers stalking down the hallway.

Lord Vitkovci threw his hand up, halting his troops, though he kept walking and joined Snow White, Angel, and the Seven Warriors in their inlet.

"Your Majesty," he bowed, persisting with the title upgrade.

"Lord Vitkovci." Snow White inclined her head in recognition. "How was the fight when you left it?"

"Going better. Lord Gossler's forces already took down two of the larger constructs—though another one showed up just as I was leaving."

"Do you foresee any difficulties in their battle?" Marzell asked.

"If you're inquiring as to whether I think they'll win, the answer is yes," Lord Vitkovci said.

"The arrival of the additional construct is troubling," Snow White said.

Fritz tilted his head. "Why?"

"Because it implies that the dark magic will continue to supply constructs until it is stopped," Snow White said grimly.

"Then we had better get moving, hadn't we?" Angel asked.

Snow White nodded. She started to step out of the inlet but hesitated. She already had a plan formed, but now she had to relay it.

It hasn't been so bad thus far. And the danger of the situation has motivated me quite well. But now I have to address a squadron of soldiers.

Snow White chewed on her lip. She didn't realize she was clenching her fists until Fritz brushed her hand with his. She blinked in surprise, and as she looked up at him, he encircled his much larger hands around her fists.

His touch seemed to clear her mind. *It doesn't matter*, she recognized. *I can be afraid. I can stutter. I can even embarrass myself. As long as the soldiers understand what we need to do!*

Snow White smiled her thanks to Fritz and took a big breath. She stiffly left the inlet and marched directly up to the soldiers.

Lord Vitkovci stood at her side with Angel and the Seven Warriors filling in behind them.

Snow White swallowed hard. She couldn't raise her eyes to look the soldiers in the face, but she managed to drag her gaze up to their chests.

"W-we received word that Queen Faina was last seen in her private q-quarters." Snow White's voice shook, and she spoke in a quiet murmur that would be inaudible for those not surrounding her. *But at least I spoke!* "We will break down the door and enter her rooms—hopefully surprising her, but that is unlikely." She took a moment to turn and point to the door to Faina's bedroom, grateful for the moment of reprieve it bought her.

When she turned back to the soldiers, she tried to raise her gaze high again, but her eyes rebelled, and instead she looked just over the tops of their heads, skimming the silver half-circle their helms made around her.

"We will likely encounter c-c-constructs—like those you have already seen," she said. She took a moment to breathe—a moment that was perhaps a little awkward due to its length. "Four of you will be selected to secure Faina. You are *not* to seriously harm her —though you will need to use force to seize her. The rest of you will do battle with constructs. The Seven Warriors will help where necessary, though they will focus on searching for the mirror."

And once they find it, I will shatter the wretched thing.

She cleared her throat, trying to move the frog that seemed to be caught in her mouth. "The four who seize the queen will be..."

Blast it, I have to look them in the face for this. No getting around it.

Snow White studied the soldiers with narrowed eyes, trying to make strategic decisions and ignore her clammy sweat. "You," she said, pointing to the biggest soldier, "You," she said, seeking out the soldier who had served as the original messenger back in the study, "and you two," she said, choosing the last two who stood with purpose but also seemed the most at ease. (They did not grip their weapons with nervousness, and their faces were free from the pinched expression of fear. With luck, that meant they would be less likely to act on impulse and accidentally injure Faina in the process of capturing her.)

When the soldiers saluted Snow White, she nodded, then carefully maneuvered herself so she was partially screened by Fritz. "Do you understand, Lord Vitkovci?" She cleared her throat and looked to the lord.

"Yes, Your Majesty. We will be ready on your mark." Lord Vitkovci bowed, then turned to speak to his men in a lowered tone.

Snow White, however, motioned for the Seven Warriors and Angel to follow her and marched up to the door. Though her shoulders hunched slightly with relief, her heart still pounded with unnecessary force in her chest, painfully thumping as if it wanted to escape.

"We're ready to enter," Marzell whispered.

Snow White frowned as she sized up the door. "Yes, about that..."

Oswald puffed up his chest. "You want me to kick it down?"

"You can't—not unless you want to break your heel," Snow White said. "The doors are reinforced against entry."

Fritz prodded the doorframe. "The hinges are on the inside of the room, so we cannot remove the door from the frame."

"We could break through it—use a pickaxe to bust a hole through it," Oswald suggested, keeping his voice at a whisper as he glanced at the solid door.

"That would work, but it would give away our position." Snow White shifted, *extremely* aware when Lord Vitkovci and his men drew closer behind them, lining up so they could swarm the room when the door was taken down.

"Then what did you have in mind?" Marzell asked.

Snow White turned to Angel.

The apprentice leaned against the wall, scratching her collar bone. "Hmmm?" she said when she noticed Snow White's gaze, then straightened. "Wait, *me*? Sorry, Princess, but that's not possible."

"I know you can do it," Snow White said.

"I'm so pleased you believe in me," Angel snorted, "but I have to correct you: I haven't the kick of a donkey or horse." She pointed to Oswald and wrinkled her nose. "Scruffy, here, has a better chance of kicking the door down."

Oswald made a sputtering noise that Snow White ignored.

"You can break the door down if you use your magic," Snow White said. She risked glancing back over her shoulder at the soldiers and immediately wished she hadn't. (They watched her with steady expressions, which was almost worse. It meant they intended to do as she ordered, and though she felt certain of her tactics, she was still skeptical of her leadership skills.)

"With my *magic*?" Angel's whisper turned into a quiet scoff. She plucked a sprig of herbs off her ever-present satchel and shook it for emphasis. "What am I supposed to do, wave some dill at it and hope the door falls in?"

"That's lavender," Snow White said.

"My magic is not going to help us here," Angel said.

"Angel," Snow White said.

The apprentice railed on—though she still managed to keep her voice lowered. "I could make it work with healing, but herbs are not meant for moving physical objects."

Snow White shifted slightly, overly aware of the soldiers' eyes that were fixated on her back. "Angel."

"I expected you would know this given your propensity to read, but then again I imagine your library doesn't have many books about magic. Regardless, you'd be better off having Oswald trot off to find a pickaxe."

"*Angel!*" Snow White hissed. She reached out and grabbed the apprentice by the collar of her tunic and yanked her closer. "Stop talking and listen to me!"

"Uh, okay," Angel said.

"I don't know what you are, but I *do* know you are not an apprentice to an herb wizard! I don't care what you want to pretend to be; I'll play along with it. *Unless* it causes unnecessary problems like it is here." Snow White growled and leaned closer and closer to the magic user with every sentence she uttered. "The queen has been—for all practical purposes—taken over. We have soldiers lined up to take her down and end this. *So break down this door. NOW!*"

Angel gulped. "Sure thing," she said weakly.

When Snow White released her, Angel brushed off her tunic —though she still gaped at her.

Snow White ignored the look and instead demurely folded her hands in front of her.

Angel eyed her and slightly shook her head. "You've got guts by the boatload when you need them, Snow White."

"I also have eyes in my head," Snow White said, aware she sounded a little snide but still too upset with the magic user's reluctance to mind terribly much.

"Very good eyes." Angel winked. "Here we go!"

Angel tossed the lavender sprig aside and eyed the door as if she were circling an opponent. She muttered something under her breath before she tossed her head at the door.

The door ripped off its hinges and flew into the room as if hit with an invisible battering ram. Even after it crashed to the ground, it skidded a few steps, its hinges scraping the stone floor.

Snow White gawked at the open door, but the Seven Warriors flooded the room, moving as silent as shadows.

Snow White pressed herself against the outside wall with Angel, letting Lord Vitkovci and the soldiers file in after the warriors.

She strained her ears, but she didn't hear any shouts of warning or clash of weapons, or even the unsettling noises the constructs made, for that matter.

Curious, she shuffled closer to the doorframe and carefully peered inside.

"Top floor clear," Fritz called, his voice slightly echoing as he shouted down the balcony.

"Bottom floor clear," Gregori sounded.

Snow White paused outside the door, then stalked inside. "You mean she isn't here?"

"Correct," Gregori nodded.

CHAPTER 19
THE THRONE ROOM

Snow White knit her eyebrows together as she scurried through the room, edging past the soldiers that cautiously poked at padded chairs and cushions. She climbed the spiral staircase as fast as she could—almost tripping at the top step as she glanced from Faina's perfectly made—and obviously not slept in—bed to her wardrobe.

"No—blast it!" Snow White hissed. She scrambled across the loft, scanning the area. "The mirror, it's supposed to be right here." She traced out its previous location where it had leaned against the wall.

"Maybe she hid it?" Angel suggested. Her voice was higher than usual, and she seemed almost frantic as she poked her head under the bed skirt.

"If it really is what is influencing her, I doubt that," Snow White said grimly.

Marzell folded his hands behind his back. "Perhaps she took it and ran?"

"Why would she do that?" Snow White asked. "Unless there is a leak among our forces, she shouldn't know I'm alive—or she couldn't have until we stormed the castle. Thank you, Fritz," she said when he pulled a large wardrobe back so she could peer behind it.

"It seems unlikely she would leave now," Rupert agreed. "Particularly since we can assume that whatever planted the mirror used Faina because he or she wants to take over Mullberg." He sneezed when he poked a vase filled with dried up flowers, and the petals nearly disintegrated at his touch.

"Then should we seek out the servants again?" Marzell asked. "Perhaps someone besides the housekeeper might better know where she is."

Snow White joined Fritz at the balcony railing and leaned her forearms against it. *Wait. When Faina attacked me here, I swear I could feel something. A different quality to the air.* She rubbed her thumb on the worn varnish. *And when we passed through the main section of the palace, there was that terrible sensation. It was far worse than what I felt here, but it has been weeks...*

"The throne room," Snow White said. She paused, but the words felt so right, she nodded with certainty. "Faina is in the throne room."

"Is this a guess or conjecture?" Wendal asked.

"A bit of both. If the mirror is making Faina as power-hungry as it seems, it is the most likely place for her to go," Snow White said. "And it felt *off* as we passed it on our way here."

"I'll back Her Highness up on that," Angel said. "There is evil lurking near the throne room. I assumed it was another band of constructs, but given that the mirror is missing, it probably was Faina herself."

"The main part of the palace was unnaturally quiet," Fritz added as he joined Snow White at the balcony. "It reminded me of the way the forest grows silent before a terrible storm."

Snow White dared to lay her hand on top of Fritz's. He moved a step closer to her.

"Very well." Gregori started down the staircase. "Let us be on our way."

Snow White followed the large man, calling out when she reached the bottom step. "Lord Vitkovci, it seems my stepmother is not here. We believe she must have moved on to the throne room."

"You wish to storm it?" the older lord guessed.

Snow White nodded. "Though I want you to send one of your soldiers to notify Lord Gossler, Lord Leyen, Lord Holdenberg, and their troops of the change in plans."

Lord Vitkovci bowed. "As you command." He swung around and gave his men a few orders while Snow White hopped over the fallen door and strode into the hallway.

Though she noticed when the Seven Warriors rearranged themselves in a protective pattern around her, she said nothing. *It will likely be necessary. I don't think it's a good thing that Faina is in the throne room. At a minimum, we are increasing the likelihood of running into constructs with all this movement.*

They left the royal wing behind them, rejoining the rest of the palace as one of Lord Vitkovci's men separated from the group and headed down a different hallway.

Snow White tilted her head as the sounds of fighting grew fainter and fainter. Conversely, the oily feel to the air came back, wrapping its fingers around Snow White's neck.

"Fritz, do you hear anything?" Snow White asked. Though she spoke quietly, her voice echoed in the unnatural silence of the palace.

Fritz tilted his head. "Besides the sounds of fighting behind us?"

"Yes."

He narrowed his eyes as he listened, then shook his head.

They marched up another hallway and were about to turn down an intersection when Fritz set his hand on Snow White's shoulder, stopping her.

The other warriors stopped as well, giving him curious looks.

Marzell opened his mouth to speak but snapped his jaw shut when Fritz held a finger to his mouth in a signal for silence.

Alone, Fritz crept ahead—as silent as a cat. He leaned against the wall and twisted so he could see around the corner. His expression didn't change, but he stayed silent as he padded back to them.

"Constructs," he whispered. "Can we take a different hallway to the throne room?"

Snow White nodded and circled back the way they had come, opting to use a set of servants' stairs to lead them downstairs instead. "There's a grand staircase that leads up to the throne room. We can access it from a lower floor," she explained as they trotted down the spiraling stone steps.

When they left the stairs, they moved through much smaller —and much less ornate—back hallways for a quiet few minutes.

At least it seems the servants made it out safely, Snow White thought as they emerged from a door meant for guards, rejoining the palace in its usual splendor.

Snow White led them through a ballroom, cutting several twining hallways off their route. She paused at the great double doors that would lead them out of the ballroom. "This opens up into the Grand Hall—which has the staircase that leads you to the foot of the throne room."

"So the likelihood of constructs out there is reasonably high," Wendal guessed.

Snow White nodded.

Marzell unsheathed his sword. "Lord Vitkovci?"

Lord Vitkovci shut the visor of his helm. "My men are ready."

Fritz gently tugged on Snow White's wrist, maneuvering her so she stood behind the Seven Warriors.

"At your command, Your Highness," Gregori said.

Snow White licked her lips. "Then let us begin."

Oswald pushed the door open, which creaked—*of course*.

The hall was darkened by the sheer number of constructs.

Thankfully, only one big one patrolled the hall, but there were more of the humanoid constructs than Snow White could accurately estimate. And every one of the constructs turned in their direction as the creaking door finally fell quiet.

"Attack!" Lord Vitkovci shouted, barreling past the Seven Warriors. His men followed behind him, spears and swords raised and helms in place.

The Seven Warriors stuck to the edge of the room, attacking any constructs that drew close, but keeping Snow White backed against a wall.

Gregori loaded bolts into his crossbow as quickly as he could. Rupert and Oswald lunged forward, carving a path through any constructs that lunged for them. (Rupert also occasionally stopped to scoop up some of Gregori's bolts for him.)

Marzell whirled a spear above his head, then stabbed it through the gut of a shadowy construct, making it lose its shape and evaporate. "What are your orders, Your Highness?"

Snow White gave up trying to estimate the number of foes they faced and shifted so she could peer up at the doors that led to the throne room. The stairway was—mercifully—free, but the doors were closed.

"We have to get up to the throne room," Snow White shouted.

"Are you mad?" Oswald howled. "We can't rush it now! What if there are more constructs in there?"

"The only way we're going to stop the constructs from regenerating is to stop Faina," Angel shouted as she withdrew a fistful of starfires from her satchel. "Shine!" She threw the crystals into the inky black sea of constructs.

The constructs hissed as the starfires rained down on them. All the constructs touched by the crystals disappeared, and those closest to the glowing lights staggered away from them, stumbling into one another as they moaned.

"Fine, but how are we supposed to get to the stairs?" Oswald asked.

Fritz squeezed Snow White's hand in reassurance, then darted forward, stabbing his sword into the writhing mass of constructs.

He moved almost faster than the eye could follow, spinning, whirling, and ducking as he slowly cut a path through the constructs.

"I guess we're going," Wendal said calmly. He skulked after Fritz, raking his daggers through a construct as if the weapons were a set of claws.

"This way, Snow White." Angel threw another fistful of glowing starfires, stirring a wave of panic among the constructs. She then grabbed Snow White by the wrist and tugged her along so they fell in line behind Fritz, the rest of the Seven Warriors closing ranks around them so they were protected.

"Angel," Snow White started.

The magic user peered over Aldelbert's shoulder and lobbed another starfire. "Hmm?"

"If we are overwhelmed, can you use your magic?" Snow White asked.

Angel cringed and almost dropped her satchel. "I don't know," she admitted. "I'm hoping with everything in me that what I've been looking for is in that throne room with Faina, and if it is..." she paused, a fistful of starfires clenched in her hand, "I might need all the magic I have to grab it," she said finally.

Snow White nodded. "I understand."

"I'm sorry," Angel said. Not for the first time, there was something about her silver eyes. They seemed timeless but also so full of *pain*. "But, it's just—"

Snow White held up a hand to forestall her, then staggered when Marzell backed into her to avoid the ebony claws of a construct. "I really do understand. I'm grateful you told me—it is merely all for strategy."

Angel pursed her lips and looked as if she wanted to say more, but Rupert staggered when three constructs attacked him at once. She squirmed to fit between him and Gregori, and stabbed one of the constructs with a glowing starfire while the young heir sliced through the other two.

Snow White bit her lip as she stood on her tip-toes to survey the fight. *We're almost to the stairs, but Lord Vitkovci's men...*she twisted uncomfortably to look back at the older lord and his forces.

They were facing the large construct—the one that was vaguely troll-like. Lord Vitkovci had one bowman in his ranks who was carefully lining up his shot as the rest of the soldiers fought off the constant wave of darkness. Half of the soldiers stood in a semi-circle, trying to guard those who were occupying the large construct for the bowman.

As Snow White watched, one of the soldiers shouted in pain when a construct slashed at his arm, opening an ugly wound. He staggered, making their protective line falter.

At this rate, they might be overrun. Can we really leave them?

The Seven Warriors reached the foot of the stairs and reorganized. Though Fritz led the way with Marzell, the rest of the warriors swiveled to protect their flank as the constructs tried to drag them back into the unrest.

"Fritz, stop," Snow White said. "We have to—"

Three sets of doors to the hall banged open, and soldiers poured in.

"*Clear the way! Clear the way! Clear the way!*" the soldiers shouted—making the war-cry sound like a roar as they cut through the constructs.

It took Snow White a moment to recognize the charging ram on their uniforms. *These are Mullberg soldiers. These are* my *soldiers!*

The soldiers swept the hall, linking up with Lord Vitkovci's men. They took the place of those among Lord Vitkovci's men who had been injured and rammed through enough constructs to let Lord Vitkovci's forces back against a wall, better protecting their flank.

Three of them darted around the large construct's feet as Vitkovci's bowman loosened his arrow. The creature didn't go down with one shot, but staggered a bit, its mouth open in anger, letting the bowman hit it twice more—finally killing it.

The battle was not won—constructs seemed to multiply before Snow White's very eyes. But as they surged at the soldiers, the front lines held, leaning heavily into their shields as they kept up their battle cry.

They might not empty the room, but they'll hold the lines, Snow White realized. *Lord Vitkovci's men will not fall, for Mullberg has rallied.*

A Mullberg lieutenant caught sight of Snow White. He pointed up the stairs, then saluted her in a clear message.

"I'd say that's our cue to keep going." The tightness around Angel's eyes relaxed some as she threw another handful of starfires into the sea of constructs.

"Your orders, Snow White?" Gregori asked.

"We continue," Snow White said. "We have to find Faina, or there will be no end to this."

Fritz started up the stairs—taking two at a time.

Snow White and the others scrambled up after him as he checked up and down the balcony before leaning against the door, listening.

"Nothing," he said when Snow White joined him on the landing.

"It must be hoped, then, that she is alone." Snow White shivered as the smoky, shadowy sensation that made her spine curl grew suffocating.

She must be here. The feeling is too strong to indicate anything else.

Snow White sucked in a gulp of air as she set her shoulders. This was it. This was their chance to grab Faina and save Mullberg—and hopefully save the continent from a world of pain.

"Fritz." Snow White stared at the doors, willing herself to be strong. "Open the doors."

Fritz leaned into the doors, pushing them open with ease.

I hope that doesn't indicate that this is a trap.

Fritz and Marzell stepped into the throne room first, with Snow White on their heels.

The throne room had changed in Snow White's short absence.

Before, the room was filled with sunlight from skylights and the glass windows behind the royal thrones. But today the sky was cloudy, and only four hanging braziers of flickering fire offered additional light. The shiny obsidian flooring that previously soothed Snow White, for it reminded her of a calm lake, now seemed as empty and hungry as the gaping mouth of an endless cave—even the white marble ram carved into the flooring seemed more of a dull ash gray. Shadows played in the room, and the elaborate gold flourishes and gems encrusted on the walls seemed more like the glittering eyes of ravenous predators.

What was most unsettling, though, were the twelve knights dressed in black armor. They were silent, though they turned to look at Snow White and the others, their blood-covered swords gripped in their black gauntlets. They were larger than even Gregori, and their armor was not made of smooth plates of metal but obsidian rock.

Constructs. They give off that same shadowy feeling—and no man would be strong enough to wear armor like that. But as we have never seen these before, does that mean they are the strongest type that can be forged?

Snow White bit her lip as she gazed past the unsettling line of new constructs and searched for her stepmother. Faina was seated on the throne of Mullberg, a cruel and foreign smile etched into her lips and a glittering crown Snow White had never seen before with points at least six inches high resting on her head.

Beside her was the mirror. Though it was beautiful—with an ornate gold frame swirled with tiny flowers and an enormous blood red ruby at the top of the frame—Snow White wondered how she had missed the coldness it radiated and the hushed whispers that seemed to stir from it.

As soon as Angel stepped into the room, she strung together an almost impressive line of curses and swear words. She jolted forward—as if she wanted to sprint past Snow White and the others—but jerked to a stop just as fast, a strange mixture of rage and fear tightening her jaw.

Seeing Faina felt like a dagger to Snow White's heart, for her stepmother—her *real* stepmother—would never look so cruel. So *dark*.

"Faina," Snow White tried to say, but it came out as a strangled squeak.

"*Snow White*," Faina said in a deep voice that was not hers and seemed ancient and murky. "Fairest of them all. How fortunate it is that you have come to *me*."

CHAPTER 20
QUEEN FAINA

Snow White wanted to tremble in fear.
That voice...this isn't a simple enemy we're facing. A rogue mage would have been better! Whatever that mirror is, it's pure evil.

She started to take a step back but shook her head. *No, I can't run. I won't leave Faina to this! But what do I do?*

"Snow White," Fritz said, his voice soft.

Snow White jerked her head up so she could meet his gaze.

"We'll follow you," he said, his hazel eyes almost glowing in the darkness of the throne room.

The phrase was deeper than it seemed to be, and Snow White felt it in her bones. *I can do this. I can—no—I will get Faina back!*

Snow White sucked in a deep breath and spoke. "It appears you have misunderstood the situation." Her voice shook a little, but it was much louder than her first greeting, and her confidence grew as she lifted her chin. "I have not come to *you*, but Faina."

Faina laughed, a harsh, cackling noise that filled the room. "You stupid child. You are too late. She is under my control, and through her, your insipid country is as well. Faina is *mine* now."

"She's yours, is she?" Snow White asked. She took a step

forward, filling the small space between Fritz and Marzell. "Then if that is the case, *why are you so afraid of me?*"

Faina rose to her feet in a sagging motion—as if she were a puppet dangling on its strings. "I do not fear stupid little girls who are so inept and useless, they cannot speak to their own people."

Seeing Faina's mouth move and deliver the insult made Snow White flinch, but she held her ground. "You're right. It isn't me you should fear," she said.

Faina threw back her head in another cackling laugh. "You think I should hold your little band of warriors in terror? How laughable!" Faina extended her arm and pointed with her black-gloved fingers. "*Attack them!*"

The obsidian knights jerked to life, moving slowly at first until they built up momentum and started for Snow White and the Seven Warriors. Each step they took made the stone floor shake.

The closest one broke into a slow jog, then jumped the last few steps, stabbing its jet black, rock-forged blade at Oswald.

The grumpy warrior blocked with his own sword, but swore and nearly dropped to his knees with the force of the strike. "Dodge their attacks," he called out to his fellows. "A few hits from them, and your arms are done for."

Rupert narrowed his eyes as he swung his sword, striking the side of the obsidian knight that still bore down on Oswald. He clenched his teeth and nearly dropped his sword. "Look for weak points," he said as he shifted his sword from one hand to the other so he could shake his fingers. "Striking them is like hitting a boulder."

"Then look lively, lads!" Aldelbert said with a breezy laugh. "For we are about to get run down—hah-hah!"

The rest of the obsidian knights closed in on them.

Snow White curled her hands into shaking fists but held her chin up and stood unwavering. *We will win this.*

Fritz stepped forward to meet two of them—sliding between

them like a shadow so they nearly collided as they tried to follow him.

Marzell uncurled his whip that he had strapped to his belt. He flicked it at the knight nearest to him so it wrapped around the knight's helm, then yanked. The obsidian knight's helm flew off, revealing inky darkness in the wavering shape of a head. The knight slowly lifted a hand to its head, but grabbed Marzell's whip when the young lord tried a second strike and yanked the weapon straight out of his grasp.

"My Lord!" Wendal shouted. He threw a rope to the blond-haired lord—who caught it with a cocky laugh.

"You are right to be my attendant, Wendal!" Aldelbert called as he crouched down across from the dagger-wielder. "You are so smart. Let us charge honorably to glory!" In their half-crouched position, he and Wendal darted past a knight, the rope stretched between them.

The knight tried to step forward, but it toddled over the rope. The weight of its rock armor dragged it down, and it hit the floor with a rumbling crash.

Gregori was not fairing as well. Though he loaded his crossbow with quick efficiency, his bolts bounced off the constructs' stone-like armor—even when he shot them in weak places like the throat or armpits.

With a growl he usually only uttered when someone tried to wake him from a nap, he tossed his crossbow aside and dodged when a knight tried to stab him. Using sheer strength, he grabbed the construct's wrist and yanked it up behind its back.

The construct's armor ground against itself as it cocked its head, then abruptly kicked back, nailing Gregori in the shin.

Gregori grunted in pain but yanked the construct's wrist higher, moving only to dodge when a second obsidian knight tried to stab him.

Rupert and Oswald fought back-to-back again. Oswald had somehow gotten a nasty cut above his right eyebrow that continuously dripped blood down his face so he had to close his eye. Rupert had no visible injuries, but after avoiding a blow from a sword, another obsidian knight kneed him in the right side. He almost slumped over and barely managed to dodge another sword stab.

Despite her warning, Angel entered the fray with a blood-curdling shout. She climbed on the back of an obsidian knight, her tongue sticking out of her mouth in concentration as she clung to its back. It swung around in an arc as it tried to grab for her. With one arm hanging around its neck, she used her free hand to push the visor of its helm open, then dropped a glowing starfire through the inky blackness contained inside.

The starfire rattled as it fell down the suit of armor. It didn't seem to do any damage, but at the very least, it unsettled the construct. It ignored Angel and staggered several steps. It planted its sword in the ground—chipping the stone flooring—and leaned against it as it shook its head.

It was so distracted that it didn't move when Aldelbert and Wendal wrapped a rope around its legs and pulled, toppling it like a tree.

"Well done—whoop!" Aldelbert skittered backwards to avoid a chop from another construct. He backed straight into the knight he had just felled, and started to pinwheel his arms as he fell.

Fritz grabbed him by his colorful collar and yanked hard, righting the lordling before a knight could stab him through.

Fritz then approached another knight in near silence, slipping around the slower-moving construct as he carefully studied it. He seemed to casually dodge when the knight tried to stab him through, and though his eyes were on the construct's head, he jumped with ease when the monster tried to kick him and missed.

He nodded as if making up his mind, then pulled his hunting dagger from his belt. In one smooth movement, he slithered behind the knight and struck the back of its helm with his palm—peeling it up—then stabbed his blade into its exposed "neck".

The obsidian knight briefly flailed and dropped its sword. Unfortunately, it recovered quickly when it tilted forward—out of range—and snapped its helm back into place.

Snow White pressed her lips together as she watched the fight. *We aren't winning, but at least we're not losing. It's troubling, though, as there doesn't really seem to be a way to beat these constructs. But if we can break that mirror,* Snow White hesitated, then nodded as she watched the seven warriors tangle with their armored foes. *The warriors will hold out—as long as I can end this.*

Snow White carefully counted the constructs, waiting until she was certain every one of them was occupied before she slipped past Fritz and ran for her stepmother.

Faina had left her throne behind and stood on the horns of the charging ram etched into the floor. Her smile was dark, and her eyes were vacant. "You really are an idiot," she said as Snow White joined her, stopping when she stood on the ram's chest. "You run freely to your doom—what a simple creature you are!"

Behind her, Snow White could have sworn she saw the surface of the mirror ripple like water in a pond.

Snow White licked her dry lips. "Why are you doing this?" she asked as she searched her stepmother's face for any sign of recognition—for any flicker of Faina's true self.

Faina shook an elegant finger at her. "Ah-ah. You're attempting to stall. In making a bid for time, you hope to distract me; it won't work." Faina pulled a black dagger from her skirts and took a step closer. "You humans think you're so clever, when you are mere ants to something like me. A few mere years, and you are gone. You are a disgusting creature, Snow White. And there is something poetic in that it is your precious *stepmother* who will be your end."

Rather than shake in fright, Snow White's heart burned.

I can be brave for Faina. I can believe in her, if not myself.

"You guessed wrong," Snow White said as she took a step closer to Faina.

Her stepmother blinked. "Wrong about what?"

"It wasn't me you need to fear, nor is it the Seven Warriors." Snow White stopped when she was close enough that she could have reached out and touched Faina's shoulder.

Faina rolled her eyes. "Then who—oh-insipid-one—am *I* supposed to fear? Your soldiers? Your grubby little do-gooder magic friend?" She flashed a feral smile that made her teeth seem pointed. "None of them can stop me!"

"No," Snow White agreed as she leaned closer. "But Faina can."

Her stepmother's face turned pinched in her rage, and the strange voice coming from her mouth erupted in an angry shriek. She swung her dagger above her head and stabbed it down at Snow White, aiming for her heart.

Snow White caught Faina by the wrist and almost staggered under the pressure of Faina's arm.

Whatever was possessing Faina must have been giving her unnatural strength, for Snow White could barely keep her arms up as Faina pressed down with greater strength, her eyes fastened on Snow White's heart as she licked her lips.

"Stepmother," Snow White said between gritted teeth as she shook with strain. "Faina—I know you would never hurt me. I know this isn't you, and I'm sorry that I left you to face this darkness alone. I am *so* sorry." Her shoulders heaved in a dry sob, and her eyes stung, but she clung on to Faina's wrists. "You held on for so long, and I never knew. I can't tell you how much I regret this! But I'm here now, and I know you can fight this thing off— even for one minute! We can still save you—you can come home!"

Faina growled. "Empty entreaties, *princess*. I already told you— Faina is *gone!*"

"Except she's not!" Snow White said with a snarl of anger that started in her heart. "I know my stepmother. She would never hurt me! She would *never* leave me!"

Faina leaned into her arm, making Snow White sweat under the pressure as the tip of the dagger nearly cut her shoulder.

This is my last stand. It's a gamble, but I would do anything to reach Faina.

"And mirror—whatever you are—you're about to learn something important." Snow White grinned as she leaned forward, ignoring the burning pain in her arm as she still held Faina's wrist above her chest. "You chose the wrong queen to ensnare because Faina is stronger than you."

Snow White released her hold on Faina's wrist. A monstrous sneer spread across Faina's lips as she jabbed the dagger straight at Snow White's heart.

Snow White clenched her jaw but didn't move because she believed.

Just as the dagger sliced through the material of her gown, the queen's expression twisted.

"NO!" Faina shouted—the strange murkiness gone from her voice. She staggered back several steps, the dagger still clenched in her hands. She shook her head, and the sick smile returned to her face.

"Struggle with all your might, little queen," she purred—seemingly to herself. "But you've already lost!" Faina toddled toward Snow White, readjusting her grip on her dagger.

Encouraged by the flicker of Faina's determination, Snow White stepped closer to her troubled stepmother. "There's so much going on, Faina, that we didn't know about. There's a struggle for the *continent*. Countries have been backsliding, but I'm not going to let it happen here. *We're* not going to let it happen. And it starts with getting you back."

Faina waggled her dagger at Snow White. "The battle for your lands is over, *Your Highness*. You lost long before you were even aware of what was going on. I've waited centuries for this chance. I will not lose again. There's no one to stop me this time."

The words made Snow White break out in a cold sweat, but she swallowed hard and held her ground. "You overreach yourself."

"Impossible," Faina snorted.

Snow White held her gaze as she took another step closer and shook her head. "In your arrogance, you underestimate your foe. Faina will beat you."

Faina curled a lip back. "On the contrary. Once I finally succeed in killing you, she will be snuffed out entirely."

"And there lies the flaw in your plan," Snow White said. "For the mother of my heart would never let you harm me." She invaded Faina's space and wrapped her arms around her stepmother in a tight hug.

Faina was boney and cold, and Snow White felt rather like she was embracing a bunch of sticks.

Please work. Please work!

Snow White kept her arms in place as Faina raised her dagger behind Snow White's back, taking careful aim at the space between her shoulder blades.

Snow White wanted to squeeze her eyes shut, but she made herself stand. She forced herself to bear witness.

Faina plunged the dagger at Snow White's back, but at the last second ripped herself away, her steps shaky. Her eyes were narrowed and angry as she stared at her hand and watched her fingers slowly peel off the hilt of the dagger until the weapon fell to the ground with a muted clatter.

"What's happening?" Faina muttered. She glared at Snow White. "You have done something to me!"

She lunged for Snow White, her mouth open in a snarl that bared her teeth. Just as an outstretched finger brushed Snow White's throat, Faina jumped backwards.

"Get away from Snow White!" she shouted. She gritted her

teeth in determination even as she clenched her eyes shut with pain.

You cannot resist, a hushed voice cooed, filling the room. *You are but a simple human, unable to fight magic.*

Faina fell to her knees, her hands curled into fists. "Maybe so," she panted. "But I'll move the world itself before I let you harm her!"

A black cloud of swirling magic surrounded Faina. She curled over herself, screaming in pain.

"Faina!" Snow White struggled through the magic—which yanked at her clothes and hair—and stretched out her hand.

Faina looked up at her, tears of pain streaming down her cheeks, and shook her head. "Run, Snow White."

"No!" Snow White shouted. She struggled to get closer even as the magic buffeted her like the winds of a summer gale. "I'm not leaving you! I'm *never* going to leave you!"

"It's too much," Faina sobbed.

"Then depend on me! You don't have to fight this alone." Snow White was nearly thrown backwards as she thrusted her right hand out in front of her, holding it out to Faina. "You don't have to protect me anymore. This time *I* will save *you*! Just trust me!"

Faina rocked in pain as the magic around her grew darker and darker, making it harder for Snow White to see her.

"Faina!" Snow White shouted, her heart in her throat. She took another staggering step forward, and tears dripped from her eyes due to the force of the winds that screamed around her. "I'm not going to give up. I'll fight this with everything I have. Mullberg will not rest until you are safe, and I will not stand quiet and let you go!"

Time seemed to drag.

I can't hold on much longer, Snow White thought as the magic still tried to drag her back. *Please—believe in me!*

Snow White sobbed and strained forward, but she felt the magic push her back a step as it grew in strength.

Human sentimentalities, the murky voice sneered. *A disgraceful trait. My magic is too powerful to be vanquished by such—*

Snow White screamed in surprise when Faina's white hand shot out of the darkness and grabbed Snow White's.

What? The murky voice sounded shocked and confused.

Deep from the center of the dark cloud, Faina growled. "I said...GET AWAY FROM MY DAUGHTER!"

The black cloud of magic dispersed, shooting back to the mirror with the speed of a falling star. It smacked the mirror's surface, making it violently ripple like a boulder tossed into a still pond.

"Faina!" Snow White scrambled to her stepmother on her knees.

Faina groaned but tried to stand on shaking legs.

Snow White helped her up, her heart threatening to burst through her chest in her elation.

It was done. Faina was freed from the mirror's clutches!

Though she stayed steady and let Faina lean into her for support, she twisted her neck, intending to shout to the Seven Warriors in her joy, but her words caught in her throat.

The obsidian knights were still attacking.

Wendal was down, crumpled against a wall, his face white and his eyes shut as Aldelbert stood in front of him, sweating as a construct rained endless blows upon him that made his arms shake.

Marzell had joined Oswald and Rupert, and while the three were still standing, Marzell had a nasty-looking slice on his thigh, and all three men were shaking with exhaustion.

Gregori panted as he scrabbled with a knight, though as Snow White watched, another construct bashed him in the shoulder with a stone shield, and he fell to his knees.

Fritz rammed into the construct attacking Gregori, but some—

time during the scuffle he had taken a blow to his side that cut through his leather doublet. The wound was slowly dying his doublet red with blood.

No—they're still attacking...but we have Faina!

Snow White's heart beat faster and faster as she twisted to stare up at the mirror.

It's surface still churned, though she could have sworn she saw a robed figure among the ripples.

What do we do? Do we retreat? Do we attack the mirror? But how?

Snow White glanced at the dagger Faina had previously wielded. She licked her lips. "I'll be right back."

"Where are you going?" Faina asked as she managed to stand upright.

"To try to stop this!" Snow White snatched the dagger and ran to the throne. Each step she took, the air felt colder, until it was so frigid she could see her breath.

Soon, it was a struggle to breathe and a fight to move.

The air burned with cold, and her teeth chattered. She stopped about three horse-lengths from the mirror, shivering uncontrollably.

If I get any closer, I'll die.

Snow White's toes turned numb, but she doggedly threw the dagger.

It struck the mirror but harmlessly bounced off.

It didn't even nick the surface.

How is that possible?

The cold redoubled, and Snow White cried out in pain.

Fog curled around the mirror, and Snow White felt something ancient and evil stir.

No! If we stay here, we're going to die.

Snow White turned on her heels and ran to Faina. "Retre—"

Before she could say anything more, Angel roared.

CHAPTER 21
ANGELIQUE

The apprentice hurtled across the room, her eyes fixed on the mirror. She ran, unflinchingly, past Snow White, seemingly not noticing as frost formed in her hair.

"Evariste!" Angel shouted. She slammed her fists on the mirror's surface.

The robed figure appeared again in the mirror's surface.

Snow White shivered in the cold, but she tried to take a step closer as she studied the figure. *It's too tall and broad shouldered to be a woman, so it must be a male. And his robes look very costly, but who is he? Unless...she said she was looking for her master?*

The man in the mirror held his palm out. Though the wind whipped outside the mirror, his blue and black robe—which was fringed with gold coins—did not move.

Angel slapped her palm on the mirror, covering the spot where his hand pressed against the inside surface.

Snow White almost yelped when a gust of wind moved her back a step, but she could still barely make out the robed man's voice.

"Angel—you have to leave."

"Not when I've just found you!" Angel argued as hoarfrost spread across her eyelashes.

"*It's too dangerous!*" the man argued. "*Please—I just want you safe!*"

"I've looked for you for *six years,* Master Evariste," Angel growled. "I'm not giving you up now."

*Choices...*the mirror whispered. The murky voice was gone, but a cold, ancient voice had taken its place.

The wind picked up again, and Snow White only heard a few snatches of the mirror's words.

Rage...Power...

Angel ignored it as she slammed her fists on the mirror. "I'm getting you out!" she shouted.

"*But you can't! Not with your current abilities—*"

Angel shut her eyes, and when she opened them again, magic flooded the throne room.

The skylights shattered, a few decorative weapons were ripped off the walls, and the doors were flung open as silvery magic filled the room in an uncomfortably bright light.

Angel's magic was cool, glittering, and *sharp*.

Snow White's breathing hitched as the magic swirled past, and it felt like she stood on pins and needles.

But the silver magic ignored Snow White, Faina, and the warriors. It converged on Angel, throwing her hair into the wind and yanking on her overly large tunic.

Snow White blinked, and for a moment she thought she saw a woman of breathtaking beauty clothed in a sparkling gown standing in Angel's spot, but when she squinted, the vision faded.

"Give him back." Angel's voice was low and wolfish as she snarled at the mirror, her silver eyes hard in her rage. She slapped her hand over its surface, and her magic briefly surged around the mirror—much like a lightning strike.

Never, whispered the mirror.

"That wasn't a request!" Angel grabbed either side of the

mirror and grit her teeth. Her magic encircled the mirror, making it rattle in its frame.

The room grew colder as the mirror resisted, and ice formed at Snow White's feet.

Angel didn't let go. She opened her mouth in a silent war cry as the magical pressure in the room built until Snow White couldn't stand anymore and dropped to her knees.

She watched—open-mouthed—as Angel put her hand *into* the mirror. The mirror's surface pooled like liquid silver around her wrist, but she pushed until her forearm was through.

"Take my hand!" she shouted to the robed man.

He said something, then put his hand in hers.

Snow White gawked—shocked—as Angel slowly drew him out of the mirror.

His hand came first, then his arm and front foot, but he gradually stepped through the mirror the way bubbles surface in a pond.

Snow White could tell Angel had to fight for every inch of progress he made.

Her silver eyes were brighter, now—almost an unforgiving white. Her hand trembled as more and more of her magic built, pooling under her feet where it took the shape of a many-pointed star...if the star were made up of sword edges, that was.

Angel shook with strain, and she sweated, but when the temperature plunged again, she roared like an angry dragon, and her magic flared.

When the robed man was most of the way out, Angel yanked on him, dragging him out and maneuvering him behind her where he fell on his knees.

Angel snapped her left leg up and kicked, and the mirror fell backwards, crashing to the ground.

(Though, as Snow White peered after it, its surface hadn't so much as cracked at the abuse.)

Her eyes *glowing*, Angel swung around and snapped her teeth at the Seven Warriors.

She was a fierce sight to behold with the wind whipping her hair and sharp bits of her magic floating around her.

She pulled her hand back as if pulling a nocked arrow back in a bow.

The room was filled with a cacophony as all the bladed weapons belonging to the Seven Warriors *and* all the construct's obsidian black swords and shields rose up into the air.

Through the open doors, Snow White could see the same happening in the hall down the stairs—weapons rose into the air, as steady and sure as if maneuvered by the invisible fingers of a master.

Angel grimaced, then thrust her fingers forward.

The weapons stabbed downward with pin-point precision.

Snow White jumped to her feet in surprise when an obsidian sword plunged straight through the belly of an obsidian knight, cutting through its rocky armor.

The knight seemed to stare down at the sword, then it fell in on itself, its armor crashing to the ground in a heap.

All the other knights faced similar fates, impaled by their own weapons.

Snow White ran across the throne room and flew down the top few stairs, watching wide-eyed as Angel's magic raised the soldier's weapons in the hall and cut through the shadowy humanoid constructs with devastating efficiency.

In moments, all the constructs were gone. The fight was over.

Angel!

Snow White charged back up the stairs, entering the throne room just in time to see the robed man enfold Angel in a tight embrace.

Angel's magic had faded away, though she was clearly sobbing as she pressed her face into the man's shoulder.

He soothingly rubbed her back and rested his chin on the top of her head.

After a few moments, Angel's heart-wrenching sobs turned into a strangled gurgle, and she ripped herself from the robed man and dashed away just in time to throw up into a vase that Snow White would be disposing of once the day was over.

The throne room was quiet—except for Angel's retching.

Snow White pushed her black curls out of her face as she inspected the Seven Warriors. They looked more than a little windblown, and their injuries were undeniable, but even Fritz's side wound was not life threatening.

We survived.

The Seven Warriors stared at each other, slightly dazed.

Snow White could feel her own shock looming behind her, but she couldn't give in just yet.

The battle might be won, but we have to do something about that mirror. And Angel needs to see a barber surgeon, as do the rest of the Warriors—particularly as it seems neither Angel nor her master are herb wizards, but they must be capable of some kind of healing given what Angel was able to do. Regardless, we have to inform Lord Vitkovci and the others of our win—and that doesn't even begin to touch the preparations I'll have to make to assure Grandfather.

Snow White shook her head and snapped down on her thoughts. *Enough. Internal babbling is just another form of shock—something I will not allow to occur just yet.*

She turned her attention to Faina, who had shakily risen to her feet and was looking around the disorderly throne room with a slight frown. When she met Snow White's gaze, she smiled—her first real smile since they had entered the chamber—and extended her arms.

Snow White tried to say something, but her unshed tears squeezed her throat, so instead she stumbled blindly to her stepmother, throwing herself into her embrace.

Though Faina was still boney, her hug was as warm and secure as ever. A hiccup escaped Snow White. "I'm sorry," she whispered. "For everything."

"My darling Snow White," Faina crooned. "You have nothing to be sorry for. Since your father died, you have been the joy of my life. You have made me immensely proud."

"But I—"

"Rescued me from a darkness I couldn't escape." Faina stepped back just far enough so she could meet Snow White's gaze and smooth a stray curl. "You have grown. But your new strength does not discredit your past struggles. Be proud of who you were, Snow White. For it shaped you for the role you took up today—the rightful Queen of Mullberg."

"Oh, no!" Snow White shook her head. "No—no. Not yet."

Faina laughed. "You rescued me and saved our country from certain danger, and *yet* you feel like you are not ready to lead?"

"It is more that I would rather not jump in all at once," Snow White said. "Easing my way in is a much better strategy." *And it will give me a chance to keep battling my shyness.*

"We can discuss it once things have been righted," Faina said in a tone that conveyed she was not going to give in easily.

But that was fine. Snow White was just as confident she'd be able to produce a sound plan for the future that not even Faina could find fault with. *But now we must pick up the pieces.*

Snow White gazed past Faina to Angel's hunched figure.

The apprentice—*mage?*—was curled in a miserable huddle. She leaned against the man—*her master?*—she had freed from the mirror, though she still kept a hand on the lip of the vase, as if she might need it again shortly.

"I'll be just a moment, Faina." Snow White smiled, glee filling every bit of her being as Faina grinned. (*Faina was back—she was better!*)

Faina winked. "Of course, Snow White," she said.

"Queen Faina!" a male voice called from the throne room entrance.

"Lord Vitkovci," Faina said as she separated from Snow White and strolled in the older lord's direction. "It seems I have much to thank you for."

Snow White pointed herself toward Angel, but she couldn't help glancing at the Seven Warriors again—Fritz in particular.

The tall forester was helping Marzell stand, and already he had reclaimed his sword from where it had dropped. He glanced over at Snow White, his eyes meeting hers with warmth and concern.

Snow White couldn't look away. In fact, the only thing she appeared to be capable of doing was beam like an idiot, though the longer she stared at Fritz, the more she wanted to gulp at the intangible but strong *thing* between them.

Another retch from Angel broke the spell, and Snow White blinked. She offered Fritz another smile when he nodded at her, then picked her way through the crumbled armor.

We'll have to do something with that mirror. Though it's quiet now, I don't believe for a moment that Angel actually defeated it. It seems more like she momentarily subdued it. But how do we lock up a magical mirror?

The thought made Snow White's forehead pucker as she scrambled the last few steps to Angel and her...man.

"Angel?" Snow White asked, slowing her approach. "Are you terribly injured? Should I call for help?"

"No," Angel said miserably as she eyed her vase. "It will pass. Eventually." She sounded glum, and her skin had taken on a sickly green hue.

Snow White bit her lip as she studied her very obviously ill friend. *She saved us all from that mirror. It seems cruel to leave her in such low health.* "Is there anything I can do to help? Could magic heal you?" She ventured.

"Nope." Angel wiped her mouth on the sleeve of her drooping tunic. "If it could, Evariste could do something."

"Ahhh, yes," Angel's companion—Evariste, apparently—said in a smooth, almost musical voice. "If I could spare Angel I would, except I'm afraid in this case, I am doubly unable to help. My magic is sealed."

Angel froze. Her eyes bulged, and she gaped like a fish. "What?" she finally croaked.

"I served as a power source for the mirror, but to keep me from escaping, I was sealed before I was placed inside it," he said.

Angel broke into a cough and nearly choked. "But it will be easy to break off, right? We'll just take you to the Conclave, and someone there will remove whatever it is that is keeping you sealed."

"I'm afraid that's impossible," Evariste said.

Angel stared at him as if he had just broken her entire world. Even her grasp on her vase loosened as her skin turned from green to white.

I get the feeling this isn't merely personal bad news to Angel but very bad news for the continent.

Snow White pressed her lips together and opened her mouth to ask more, but behind her, the Seven Warriors shouted.

"Guards up!" Marzell yelled.

Snow White whirled around in time to see the last of four gray-clothed figures leap in through one of the broken windows.

The tallest of the figures balanced a globe of churning fire between his hands, which he lobbed at Angel, Evariste, and Snow White.

Snow White raised her arms to shield her face, but Angel lunged at the fireball with her hand extended.

Snow White felt the heat of the fire as it zoomed closer. It was abruptly blocked by the wall of the shattered obsidian armor Angel had raised just in time. Instead, it crackled and spattered against the rock surface.

"Snow White!" Fritz roared.

Once again, wind stirred Angel's hair as she raised the jagged weapons of the fallen constructs. "How did they get here so quickly?" she growled. "I *just* freed you!"

"I don't think they're here for me," Evariste said lightly.

With a quick hand movement from Angel, the wall lowered just enough for Snow White to peek over it.

The magical invaders had crowded around the mirror. One of them picked it up with ease, as if the full-length mirror with its intricate frame weighed less than a straw basket.

Angel rattled off a string of curses. "They're taking the mirror!" she said between growled profanities.

Evariste arched his eyebrow. "Has Stil been hanging around you during my absence? He's the only one I can think of who would know such creative language."

"Stay down—both of you!" Angel snapped. She jumped over her temporary wall and wiggled a finger at the obsidian swords that still hung in the air.

The swords swiveled slightly, then slammed at the thieves as they hauled the mirror back to the broken window.

One of the invaders shouted something and yanked up his arms, peeling the layer of (expensive) obsidian stone off the floor so it half curled around the group, protecting them from Angel's attack.

The fire mage formed another ball of fire, but before he could launch it, he collapsed to his knees, a crossbow bolt buried in his bicep.

"Now!" Marzell shouted.

Wendal threw three daggers, and Gregori released another bolt, but the invader who had ruined the floor hurriedly peeled up more of the stone tiles.

One of the gray-clad thieves hopped out through the window. The one carrying the mirror tried to shove it through, but it was too wide.

Angel hacked at them again, this time directing the obsidian swords in a wide slicing motion.

The thieves ducked behind their solid shelter, barely avoiding her attack.

Angel rammed the weapons into the stone wall with such force that one of the weapons cracked, then crumbled into shards.

We need to call for backup!

When there was a brief lull in the fight, Snow White took a cautious step out from behind the side of the wall. "Lord Vitkovci!" she shouted—though she could barely hear herself over the crunch of Angel slamming the obsidian wall again.

The man carrying the mirror crept out of the shelter long enough to try rotating the mirror as his companion that seemed to have an affinity for rocks provided cover.

Using his magic, he catapulted chunks of rock as big as melons, lobbing them at Angel, Snow White, and Evariste.

Angel ducked one lump, and too late, Snow White realized the rock was going to hit her.

She tried to dive behind the wall, but she knew she wasn't going to make it in time. She cringed, stiffening herself for the painful crunch.

A shadow fell over her, and she glanced up to see Fritz, bearing a shield, slide between her and the rock. The rock dinged off the shield, though the force with which it hit the forester made him grimace.

"Get behind the wall," he said to Snow White, who was already crawling the short distance back to the shelter.

Fritz joined her there, removing the shield to toss it aside before shaking out his likely bruised arm.

"Thank you," Snow White said.

Fritz nodded and smiled at her with his eyes before he swiveled into a protective crouch at her open side.

Snow White inhaled deeply, then risked peeking over the top of the wall of armor again.

She looked just in time to see the man finally flip the mirror so he held its edge and could carry it through the window with ease.

The wounded fire user and the one with the affinity for stone jumped after him, their gray clothes flapping noiselessly as they dropped out of view.

"NO!" Angel roared. She ran up the marble shell and jumped through the open window.

"Angel, wait!" Evariste shouted. He sprinted around Angel's wall, darting toward the open window—Fritz and Snow White on his heels.

But even before they reached the window, Snow White heard a retching noise, followed by more cursing.

When Snow White peered through the jagged opening, she could spot the gray figures running across the rooftop of a lower wing of the castle.

Angel was collapsed on the roof, half snarling, half sobbing. She tried to stand, but her legs seemed unable to hold her, and she dropped with a muffled oath.

Evariste leaped through the window and landed at her side in a crouch.

"They got away," Angel said in a dead voice. "I couldn't stop them."

"Angel, you just expelled a huge amount of magic in rescuing me. It wasn't your fault," Evariste said as he picked a piece of glass from Angel's hair.

"It doesn't matter. That was the mirror the Chosen wanted! That's the mirror the Snow Queen buried," Angel groaned.

Snow White didn't quite understand everything Angel was talking about, but she knew it was bad news.

"Lord Vitkovci!" Snow White shouted this time as she spun around. "Send your soldiers after those men! I want Juwel closed, and all guards to search for those intruders."

Lord Vitkovci—who stood protectively in front of Faina—bowed. "Yes, Your Majesty!" He hurried down the steps outside the throne room, roaring for his men.

Snow White gazed around the broken throne room and took

in a shuddering breath. The chamber was ruined. Not a single window had gone unscathed, and much of the flooring was cracked, if not peeled off.

But it was a cheap price to pay for the return of Faina.

It's over—at least my part of this fight is. Despite her orders to Lord Vitkovci, Snow White knew the chances of recovering the evil mirror were miniscule. But if they could uncover any additional information about the men who had grabbed the mirror, the search would be worthwhile.

There's so much to do—both in Mullberg and to inform the other countries of what has occurred here. Where do we even begin?

Snow White was startled from her thoughts when Fritz took her hand.

Surprised, she glanced up at him.

Fritz smiled and bent over slightly so he could whisper in her ear. "Breathe," he said. "You saved Faina."

"Yes." Snow White let herself lean slightly into him, and the tension in her shoulders eased. "She's safe—and Mullberg is safe."

"And *you* are safe. You did this."

She shook her head. "No, we all did. I couldn't have done this without you or the other warriors—or the lords."

"And we couldn't have done it without you leading," Fritz countered. "You *won*, Snow White. Against all odds—against what others tried to tell you. We triumphed."

Snow White finally smiled as her eyes fell on Faina. "We did."

Her stepmother's eyes were crinkled with worry as she smoothed the skirts of her black gown. She smiled, though, when she noticed Snow White's attention. (However, Snow White could tell the moment Faina realized she was leaning against Fritz, for she tilted her head and narrowed her eyes slightly.)

There really is so much to do…but perhaps I could be forgiven for prioritizing this one thing.

Snow White blushed as she pressed her lips together. "Can I introduce you to Faina?"

"You want to?" Fritz asked.

Snow White frowned up at him, her eyebrows puckering. "Of course!"

Fritz chuckled—a quiet sound Snow White could barely hear. "Then lead the way."

Snow White nodded and, still holding Fritz's hand, marched toward her stepmother, wondering how she was going to bumble through this conversation.

"Faina? I'd like you to meet someone…"

CHAPTER 22
A DIFFERENCE OF HEIGHTS

Snow White sat in contented silence and watched the soldiers who had marched on the palace start off another round of toasts to her, Faina, and the Seven Warriors.

The soldiers were seated at various tables around the still mostly empty feasting hall, but their mirth and happiness filled the room until it brimmed with noise and cheerful laughter.

Angel, her rescued companion, and the Seven Warriors all sat with Snow White and Faina at their table, but they shouted to the lords and the soldiers seated at the other tables anyway.

In fact, Lord Leyen was tipped back in his chair so he and Marzell could exchange a brief conversation as Leyen sat on the edge of the two tables his men had claimed. Lord Holdenberg sat in the middle of his forces, roaring with laughter and bright red with good cheer.

Lord Gossler was absent—he had been hurt badly enough to warrant a night in the infirmary, though he heavily protested the idea—and Lord Vitkovci was missing as well, given that he had rushed off to Hurra to wait for and explain to Snow White's grandfather, Lord Trubsinn, all that had happened. However, his men, as well as Lord Gossler's, were still present.

In fact, Snow White had an inkling it was Vitkovci's men who helped Oswald pull the greatest prank of the night: a gray horse with its mane tied up in ribbons and braids stationed at the back of the room, hitched up to an elaborate carriage that held a great many beer kegs.

The horse was unbothered by the noise and stood with one hoof cocked, though it did swing its head around to watch whenever soldiers came to unload another keg. (Rupert and the so-helpful-soldiers seemed to think the horse would get lonely by itself, for some time in the middle of the feast, two miniature donkeys were procured and were tethered by the patient steed. Though that also might have been Rupert's competitive streak showing.)

Someone was playing the violin loudly enough to be heard over the clanks of dishes and boisterous laughter, and it seemed the room was only going to grow louder as the night progressed.

The noise was enough to give Snow White a headache, but she sat in her chair—stuffed to the gills with all her favorite foods the kitchens could make on such short notice—and observed the festivities.

They deserve this, after what they've faced today. And in a strange way I'm grateful for all the fuss and sounds. I'm almost afraid that this is all a wonderful dream, and I might soon wake up.

Above all the noise was a terrible, wheezing/laughing-like sound.

But then one of those donkeys bray, and I know it's real.

Oswald was crouched next to one of the aforementioned donkeys, patting its neck as he chatted with a few soldiers.

Surprisingly, it was Rupert who was passed out on the table while Gregori was still bright-eyed and smiling.

Aldelbert had taken his antics to a new level, though, and was dancing on top of a table with Wendal. (Snow White had feared this might offend Faina until the lord and his attendant *almost* managed to talk her stepmother into joining them.)

But where is Fritz?

Snow White searched, but she didn't see the quiet forester anywhere. She slipped from her chair—smiling at Faina when her stepmother glanced her way—and turned around, looking for any convenient shadows.

There! A mass of shadows by the balcony door.

Snow White gripped her skirts as she wove between two tables, making for the rim of the room. Sure enough, as she had predicted, Fritz was cloaked in the shadows, seated on the edge of an elaborate stone windowsill.

"I had wondered where you were," she said by way of greeting.

Fritz slightly bowed his head and straightened from his spot so he stood upright. "And you have found me."

"Yes." Snow White awkwardly stared at his chest.

So...what now? I didn't have anything to say to him. I just wanted to see him.

Snow White chewed on her lip.

"It is quite loud," Fritz said.

"Hmm? Oh, yes. Rather overwhelming, too." Snow White laughed awkwardly. "This might be the loudest party we've ever held in here—including the ones in which the room was filled."

Fritz glanced at the window, where the sky was streaked with the last rays of orange-gold light from the setting sun. He held out his hand—which Snow White took without hesitation—then effortlessly slipped through the shadows, leading the way to a balcony door not far away.

Snow White followed him outside, though the cold night air made her shiver.

Instantly the noise of the feasting hall grew muffled and quiet, and Snow White felt like she could practically *think* more clearly in the new silence.

Fritz had led her out to one of the side balconies—this particular one jutted out over a large pond that was decorated with a statue of a knight bearing a shield and sword. She could see the other balconies—all unconnected, except for the main balcony that led down to the viewing area by the pond and opened up into a courtyard that bridged the gap between the feasting hall and the guest wing.

Fritz tugged his cloak off his shoulders and held it out to Snow White.

She cleared her throat and hoped her blush wasn't visible in the dimness of twilight. "Thank you." She took it and slung it across her shoulders, snorting when the cloth draped on the ground thanks to their rather marked height difference.

It was warm, though, and it smelled faintly of leaves and the wind—like Fritz.

She smiled up at the forester—tipping her head back so she could properly meet his eyes.

He rewarded her with his gentle yet sincere smile—the one that made him go from mysterious to charming.

And as Snow White stared up at him, she came to a horrible realization. *Soon, I will have to bid Fritz farewell now that all of this is finished. But I can't. I love him!*

It made her good humor depart.

I should tell him that I'll miss him. No, not should, I need to! Or, truly, I should thank him for all his help and everything he has done for me. Although perhaps that is presumptuous to assume it was for me and instead I should say everything he has done for Mullberg?

"Snow White," Fritz said, breaking the silence and Snow White's frazzled thoughts.

"Yes?" she asked in a breathless yelp.

Fritz adjusted his stance so his legs were positioned wider, in an almost military posture. Snow White could see a thoughtful frown settle on his lips thanks to the rising moon.

Oh, this can't be good. Is this where he tells me he's an honorable hero who will take his leave now that he has finished his quest?

"Faina has been saved," he said. "We have accomplished the task you asked us, the Seven Warriors, to aid you in."

No, no, no! I didn't want to be right about this! *Quick, distract him—don't let him ask permission to leave!*

"Uhhh," Snow White managed to say.

"Which is why I ask permission—"

DON'T JUST STAND THERE—SAY SOMETHING!

"To stay and serve you," he said.

Snow White nearly spit out her refusal, but just as the "no" was on the tip of her tongue, his request finally caught up with her thoughts.

To stay with and serve? Is this a prank—like the horse and donkeys inside the feasting hall? She rapidly blinked, then squinted up at the tall forester. He gravely met her eyes. *No, he definitely means it. But, wait, is he asking for a position?*

"Why?" Snow White asked in a strangled voice.

Fritz held her gaze. "Because I love you."

Snow White had to mentally replay his response at least twice before she was certain she had not—in her whimsy—misheard him. "You *love* me?" she asked, her voice squeaking.

Fritz nodded.

Snow White stared open-mouthed at him, her supposedly clever mind utterly silenced in shock.

"If my feelings make you feel uncomfortable, I can assure you that no matter how you feel in return, I still want to serve you—to guard you," Fritz continued.

"No, no—I mean, yes—wait." Snow White could have slapped herself for the extra dosage of awkward. *Just when I hoped I was a little better.*

Snow White held up her hand, signaling for a pause, then sucked in a breath of the cool night air and coughed. When she finally gazed up at Fritz again, she found she couldn't look into his eyes and speak—it made her freeze like a startled deer—so she settled for staring at the lobe of his right ear.

"Y-your request is quite noble, and I-I-I—" She paused and pressed her lips together as if she could will herself to speak better. She risked glancing at his eyes again and noticed the slight line of concern wrinkled at the corner of his eyes.

Oh no—he thinks I don't return his feelings!

Without thinking, without hesitation, she blurted out, "I love you, too!"

Fritz blinked, and Snow White breathed a little easier.

There. I said it!

"You love me?" Fritz slowly repeated, as if tasting the flavor of the words.

"Yes," Snow White said, her words coming more smoothly now that the worst was behind her. "I knew for certain once you woke me up from the spell the apple had put on me."

Fritz adjusted his cloak on Snow White's shoulders so it didn't sag in such a lopsided matter. "When I returned from the Conclave and saw you...I knew if I ever got you back, I *had* to tell you."

"You don't mind that I'm a princess, do you?" Snow White bit her lip as she peered up at him.

Fritz arched an eyebrow. "Do you mind that I am a forester?"

"No, but you're more than that—you are one of the Seven Warriors, and the most heroic and noble man I know."

"But I won't be able to help you rule," Fritz pointed out. "I have no interest in becoming a real monarch. I'll stand with you and guard you until my dying breath, but I'll never be like a Minister from that Cabinet of yours."

"That doesn't matter," Snow White said, blinking in surprise when she realized it was true.

Fritz cocked his head and waited patiently.

"I have the necessary knowledge, and I've been raised to become a just queen," Snow White said. "I don't need more advice—I have my books and advisors for that—I need you: a safe place."

She mashed her lips together and managed to resist touching

him for a few pathetically short moments before she poked her hand out of his cloak.

Fritz caught it and intertwined his fingers with hers. "What do you mean by that?"

"Today was the perfect example," Snow White said. "You saved me on more than one occasion, and whatever strategy I decided upon, you enacted. That's what I need—not a fellow noble to conspire with, but a hero—a *warrior*—who can protect me." She swallowed and almost choked when Fritz rubbed his thumb on the back of her hand. "And maybe one who will believe in me when I'm having a hard time mustering the courage to speak," she added in a voice barely above a mutter.

Fritz's charming smile was back. "I will *always* follow you, Snow White, wherever you lead." The smile morphed into a dark glare that Snow White was certain would have made a knight tremble in his armor. "And I will stop any who dare threaten you, my just and clever queen." He bowed formally over her hand.

"We'll be an unusual pair," Snow White said. "Or rather, unusual rulers. Father and Stepmother were the very picture of the stories you hear as a child—the handsome, good King and his beautiful and kind Queen." She frowned a bit. "Instead, we will be the bookish-and-perhaps-passive-but-overly-aggressive queen and her silent-protector king. But...that's the kind of person I am."

"Yes," Fritz agreed, "and that's the woman I fell in love with."

Snow White winced. "I cannot mentally conceive how that happened. I can't speak a clear sentence to save my life, and I blush too much."

Fritz tugged on Snow White's hand, raising it to his lips. "I rather enjoy your blushes. But it was your loyalty to Faina that first caught my attention." His lips brushed the back of her hand. "Though you were terrified, you pushed yourself for her sake. And then, it became clear how brilliant you are."

"I didn't repulse you when I tore into the lords?" Snow White asked.

Fritz smiled—not his usual warm smile, or even his charming one. Something that was distinctly *more* and perhaps almost had a flirtatious quality to it. "Snow White, you are beautiful at every moment. But witnessing you demand the respect owed to you..." His smile grew. "*Beautiful* is too tepid of a word to describe it. You were *stunning*."

Snow White felt like her cheeks were on fire with the strength of her blush. *He obviously is unhinged—who could call me stunning?—but I'm not going to question it and will instead count it as a blessing.*

He started to bend his tall frame and lean over, but Snow White held up a hand to forestall him.

"Just...just...one moment." Snow White scurried over to a stone bench shoved against a railing and climbed onto it. She almost tripped on Fritz's cloak, which was still thrown round her shoulders, before she was able to extend a hand and beckon him closer.

The unusual edge to Fritz's smile intensified as he stepped across the balcony, stopping so closely that his shins bumped the edge of the bench.

"Now we're nearly the same height." Snow White couldn't help her idiotic smile as she slipped her arms around Fritz's shoulders. "Otherwise, you might pull a muscle in your neck or back."

Fritz leaned in closer, so his breath fanned across her cheeks. "Thank you for your concern. Is there anything else I should be aware of?"

"Um," Snow White said as her eyes fluttered shut.

Fritz chuckled and didn't give her any time to respond. He pressed his lips to hers in a kiss that Snow White would remember forever.

It was a surprising kiss, for it was a *searing* kiss. Snow White had thought Fritz would be soft like a flower brushing her lips.

That was not so.

Though he was gentle, there was a great deal more fire in their kiss, to the point she felt her limbs lose all weight-bearing abilities.

She leaned into him, practically sagging all of her weight into his chest. But he didn't seem to mind. He wrapped his arms around her, and Snow White knew she was loved, and she would be safe as long as her forester—her warrior—breathed.

Even after he withdrew, Snow White flopped against his chest.

"That was something I never read about," she said thoughtfully.

Fritz laughed—a rumbling sound Snow White could actually *feel*, planted against his chest as she was—and adjusted his arms so he was able to lift her clear off the bench with only the smallest of winces from his half-healed side wound.

"I hope it was satisfactory?" he teased.

Snow White—aware she was glowing bright red thanks to her cursed blushes—busied herself with fixing the collar of his shirt. "Well. More study might be necessary."

Fritz smirked and spun in a tight circle that made her laugh and again ring her arms around his neck.

Snow White had been born into a world of love. And that world had just grown a lot…taller.

EPILOGUE

Snow White, bearing a tray filled with three steaming mugs, tip-toed through Faina's private parlor, carefully edging around the snoring Seven Warriors.

The men were passed out in various uncomfortable looking positions, sprawled out on the Queen's dainty furniture. (She was positive Oswald was going to wake up with a creak in his neck as he was passed out in an arm chair, his head tilted back as he loudly snored. Marzell wasn't likely to fare any better given that he was huddled on a mere rug.)

Though sunlight snuck into the room around the edges of the velvet drapes, they slept on—fatigued from a night of festivities and *days* of being on edge.

Snow White stopped and gazed around the parlor with love warming her heart.

The Seven Warriors had done so much for her already, and yet when she had asked if they would sleep in Faina's parlor that night —a comforting presence and promise of safety—none of them had refused, as exhausted as they were.

Angel, and her companion (master?) Evariste were there as well.

In fact, the magic user—who hadn't yet explained much as she had been busy speaking to Evariste most of the evening—was the only one awake out of the bunch.

She stood, leaning against the wall, her silver eyes watchful despite the dark rings around them.

As far as Snow White was aware, the magic user hadn't slept all night. *I think she's afraid those thieves might come back for Evariste.*

Snow White sidled up to Angel and held out her tray, offering her a mug of mulled wine.

Angel took one, sniffed it, then shook her head.

"It's sweetened and spiced," Snow White whispered as Angel tried to set the mug back on the tray.

"It might make me sleepy," Angel whispered back.

"The warriors will wake up soon. They'll take over guard duty," Snow White promised.

Fritz—either already awake or stirring at the sound of her voice—opened his eyes and nodded.

Angel glanced at her companion—Evariste was seated on a chair he had turned around to face her.

He also opened his eyes. "Sleep, Angel," he said, his musical voice soft.

Angel pressed her lips together, but she took a sip of the hot drink. "Any news on the mirror?"

Snow White shook her head. "I spoke to the leaders of the royal guard: nothing. Juwel was searched as well, and though we have witnesses who saw the thieves leave the palace, they lost track of them outside these walls."

Angel sighed. "That's what I feared. They likely used magic in some way or another." She narrowed her eyes, then tipped her head back against the wall.

Snow White paused, then reached out with determination and set her free hand over Angel's. "Thank you; and I'm sorry."

"The mirror, Evariste, none of this was your fault." Angel studied her companion, who hadn't returned to feigning sleep and instead watched her with mismatched eyes—one blue and one green. "In fact, I don't think I could have freed him if it weren't for you." Angel offered her a tired but sincere smile.

Snow White nodded. "Will you tell me everything...later? After you've slept?"

Angel nodded. "Whenever that is."

Yes, it's time to pass that mantle. "Fritz?" Snow White called out.

Her handsome forester was already on his feet, having predicted her request. He nudged Marzell with his foot as he set a hand on Rupert's shoulder.

The two warriors started to stir, blinking and groaning as they awoke.

When he had their attention Fritz said simply, "Our turn."

Marzell muffled a yawn. "That's about right," he agreed as he peeled himself off the ground. "Come on Oswald, Wendal, Aldelbert."

Aldelbert leaped off his sofa with an amazing surge of energy. "Let us greet the morning sun and embrace our glory for the day!" he declared.

Oswald groaned, but Wendal stood and jumped over Gregori —who was slowly rousing himself. "As My Lord orders!" Wendal said.

Snow White shared a secret smile with Fritz before she started for the staircase, climbing the stairs that led to Faina's loft-bedroom. She paused on the top step, peering through the dim light at her stepmother's bed.

Faina yawned and stretched on her mattress. "Snow White? Is that you?"

"It's me, Stepmother." Snow White adjusted her hold on her tray as she sat down on the edge of the bed. She offered her stepmother one mug then took the other for herself before setting the tray aside.

"The Warriors are changing guard duty?" Faina guessed as Aldelbert's laughter and Gregori's deep grunts reached them.

"Yes," Snow White said. "Angel needs to sleep. I think her friend does, too—I'd be surprised if he slept at all. When I tiptoed through the parlor this morning to procure these—and to talk with some guards—he was watching her whenever she wasn't looking his way."

"They have a story to tell—and a shared history." Faina hummed as she sipped her drink.

"Yes," Snow White agreed. She inhaled the wine's fruity, spiced scent, and traced a patterned swirl on the brocade bedcover. "Faina..." She paused.

Do I really want to know the answer to this question? She sucked in a deep breath. "Do you remember—or perhaps were you *aware*—of what happened while the mirror had you in its thrall?"

Faina thoughtfully tilted her head. "In the beginning, no. I knew something was wrong, but I didn't know what. It wasn't until you left that I realized something was controlling me, and by then it was too late."

"Do you know, then, exactly what motivated the mirror, or who gave it to you?" Snow White asked. When Faina cocked an eyebrow, she added, "Anything would be helpful. There is much going on throughout the continent that we weren't aware of, and so much darkness. Prince Severin of Loire is leading a resistance of sorts."

Faina nodded and rearranged the pillows mounded at her headboard. She scooted over, then patted the space next to her.

Feeling like a little girl, Snow White carefully balanced her mulled wine and scrambled onto the bed as well.

"That mirror...whatever it was, it's ancient," Faina said. "When you refer to the trouble continent wide, is that the Chosen group you mentioned last night when talking to Lord Vitkovci and the others after the battle?" She asked, referring to the multiple meetings Snow White had held before the evening feast.

"Yes."

"This mirror is not *with* them," Faina said. "I think the

Chosen gave it to me and planted it in our household, but the mirror is old and terrible, and it has magic that no longer walks our lands. Simply put, it wishes for the destruction of mankind. The Chosen may believe they can harness it for their own purposes, but I am not convinced."

"The Chosen don't control it?" Snow White asked.

Faina shook her head. "The Chosen wanted Mullberg under their sway—it is why they sent the mirror to me. But the mirror is what drove me mad, and the mirror is what longed to hurt and kill you."

"Because I'm the heir, and soon to be queen?" Snow White asked.

"No," Faina said.

Snow White stopped with her mug half raised to her lips, her eyebrows furrowed in surprise. "No? Wasn't it because they feared I would challenge your regency and remove you from the throne?"

Her stepmother shook her head.

Snow White set her cup down, surprised. She couldn't fathom another reason why the mirror wanted her dead—it had never occurred to her there would be any other reason for the attacks against her. *If it wasn't politically motivated, what else could it be?*

"But you fought the mirror for so long," Snow White said. "When I ate the apple, the mirror—through you—complained that it had taken years to wrestle control from you."

Faina cringed. "Ahh, yes, the apple. That was the mirror, working to circumnavigate your intelligence and my stubbornness, I'm afraid. I'm so sorry, Snow White. I never wanted to hurt you."

Snow White leaned against her stepmother, warmed when Faina slipped an arm around her shoulders and squeezed. "There is nothing for you to apologize for, Faina. That wasn't you, but the mirror..." she trailed off, finally piecing together what Faina had said. "Circumnavigate?"

Faina sank deeper amongst her pillows. "It was the only way it could get me to directly hurt you—which was necessary because you kept outsmarting the constructs the mirror sent."

Snow White stared at her still steaming wine. "Yes. Because whenever it tried to attack me using you, you would stop yourself, so the poison was necessary. It was less of an attack when compared to a blade to the heart—as it had tried before." She puckered her lower lip slightly in thought and raised her gaze to Faina. "*That's* why it was so intent on killing me, wasn't it? It had nothing to do with politics. It was all because you would fight off the mirror *for me*."

Faina nodded.

Snow White wrestled with the thought for a moment longer. "But you just said the mirror was dark and uncontrollable. You stood against that, for *years*, and you sacrificed yourself...for me?"

Faina's eyes were glazed with unshed tears as she smiled at her. "You are my daughter, Snow White. I didn't give birth to you, but I love you. I would *never* let anything hurt you."

And so her stepmother—sweet, warm Faina—had fought off an ancient magical artifact of unimaginable black magic and endured years of pain and agony...because she loved Snow White.

Snow White's eyes stung with tears, and she again leaned into Faina. "I love you, too."

"I know, darling." Faina set her mug aside and gently patted Snow White's back. "You show me that with everything you've done. I'm so proud of you, and so thankful to call you my stepdaughter. And I will *always* fight for you."

The Queen and Princess hugged and wept tears of joy, laughing and enjoying each other's company. Several minutes passed before Faina cleared her throat and dried her tears.

"So," she began. "When are you going to tell me more about that forester boy of yours?"

SNOW WHITE

NEVER—EVEN in her most optimistic dreams in which she saved Faina and everything was rosy—did Snow White ever think she would address not one but *two* powerful enchanters. (Or, as she was a stickler for proper terms, an enchanter and an enchantress.)

"If we leave for Loire within an hour, we'll make good time," Angel said.

No, no—her name is Angelique, and she is a Lady Enchantress, Snow White mentally corrected herself. After Angelique had finally gotten a decent amount of sleep, she and Evariste had explained their story—and their rather honored positions.

Angel had also undergone quite the transformation since recovering her companion, Lord Enchanter Evariste.

While staying with Snow White, Angelique had used illusion magic and props to change her physical attributes. Now she was taller, her features fuller and more pronounced, and her silver eyes were even brighter. She was more beautiful now—almost breathtakingly so—and she smelled faintly of flowers—but she still had her devil-may-care attitude. (And she had traded her poor-fitting tunic for a dress that, Snow White was interested to see, sparkled and changed colors at an intermittent basis.)

No small wonder she kept getting herb names wrong and did strange things as part of her "herb magic."

Snow White slightly pursed her lips as she studied the magical pair. "You still do not plan to stop by the Veneno Conclave on your way to inform Prince Severin and Prince Lucien of what occurred here?"

Angelique shook her head. "Severin needs to know first—he'll actually do something about it," she said. "I doubt the Conclave would do much more even if we did tell them, and they'll fuss over Evariste's return and waste time we don't have."

Snow White nodded and shifted her gaze to Evariste.

The young Lord Enchanter had not changed out of his elaborate and beautiful blue and black cape, and as he moved, the coins that hung from the hem jingled.

"Whatever Angel thinks is best," he said when he realized she was waiting for his input. "I've been locked in a mirror for years. I really haven't the faintest clue what has transpired in my absence."

Though he spoke in an open tone, and his expression was pleasant and calm, as Snow White glanced back and forth between the sharp-tongued Angelique and her master, she couldn't help but ponder.

I think they may be more well-matched than one would be led to believe. For although he looks so friendly, Lord Enchanter Evariste seems rather similar to Angelique. He is putting on a front—though I can't say what for or in what way.

"I see," Snow White said. She glanced around the hall—which had become something of the temporary receiving room since the throne room was still in shambles. "I cannot say I blame you—for we freed Faina nearly two days ago, and we have not yet received word from the Veneno Conclave representative we sent Fritz to notify even before I ate the spelled apple."

"Yes." Angelique frowned. "It is disappointing."

Sensing the topic disturbed the enchantress, Snow White awkwardly cleared her throat. "I h-hope you two have a safe journey."

"It would be a fast one—if I had access to my magic," Evariste said ruefully.

"It will still be quick." Angelique rubbed the back of her neck. "Pegasus can bear us both."

"I must add my thanks for your willingness to carry my letters and reports to the princes of Loire," Snow White said. "And please...if you could ask for mercy on our behalf when you explain why we failed to attend the Summit, I would appreciate it."

"Don't worry your pretty head, Snow White," Angelique drawled. "Severin will understand. Rather, he's going to be grateful for everything you've accomplished this spring."

Snow White frowned slightly. "I freed Faina, yes, but the mirror is gone."

"Perhaps," Angelique said. "But you stopped what would have been a major blow to the continent when you saved your stepmother and held your country together."

Snow White folded her hands together to keep from twitching her skirts. "If you say so, Lady Enchant..." she trailed off at the dark look Angelique gave her.

"Snow White," the enchantress said with a glare. "I have already told you: I have lent you clothes, we have slept next to each other on the ground, and you have seen me at my scruffiest. There is no need for formalities between us. It's just Angelique—or even Angel!"

Evariste chuckled slightly. "Thank you for your hospitality—and for mounting the attack that resulted in my freedom, Your Highness," he said to Snow White.

"It was the least I could do, Lord Enchanter Evariste," Snow White said. "I am sorry I did not move sooner or that I never saw you in the mirror. I might have done something earlier then."

The enchanter shrugged. "I could only appear when dragged forward by the mirror—or by magic, as Angel showed. As the mirror was choosing to shield its presence from you, there is no way you could have known."

"Still, it's rather disheartening."

"And aggravating," Evariste agreed with a sunny smile. "But I am free now—even if I don't yet have my magic back."

"Yes, that is the one thing that would tempt me to stop by the Conclave first if it weren't so important we update Severin." Angelique grimaced. "Surely someone at the Veneno Conclave will be able to break the seal placed on you."

"We shall see," Evariste said simply. "Your Highness, if you'll excuse me, I'll go summon our mount. Thank you again for all you have done."

"Go with safety, Lord Enchanter," Snow White said. "I hope

your magic returns to you soon."

The Lord Enchanter slightly inclined his head, then turned around and strode off, his cloak furling around him.

Snow White frowned thoughtfully. "He really is your master?"

"Yep—though he's been absent for six years, I never received my title, so I'm still an enchantress-in-training." Angelique glanced over her shoulder so she, also, could watch her master stride off.

"You two don't seem to be a...typical combination," Snow White said hesitatingly.

"You mean because Master Evariste is barely older than I am?" Angelique asked.

Snow White nodded. "I thought generally an apprenticeship was when older magic users took on the younger generation to teach them."

"You're not wrong," Angelique said as she ran a hand through her brown hair—it was still shoulder-length, though it was markedly silkier and shinier. "It's mostly due to Evariste. He was considered a prodigy and obtained the title of Enchanter when he was still a child. He only took me on out of pity."

Snow White opened her mouth to ask Angelique what she meant but hesitated when she noted the pained expression in the enchantress's eyes and the bitter twinge to her smile. She swallowed her question and chose a different route instead.

"When all of this is over, Angelique, I hope you will return to Mullberg and stay with me," she hesitated, her hands growing a little clammy as she dimly wondered if she was overstepping her bounds. "That is, I should like to get to know more about you as I consider you a..."

Angelique's smile turned warm. "I would be delighted. After all, we *are* friends."

Snow White couldn't stop the bright grin that spread across her lips. "Yes," she agreed.

Angelique stepped forward and embraced Snow White, filling

the air with her floral scent. "Stay safe, Snow White—though I am certain your dark guardian will allow no harm to come to you," she teased when they separated.

Snow White furrowed her brow. *Dark guardian...oh!* She twisted slightly to glance behind her.

Sure enough, Fritz stood in the shadow of a marble pillar not ten feet away. Though he watched the room with his hazel eyes, he seemed to feel Snow White's gaze on him, for he glanced her way and offered her a smile that made her toes curl.

"Um, yes. Of course," she shyly muttered.

Angelique laughed and ruffled Snow White's curls. "The pair of you are quite adorable. I wish you happiness there, as well." The lady enchantress started to walk away, her full skirts rippling. "You can expect a courier from Severin as soon as I relay your words to him. Watch for one," she advised.

Snow White nodded. "Indeed. I wish you well during your time in Loire and at the Veneno Conclave."

"Thank you," Angelique grimaced. "I am sure I shall need it." She winked, then was gone, gliding out of the hall and joining her master in the sunny courtyard.

Snow White exhaled deeply and shook her head.

Angelique is my friend—and she still has her playful and sarcastic personality. But there's a power to her now that I wasn't aware of before. She must be extremely talented at illusions, for I have no idea how she hid it so well.

She took a moment to gather her wits—for she would need every bit of her intellect for what came next: a meeting with the Cabinet.

She searched out Marzell and Gregori. They stood off to the side, speaking animatedly (or at least in Marzell's case he was animated. Gregori looked like he might pass out if he got the chance to sit down) with Snow White's grandfather.

He was also attending the meeting. Snow White wasn't certain if that was a good thing or bad, given that the meeting was supposed to discuss The Chosen and everything she had learned from Prince Severin's report and Angelique, as well as what had happened to Faina.

Unbidden, her eyes drifted to her stepmother.

Faina wore a bright pink dress, and already she was looking better, healthier. She listened with an amused quirk to her lips as Aldelbert loudly instructed her in the ways and methods of his "glory stretches," while Wendal voiced his support.

At one point, the queen laughed and said something to the sunny lord, for he puffed up his chest and beamed when she finished.

That's right. Faina will be there with me. The thought made Snow White stand a little straighter. *I've learned my lesson after our near collision of wills with Lord Vitkovci, and I will not allow my ministers to gainsay me in that we must act against the Chosen, but...I do feel ill just thinking about the meeting.*

"You'll do well," Fritz said, having soundlessly approached her.

Snow White held out her hand and only blushed *a little* when Fritz took it. "How did you know I was thinking about the meeting?" she asked.

"Given that it is the next event on your schedule, and the depth of the wrinkle in your forehead has increased, it was an easy guess." Fritz had to hunker down so he could kiss her forehead—likely right on the aforementioned wrinkle.

Snow White's blush deepened. "I see."

"You'll do well," he repeated.

Snow White took in a gulp of air. "I'll try."

Fritz raised an ashy brown eyebrow. "We have had this conversation in several variations, but I can repeat it again. You've improved so much already in a very short amount of time."

"I have a long way to go, though," Snow White said. *But at least I don't think I will get sick in front of everyone as I have on occasion in the past.*

"You've learned to walk. You're now beginning to jog," Fritz said. "That does not mean you can belittle yourself for being unable to run."

Snow White cracked a smile at the familiar illustration, but their conversation was interrupted by Rupert and Oswald.

"This here is why I liked our agreement to live in the woods," Oswald said.

"You enjoy limited bathing?" Rupert asked boredly as they strolled past Snow White and Fritz.

"No! I hate these prissy clothes!"

Despite his protests, Oswald had been dressed in a silk tunic and was only allowed to carry two weapons. He frowned down at his shoes—which had bows on them—and almost seemed to draw comfort from Rupert's snark.

"It is restricting," Rupert acknowledged, "but not unexpected. Besides, we only are made to dress like this in court."

"I still don't like it," Oswald grumbled. "Angel told me yesterday there was going to be a party tonight, and I'll have to *dance*!"

"You are the third son of a noble. You are expected to follow court rules," Rupert reminded him.

"Yeah, well maybe I'll leave and go someplace where I'm *not* considered a noble!" Oswald declared.

Rupert strolled away, leaving his fellow warrior to follow behind him. "The chances of that place actually *wanting* you are rather slim given your disagreeable personality and questionable sense of hygiene."

Oswald stomped after him. "As if *you* have people beating your door down with offers, Lord Sick-a-lot!"

Snow White smiled slightly at the interchange. She watched the odd pair plop down on a velvet padded bench before her gaze roamed to Wendal and Aldelbert—still displaying his "stretches."

"I'm glad you all stayed here in Juwel," Snow White admitted. "I knew you would, but I did not know about the other warriors. I thought they might choose to slip off."

Fritz pensively watched Aldelbert fold in half and speak to Faina while peering between his own legs. "You are giving them everything they have wished for: the chance to fight back against the monsters and forces that have attacked Mullberg."

"I suppose that's true," Snow White said.

"It is also likely due to our shared comradery with you," he added.

Warmth bloomed in Snow White's chest. "I'm grateful for them—and for you. I'm thankful for your support. Especially given that the advisors won't be happy when I tell them Faina is to remain Queen until I reach twenty, as the original agreement said."

Fritz nodded.

"You don't think I'm needlessly delaying my coronation?" Snow White asked, glancing up at her forester.

"No," Fritz said. "Because you will fill that time preparing for the Chosen instead."

"Exactly," Snow White said grimly. "War is coming. And this time, I will not let Mullberg be caught off guard."

"You think it will become big enough to be called a war?" Fritz asked.

"I'm afraid so," Snow White said. "Because these conflicts and plagues upon our countries won't stop. Not until that mirror is destroyed," she said grimly.

Fritz watched her for a few thoughtful moments, then shifted his gaze and nodded at her grandfather. "If you can repeat those words in your meeting, I don't think anyone would dare naysay you."

Snow White cracked a smile. "If I can manage it, yes. My ministers are smart. I'm just afraid I might have to get a little rough to make them—particularly my grandfather—hear me."

"You handled Lord Vitkovci and the others well." Fritz tilted his head and smiled at her with his eyes. "You will do equally as splendid here."

Snow White frowned a little. "Perhaps, but I would rather *not* have a reputation as the Tyrant Queen of Mullberg."

"Never," Fritz assured her. "Aldelbert would tell you before you grew close to such a thing."

Snow White laughed. "He would," she agreed. "He would inform me my rule is impinging upon his quest for greatness and glory." The thought made her laugh a little more, bringing relief to her tense muscles.

I needed that, she realized as she gazed up at Fritz. *And he knew exactly what to say.*

He may not be a prince, or the son of nobility...but he is better. He is Fritz, my forester, supporter, and protector. He's exactly what I need, and with him at my back, I really don't have anything to fear. Not even embarrassing speeches.

"It seems Marzell believes we should move on to the meeting," he said, nodding at his friend.

The young lord tilted his head questioningly at them, then motioned for them to join him, Gregori, and Snow White's grandfather.

"Then we shouldn't keep them waiting, I suppose." Instead of sighing, like she would have not long ago, Snow White lifted her chin. "Come along, Fritz. Let's go rattle some lords."

Fritz offered her his arm, and together, the princess and her forester crossed the hall, unaware that they had changed the fate of many and would continue to do so with Mullberg's addition to the alliance.

For Snow White was correct. War was coming, and it would be worse than anyone could have predicted.

The End

To learn what happens to the rest of the continent, check out *The Fairy Tale Enchantress: Apprentice of Magic.*

A MOTHER'S RESPONSIBILITY

A Mother's Responsibility
A Snow White Short Story

FAINA WAS NOT ENTIRELY certain how she felt about Fritz.

She was aware he stood with Snow White when Faina was otherwise incapacitated. And she knew perfectly well he had shielded Snow White and protected her from threats: both physical and perhaps emotional. And yet.

And yet.

As Snow White's stepmother, she couldn't help but feel that everything had happened rather...*fast*. Not to mention she was not particularly pleased that it had all occurred without her on hand to observe.

Afterall, having Snow White fall in love with a strange forester in less than a month without Faina present to ascertain the man wasn't an axe murderer was not exactly how she had pictured her stepdaughter's love story unfolding.

Moreover, Fritz was not the sort of man Faina would have picked out for Snow White.

To begin with, he was about as talkative as a rock. And while Faina was not one who cared much for family lines or pedigrees, as a common forester he unfortunately had no family history for her—or her spies—to snoop through.

Additionally, he could do very little for Snow White and her future role as Queen except protect her. While Faina deeply appreciated knowing Snow White would undoubtedly be safe from now until the day Fritz died, she had always thought that Snow White would end up with a confident man who could help her rule Mullberg.

But Snow White has grown much during my... incapacitation. She has come into her own, and has gained a new kind of confidence. One I'm very glad to see as it has made her happier and will undoubtedly make her a better queen. Because of that, it is possible Fritz may be a better husband for her than the sort of man I was picturing. Still...

"If he harms one hair on her head, or makes her cry, I shall have him scalped." Faina announced to her maidservant.

The attendant peered cautiously at Faina, "Are you referring to Master Fritz, again?"

"Yes."

The maidservant nodded understandably and clucked as she patted Faina's hand. "Don't your worry, Your Majesty. As the mirror's influence on you continues to fade, such disturbing thoughts will soon no longer trouble you."

Faina pressed her lips together but said nothing more.

This has nothing to do with the mirror's influence, and everything to do with the fact that I will kill anyone who harms my stepdaughter. Ignoring the fact that she is my precious daughter, I have many people to answer to for her happiness and love.

There were, of course, Snow White's deceased father and paternal grandparents, but most of all there was Snow White's mother. And though Faina had never met Snow White's mother, she had a great deal of respect for the late queen. She was aware of what a precious gift the queen had left her in the form of Snow White, and she had no intention of betraying the responsibility her position as Snow White's stepmother represented.

Regardless, Faina still wished for Snow White to marry for love. And really, Fritz hadn't done anything to arouse her suspicions, besides the manner in which he had seduced her stepdaughter. (Because could you call a love story played out over a few short weeks anything except a seduction? No! Never mind that Faina's romance with the late King Matvey had played out in a similar timeframe....)

THOUGH FAINA DID NOT VOICE her concern to Snow White, she had no such reservations in speaking frankly to Fritz.

"I don't really know that I like you," Faina told the taciturn forester over breakfast—in the early light of dawn, before Snow White arrived.

Fritz tilted his head. "I beg your pardon?"

"You seem like a fine young man," Faina continued. "But as Snow White's stepmother I reserve the right to be reluctant in forming a positive opinion about you."

Fritz blinked slowly, and the calm—or perhaps unemotional?—expression on his face did not so much as twitch. "Good," he said.

It irritated Faina that she thought better of him for that reaction.

IN THE END, it was Snow White's maternal grandfather who offered Faina the right mix of wisdom and assurance.

"Snow White is a clever girl, is she not?" Lord Trubsinn asked.

Faina sat up straighter in her arm chair. "Snow White is more than clever. She is dazzlingly brilliant!"

Lord Trubsinn chuckled. "But of course," he said. "Which means we can trust her judgement on this forester fellow."

Faina drummed her fingertips on her armchair. *I had not thought of it that way. But it's true, Snow White would never pick an unscrupulous husband. She'd see through him in an instant, and she would never do something that would put the country as risk.*

"Not that it matters," Snow White's grandfather continued. "Because she'll still have you by her side. And with her forester to protect her back, and you to stand with her by the throne, woe befall whoever is stupid enough to oppose her."

The thought of being allowed to continue to watch over Snow White made Faina smile, but she also realized that the statement was true about Fritz as well.

Faina had witnessed a courtyard practice session held by the Seven Warriors.

Fritz had undoubtedly been the best fighter of them, and Faina would be hard pressed to find a better warrior amongst her soldiers.

He will protect her...in a way that is perhaps far more important in these dark times as the Chosen lurk about. Besides, Snow White is able to rule alone. She has the ability, and I think she will continue to gain the necessary confidence—with help from Fritz.

"Perhaps I will like my future son-in-law after all." Faina smiled wryly at Lord Trubsinn, and added rather mischievously, "but there is no need for him to know that."

The End

THE ROYAL MULLBERG CABINET

The Royal Mullberg Cabinet
A short story

THINGS HAD CHANGED DRASTICALLY for the minsters of the Royal Mullburg Cabinet. Over the span of a few short weeks, their queen—to all appearances—went mad, and the princess had gone missing. As the country seemed to spin out of control, and with Lord Trubsinn threatening to scour the country in search of his granddaughter, things had seemed hopeless and grim.

And then Snow White had returned.

Marching on Glitzern Palace with four lords under her command—not to mention the Seven Mule-Headed Idiots—Snow White drove back the darkness that had plagued Queen Faina and essentially reclaimed the country.

While the minsters were thrilled Snow White had saved them all, they quickly realized the Snow White that had emerged from the near wreckage of their country, was not the same tongue-tied princess they had seen at the last Cabinet meeting.

"Your strategy and planning were brilliant, Your Highness," Lord Dalberg declared.

"Indeed!" Lord Kleist chortled. "You saved the country from potential disaster, and in one swoop ripped off the mask of the Chosen and revealed their presence in Mullburg!"

Snow White smiled shakily. "I am g-glad you approve of the tactics I employed," she said with only the slightest stutter. (Though she still looked like she might faint if they asked her to give a speech.)

Lord Dalberg nodded sagely. "Yes, of course! You did so well, I do not believe a general could have done better himself!"

"How did you get Lord Vitkovci and the others to help you storm Glitzern?" Lord Sparneck enquired.

Snow White looked a little ill at the thought and glanced up at Fritz, the forester that now shadowed her every step. "Um," she said.

"It is no matter," Lord Kleist stated. "It is remarkable what you have been able to accomplish! As your minsters, we are both pleased with your direction and honored to continue serving you." He bowed slightly with his words.

"However!" Lord Sparneck rumbled. "We are disappointed you did not seek us out when you fled. Though your strategy and plans worked, you were put in an unnecessary amount of danger."

Snow White slid down deeper in her chair.

"Which is why we ask, Your Majesty, that next time you do something this risky, you seek counsel with us first." Lord Dalberg added.

Though Snow White's expression did not shift, she seemed to sit up straighter in her chair. "Is that a request, or an order?" she asked, all traces of shyness banished from her voice.

Lord Dalberg and Lord Kleist exchanged surprised glances.

"It is merely strongly worded and strongly recommend advice," Lord Sparneck said stupidly. "Advice you should follow," he finished with a grandfatherly smile.

The smile seemed to have no effect on Snow White, for she frowned slightly at the lords. "After all I managed to accomplish in such a short amount of time—which you have just stated yourselves, other leaders of the country would be hard pressed to pull off—you suggest to me that I *hide* behind you?" Her pretty blue eyes were harder than ice as she unflinchingly stared them down.

Lord Kleist was now fairly certain he knew how Snow White had won support from Vitkovci and the three other lords.

꼬

SNOW WHITE HAD CHANGED—ARGUABLY for the better, though it would take some time to get used to the cunning confidence still clothed beneath her shy smiles. But the palace had changed as well. Once, it had been a place of austerity and beauty. Though Faina and Snow White were somewhat famous for being gentle, kind, and joyful rulers. It had been a place of respect and peace.

These days, it was hard to turn a corner without running into one of the Seven Loafers raising up one matter of a ruckus or another in the palace corridors.

"Your Majesty," Lord Sparneck said as he bowed in respect to the Queen Regent.

Faina roused herself from where she had been dosing in the sunshine, seated in an armchair placed in the palace gardens, with five of the Seven Hermits mulling around her.

"Yes?" she asked with a smile.

Lord Kleist squinted as he watched Lord Aldelbert saunter past.

"Come, Wendal!" Aldelbert bellowed. "We must hurry, so you can capture my greatness in this beautiful morning light."

Lord Aldelbert's attendant traipsed behind him bearing a canvas and what appeared to be a set of paints. "As you say, My Lord!" Wendal cheerfully agreed.

The lord and his attendant narrowly missed colliding with

Rupert and Oswald, who were daring to bare their blades in a fight that was dangerously close to Queen Faina.

The two kept darting around like a pair of disreputable squirrels, and had managed to shave off the tops of three different hedges with their antics.

"Out of the way, Aldelbert," Rupert growled. He kicked out at Oswald, hitting him in the kneecap so he tumbled to the ground.

Oswald rolled to his feet, and thrust a budding tulip in Rupert's face. "Block this, Lord Fragile!"

The affect was instantaneous, and Rupert sneezed directly into Oswald's face.

"You did that on purpose!" Oswald shouted.

"It was a lesson for you." Rupert stabbed his wooden sword and smacked Oswald in the ribs. "Use every weapon you have to your advantage."

"Quoting wisdom now are you?" Oswald scoffed. "I give you two more weeks here in the palace, and soon you'll be reciting poetry with the ladies and mincing around in silks and satins!" He nearly backed into Lord Kleist, who sputtered.

"I beg your pardon!" Lord Kleist huffed.

"Sure," Oswald said. Before they could lecture him on his manners, he threw himself into a cartwheel and tackled Rupert.

Lord Kleist scowled as he brushed off his doublet and puffed breeches.

"Your Majesty," Lord Dalberg said with a charming smile. "You are looking well rested."

"Thank you. Would you like to tell me what has brought you to my peaceful garden?" Queen Faina asked—seemingly with all seriousness even as Lord Aldelbert laughed when the still wrestling Rupert and Oswald nearly knocked his attendant's canvas over.

Lord Dalberg's smile crystalized. "Well..."

"It has been over three weeks since you were saved and the castle was cleared," Lord Kleist said.

"Indeed," Faina agreed with a tip of her head.

"Don't you think...that is to say..." Lord Kleist hesitated as he tried to find the right words.

Lord Sparneck apparently had not learned his lesson, for he rather stupidly blurted out, "Isn't it about time we send the Seven Hermits away?"

When Faina raised a slanted eyebrow, he gulped.

"That is, I meant to say, the Seven Warriors," Lord Sparneck lamely amended.

"I'm afraid, Lord Sparneck, that I disagree with you," Faina said.

"Oh?" Lord Sparneck weakly asked.

"Indeed." Faina stood and elegantly twitched her skirts into place. "The Warriors supported Snow White when she rescued me, and based on the reports Snow White has accumulated, they have protected Mullberg for months as they hunted down the evil creatures and monsters my own troops could not find. I owe them a great debt of gratitude, and as such I will host them here in Glitzern as long as they would like."

She smiled serenely at the ministers who had assembled.

The ministers balefully looked past her, where the warriors tumbled.

Rupert coughed when Oswald nailed him in the stomach, knocking the air out of him and making the pale lord stagger a few steps.

"If you two knock into me, I'll flay both of you," Wendal warned as he mixed paint colors.

"Their renewed vitality can only be due to my glory stretches," Lord Aldelbert declared.

"Hah!" Oswald snorted when he ducked a punch from Rupert and skirted backwards. He, unfortunately, wasn't watching where he was going and as a result the backs of his legs hit a stone bench, making him fall backwards onto the dozing merchant heir, Gregori.

Gregori awoke with a snarl that would not be out of place in a bear den, and it was quite some time before any semblance of peace returned to the gardens.

BESIDES THE CHANGES to the princess and the palace, the ministers of the Royal Mullberg Cabinet were discovering that their vision of the future had drastically changed as well.

They realized this—with a small amount of shock—in the middle of a magnificent banquet thrown by Queen Faina.

"I've been thinking," Lord Sparneck said as he twirled his cutlery between his fingers.

Lord Dalberg—who had been watching Princess Snow White greet a noble lady with her ever present Fritz-shadow—turned to look at his fellow minister. "Of what?"

Lord Sparneck set his knife down and tapped the table. "Is this an engagement dinner?"

Lord Kleist choked on his wine. He set his cup down with a clack and thumped his chest until he managed to get out, "Gaping Gads, man, *what* are you speaking of?"

Lord Sparneck nodded to Snow White and Fritz. "Surely I am not the only one who has noticed the signals between those two. They clearly care for each other—which means if *we* can see it, our shy princess has already spoken to Queen Faina about the matter."

Lord Dalberg scratched his chin. "Queen Faina has been taking great pains to introduce him to many of the respected and famous members of nobility this night…"

"And on the rare occasion Fritz is not standing behind Snow White—or shadowing his ruffian-companions—I have seen him with Lord Trubsinn," Lord Sparneck continued.

Lord Kleist, shocked by this revelation, wildly shook his head. "But, but they haven't announced anything yet!"

"No, but it likely means they are easing him in," Lord Sparneck said. "Our Princess is bright. She knows it wouldn't be wise to announce an engagement to a stranger so close on the heels of Faina's...episode."

"A forester, eh?" Lord Dalberg cocked his head as he watched the princess and her beau slide away from the blue-blooded lady they had been speaking with and make for the shadows. "At least we know he is heroic."

"I always pictured a charming young noble for our princess," Lord Sparneck stated. "But after working with her these past few weeks, I am forced to admit she likely does *not* require a husband with social backing to strengthen her power." He ended with a bit of a shudder.

"The boy does have a good head on his shoulders," Lord Kleist said finally. "Though he can be as frightening as a phantom as he ghosts around behind her."

"That might work to her benefit," Lord Dalberg said. "He's so intimidating, I don't imagine any rogue with half a brain would willingly try to harm her in his presence."

Lord Sparneck snorted. "I think a *black mage* would think twice before crossing paths with him. The man has the battle instincts of a seasoned knight."

"Agreed," the lords chorused.

"And it could be worse," Lord Kleist said. "She could have fallen for Lord Aldelbert."

The ministers shivered in fear as they glanced in the direction of the blond-haired lord.

Aldelbert stood at the far side of the room and appeared to be reenacting some kind of fight for three giggling ladies judging by the way he brandished a serving tray at an empty suit of armor.

"Yes," Lord Sparneck said. "It could be *far* worse."

THINGS HAD CHANGED DRASTICALLY for the Mullberg Royal Cabinet, and it would take time to adjust.

But the more they witnessed the changes in their future queen, and the more they learned about the actions of the Chosen and the state of the continent, they suspected that *perhaps* this new future was better than what they had expected.

...Even if the Seven Warriors still loitered around the palace.

The End

ACKNOWLEDGMENTS

Snow White is the last book in this arc of the Timeless Fairy Tale series, and the last heroine as well. Since *Beauty and the Beast* I knew I wanted *Snow White* to be based around the loving relationship between a step-mother and step-daughter, but it wasn't until later in the series that I realized I wanted to make Snow White a shy bookworm.

She's a stark contrast to Elle—the bold intelligencer—or any of my other fairy tale heroines who all tend to be more on the outspoken and courageous end of the spectrum. But Snow White is the perfect heroine to close out the series.

Fairy tales teach us that good will triumph over evil and love prevails. But my Snow White teaches you that one does not have to be skilled in combat, charismatic, or even strong to win this war. Sometimes it's the warriors of a different sort that create the biggest change.

And that's why, with the end of *Snow White*, I want to thank my Champions. Because you stood up for this series and stayed with me, Timeless Fairy Tales became more and more known, and our community has grown.

Thank you. No matter what kind of hero you are, I have needed you and I'm so grateful that you fought for me.

The adventures in this world aren't over, rather, they've only just begun. And there's no other group of readers I would rather explore future stories with than you all.

Thank you for reading.

OTHER BOOKS BY K. M. SHEA

The Snow Queen:
Heart of Ice
Sacrifice
Snowflakes: A Snow Queen Short Story Collection

Timeless Fairy Tales:
Beauty and the Beast
The Wild Swans
Cinderella and the Colonel
Rumpelstiltskin
The Little Selkie
Puss in Boots
Swan Lake
Sleeping Beauty
Frog Prince
12 Dancing Princesses
Snow White
Three pack (Beauty and the Beast, The Wild Swans, Cinderella and the Colonel)

The Fairy Tale Enchantress:
Apprentice of Magic
Curse of Magic

The Elves of Lessa:
Red Rope of Fate
Royal Magic

King Arthur and Her Knights:
Enthroned
Enchanted
Embittered
Embark
Enlighten
Endeavor
Endings
Three pack 1 (Enthroned, Enchanted, Embittered)
Three pack 2 (Embark, Enlighten, Endeavor)

Robyn Hood:
A Girl's Tale
Fight for Freedom

The Magical Beings' Rehabilitation Center:
Vampires Drink Tomato Juice
Goblins Wear Suits
The Lost Files of the MBRC

Other Novels
Life Reader

Princess Ahira

A Goose Girl

Second Age of Retha: Written under pen name A. M. Sohma

The Luckless

The Desperate Quest

The Revived

ABOUT THE AUTHOR

K. M. Shea is a fantasy-romance author who never quite grew out of adventure books or fairy tales, and still searches closets in hopes of stumbling into Narnia. She is addicted to sweet romances, witty characters, and happy endings. She also writes LitRPG and GameLit under the pen name, A. M. Sohma.

Hang out with the K. M. Shea Community at...
kmshea.com

Made in the USA
Coppell, TX
07 October 2020